T0096039

HITLER
IS
ALIVE!

HITLER
IS
ALIVE!

EDITED BY
STEVEN A. WESTLAKE

MYSTERIOUSPRESS.COM

OPEN ROAD
INTEGRATED MEDIA
NEW YORK

Collection copyright © 2016 by National Police Gazette Enterprises, LLC

Original articles copyright © 2015 by Mitchell Azaria

Cover design by Mauricio Díaz

978-1-5040-2215-6

Published in 2016 by MysteriousPress.com/
Open Road Integrated Media, Inc.
345 Hudson Street
New York, NY 10014
www.policegazette.us
www.mysteriouspress.com
www.openroadmedia.com

CONTENTS

HITLER
IS
ALIVE!

HOW ADOLF HITLER REMAINED ALIVE UNTIL THE 1970s

A *Police Gazette* Primer

Nearly two centuries ago, the *National Police Gazette* made history as North America's first-ever tabloid. Its groundbreaking, no-holds-barred style changed journalism forever, and it would go on to become one of the continent's five longest-running periodicals.

During the 1800s, while the underbelly of America was hidden beneath the skirts of Victorian purity, the *Police Gazette* delighted in foisting in-your-face stories of adultery, boozing, drug taking, corruption, and gambling onto a shocked public. Tom Wolfe, a literary groundbreaker himself, observed that "Victorian concepts of dignity were simply trampled on in the *Police Gazette*. . . . Yet its writers did provide a look at a side of American life that more serious and fastidious writers, including the major novelists of the period, never approached."

The *Gazette* reported it all with a quirky sensibility that is still present in media today. Its graphic pictures and articles were presented with a—not too visible—wink; some sort of punch line was never very far from anything published in the *National Police Gazette*. So when James Joyce had his characters in *Ulysses* "giggling over the *Police Gazette*" he may not have realized how very much to the point this was.

In the 1880s, for example, the *Gazette* cheerfully reported on the adventures of its "religious editor." Whether he was depicted being sexually aroused by the sight of Oscar Wilde's legs, blown up by an alcohol-soaked minister, or visited by a member of the Society of Clerical Kleptomaniacs, the *Gazette*'s religious editor always maintained the height of decorum and integrity befitting one of the "*Police Gazette* species." Of course, the *Gazette* had no religious editor. Religious America hated the *National Police Gazette* with a passion, seeing it as the most dangerous force for the corruption of youth and degradation of the morals of responsible adults the country had yet known.

This blurring of the distinction between real and fake news correspondents—not to mention real and fake news—became a *Police Gazette* specialty. *The Daily Show*, *The Colbert Report*, Sacha Baron Cohen—even the old *SPY Magazine*—all have a direct ancestor in the *National Police Gazette*. So it is no surprise that 170 years since it was first published, the *Gazette*'s keen observation of America has made the magazine hip again.

Internet humorist Seanbaby recently published his "6 Reasons the 'Police Gazette' is the Craziest Magazine Ever" at Cracked.com, which elicited comments ranging from shocked to disgusted to a profound desire for the return of such a "wonderful magazine." He got the tone just right, as this is exactly the response the *Gazette* evoked from readers when it was at its best. The closest correlation we have today would be a Howard Stern fan in the 1990s trying to explain to a nonbeliever how Stern really was NOT racist, sexist, or homophobic, and was actually hysterically funny and even provided a valuable service to society.

Yet, despite its low-brow reputation, a few heavyweight thinkers have tried explaining the *Police Gazette* over the years. Tom Wolfe is quoted above, while author and editor H. L. Mencken wrote "The Europeans, the English in particular were quick to see through the cheap yokel disesteem in which [the *Gazette* and its owner Richard K. Fox] were held and to estimate the fellow in the terms of the peculiar genius that was his. . . . [H]e was regarded on the Continent as the most enterprising, the most audacious and the most thoroughly honest of the American editors of his day."

The *Police Gazette* was the first publication to see through the hypocrisy of the times and give the people what they wanted without the non-load-bearing facade of self-importance. The *Gazette* mocked self-important posturings in American society with everything from features on corrupt religious leaders in its "Crimes of the Clergy" column to referring to itself with a satiric grandiosity that would make Stephen Colbert blush. "The POLICE GAZETTE first—Our Country next," declared one religious-editor dispatch.

Ironic pomposity aside, however, a list of the *Police Gazette*'s accomplishments reads like the Big Bang of pop-culture journalism. The *Gazette* invented or perfected the illustrated news weekly, the illustrated sports weekly, the newspaper sports department, comprehensive theater & entertainment coverage, the celebrity gossip column, Guinness World Record–style chronicling of crazy human achievement, the mainstream girlie magazine, the men's lifestyle magazine, and the sensational/tabloid journalism we know today. Joseph Pulitzer, who came to New York six years after Fox began using the *Gazette* to revolutionize journalism and pop culture, spoke of the substantial influence the *Police Gazette* had on his own approach to revolutionizing the daily newspaper.

Of course, a publication like this could not help but also perfect the art of the sensational headline, and article toppers like "Battle with Corpse-Eating Cats" or "Insane Asylum Horrors" kept the pages turning. So it was, six years after the alleged death of the person most directly responsible for the deadliest war in human history, the *Police Gazette* first presented evidence that "HITLER IS ALIVE!"

Like Flannery O'Connor's Misfit, who needed to see the acts of Jesus with his own eyes or else there was "No pleasure but meanness," the story told to us about how the demise of the worst—or best, if it's a measure of skill—mass murderer in history is maddening for its lack of our having seen it with our own eyes. Similarly, the bullets of *Star Trek*'s O.K. Corral gunfighters, though imaginary, could still kill you if you had even one quark-sized bit of doubt that they were not real, illustrating it only takes one tiny crack of doubt to open up a canyon of fear. And riding into that canyon, like a donut salesman at an

Overeaters Anonymous meeting, came the *National Police Gazette*, ready, willing, and able to fill the canyon to overflowing . . . and then some. If one article about how Hitler escaped death and was planning a comeback was good, then several dozen had to be that much better!

The *Gazette*'s coverage of Adolph Hitler began predictably enough. In June 1939, even before the start of the war in Europe, the *Police Gazette* published an article proving Hitler was a raging homosexual. Then, following oddly little coverage during the war itself—perhaps the real-life absurdities reported daily in the newspapers were enough—a portent of things to come was published in the October 1946 issue. A caption under the photo of a Führer lookalike begins "Is Hitler Dead?" But, except for an article in September 1947, it would be another five years before the *Gazette* revisited the Hitler subject. And this time it would be revisited with a vengeance.

For those keeping score, from 1951 to 1968 the *Police Gazette* published seventy-six Hitler-related articles—including thirteen excerpts from Alan Bullock's respected biography *Hitler: A Study in Tyranny*—and featured him on the cover thirty-seven times, not counting a few more covers where his name was only mentioned in small print. During this period, a prominent Hitler grabber appeared on a *Gazette* cover an average of over twice per year.

Adolph Hitler being proven alive ended up the longest running gag in the long history of the *National Police Gazette*—all of it, of course, done with a completely straight face. Journalist and former *Gazette* employee Edward Van Every had lamented during a weak stretch, "The *Gazette* ceased to be funny when it started to take itself as a joke." But his worry during the Hitler series for the most part was dodged, in spite of the increasingly obvious comic device of repeating something to the point of absurdity.

So at the risk of beating a dead Führer, presented here all in one place for the first time, the collected wisdom of the investigative staff of the *National Police Gazette* on just what happened to the most notorious figure in a millennium of human history.

Hitler Is Alive?!

Our story opens with submarines—mysterious objects under normal circumstances—that suddenly appear off the coast of Argentina in July and August 1945. They are Nazi subs, the U-530 and U-977. Why are they there? And what were they doing for the three months prior to their arrival?

Besides being Adolph Hitler's personal physician, who was Dr. Ludwig Stumpfegger? And did he develop a mysterious procedure called the "silk-cord operation" that could temporarily paralyze parts of the human brain? What role might this operation have played in the disappearance of Hitler?

Did Hitler escape to "a place sufficiently uninhabited, remote, and immense to make it practically impossible to find him?" And what was that place?

Zombies, epic underwater journeys, ice-palace fortresses of criminal masterminds . . . It's all here in the first great blast of *Police Gazette* Hitler-Is-Alive reporting. Then, as the series was beginning to stretch the reader's willing suspension of disbelief into the thinness of a bubble, the cavalry comes over the hill in the person of Colonel William F. Heimlich, a high-level member of the first US intelligence team to enter Berlin at war's end.

Having been personally involved in the search for Hitler evidence, Heimlich provides the verisimilitude in his own bylined *Police Gazette* article that had been lacking in some of the previous articles. Heimlich declares "No insurance company in America would pay a death claim on Adolph Hitler." This imprimatur from a respected former official of the US government gives the *Gazette* gas and the magazine floors it from that point on.

The *Police Gazette*, which showed the way with so many journalistic innovations, here creates the conspiracy theory as Oak Island excavation, a bottomless pit of conjecture that's impossible to resolve and, by definition, cannot end! Everyone from JFK assassination buffs to 9/11 truthers should bow down and pay homage.

EXCLUSIVE SCOOP!
HITLER IS ALIVE!

Officially Adolph Hitler and his mistress Eva Braun, were reported to have taken their departure from life in a double suicide pact. The bodies, placed in a ditch filled with gasoline, were supposedly burned in the courtyard of the Reichschancellery.

In this issue the Police Gazette *starts publication of the sensational findings of an investigation made throughout Europe and South America by competent investigators into the strange mystery of Adolph Hitler's alleged death.*

This world-wide investigation has unearthed amazing revelations to displace this theory. Former heads of the Wehrmacht, who are spread all over the world, and certain Nazis, still being sought, were interviewed. The extensive inquiry reached into the far corners of the world.

So sensational and world-shaking are the results of this probe that the Police Gazette feels obligated to present all the data to its readers in a series of exclusive articles.

When news of the probe reached Lieutenant Heinz Schaeffer, former commander of the German Submarine U-977, he came voluntarily from Argentina, where he now lives, to the Paris office of the investigators. He was the commander who surrendered to Argentine authorities at Mar del Plata in August, 1945, after having spent three and a half months on a mysterious sea voyage.

The German naval officer involved denied spiriting Hitler away, but could not—or would not—explain his long and mysterious submarine voyage at war's end. Nor would he disclose the unexplained luxury condition of one U-boat.

Lieutenant Commander Schaeffer made the following statement which, incidentally, in no way invalidates the findings which will be presented in these articles.

"It has been claimed that I carried Adolf Hitler, Eva Braun and Martin Bormann aboard my submarine. That is untrue. Also, I was subjected to lengthy interrogations on this point by the American and British authorities. Finally, the latter accepted my explanations and freed me and my crew.

"The truth is that I went to Mar del Plata, like the U-530 which preceded us, in order to escape internment.

"At the time I received command of the U-977, in April 1945, the Russians were approaching Berlin and the Americans already had occupied most of the French ports. My superiors ordered me to Norway. I arrived there the day Admiral Doenitz took over as head of the German Reich. On May 2 we received orders to surface, hoist the white flag, return to our bases and wait there for the Allies.

"I told my crew that we had two possibilities:

"(1) to scuttle our submarine in the Channel, make for the English coast in our lifeboats and surrender;

"(2) make for a country which had remained friendly to Germany.

"Since I had friends in Argentina, I suggested that country which was approved by the crew. Sixteen of the men who were married preferred to return. I put them ashore on the Norwegian coast and then turned the bow of my vessel towards South America."

We asked Commander Schaeffer at this point: "Did you have sufficient provisions for such a long voyage?"

He said, "Yes, only a few days earlier we had taken aboard cases of canned foods at a depot in Denmark."

A lucky coincidence, indeed.

Heinz Schaeffer then went on:

"I knew that the ocean was patrolled by American planes. For that reason I decided to travel submersed. Our boat was equipped with Schnorkel which enabled us to travel under the surface by using our diesels.

"We could have lightened our boat by shedding our torpedos. However, I held on to them. I was afraid we might be charged with having sunk ships after the armistice.

"We traveled submersed for sixty-six days. Sixty-six days of superhuman suffering.

"My crew of 31 sailors took turns in falling sick.

"By the time we had left the danger zone they had been reduced to human debris.

"We surfaced in the vicinity of the Cape Verde Islands.

"From there on the voyage was pleasant and on August 17 we entered the Port of Mar del Plata."

Nobody maintains that Hitler was aboard the U-977. Our staff investigator also established that fact. However, as we shall see very soon, the U-977 as well as the U-530 were stated to play different roles than that of transport vessels.

The statement of Commander Heinz Schaeffer fails to shed light on several points on which we vainly tried to get satisfactory explanations.

For instance, is it plausible for a captain to condemn his crew to two months of superhuman suffering—merely to escape captivity?

On the other hand, the U-977 left Norway May 2 and arrived around July 8 in the vicinity of the Cape Verde Islands. Why did the vessel take two and a half months to reach Argentina? We stress these baffling details, because in the course of the series of articles which starts in this issue, the staff of investigators will present a proper explanation.

Surrender by the U-530

"Hello," an excited voice came over the phone. "This is the United Press. A German submarine has just surrendered to Argentine Naval authorities in the port of Mar del Plata."

This conversation took place July 10, 1945. The capitulation of the Reich already was history and the three Great Powers were making last-minute preparations for their meeting at Potsdam. Thus it was no wonder that this unexpected news created a sensation not only in Buenos Aires, but also in London and Washington.

Subsequent stories confirmed that first piece of news and around noontime an official communique of the Navy Ministry announced the vessel in question was the German submarine U-530.

The commander's papers identified him as Captain Otto Wermutt. He was the last to leave his boat. On shore he handed over a small valise containing the flag of the submarine as well as the ship's papers. His youth created general attention. It was later learned that he was only 25 years of age. His second in command, Captain Karl Felix Schubert, was still younger, only 22. Both officers and enlisted men seemed unusually young, some of them mere children.

The crew of the U-530 appeared tired, but not undernourished.

The first officials who came aboard established that the boat's entire complement of 54 men still had a rather large store of food, despite their long voyage. In turn, a surprisingly small amount of fuel was found on board the submarine. Incidentally, at the moment of surrender the vessel was partially disarmed. It lacked the forward (bow) cannon as well as two large-caliber anti-aircraft guns. These it was supposed, had been dumped overboard when the captain had decided to surrender. On the other hand, the hull of the submarine was partially denuded of paint and generally covered with dirt, sure signs of an extended voyage on the high seas.

"No important Nazi bigwig arrived on the U-530," the Buenos Aires evening papers announced in large headlines, thus furnishing a clear answer to the question asked by all. Meanwhile, another question raised was whether the U-530 was responsible for the sinking of the Brazilian cruiser *Bahia*, whose survivors arrived that same morning at the port of Recife. On the other hand, rumors were heard everywhere to the effect that some of the Nazi Chieftains had landed on the coast of Patagonia. These landings, it was alleged, had been made by means of rubber boats in the region of Necochea.

Four and a Half Months at Sea

The next day, the mystery was cleared up by a second communique issued by the Navy Ministry which stated as follows:

(1) Investigations established that the German submarine which surrendered to the authorities of the Mar del Plata base was not responsible for the sinking of the Brazilian cruiser *Bahia*.

(2) No German political or military leaders were on board the aforementioned submarine.

(3) Prior to having surrendered to the authorities, the submarine did not disembark anybody along the Argentine coast.

(4) All persons who did come ashore were members of the crew of the submarine, in accordance with the official register submitted.

At Mar del Plata the arrival of the German submarine created unusual excitement.

Following inspection visits by the Naval Attaches of Great Britain and the United States, it was learned that in accordance with information furnished by the Captain the U-530 had left Germany on February 19, 1945 and sailed northward to Norway. From there it left on March 13 in the direction of the North Atlantic. When the surrender order issued by Admiral Doenitz became known on board, Captain Wermutt decided to continue his voyage to the coast of Argentina and surrender at Mar del Plata.

These statements, together with additional information concerning the person of Captain Wermutt and his career as submarine commander were soon published by the papers. Yet, there was the fact that the U-530 had traveled on the high seas for almost four and a half months.

This fact, in itself, could not fail to attract considerable attention. The modern German submarines like the U-530 which had been constructed in 1942 were equipped with completely new devices which enabled them to cruise for months on end far away from their bases. They were Schnorkel-equipped, the Schnorkel being a respiratory device which made it possible for the submarine to stay submersed and travel under water for 70 consecutive days. Thus, it was not the fact of the prolonged voyage on the highseas which attracted so much attention, but the question which logically followed, namely:

What had been the activities of the U-530 during those four and a half months, from the day it had left its base to the day of its surrender at Mar del Plata?

This question was asked not only at Buenos Aires but also in London. There the news of the submarine's surrender created consternation at the Admiralty, whose spokesman had only recently stated that the seas of the globe could again be traversed in absolute safety. When no official communique was forthcoming in the British capital, a naval commentator did not hesitate to speak of "an ocean mystery which is open to numerous conjectures." One month before it had been assumed that the last German submarine had been accounted for. Then, on June 3, one of these vessels was disarmed by its crew off the northern coast of Portugal.

The news of the surrender of the U-530 created in London the effect of a bombshell and promptly provoked lively disputes in naval circles, where the presence of a German submarine in Argentine waters was explained by one of two theories:

(1) Under orders of its fanatical commander, the submarine had continued to carry on the war on its own account as long as possible, without heeding the orders issued by Doenitz.

(2) The submarine had been selected for the secret transport of a high Nazi personage to Argentina with the hope of finding refuge there.

Soon it became evident that both theories were ill founded. Few facts were known concerning the political convictions of Commander Wermutt. However, inspections of the technical installations on board the vessel showed beyond doubt that the U-530 not only had not sunk the *Bahia*, but had in fact not engaged in any warlike action during the last phase of its voyage, that is, at least not since the day when the capitulation order had been issued.

With regard to the second theory, the official Argentine statement was absolutely clear: it was based on the result of inquiries carried out in the most conscientious manner. Yet, one question remained unanswered: What had the U-530 been doing during its long voyage and why had it come to Argentina to surrender?

The Mystery Cigarettes

There seemed to be no satisfactory answer to this question nor to several others that cropped up in that connection. The crew of the submarine underwent repeated questioning, with no result. Their statements agreed perfectly with the documents produced and with the stories of their officers. Their replies were perfectly coordinated, as if they had been carefully rehearsed or—and there is always that possibility—as if they actually embodied the truth.

Nevertheless, three days after the arrival of the U-530 at Mar del Plata only a handful of people believed in the declarations of Captain Wermutt and his crew. For in these uniform recitals there were several obscure points which yet required explanation. Without going into any lengthy investigation, there was the obvious fact that *the submarine could not possibly have undertaken the long and dangerous voyage from Norway to Mar del Plata for no other reason than to arrive "on the hospitable shores of Argentina," to quote the Captain of the vessel.*

Certain details continued to arouse the public interest. The U-530 was of limited tonnage. Its normal complement could not have exceeded 27 men. Since the second year of the war, German submarines of the U-530 type used to carry no more than 18 and sometimes only 16 men, in view of the lack of manpower which permanently beset the Reich submarine arm. Why, then, did the U-530 at the time of its surrender carry three times the complement of the war years?

Why did Captain Wermutt's vessel carry 54 men aboard? Why was the majority of the crew so surprisingly young?

Experts who inspected the vessel were able to establish that the supplies on board were rather ample even for such a large crew. They also found that the ship carried only an insignificant number of torpedos and other munitions. In all probability, the war materiel had been reduced in quantity so as to gain space for such a large crew as well as for the necessary food supplies.

Another mystery which balked satisfactory clarification: one compartment of the submarine yielded a rather large quantity of cigarettes. The naval inspectors were surprised to find such a large stock of cigarettes on board the U-530. And without doubt they raised eyebrows when Captain Wermutt told them that 'on his arrival he still had 10 cartons of cigarettes per man aboard.' As a result, there were found 540 cartons of cigarettes on board and maybe more.

Imagine the surprise of naval technicians—in view of the fact that no smoking is permitted in the interior of a submarine. As a rule, submarine crews don't smoke and the Germans are no exception to that. And this abstinence became quite evident during the internment of the U-530 crew near Mar del Plata at a summer camp, which happened to be vacant: they didn't smoke, even though they had disembarked.

A Phony Captain?

All these facts indicated that the U-530 was truly an unusual submarine. It carried a large complement, plenty of food supplies, a large store of cigarettes and little war materiel. It had not conformed to the capitulation orders and it had undertaken such a long and perilous voyage for the sole purpose of surrendering to the Argentine port authorities.

Truly, this story smelled phony. On the other hand, the truth failed to be unearthed. Officers and men of the U-530 continued to repeat their initial statements with the precision of a phonograph record and without any contradictions. Yet, the naval authorities dared not be satisfied with these well-tailored stories.

And so, on the morning of July 13, the Argentine flag was hoisted on the conning tower of the German submarine and Argentine war vessels and planes left the Mar del Plata base to search the coastal waters for other German naval units.

That search yielded no positive results. Investigations were also undertaken throughout the Necochea region where several persons insisted they had observed the landing of a rubber lifeboat several days prior to the surrender of the submarine. A new crop of rumors sprang up but soon subsided. *Yet some people persisted that Captain Wermutt was not the real captain of the submarine.*

The most persistent rumors concerned alleged landings of Nazi bigwigs on the coast of Patagonia. True, in view of the enormous length of the Argentine coastline, the U-530 could have carried out shore landings by means of rubber lifeboats. However, the results of the investigations did not support such theories by a single shred of evidence. During the period which has elapsed since, all conjectures of this sort have been thoroughly demolished. It is safe to state that beyond any reasonable doubt, *no person was put ashore along the Argentine coast by the U-530.*

If such conjectures had proved well founded, it would have undoubtedly caused new investigations and certainly would have resulted in official steps on the part of the United States and Great Britain with the Argentine Government.

On July 14, 1945 a naval commentator declared: "The truth concerning the U-530 will be found only in the German naval archives." He is probably right.

It is not known whether the Allies succeeded in getting hold of the pertinent Reich Naval records and whether those records explained the nature of the last mission of the submarine seized at Mar del Plata. News dispatches announced that the American and British Governments would hold consultations on the case of the U-530 on the basis of reports from their respective naval attaches at Buenos Aires.

But a few weeks later it was learned that the submarine which had surrendered at Mar del Plata actually was not the real U-530 at all.

HITLER IS ALIVE!

Second of a Series

As related in the preceding installment, the German submarine U-530 entered the Argentine port of Mar del Plata on July 10, 1945 and surrendered to the Argentine authorities.

Several days later, on July 19, 1945 Admiral Eberhardt Godt, Commander in Chief of Submarine Operations issued this statement at Kiel, Germany:

"The U-530 did not leave Germany on February 19, 1945. As a matter of fact, the boat was still at Kiel on March 3. On that date it left Kiel for Norway."

This statement by Admiral Godt later confirmed by Admiral Helmuth, former Commander of the German Battle Cruiser Hipper and ex-Chief of Small Combat units, squarely contradicted the stories told by Capt. Otto Wermutt, Commandant of the U-530, to the Argentine authorities.

Did Wermutt Lie?

Wermutt's tale was contradicted even more strongly by another German naval officer, Capt. Kurt Langer who until the middle of 1944 had been in command of the U-530.

In an interview with newspapermen, Langer stated that "the U-530 actually leaked water at the seams and could no longer be considered seaworthy.

"In fact," he went on, "the U-530 was an unlucky submarine. Its stern had been smashed by an American tanker on Christmas Day of 1943 when I was attacked on the eastern shore of the Panama Canal. It was a sheer miracle that I managed to get back to my base.

"It seems unbelievable to me that such an old and worn ship could have made the trip to the Argentine Coast.

"If Hitler and Eva Braun escaped from Germany aboard a submarine," he concluded, "they hardly could have made this voyage aboard the U-530."

But the U-530 which surrendered at Mar del Plata, was not at all an "old and worn ship" which leaked water through its seams.

As a matter of fact, it was a recently designed, completely new boat and in excellent condition to have made the long journey across the Atlantic.

Thus, *all evidence points to the fact that the U-530* which surrendered at Mar del Plata *was not the same submarine of which Captain Langer spoke.*

In other words, the ship at Mar del Plata *was a different unit*, though of the same class as the original U-530.

Somewhere along the line, a switch had been made and a new ship had been substituted for the old U-530.

What reason was there for this switch?

Obviously, it was to confound any subsequent investigations. What actually seemed to have happened was this: while the real U-530, that "old and worn ship", was being overhauled at Kiel for departure scheduled on March 3, its double had left Germany as early as February 19 to carry out the mission entrusted to it. It is entirely feasible that this switch was carried out in a secrecy which tricked even Admirals Godt and Helmuth, especially since the secret orders heretofore seem to have come from the Supreme Army Command of the Reichwehr.

Thus, all German naval officers quoted previously may have spoken the truth. Commandant Wermutt may have been sincerely convinced that his boat was the real U-530. And Captain Langer and Admirals Godt and Helmuth also may have been entirely sincere when they asserted that the real U-530 was on February 19 still at Kiel.

Did the Allies ever succeed in proving a switch? This is a moot question, since no statement on this subject was ever published.

Nevertheless, the British Admiralty must have entertained suspicions as to the real state of affairs. On July 18, 1945 its spokesman told the press in London that "no official calculation has been undertaken as to the number of remaining German submarines." At about the same time a London naval commentator freely admitted "With respect to the German submarine problem even the Admiralty's secret intelligence branch despite the information available, is unable to express itself with absolute certainty."

Strange Events

With the U-530 and its crew interned at Mar del Plata, the Argentine Naval Authorities decided on July 17, 1945 to place that sub at the disposal of the United States and Great Britain.

That same day, July 17, news was received in Buenos Aires of strange observations made by inhabitants of the village of San Clements del Toyo, situated to the north of Mar del Plata.

These villagers claimed to have seem the shape of another German submarine silhouetted against the horizon far out at sea. A few of the observers even claimed to have spotted TWO subs and that one of them appeared to have run aground not far from the shore.

Upon receipt of this news the Argentine Navy Ministry dispatched several airplane squadrons and various ships to the scene. But despite intensive searching no submarines were spotted. As a matter of fact, weather conditions in the warm of a thick fog hampered the search considerably which rendered the job of the combined naval and air units so difficult that it was soon broken off. Yet, and extensive area was covered.

Also, numerous beach patrols were organized immediately along the coast in order to prevent any landing attempts. Simultaneously, Argentina's Federal Police launched several investigations among the country's German colonies.

The net results were zero.

No submarines were sighted and no landings were discovered along the coast.

A week later, on July 24, the US Government at Washington announced it had dispatched army planes to Mar del Plata in order to bring the crew of the U-530 to the US The same communique added that the U-530 would be towed to an American port.

The news was bound to create a sensation. Though the war had ended three months earlier, the US seemed in great haste to intern within its borders the crew of the U-530. This contrasted with the leisurely manner in which the crew of the Admiral Graft Spee had been carried off at the height of the war.

Suffice it to say that no official statements were ever issued concerning the interrogations of the crew of the U-530 by the US authorities. Rumors had it that both officers and men were subjected an intensive questioning. But the results still remain to be aired.

Appearance of the U-977

A little over a month after the surrender of the U-530, on August 17, 1945 the Argentine Naval Ministry issued to the press two communiques.

"Today, at 9:20 a.m.," the first communique, from "a German submarine, seemingly of the type of the U-530, surrendered to Argentine Naval units on patrol off Mar del Plata. The aforementioned submarine entered Mar del Plata at 11:15 towed by the Dredge M10 and escorted by a submarine of the country's Navy. Thereupon the crew was taken ashore. At present, a security watch is being stationed on board."

The second communique added:

"The German submarine now lying at anchor in the port of Mar del Plata is the U-977 of 600 tons. Its crew is made up of 32 men, including four officers. The boat was commanded by Lt. Commander Heinz Schaeffer who at present is aboard the S.S. Belgrano."

During the next 48 hours it was revealed that the U-977 had been spotted approximately eight miles east of the port of Mar del Plata. It was sighted by Argentine Naval Units on patrol in this area as well as by a local fishing boat. The S.S. Commodore Py and other vessels approached the sub and ascertained that it was German. Thereupon the sub's commander indicated his readiness to surrender. The ship was then escorted to the base where officers and enlisted men were immediately interned and subjected to preliminary questioning.

Important contrasts were observed between the new arrival and the U-530 which had surrendered over a month earlier.

The U-977, seemingly of the latest design and equipped with the latest type of navigating and other instruments, was not disarmed. It even possessed equipment in the form of a chemical substances which, when released into the water, would stay submerged and there create subsurface bubbles so as to lend the impression that the submarine had sunk.

Concerning the itinerary of the U-977 as recorded in the ship's log book, the Argentine Naval Ministry on the eve of August 18 issued the following communique:

"Documents found aboard the German U-boat U-977 seem to indicate that the ship left Kiel on April 13, made Oslo and left there on April 22, then touched Christiansund and left there on May 2. On the Norwegian Coast it disembarked 16 men, all noncommissioned officers, who were married and had families in Germany. Next the ship traversed the blockaded zone of the Atlantic by slipping through the Faroe Islands and Iceland. From there it traveled a southerly course, passed to the west of the Charies and in between the Cape Verde Islands. Thereafter it surfaced, passed near the cliffs of San Pablo, then followed the Brazilian coast, but out of sight from the latter and at an average distance of 180 miles, and made for Mar del Plata."

From the above communique it would appear that the U-977 had been on the high seas for more than three and a half months, without engaging in any belligerent act, just like the U-530.

Now Commandant Schaeffer of the U-977 stated that he had no personal acquaintance of Capt. Otto Wermutt of the U-530 and his officers.

But he DID admit that he knew about the surrender of the U-530 to the Argentine naval authorities at Mar del Plata. This news had been received by the radio on board the U-977.

Now arises this question: why did Captain Wermutt and the U-977 wait five additional weeks before following the example of the U-530 in surrendering at Mar del Plata?

The rest of the story of the U-977 is comparatively uneventful. The crew was taken to Garcia Island and from there transferred by planes to the US As in the case of the U-530, the results of their interrogations were never published.

An Unknown Mission

Despite the official silence cloaked around these two mysterious Nazi subs, the following conclusions are self-evident:

(1) After leaving Germany, both the U-530 as well as the U-977 touched Norwegian ports, then set their course for the South Atlantic, both traveling almost identical routes.

(2) Both boats were on the high seas for approximately three and a half months, without their officers being able to account satisfactorily for their activities during that period.

(3) Both commandants failed to comply with the surrender orders issued by Admiral Doenitz. Nevertheless, they did not engage in any acts of war.

(4) No satisfactory explanations were given by either sub for their motives to surrender. Although Capt. Schaeffer of the U-977 had received the news of the surrender of the U-530, he elected to remain at sea for another 5 weeks prior to surrendering HIS ship.

(5) Despite the U-977 being fully armed, both submarines apparently had been used for transport instead of combat. This is also borne out by their rather full complements and by the surprisingly large food stores on board.

(6) In both submarines, officers as well as enlisted men were young and had no families.

(7) The ship headed by Commandant Wermutt obviously was not the original U-530, as seen from the statements of Admiral Godt and Capt. Langer.

(8) Actually—and we again stress the point—not only the U-530 and the U-977 were prowling the Atlantic *after* Doenitz's surrender orders. There was a third sub—or, chronologically speaking, a first one.

As early as June 4, 1945 it had been announced by the British Admiralty that a German submarine had appeared that day off Leixoes, Portugal. The crew, numbering 47, disarmed and scuttled their ship and then surrendered to the Portuguese authorities. Its commander stated that the ship had followed a course which later on was traveled by the U-530 and U-977, but had decided upon surrender to the Portuguese authorities because its hull and engines were badly in need of repairs.

The above seems to indicate that at the time of Germany's collapse, a number of subs had left German ports, their identity either real or faked, in order to touch first Norwegian ports of call and then to embark for the South Atlantic on missions of mystery.

Nevertheless, the mystery of these Nazi subs prowling the Atlantic even after the end of the War is bound up with the greatest mystery of all time: the survival and hiding place of Adolf Hitler, in whose death neither the highest diplomat in America nor England nor Russia believes.

As a matter of fact, the strange story of these German subs which surrendered in Argentina and Portugal starts in the underground fortresses of the Nazi Chancellery.

In the Bunker of Adolf Hitler whose criminal hand seven years earlier had set the torch of war to the world, there was hatched one of the supreme hoaxes of all times.

HITLER IS ALIVE!

Third of a Series

**"I shall die defending Berlin," boasted Adolf.
But the FANTASTIC EVIDENCE proves that HE LIVED!**

Editor's Note: During the summer of 1945, a few months after the supposed death of Hitler in the ruins of Berlin, two Nazi submarines appeared at the Argentine naval base of Mar Del Plata and surrendered to the local authorities.

The officers were unable to account for the purpose of their voyage across the Atlantic which they claimed had taken several months. Also, the subs carried aboard abundant food supplies and their crews were made up of mere youths.

Investigation was launched immediately, but the mystery surrounding these submarines still persists. Allegedly these strange craft play a part in the survival of Hitler.

On April 30, 1945 the battle for Berlin entered its last stage. The entire city was in flames and the ground trembled under salvos of 15,000 cannon with which Soviet General Yukov had ringed Hitler's Capital. Illuminated by flickering flames, combat continued throughout the night with a ferocity seldom witnessed. At dawn the Russian flag was fluttering over the hollow, ruined shell that remained of what once had been the Reichstag, Germany's Capital.

Where was Hitler? He was said to be directing the defense of Berlin from his underground shelter below the Nazi Chancellory. But the Allies doubted this.

Nevertheless, in the early morning hours of April 30, the London Daily Mail blared forth in giant headlines:

Hitler Dying; War May Be Over Today

This prediction was based on a piece of news received by Wilson Broadbent, diplomatic editor of the paper, who quoted a high Whitehall official as having told him: "Hitler is dying and may already be dead." The official had added that in his opinion the European war had come to an end. The *Times*, generally considered the most reserved newspaper in the world, ran the following news item: "Hitler is on the brink of death as the result of a cerebral hemorrhage." The paper added that this news was based on information supposedly released by Himmler.

A Piece of Clever Staging

During the afternoon of May 1, 1945 the Hamburg Radio Station suddenly interrupted its program and began transmission of solemn Wagnerian music. After the funereal strains of Twilight of the Gods, the announcer stated:

"Attention: In a few seconds we are going to broadcast a grave, but important message addressed to the German people. But first, the Seventh Symphony by Bruckner."

The Bruckner piece concluded, the announcer resumed:

"German men and women: Our Fuehrer Adolf Hitler died this afternoon at his post of command in the Chancellory of the Reich, fighting to his last breath against Bolshevism."

Later, the same German radio station announced that Admiral Doenitz, Commander in Chief of the Reich Navy, had assumed Hitler's functions. Thereupon, the radio transmitted a proclamation by the new Chief of State, exhorting the German people to "keep the oath they had sworn to the Fuehrer while the German Army fought on to save the Reich from deadly peril!"

Thus, everything seemed to jibe perfectly. Hitler, falling amidst the burning ruins of Berlin, had already written what was to become the first chapter of the Fuehrer Myth.

But suspicions already were rife Many observers doubted that the Nazis' own story of Hitler's death could be accepted without reservations.

The Russians displayed frank skepticism in the face of the melodramatic announcement. Tass, the official Soviet news agency, termed the news of Hitler's death "just another Fascist trick," and Moscow promptly stated that "in propagandizing the news of Hitler's death, the Nazis schemed to make it possible for the Fuehrer to leave the stage and retire into the wings."

On the morning of May 2, 1945, Allied General Headquarters published the following communique:

"On April 24 a conference took place at Luebeck between Count Bernadotte, President of the International Red Cross, and Heinrich Himmler. In the course of this talk Himmler acknowledged that Hitler was mortally ill, perhaps already dead.

"General Schillenburg who also participated in these talks, added that Hitler had suffered a brain stroke."

Thus, the announcement by Doenitz that Hitler had died a hero's death in contradiction to the statement made by Himmler and Schillenburg.

By May 2, 1945, however, both British and American leaders were fully convinced that Hitler was dead. They discarded the Doenitz version of Hitler's heroic death, but they nevertheless were certain Hitler was no longer alive.

With respect to Himmler and Schillenburg, how did they know what occurred in Berlin at the critical hour? Either they may have been uninformed—or they may have lied, a possibility which emerged a few days later.

In an order of the day released in the afternoon of May 2, 1945, Marshal Stalin announced the fall of Berlin.

At the same time, the victorious troops began to search systematically among the ruins of Berlin for the body of Hitler. Starting from the Reich Chancellory where the General underground Headquarters of the Fuehrer had been located, they fanned out in all directions.

They also searched for the body of Goebbels.

Faint or Suicide

According to a news item broadcast by Radio Moscow on May 3, the Director General of Nazi Propaganda, Dr. Hans Fritsche, who had been captured by the Russians, had stated that Goebbels had committed suicide. As the fall of the capital seemed imminent, Fritsche related, Goebbels had first killed his wife and children and then taken his own life. Fritsche also asserted that Hitler had died as the result of Soviet shells and that his body was entombed in a place which it would be impossible to locate.

While the world enthusiastically celebrated the fall of Germany, hopes of finding the principal culprit or at least his body soon waned. It seemed as if developments bore out Fritsche. Despite systematic searching, the body of Hitler failed to turn up.

On May 8, a communique issued from Headquarters of the 2nd British Army announced that according to information furnished by a Soviet General, the Russians had found under the ruins of the Chancellory a corpse which seemed to be Hitler's. Furthermore, all the servants attached to the Chancellory asserted that the corpse was Hitler's, except one who said that it was a chef's who had been killed because he was mistaken for the Fuehrer. He also said that Hitler wasn't dead, but had fled from Berlin.

On May 7, the theory that Hitler had suffered a brain stroke was categorically denied by Dr. Erwin Giensing, a German Army doctor and nose, ear and throat specialist. Interrogated by the Americans, Giensing said he had examined Hitler thoroughly on February 15, 1945 and that there was not the slightest probability that Hitler had died from a cerebral stroke.

Giensing stated also that in the course of his last examination he found Hitler's blood pressure normal, his lungs healthy, and that, in general, his health for a man of his age was exceptionally good.

Soon the Russians began to show indications of skepticism with respect to Hitler's cadaver. On May 10 a Soviet spokesman stated curtly: "At least four corpses were found in the ruins of Berlin, any one of which could be Hitler's. However, none has been identified in a manner which would establish Hitler's identity beyond reasonable doubt."

Meanwhile Erich Heinz Kempke, ex-chauffeur of the Nazi Dictator, declared that he had assisted at the cremation of the corpses of Adolf Hitler and Eva Braun.

Kempke told his story on June 20 at Berchtesgaden to the United Press which quoted him as stating in effect that Hitler and Eva Braun had been married April 11 and committed suicide on April 13 in an under-ground apartment in back of the Chancellory at Berlin. Kempke claimed that shortly before dawn on April 13 he had carried the body of Eva Braun from that apartment after she and Hitler had died from shots with a Walther pistol.

According to the United Press, Kempke named as witnesses to the cremation of the bodies of Hitler and Eva in the Chancellory, in addition to himself, Bormann, Goebbels, Otto Guesche and Heinz Linge, two personal aides to Hitler, as well as two others whose names he did not recall. He also said that shortly before Hitler's and Eva's suicides, the Fuehrer personally ordered Guesche to attend to the cremation of their bodies so that they would not fall into Russian hands.

Thus, according to Kempke, Hitler and Eva died on April 13. Yet, there seems to exist indisputable proof that they were still alive on April 22 when the last Council of War was held in Hitler's subterranean Fortress with Marshal Keitel, General Jodl and Martin Borman participating.

Stenographer's Story

Hitler's personal stenographer, Gerhardt Herrgeselle, who had surrendered himself and his notebook to the Americans, provided the Allies with a seemingly accurate description of the stormy underground meeting of April 22.

According to Herrgeselle, Hitler retired to his quarters in the Chancellory on January 16, and from April 1 on all meetings of importance were held in his underground bunker. Hitler and Eva lived in two tiny apartments adjoining the meeting chamber. The apartments were lit and heated by electricity.

A few weeks prior to April 22 Hitler declared: "We shall fight to the last square foot of German soil."

As a result, it was generally expected that he would fix the date for exchanging his head-quarters in the underground bunker for the comparative safety of the "National Retreat" in the Bavarian Alps.

"On April 20, around noon," Herrgeselle stated, "Chief of Staff Krebs who had succeeded Guerian, declared that the situation of Berlin was critical. As a result, Hitler gave orders for the majority of his Headquarters staff to be evacuated to Berchtesgaden. Only a small part remained behind in Berlin."

On April 21, Russian shells began to fall among the Government buildings in Berlin.

The Last Council

"On April 20, around noon," Herrgeselle stated, explosions of Russian shells could be heard clearly in Hitler's underground shelter. Half an hour later the Fuehrer sent word to Keitel, Jodl and Bormann that he wanted to see them in the meeting chamber. Herrgeselle too was ordered to report for taking notes.

The meeting, which was to be the last War Council of the Nazi High Command, began with Hitler saying:

"I realize that all is lost. I shall stay in Berlin. I shall die here in the Chancellory because I believe that in this way I can best serve the German people. They must be inspired to continue the struggle."

His listeners repeatedly urged him to evacuate and reminded him of his own statement that, "we shall fight to the last square foot of German soil."

But Hitler remained firm: "I shall stay here," he said.

Keitel, Jodl and Bormann then told him that they would not leave him in this hour.

But Hitler ordered: "Go to South Germany."

Thereupon he arose, indicating the Council was ended.

Thus, according to Herrgeselle, Hitler decided to die in Berlin. The Fuehrer's personal stenographer was convinced that he and Eva Braun had died under the ruins of the Chancellory. He discounted both the theory of Hitler's brain stroke and that of his and Eva's suicide. In accordance with the Fuehrer's orders, Herrgeselle and another stenographer were evacuated by plane from the Gatow airdrome near Berlin on April 22.

Herrgeselle concluded by stating that a few minutes before he left Berlin for the airport, Eva Braun Handed him a small package to deliver. He believed it contained a ring as well as a long letter, to whom he didn't know. The package was addressed to one Lt. Mueller, an aide to Martin Bormann.

Herrgeselle's story, which was in effect corroborated by both Keitel and Jodl, confirms the fact that Hitler and Eva were still alive on the 22nd of April.

As to Kempke's tale, he admitted under questioning that at the "cremation" he had seen only a casket draped over by a Nazi war flag. He had not seen the Fuehrer's body.

We believe that the Wagnerian music, the sensational communiques and "eye-witness stories", the many corpses and the "cremation" are but bits of Hitler's plan to simulate his death.

He would have succeeded in the deception except for one detail which he overlooked.

HITLER IS ALIVE!

Fourth Installment

Der Fuehrer Marries Eva Braun
and plans their escape from Berlin.

Editor's Note: Official Allied reports said that Hitler and the beautiful Eva Braun had committed suicide and been cremated in the ruined Reich Chancellory at Berlin. But an intriguing rumor circulated in Europe—and on top levels—that the suicide was a hoax, a brilliantly conceived smokescreen behind which the most-sought-after couple in the world had fled to escape Allied justice.

Suddenly the rumor became something more when two Nazi U-boats—one of them luxuriously furnished—came out of nowhere at the Argentine naval base of Mar del Plata and surrendered to the authorities. This was late in the Summer of 1945—months after Germany had capitulated and the shooting war had ended.

During the early part of July 1945 English and American war correspondents for the first time obtained permission to visit the site of the alleged suicide of Hitler.

The British journalists did not hide their skepticism concerning the many versions relative to the Fuehrer's death. Their opinion as a group was expressed in the following Reuters dispatch datelined: Hitler's Underground Bunker, Berlin, July 5, 1945:

"The story of Hitler's death is a yarn which has no point. The charred body found by Red Army Officers and examined by experts was not that of Hitler. It was the body of one of his doubles and at that, one of his second-rate doubles, according to an officer on the staff of Marshal Youkov who conducted this Reuters correspondent through the ruins of the Chancellory.

"'So far no trace has as yet been found of a Body resembling Eva Braun,' this officer added. 'We are so certain that the corpse found is not that of Hitler that orders have been issued to re-inter it in the garden of the Chancellory.'"

The Famous English Report

The official English report, published Nov. 1, 1945, attempted to detail the circumstances concerning the deaths of Adolf Hitler and Eva Braun. However, the report was far from convincing and as a result, doubts concerning its accuracy continued to linger.

On the evening of April 23, according to eye-witnesses interviewed by the English, Hitler received at his bunker Reichs Armament Minister Speer. The Fuehrer told him of his suicide plans and asked that his body be cremated.

By nightfall on April 26, Hitler received the Commandant of Berlin, Ritter von Greim, to whom he communicated the same plans concerning his suicide. The Fuehrer added that he had taken measures to insure the complete destruction of his and Eva Braun's bodies, so that "they would not fall into the enemy's hands and so that nothing recognizable would remain."

On April 29, as the Russian tanks rumbled onto the Potsdamer Platz, Hitler in desperation ordered an attack by the Luftwaffe which, however, had disintegrated. Also he sent Doenitz a wire full of recriminations. That same evening Hitler married Eva Braun in the small conference room of his underground bunker.

After the ceremony the newlyweds retired to their apartment for a macabre supper. One of Hitler's secretaries has stated that the table conversation revolved around the suicide plan and that the bride was so depressed she left the table. When she had gone, Hitler ordered his favorite Alsatian dog destroyed.

At 2:30 a.m. Hitler summoned some 20 persons from the neighboring ruins and officially said goodbye to them, shaking hands with everybody. A little later, upon orders of Hitler, two liters of naphtha were placed at the entrance of his bunker.

On the same day, at about 2:30 p.m., Hitler and Eva made the rounds of their bunker, saying goodbye to all others. Next, Hitler and his wife again retired to their apartment. There Hitler fired a shot, presumably into his mouth while Eva Braun swallowed a lethal dose of poison.

Thereupon the bodies were taken to the garden adjacent to the entrance of the bunker. They were carried by Goebbels and Bormann and probably by Dr. Stumpfegger, Hitler's personal physician, as well as by others. Hitler's blood-covered body was draped in a flag.

The two bodies were placed side by side about three yards from the bunker entrance, then drenched with naphtha. Constant shelling by Russian artillery forced the party to seek shelter in the very entrance to the bunker. From there a rag soaked in burning naphtha was hurled at the bodies.

While the group stood at attention in the bunker entrance, the bodies began to burn. After a last salute to the Fuehrer the party retired into the bunker proper.

There is no indication as to the time it took for the two bodies to burn. One of the witnesses has said that they burned until nothing whatsoever remained.

In conclusion the official report stated:

"Proofs are not complete, but they are positive, circumstantial and gathered from independent sources. There is no proof that Hitler is still alive. Rumors to this effect have been studied thoroughly with the result that they have been found baseless."

Who Was Eva Braun?

Hitler had known Eva Braun since 1929. The daughter of a professor, she was apprenticed to Heinrich Hoffmann, the Fuehrer's personal photographer. At that time she was about 20.

Thanks to precautions taken by the Gestapo, Hitler's affair with

Eva was kept secret for about 12 years. Nobody dared talk about her and magazines and papers never printed her picture. She never held any official post nor accompanied Hitler to any public receptions. Even when Hitler attended performances of his beloved Wagnerian operas, Eva remained at home. She officiated only at private gatherings in company with Emmy Goering and Mrs. Goebbels.

She didn't use lipstick nor did she smoke in the Fuehrer's presence and there were tearful scenes before she got permission to wear high-heeled shoes, especially brought for her from Paris. Otherwise, she dressed to suit Hitler's taste. On February 6, her birthday, Hitler invariably presented her with a valuable jewel.

At Berchtesgaden, in the evenings or when it rained, Hitler and Eva Braun played cards in front of the fire place while a servant played softly on his accordion in the background of the large living room.

Hitler always treated her as if she were his little daughter while she respectfully addressed him as "My Fuehrer" and never spoke to him frivolously.

Thus, Adolf Hitler, puritan demigod and bachelor of mythology of the Third Reich, kept a secret mistress, just like any second-rate politician. He managed to deceive the German people and the entire world for more than 10 years, by assuming an air of austerity which was almost entirely simulated.

Dr. Stumpfegger

The official British report is purely circumstantial, since various "eye-witnesses" were in complete disagreement as to the exact date of Hitler's suicide which, according to the British, occurred on April 30.

It is logical to assume that Hitler had planned his flight and that he felt considerably relieved as soon as he was in the company of people who had been entrusted with the project. On April 22, Hitler had ordered his General Staff south. Also, he managed to keep Keitel and Jodl away from the Chancellory. By announcing his proposed suicide, Hitler managed to remove from Berlin all those who might have hindered his flight plan.

Furthermore, the minute details furnished in the report with respect to the "macabre wedding night" are interesting. This account fixes the date of Hitler's marriage to Eva Braun as the evening of April 29, with nothing as basis for that assumption except statements by various people. However, in the alleged marriage certificate which was found subsequently, the date and place of marriage are stricken out. And as to the final scene, nobody saw Hitler's body because it was draped with a flag.

But even the English report admits the attendance of a person at the funeral whose presence there is not easily explained—if it can be explained, at all.

That person was Dr. Stumpfegger, personal physician to Hitler.

Dr. Stumpfegger had perfected what he called the "Silk-Cord Operation." This operation, technical details of which have never been revealed, was perfected in numerous experiments at Havesbrueck on prisoners whom Stumpfegger committed to a state of paralysis and then returned to their normal state by means of surgical treatment. According to other Nazi doctors, Stumpfegger pursued his experiments with such success that was able to cause certain forms of brain paralyses in his victims and was equally able to restore them to health.

Towards the end of March, 1945, Stumpfegger suddenly left Ravensbrueck with all instruments necessary for a "silk-cord" operation and took up residence in Hitler's bunker.

Why?

Nobody seems to have given a plausible explanation. But some of those who spent the last days with Hitler at the Chancellory told the following story:

As the Russian artillery barrage on the ruins of Berlin grew in intensity, the few women who, due to the nature of their jobs, had to remain in the Chancellory, were led every night to the most secure part of the building: the private sanctuary of Hitler.

There, at 2:30 a.m. on the morning of May 1, word spread that the Fuehrer wanted to say goodbye to them. The women were surprised, since it was generally assumed that Hitler had removed himself from the scene several days before.

Thereupon, the women lined up outside Hitler's private apartment. Soon someone announced the coming of the Fuehrer and on the scene appeared Dr. Stumpfegger in his white surgeon's blouse. With him was a person who seemed semi-paralyzed. That person rigidly shook the hands of every woman and finally withdrew into the Fuehrer's private apartment. Not a word was spoken during the entire scene. Although it had been said that Hitler wanted to say goodbye, the person did not speak a single word. When some of the women addressed him, he didn't answer.

This person could have been one of Hitler's doubles who had been transmitted into a semi-paralytical state by one of Dr. Stumpfegger's silk-cord operations.

The women as a whole thought it was Hitler. One remarked, "I am sure it was the Fuehrer. But he had changed. Maybe he had been injected with drugs. His eyes were glassy and seemed unable to focus. His spirit was different. But it was the Fuehrer all right."

The Russians expressed the opinion that everything had been set in motion for a gigantic plot to facilitate Hitler's flight.

"We know that Hitler had doubles," one of Marshall Youkov's aides stated. "Several of them were killed at Berlin. Also, I want to make it clear that I am certain we have NOT found the corpse of Hitler."

Commandant Deodor Pletonov, the Russian officer in command of the Berlin sector which took in the Chancellory, himself was at the head of the first Soviet troops who penetrated into the building. At the entrance they came across a charred body which was supposed to be Hitler's. Pletonov said, "The body was not that of Hitler's. It was one of his doubles."

From a study of the foregoing, we know that:

(1) Two bodies were cremated in the Reich Chancellory in the early afternoon of May 1.

(2) Nobody at any time got a closeup of the corpses supposed to be those of Hitler and Eva. Both were draped in flags.

(3) The man in the company of Stumpfegger on the morning of May 1 was semi-paralyzed, and his movements were limited to shaking the hands of about a dozen women. These women said that the person was Hitler, although "he appeared changed and his eyes were glassy."

(4) The women were summoned to say goodbye and to testify later that they had seen Hitler a few hours prior to his "suicide," thus serving as alibi witnesses for Hitler.

There is no doubt that this miserable double who appeared as semi-paralytic and who was unconscious and deprived of his will-power, was later eliminated by means of a pistol shot, then wrapped in a flag and cremated in the company of a body supposedly that of Eva Braun.

In the meantime, where was the real Hitler? Undoubtedly, he was already a long way from the Chancellory, the same building which General Jodl on April 22 had nick-named a "mouse-trap."

Hitler could have escaped by plane from the Gatow Airport, located 13 kilometers from the center of Berlin, as late as April 27, when the airport was taken by the Russians.

Or Hitler and Eva could have escaped even later. They could have taken off directly outside the gates of the Chancellory where the Charlottenburg Highway could have served admirably as runway.

In fact, although the Charlottenburg Highway was under the fire of Russian artillery, Hitler could have taken off from there as late as April 30. A plane piloted by the Nazi Aviatrix Hanna Reitach and carrying as passenger General Ritter von Greim took off from the highway as late as the early hours of April 30.

On June 9, 1945 Marshal Youkov announced that Hitler and Eva Braun had been married shortly before the fall of Berlin. Several days later, a Stockholm dispatch stated that Eva Braun had two children, a son and a daughter, both of whom had been born during her long affair with Hitler.

Hitler reportedly became a father for the first time during the night of January 1, 1938. Eva Braun bore him a son in a maternity pavilion at San Remo, Italy. During the preceding month she had not been seen, as usual, driving through Berlin in her car.

Several hours after the birth, it was announced to Japanese journalists in Berlin in a short, unofficial statement by General Bansai, Japanese military attache. Very soon afterwards, the Japanese Ambassador summoned the correspondents to his office and said the statement had been without any factual basis. Also, he asked them to give their word of honor not to speak about the matter and especially not to breathe a word about it to their colleagues of the foreign press in Berlin.

But the Berlin correspondent of *Nichi Nichi*, leading Japanese daily, decided not to keep silent. At least, he felt not bound to silence if the news was inaccurate. And so he decided to go to Munich where Eva Braun's father lived and where also the informant of the Japanese military attache resided.

In the course of a long talk with Eva's father, the latter said, "There is no doubt that the Fuehrer intends to marry my daughter. That she has borne him a son or is about to do so is of little importance. The important thing is that Hitler shall not die without a successor."

The correspondent returned to Berlin and called on his Ambassador. He told him of the result of his trip in the hope that the diplomat would relieve him of the oath of silence. On the contrary, the Ambassador enjoined him not to reveal a single word on the matter.

Another correspondent states that on the eve of January 1, 1939, an official of the Reich Chancellery was arrested for having stated at a party, "Today, the son of the Fuehrer celebrates his first birthday. Let us drink to his health."

But where are Hitler's children? After the fall of Berlin a former attache of the Swedish legation who had remained in close contact with Hitler's headquarters during the siege of the Reich Capital, revealed that Hitler's children were living with Eva Braun's parents in Bavaria. He added, "It is believed that when Hitler left Berlin on April 8 or 9, he did so not only in order to take Eva Braun out of Berlin but also to say goodbye to his children whom he wanted to be in a safer place. He spent 3 days in Bavaria at a time when his presence in Berlin was more than necessary."

HITLER IS ALIVE!

Fifth of a Series

What happened to Adolf's three trusted messengers?—Why did Hitler write two testaments?—The Allied Headquarters continue to unravel the great mysteries surrounding the Fuehrer's strange vanishing act—Where's he hiding out now?

The Nazi scheme was unfolding now and succeeding perfectly, having been conceived with typical German thoroughness. While the certainty of Hitler's death had "crystallized" in world opinion, the underground activity of Martin Bormann in Germany had maintained its hold over a large part of the population. And this despite the many rumors that Martin Bormann had been killed trying to escape from the Reich Chancellory when his tank was blown up by a Russian shell.

There were a large number of "eye-witnesses" who asserted they had seen Bormann in Austria, and later in South America. Others professed to know that he was engaged in reorganizing the cadres of the Nazi movement.

At the time when the rumor of Bormann's capture circulated—a rumor which was inaccurate—the General Headquarters of the Third US Army announced at Nuremberg that the last will and testament of Hitler as well as his marriage certificate, dated Dec. 29, had been found. The following day the Allied military authorities published the texts of these documents and revealed the circumstances under which the documents had been found.

Actually, the four documents were Hitler's private testament (last will); his political testament; a note from Goebbels; and the marriage certificate of Hitler and Eva Braun. According to the declarations of an official of the British Intelligence Service, these documents fell into Allied hands under strange circumstances.

"During the nights of April 27 and 28," this official declared, "as the Soviets approached the center of Berlin and liaison between the various Nazi forces had been cut off entirely, the Fuehrer insisted that Walter Wagner, an official of the Berlin City Administration, should perform the civil marriage which apparently took place on April 29, at 3 a.m. Immediately after the ceremony, Hitler dictated to his secretary first his own last will and then his political testament. A little later, at about 10 a.m., three trusted messengers were selected and ordered to take copies to Admiral Doenitz at Flensburg and to Marshal Schorner who, at this moment, directed Nazi resistance at Prague. The third copy was reserved for posterity.

"Also," the British Intelligence Service officer continued, "a telegram was sent to Doenitz informing him that the documents were on their way. Nevertheless, the three messengers never arrived at their destinations and until the first days of December, 1945, nobody had found out just what had happened to them, despite the concerted efforts of the Allies to solve this riddle.

"Finally, these three messengers were arrested by the Anglo-American authorities. They were Heinz Lorenz, Willy Johann Meyer and Wilhelm Zander. The latter also went by the name of Paustin. Lorenz was an employee of the Propaganda Ministry, belonging to the staff of Martin Bormann.

"These three messengers had left the Chancellory through a secret passage and made their way towards the zone which was in Allied hands, traveling at night and hiding by day. They finally got to the outskirts of Hanover where they separated. There they learned that German resistance had collapsed, whereupon they decided to return to their own homes. Nothing was learned on that subject until early in December, 1945, when British agents in their zone of occupation arrested a man for carrying false identification papers. When the man was searched, there was found in the shoulder-padding of his coat a complete set of the much wanted documents. The man's identity was then ascertained: he was Heinz Lorenz, one of the three messengers.

"Thanks to the documents furnished by Lorenz, British intelligence agents were able to begin the search for the two other messengers. Willy Johann Meyer was found and arrested on December 29 at Iserlohn, but he refused to tell what had happened to his set of documents. Next the hunt concentrated on the last missing messenger, Zander. Information furnished by members of his family enabled the Allied authorities to trace him to the little Bavarian town of Tegernsee where he had lived under the name of Paustin with his girlfriend, Martin Bormann's ex-private secretary.

Arrested, Zander-Paustin immediately admitted that his set of documents, including Hitler's marriage certificate, was secreted in a filing cabinet of the local elementary school, around the corner from the official headquarters of Gen. Lucien Turscott, in command of the 3rd US Army. The documents in question were located in the school on December 28, the day of Zander-Paustin's arrest. They turned out to be faithful duplicates of the set found on Lorenz."

The documents were kept in the inimitable style of "Mein Kampf." The last will was entitled "My Last Will and Testament" and consisted of two parts, both written on excellent paper and bearing the signature of Adolf Hitler at its characteristic angle. On the letterhead appeared the Swastika. The marriage certificate consisted of one paragraph only, typewritten on ordinary bond paper.

The political part of the Last Will, which was made available to the press, contained the following significant information:

"Inasmuch as our forces are already too weakened to resist the enemy's concerted attack and since our own resistance is reduced gradually by leaders who are blind and incapable of initiative. I desire to share the fate of millions of citizens of this city who have decided to remain here.

"I shall not fall into the hands of the enemy and furnish a spectacle for amusement of masses of hysterical Jews. Instead, I have decided to remain at Berlin and to commit suicide of my own free will as soon as I shall be convinced that I cannot any longer maintain my position as Fuehrer (Leader) and Chancellor. I die with a glad heart, thinking of the immemorial feats of my soldiers at the front, of the women of Germany, of our peasants and workers. And I also think of the historical role played in history by the German youth which bears my name (Hitler youth).

"From the bottom of my heart I wish to thank them all. And I hope that they will not give up the fight but continue the struggle against the enemy of our Fatherland, in accordance with the principles of the great Clausewitz (military leader and strategist of the early 19th century). The sacrifice of my soldiers and my comradeship with them is the germ which one day will blossom into a glorious revival of National Socialism.

"Prior to my death, I herewith expel from the Party Ex-Marshall of the Reich Hermann Goering and I herewith strip him of all the rights and privileges conferred upon him by the Decree of June 20, 1941 and earlier by my Reichstag speech of September 1, 1939. In his place I herewith appoint Admiral Doenitz, President of the Reich and Supreme Commander of the Reich Forces.

"In the desire to give the German people a Government composed of honest people as well as for the purpose of continuing the war by all means, I herewith designate the new German Cabinet as follows: President, Doenitz; Chancellor: Goebbels; Minister of the Party, Bormann; Minister for Foreign Affairs: Seyss-Inquart; Minister of the Interior: Gauleiter Giesler; Minister of War: Doenitz; Supreme Commander of the Army: Schoener; Supreme Commander of the Navy: Doenitz.

"May they always be imbued with the conviction that our aim of bringing about the National Socialist State represents the crowning achievement of centuries and that this aim implies the obligation to serve the Fatherland before serving themselves. I herewith command all Germans, all National Socialists, men as well as women, all soldiers of the Armed Forces, to be loyal to these men and to obey the orders of the new German Government.

"Furthermore, I command my people to hold on to the racial laws to the very end and to resist forever the poison which penetrates all nations. International Jewry.—Berlin, April 29, 1945 at 4 a.m. Signed: Adolf Hitler. Witnesses: Goebbels, Wilhelm Bargdorf, Martin Bormann, Hans Drebbs."

In an appendix to the political testament of Hitler, Joseph Goebbels, Minister of Nazi Propaganda and new Chancellor of the Reich, has laid down the reasons which forced him to go on living after Hitler's death . . . these reasons being his obligation to Hitler to serve in the new German Cabinet.

To the certificate of marriage was attached the photo of a little boy aged approximately 12 years and showing a remarkable likeness to Adolf Hitler. The Allied authorities were certainly surprised when they stumbled on this document.

Despite the fact that the Chief of intelligence of the 3rd US Army termed those documents genuine, certain doubts cropped up and inquiries were made. Finally, however, it was stated officially that the last will and the marriage certificate were authentic.

There is no doubt that the last will of Hitler was an authentic Nazi document. From the first line to the last, it breathes the spirit of "Mein Kampf." It reverberates with the perennial intentions of Hitler concerning his love for peace and his hatred of the Jews— both themes representing the real thread in the strange career of the Nazi dictator. IT IS AUTHENTIC, INDEED, AND UNDOUBTEDLY WRITTEN BY HITLER SO AS TO CONVINCE THE ALLIES OF HIS DEATH AND TO CREATE A MYTH AROUND HIS PERSON IN GERMANY.

Furthermore, Hitler's last will and testament was written for the purpose of publication. As it turned out, this aim was fully achieved by the Nazis. The ease with which these papers were "discovered" hits the eye. Furthermore, the capture, or rather the surrender of Heinz Lorenz who carried "false papers" plus the duplicate set of the papers must evoke the strongest suspicions, THE LAST WILL OF HITLER AND ITS COMPANION DOCUMENTS WERE FOUND BECAUSE THEY HAD BEEN INTENDED TO BE FOUND AT THAT MOMENT. By whom had that been planned? By Martin Bormann perhaps?

Adolf Hitler's "last will and testament" is inescapable proof that the person who in the night from April 30 to May 1 took leave from the personnel in the Chancellory bunkers of Berlin, WAS NOT THE REAL FUEHRER. How could it otherwise be assumed that the semi-paralyzed person who "appeared doped and glassy-eyed" (as explained in a previous issue of *Police Gazette*) had had the necessary ability on the preceding day (the last will was dated April 29) to conceive as precise a document as the Fuehrer's "last will"?

No, that semi-paralyzed, doped person was not the Fuehrer, but a double. The real Fuehrer, after having issued and signed his message of hatred, cold revenge and pathetic appeal for a revival of the Nazi spirit, had abandoned the "mousetrap" which had become too dangerous for him. Instead, Hitler fled.

Hitler took off in a fast plane either from the Gatow airport or directly from outside the Chancellory, using the wide Charlottenburg Highway as a runway. To Bormann, Goebbels and Stumpfegger he left the task of staging the funeral of his double, who had been assassinated. Their task achieved, these three also fled.

Goebbels and Stumpfegger had various choices, among them that of joining Hitler and Eva and the rest of their entourage at a convenient rendezvous. Bormann, however, preferred for the time being to remain in the Reich in order to lead his secret underground movement and to direct the plans for staging the greatest hoax in all history: the disappearance of Hitler.

On June 26, 1945, almost two months after the flight of the Nazi dictator, there came from the air the voice of a mysterious radio station which announced:

"Attention, Germans. Hitler is alive and safe."

It was a clearly broadcast message lasting but one minute and impossible to trace. After opening with the above words, the mysterious announcer said:

"The false friends who surrounded Hitler have been foiled. They are all either dead or in prison. And the power which induced them to carry on their cabal was but short lived. Now the Fuehrer has surrounded himself with but a few of his most tried aides and is beyond the reach of the enemy. And the message he sends to his German people is this: "From the darkness the light will shine anew."

Martin Bormann had begun his work.

MARTIN BORMANN was spotted in Chile in 1948 by a former acquaintance Deputy and for several years a refugee in South America.

This man together with a party of friends was riding horseback in the vicinity of an Indo settlement when they met three other riders. These riders were dressed in the gaucho fashion and wore large-brimmed hats shading their faces. Pulling his gun the former friend approached the man in the center who seemed strangely familiar to him: it was Martin Bormann.

Bormann recognized him, then turned to his party and cried: "at the gallop."

Thereupon the party cantered off at full speed toward the Argentine frontier.

Several days later it was learned that Bormann was living in Chile under an assumed name.

A Nazi refugee in Chile who made inquiries concerning Bormann reported:

"In strict confidence, Bormann has returned to Europe. He is hiding in Spain until his hour should come. The conflict with

Russia is inevitable and then Martin Bormann's day will come, too. His friends here have spread the rumor that he had died in the course of his flight from the Reich Chancellory in Berlin!"

Several days later, Paris-Presse published the following story:

"Bayonne—The Police Bureau of Identification has photographed the complete set of paintings recently found near the frontier. The set will be forwarded shortly for exhibition in the National Museum. One of the canvases bears on its back the inscription: Martin Bormann, Reichleiter, Munich, and speaks for itself. There are rumors that Martin Bormann, allegedly a refugee staying in a secret hiding place in Spain, might have tried to retrieve some of his belongings and that the consignee in Madrid might well have been one of the members of the secret organization known as Free Germany with headquarters in Madrid.

"Objects of art of this kind are now being smuggled constantly by elements operating in the Franco-Spanish border region. It may be supposed that some of the German ships which now are engaged in transporting lumber from the part of Bayonne, may have dropped some such cargo in the Bay of Ilbarritz where they could be fetched later on by some mysterious party."

Nevertheless, one thing seems to be certain:

Martin Bormann was in Spain.

A MEMBER of the French Intelligence Service, in an exclusive interview, declared:

"In May, 1945, I happened to be at La Rochelle (a French naval base and port on the Bar of Biscay). I learned there that a mysterious submarine had entered La Pallice Naval Base on May 3, in order to refuel and to restock food. For reasons which were not explained to me, the entire personnel of the base had been given leave that day. Only the Admiral was on hand to receive the commandant of the sub.

"Questioned by me on this mysterious vessel, the Admiral told me that he couldn't tell me anything about the sub, except one detail: the ship was covered entirely with rubber as protection against magnetic mines . . .

"My immediate impression was that on board the mystery sub were Hitler or Martin Bormann. Today I am convinced that on board this sub Hitler and Eva Braun sailed for South America . . ."

HITLER IS ALIVE!

Sixth of a Series

Hitler's Shangri-La is a refuge, which is both sufficiently immense and remote to make it impossible to conduct a search for him. Fantastic as it sounds, that land exists today!

In his political "Last Will and Testament" (see previous installment) Hitler had bragged:

"I was never beaten—I was betrayed."

And now he was thirsting for revenge.

He was planning his comeback and the resumption of his work, just as he had done during the bleak days of 1923 when the failure of his ill-fated "putsch" had forced him to start all over again, using new methods and plans.

In 1923 Hitler also had fled. But six months later he was captured, due to having taken insufficient precautions and was committed to the relative comfort of Landsberg jail.

Had Hitler this time made preparations, better preparations for fleeing before the victorious Allies from whom he couldn't expect mercy?

The answer is: Yes. There is proof of that, both circumstantial and concrete.

But first of all, there are the telling words uttered by Admiral Doenitz in 1943:

"The German submarine fleet is proud of having built for the Fuehrer in another part of the world a Shangri-La on land, an impregnable fortress."

Strangely enough, Doenitz's words were soon forgotten in the torrent of subsequent events. No mention was made of that utterance in the press commenting on Doenitz's succession to Hitler as Reich Fuehrer on May 1, 1945.

Only from time to time the matter cropped up, like sudden flashes in the dark. Thus when the Norwegian traitor Vidkun Quisling faced his judges he cried in a desperate plea for his life: *"I believed I fought for a just cause and I refused to run away from my responsibilities when the Nazis, shortly before their final collapse, offered to convoy me aboard a German submarine to a safe refuge."*

But there is no doubt that the submarine was the only means by which Hitler could have been able to flee the European Continent. The airplane was no longer a safe means of flight, in view of the superiority of the Allied air arm and also in view of the vast, invisible radar net which enmeshed the sky over Germany.

In contrast, the submarine did not only enjoy an infinitely larger radius of action, but also, practically enjoyed immunity—if it refrained from warfare action. From the second year of the war on, a fairly large number of German submarines had operated in the vast reaches of the Pacific and in some cases had been away from their bases for over a year. They were capable of descending for a depth of more than 200 meters and could cruise in a submerged state for weeks without coming to the surface, according to information given out by the British Admiralty.

It is silly to believe that Admiral Doenitz could have been unaware of such organized flight plans. A task of such nature involved a certain number of submarine units and could never have been accomplished without authorization of the supreme Commander of the Nazi submarine arm.

Doenitz most certainly was fully aware of Hitler's plans to escape. Witness his ominous words spoken towards the end of 1943 and cited above.

Actually, Doenitz was far from being a "simple sailor at heart and good-natured", as he had been pictured by friendly sources. On the contrary, he was one of the most formidable figures in the galaxy of the crumbling Third Reich. Implacable, fanatic, experienced and possessed with unbelievable energy, he was more Nazi than any of the other high officers of the Nazi war fleet.

Furthermore, Doenitz enjoyed the fullest confidence of the Fuehrer and was at any time able to come and go as he saw fit at Hitler's Headquarters.

According to British commentators, Doenitz was one of the "mystery men" of the Nazi Hierarchy. In fact, he is said to have also operated under the pseudonym of "Admiral Canaris", Chief of the Nazi Counter-intelligence, whose identity has never been revealed.

There were sufficient grounds for such theories.

During the first World War, Doenitz was one of the most clever submarine commanders of the German War Fleet which then was commanded by Admiral Tirpitz. Nevertheless, during a brave, but careless attack against Allied shipping. Doenitz's vessel was torpedoed and sunk. He was taken prisoner on October 14, 1917 and sent to a prisoners' camp near Manchester where he began to fake symptoms of incurable madness. Six months later he was returned to Germany with a group of disabled prisoners. Hardly had Doenitz touched German soil when his 'madness' vanished.

It is strange that so little attention has been paid to the fact that at the crucial moment when the very existence of Nazi Germany seemed in the balance, the helm of the Third Reich was entrusted to a naval person, instead of to an army man, an aviator or to a politician-diplomat. The surrender talks were initiated not by Keitel of the Army or von Ribbentrop of the Foreign Office, but by Admiral Doenitz of the Fleet.

Why? Because it was necessary that in the critical days of Hitler's flight, Doenitz should be in command of the overall situation.

According to Hitler's carefully drawn and long-prepared escape plans, the submarine convoy which was to transport Hitler and his entourage southward, was to meet at "some point along the Norwegian coast". Here the embarkation of the Fuehrer and his aides was to occur sometime between April 22 and May 2, 1945.

The above is not simply based on conjectures, but on indisputable facts. The submarine which surrendered at Leixoes, Portugal, on June 4, 1945 as well as the U-530 and the U-977 both of which surrendered at Mar del Plata, Argentina, came from Norway. All three had left Norwegian ports prior to undertaking their mystery trip to the South Atlantic.

Then there is the testimony of the documents found on board the U-977 and corroborated by its Capt. Schaeffer and his officers and men. The U-977 had weighed anchor in the German port of Kiel on April 13th, 1945 and gone to Oslo. It left Oslo Fjord on the 22nd of that same month and went to the Norwegian base of Christiansund where it remained until May 2 when the sub got underway again, beginning its southward journey.

All three subs, the one which gave up at Leixoes, the U-530 and the U-977, belonged to that "phantom convoy" whose task it was to convoy the Fuehrer southward to an *already prepared refuge*, the existence of which had been hinted at by Doenitz towards the end of 1943.

Neither Commandant Wermutt nor Capt. Schaeffer could reveal anything concerning the nature of their mission, since they did not know a thing about it. They did not know whom they followed or escorted nor where they were bound for. *They had received from their superiors sealed orders to the effect that they were to follow a predetermined route towards the South Atlantic,* always traveling submerged.

They, as well as the other units of the convoy, had been expressly forbidden to use their radio, even for intercommunication, so as not to reveal their whereabouts. They were to follow the submarine flagship as closely as possible, guided only by their earphones.

This then was the "phantom convoy" which traveled southward, mute, blind, unseen and unheard, led only by the one vessel which knew its plan and purpose and final destination. It did not matter if one or several of them would be impelled by storms, or would suffer damage impairing their maneuverability and become separated from the convoy. The risk of losing several of the units during the long trip had been foreseen. It did not matter—as long as none of the officers knew anything about the true nature of the "phantom convoy" so that they could not reveal the plan.

And this was what happened to the Leixoes-surrendered sub as well as to the U-530 and the U-977. The first suffered serious engine trouble. The other two were most probably isolated from the main convoy by storms, since their engines and other sailing equipment were found to be in perfect order. It seems safe to calculate that this piece of bad luck occurred in 1945, probably in the South Atlantic, approximately 40 degrees southern latitude.

Furthermore, the fact that the U-530 and the U-977 were separated from the rest of the "phantom convoy" explains clearly why these two subs. roamed for so long in the South Atlantic before their commanders decided to turn towards Mar del Plata and surrender. They had been forbidden to use their radios. Yet, they continued to keep on their course in the vague hope that some units of the convoy would turn around and come searching for them. The security measures prescribed for the commandants of the convoy were so stringent that they deprived the individual captains of any chance to make for a prearranged rendezvous point in case they should find themselves dispersed for unforeseen reasons. To act otherwise would have been imprudent: it would have meant taking unjustified risks which could have compromised the entire scheme.

The convoy units had been ordered to refrain from any warlike actions. They were not to use their cannon and their torpedo tubes except when actually attacked and then only to protect the submarine flagship. However, no such contingency materialized. The convoy was not attacked and the two subs which surrendered at Mar del Plata arrived with their arms and munitions intact.

That it was the "double" of the U-530 and not the authentic U-530 which surrendered at Mar del Plata confirms plainly that the convoy had been prepared with the greatest secrecy and that most of the Nazi Naval Chiefs did not suspect its existence. It seems safe to assume that quite a number of subs which formed the convoy were doubles of Nazi subs which at that time were operating from various German bases. This was an easy way to fool the victors as well as the leaders of the vanquished German Armies.

What was the final goal of the two German subs which surrendered at Mar del Plata? Where did the "phantom convoy" travel to? In what part of the globe was the "Shangri-La" which had been constructed by the Nazi submarine fleet and which had inspired the aforementioned boasting on the part of Doenitz late in 1943?

Although it might seem obvious, Hitler could not have escaped to Japan. At the time of the flight, relations between Berlin and Tokyo had been strained since the Japanese Warlords had refused categorically to attack Russia in order to save the hard-pressed Nazi armies. On the other hand, it is well known that the Fuehrer himself cordially detested the Japanese and that he had not the slightest confidence in them.

Also he could not have taken refuge in any neutral country. No Government, regardless of what its principles and politics might be, would have assumed the responsibility of granting refuge within its territory to Adolf Hitler. To grant asylum to "World Criminal No. 1" would have in itself constituted a grave affront and defiance of the Great Powers and might have brought about an armed conflict which could have resulted only in the final capture of Adolf Hitler. And if the Fuehrer had entered secretly a neutral country or one of its colonies, even under a disguise, he would have ever been in danger of being spotted. No, the Fuehrer did not devise such a hiding place from which to plan ultimate resumption of his power through preliminary underground activity. And this was not the kind of refuge Doenitz had hinted at in his notorious boast.

Actually, there was only one country, both remote and practically deserted, which could have been considered. The construction of a Shangri-La which at the same time was an unimpregnable fortress, took a considerable time. Furthermore, it had to be hidden, regardless of where it might have been. Thus there remains the possibility that Hitler's refuge might have been established on an island, located in some remote part of the world.

A number of times there have been rumors that German submarines, in the course of their wartime roamings, had discovered some faraway, island and that they had established there a refuge for the Fuehrer.

Such a theory is that and nothing else.

But where did the Fuehrer and his convoy travel?

If he did not go to another continental country nor to any island, where did he go?

In other words: Does there exist in any part of the globe a sufficiently uninhabited, large enough space where it would be practically impossible to find Hitler and his entourage? Is there a refuge which is simultaneously sufficiently remote and immense enough so that it would be practically impossible to carry on a search for him?

Yes, that land exists, although it may seem improbable.

And not only does this place exist, but the Germans—and we shall prove this to be so—began to fit it out suitably as early as 1940.

HITLER IS ALIVE!

Seventh of a Series

The place where Hitler sought refuge comprises a surface of fantastic expanse—6,205,000 square miles, much more than the area of Europe. This land is the Antarctic, the Seventh Continent of the world. Its inhospitable regions are difficult to enter and are not inhabited by any other human beings.

This, then, was the ingenious element of Hitler's plan of flight: instead of seeking an isle, here was an entire continent available as Hitler's Shangri-La. As unbelievable as this idea appears at first glance, it was the result of calculation.

The logic in the Nazis' train of deliberation readily foresaw that the Antarctic would serve as an ideal hiding place for the Dictator because *it was far from the inhabited world*, just as remote as another planet. Here the Fuehrer could exist in absolute safety and here he could *once again plan his revenge, his comeback at an hour when events would be favorable.*

The idea to create for Hitler an absolutely safe refuge was the decisive factor in the choice. For the Nazis foresaw that even if Hitler's presence in the Seventh Continent were known, a *search for him would practically be impossible.* How could the Allies search every nook and corner of this vast expanse, with its plains, valleys, mountains and glaciers covered with ice and snow? Thousands of polar explorers with suitable equipment would be required to explore even a trifling slice of this immense territory.

And the Nazis did not intend to render Hitler's hideout visible from the air.

If one wishes to analyze further the Nazi scheme and its development, a brief examination of the known facts concerning the South Pole would be in order.

In 1823 the English seafarer James Weddell, at the head of an expedition of seal hunters, penetrated the Antarctic Circle and got as far as 75°15 latitude. According to his report, "The ice in this region had completely disappeared, the temperature was mild, birds were observed flying around the ship and groups of whales frolicked in the wake of the craft." This unexpected change in climate surprised Weddell and his sailors, especially since the temperature continued to increase the farther south they penetrated.

"I should have liked to proceed sailing south-ward," Weddell added, "but considering the season was already advanced and since we had to cross again a sea studded with ice-covered islands, I could do no better than profit from a favorable wind for our return."

Actually, the real period of Antarctic exploration began in the 20th Century when aviation facilitated exploration on a large scale. Sir Hubert Wilkins, operating from a base set up on the Isle of Deception, succeeded in flying over the Seventh Continent in 1928. His feat was repeated in 1928 through 1930 by planes of the Byrd Expedition.

With its wealth of technological equipment and modern resources, Commander Byrd's expedition eclipsed all previous enterprises. He set up a comfortable base in Whale Bay and called it Little America. From there he maintained communication with the rest of the world by means of his radio station. Five years later he returned to Little America with personnel and equipment even more numerous than that of the earlier expedition. He brought with him tractors and airplanes of several types, including even a helicopter. The personnel of his expedition did not succumb to scurvy, that terrible scourge which haunted the polar explorers of old. Instead, they enjoyed all the comforts of civilized life, not excluding a movie theatre.

Despite the numerous South Polar expeditions in the course of our century, the Antarctic Continent is still largely unexplored. It is safe to state that the explored sections of its regions do not exceed 10% of its total surface. In other words, the situation up to the present may be summed up as follows:

(1) What we have here is a Continent of its own. This Continent is situated within the Polar Circle (66°32'33"), on a peninsula known as Graham Land.

(2) Approximately, this Continent is located at a distance 5,600 miles from Africa, 4,760 miles from Australia, 1,870 miles from the southernmost point of South America.

(3) This Continent comprises not just ice-covered surface like the Arctic regions. Instead, we have here a veritable Continent, with plains, valleys and mountains. It is believed that the mountain chain extending from the Weddell Sea to the edge of Ross Sea, where Little America was located, actually is but the extension of the Cordilleran Andes. The most elevated peaks among these mountains attain heights of around 15,000 feet. On the other hand, it is believed that the eastern zone of the Antarctic Continent formed almost entirely by a high plateau locate approximately 9,000 feet above sea level.

(4) According to calculations by geographers, the surface area of the Antarctic Continent exceeds five million square miles. Thus, this continent is much larger than Europe.

(5) Outside of penguins, certain insects and lichen which abound on the slopes of the volcano Erebus, there is practically no fauna or flora in the vast reaches of the Seventh Continent.

(6) The temperature in the interior of the Continent is approximately around 0° Fahrenheit during the Summer. It drops to about 20° below zero, but usually it never falls below –30°. Temperature studies undertaken by meteorologists of the Bruce, Borchgrevink, Scott and Schackleton expeditions have shown that the cold reaches its maximum of intensity during July, when it hovers around 16°–20° Fahrenheit.

(7) Aside from the temperature, which is higher than the Winter temperatures prevailing in certain regions of Northeastern Europe, strong winds—swelling to whirlwinds and even hurricanes—cause human beings the gravest discomfort in these Antarctic regions, especially during the Winter season. But generally the air is dry, extremely pure and healthy throughout the entire Continent, according to abundant testimony.

(8) It is known that the soil of Antarctica is extremely rich. Both Charcot and Shackleton found on the surface numerous deposits of iron, copper, felspar, coal, peat and other ores, despite the fact that they were not briefed to undertake geological exploration. Admiral Byrd's three expeditions have enlarged our store of knowledge in this respect. Aside from vast deposits of coal and iron, he established the presence of more than one hundred different mineral ores on the surface. It is believed that among the vast geological treasures of Antarctica are large quantities of uranium, the element which is of paramount importance in connection with atomic research and production.

Thus, with its more than five million square miles, the Antarctic Continent is yet unknown land. Here is a vast, remote and barely accessible region which, in addition, was completely uninhabited. *Here, then, there offered itself the ideal hiding place for Adolf Hitler and his aides.* Once there, it would be practically impossible to flush him out. At any rate, at this point, there are the following questions to be answered:

(a) Was Hitler's group able to reach the Antarctic Continent?

(b) Are there proofs or indications that he traveled in the direction of Antarctica?

(c) Were the Fuehrer and his aides able to live all these years in the inhospitable reaches of this Continent?

(d) Did the Nazis undertake preparations for the construction of Hitler's refuge in Antarctica?

To answer these four questions satisfactorily would furnish an explanation not only of the mystery of Hitler's disappearance but also of his present whereabouts, of the final refuge where the man from the tiny town of Braunau, Austria. waits for the proper moment to make a comeback on the stage of world history.

The Strange Expedition

Concerning the first question, it can be stated beyond the slightest doubt that Hitler and his group reached the Antarctic Continent without any difficulty. During the larger part of the trip, which was negotiated under water, the phantom convoy in this fashion could have avoided a blockade—only there was no blockade to be evaded. Once the convoy had arrived in the Antarctic zone, there was no fear of the presence of anybody who might have reported its presence. True, on certain points of the Antarctic Continent existed a US based and a British mission. However, the Nazis knew the location of the latter and took pains to keep at a distance.

The fact that the U-530 and the U-977 surrendered at Mar del Plata, Argentina, is stark proof that the phantom convoy went southward, in the direction of the Seventh Continent. In examining the itinerary covered by these two Nazi subs from their departure from Norway, the sole conclusion which can be arrived at is that the line traced thus far was broken at the latitude of Mar del Plate and that its extension would undoubtedly have led the rest of the convoy to the Antarctic. Where would the line have terminated?

The history of the expeditions carried out in the 20th Century furnishes the most eloquent proof that a group of persons under certain conditions could exist in these regions throughout the entire year.

The Byrd expeditions have demonstrated the miracle of technological progress as applied to survival in these remote corners of our globe. The members of these expeditions did not suffer any privations. Photographs of the members of these expeditions, showing them with bare upper bodies caressed by the Antarctic sun, show in irrefutable manner that the human being, if equipped with proper resources, can exist throughout the entire year in the vastness of Antarctic Continent without any damage to his health and without the necessity of lowering his living standard.

It is safe to assume that the Nazis did everything in the way of preparations so as to construct a comfortable refuge in this *Seventh Continent.*

And there are proofs. Even if we disregard Doenitz' assertions concerning that "paradise on land" and "impregnable fortress" which had been constructed for the Fuehrer by the Nazi Navy, there are additional facts of circumstantial evidence.

Toward the end of the second expedition by Byrd, and after the Ellsworth expedition which explored a zone that was later on claimed by Australia, the Norwegians, the British and even the Japanese seized parts of the *Seventh Continent.* All this happened during the years preceding the second World War. Then on January 2, 1938, it was announced at Moscow that preparations had been concluded for a South Polar expedition under Vodopyanov. But this venture never came off. On the other hand, a German mission appeared in the Antarctic Continent toward the end of 1938, without any previous announcement. It returned the following year. This expedition caused world-wide surprise.

"In carrying out this mission, I have merely executed the orders of Marshal Goering," declared Capt. Alfred Ritscher, after his return to Hamburg on board the Schwabenland on April 12, 1939.

According to this officer's statement, the purpose of the expedition had been to study the feasibility of whaling in these international waters, since the Reich was much in need of all sorts of fats.

It so happens that the motor vessel Schwabenland was not an ordinary ship. It was, rather, a floating island. It belonged to the Lufthansa, which had placed the vessel, with its complement of technicians and planes, at the disposal of the expedition. There were two planes on the Schwabenland, both amphibians weighing ten tons each. Among the flight personnel attached to the Schwabenland were fliers who had experience in Arctic aerial reconnaissance. They now were able to collect photographic aerial surveys of large and previously unmapped stretches of Antarctica. For their specific mission these planes had been equipped with powerful Zeiss cameras.

With typical German arrogance, Capt. Ritscher let the cat out of the bag when he made his statement concerning his aerial reconnaissance activities over the South Pole:

"For the first time German planes flew over the Antarctic Continent. Under extremely difficult conditions, they landed in the vicinity of the South Pole and there raised the German flag designating the sovereignty of the Reich. Every 25 kilometers our planes dropped pennants with the colors of the Reich and thus marked the boundaries of their flights. We covered an area of about 600,000 square kilometers. Of these, about 350,000 were accurately photographed, thus yielding a suitable map of the region."

In other words, Ritscher had started out to study whales and had ended by staking out for the Reich some 600,000 square kilometers. He frankly added that the territory mapped out by the Schwabenland expedition was situated between 11°5' west and 20° east longitudes and that it reached the coast near 70° southern latitude and approached the South Pole at 76°5'. "From the latter point," Ritscher added, "there rises a vast plateau at an altitude of about 12,000 feet which extends toward the South Pole. And within this territory mapped by our planes there rise mountain ranges up to a height of an additional 9,000 feet."

Soon after this the curtain rose on the tragedy of the second World War. The little Nazi pennants dropped in the icy wastes of the South Pole were generally forgotten.

But the Nazis had not forgotten.

During the first phases of the World War, their submarines prowled the North Atlantic, inflicting terrible damage on Allied shipping. Yet they refrained from any hostile acts throughout the South Atlantic, where commentators thought these bases were along the extreme southeastern coast of South America.

Actually, the Nazi sub lairs were located much farther south, most probably on the very shores of the Antarctic Continent. These bases were destined to play a double role. When, toward the middle of 1940, Nazi subs suddenly ceased to operate, these bases changed into depots for accumulating the vast stores of material required for the subsequent setting up of Hitler's refuge. Clothes, food, fuel and every other conceivable item necessary for survival and for comfort were stored here. For the transportation of these stores, submarines were used exclusively. Undoubtedly, Doenitz' cryptic remark about the "paradise on land" referred to that phase of submarine operations.

Then, in August, 1940, Dr. Wohlwill, Director of the Reich Institute for Metals, launched an appeal to German technicians for construction of nonferrous metal which could be safely exposed to temperatures below 60°. We know that iron, when subjected to temperatures of less than 60°, becomes extremely brittle because its inner structure is subjected to fundamental changes.

But where did the Nazis have any use for nonferrous constructions designed to resist low temperatures?

Previously, some observers suggested Spitzbergen. Actually, it was the South Polar region where, since the middle of 1940, the Nazis had started to amass planes, tractors, sledges, gliders and all sorts of machinery and materials. Here, then, was to rise the Fuehrer's new Berchtesgaden.

For the next four years, Nazi technicians and workers built here the Fuehrer's Shangri-La. They scooped out an entire mountain and constructed a facsimile of the hollow mountain of Berchtesgaden, Hitler's ill-famed Eagle's Roost in the mountains of the South Bavarian Alps. The new refuge was practically impregnable and completely camouflaged.

With the ingenuity of modern construction science, the Nazi engineers built a number of shelters completely protected against cold. Inside his magic mountain Hitler and his staff were able to grow their own vegetables and fruits in artificially-heated beds of black soil, also imported from the Reich. They could raise their own poultry and cattle. No doubt the Nazis had stored here thousands of tons of oil, naphtha, clothing, linen, medicines, canned foods, vitamin tablets, distillation apparatus, planes, tractors, arms, radio station equipment and all other things—in brief, everything so as to make it possible for Hitler and his aides to live here, if necessary, dozens of years.

HITLER IS ALIVE!

New Exclusive Evidence

Many top American and foreign military officials agree with the *Police Gazette*'s contention that Hitler's death was faked. Signing of German peace treaty will pave way for his return— legally a free man!

"No human being can say conclusively that Hitler is dead."

This was the statement on Oct. 12, 1945 of Lt. General Bedell Smith, World War II Chief of Staff to General Eisenhower and today Director of the top secret American Central Intelligence Agency. General Smith, postwar American Ambassador to Moscow, is now chief of all secret service agencies connected with foreign affairs in the United States.

There is no man in the United States today whose word carries more authority on the explosive subject of Adolf Hitler being alive, yet it was not until the recent *Police Gazette* series of exposes, indicating that the Fuehrer was not dead, that the following facts emerged:

(1) Hitler, for strange and mysterious reasons, has never been tried in absentia by the Allied governments.

(2) A peace treaty will soon be signed with the Bonn Government of Western Germany—such a treaty will automatically end legal prosecution of war criminals.

(3) The Allies are now rearming Western Germany, and, after the signing of the Peace Treaty, there is nothing, literally noth-

ing, to prevent the triumphant return of Adolf Hitler to assume
his fanatical leadership again.

This would be more electrifying and dramatic than the historic "Hundred Days" following Napoleon's return from Elba; it
would upset the calculations of both the Western World and Stalin, because the appearance of Hitler might once again unite both
Eastern and Western Germany. There is no doubt that it would
throw confusion into Central Europe, and the *Police Gazette* is the
first periodical on either side of the Iron Curtain to present this
astonishing truth:

Although both the Russians and the Western Allies are about
to conclude a peace treaty with their areas of Germany, neither has
tried Hitler in absentia, neither has offered evidence that the Fuehrer is dead, and both admit there is no proof of such assumption.

Why?

There are several plausible explanations: first of all, President
Truman declared at his press conference on May 2, 1945, that he
was certain Hitler was dead. It now emerges positively that he had
no proof of this when he made the statement. This line was considered politically advisable at the time in order to hasten the sub-
mission of the German people. That it had no basis in fact was
admitted by the staff officers of the American army in Germany.

As far back as October 12, 1945, six months after Hitler's supposed death and following numerous investigations, no less a military leader than General Dwight D. Eisenhower reported:

"There is every presumption that Hitler is dead, but there is not
a bit of positive proof. The Russians (who occupied Berlin before
American forces) have been unable to unearth one single bit of tangible evidence of Hitler's death."

Thomas J. Dodd, Chief of the US Trial Council at Nuremburg,
declares today, "No one can say he is dead."

Major General Floyd Parks, who led the first air-borne division
into Berlin on July 1, 1945, and became Commanding General of

the United States sector in Berlin, also told the *Police Gazette* that in the light of all available evidence he had received, Hitler may very well be alive.

"I remember being present on several occasions when Marshal Zhukov, the Russian Commander told how he had entered Berlin two months before, and conducted the on-the-spot investigation at the Reichchancellery bunker into the report of Hitler's death. Zhukov was strongly of the opinion that Hitler might have escaped. There was no conclusive evidence that Hitler had died."

The world first heard Hitler was dead when Grand Admiral Doenitz announced over the Hamburg radio on May 1, 1945 that the Fuehrer had died a "hero's death," leading his troops in defense of Berlin, and that Hitler had appointed him as his successor to the Supreme Command.

This announcement surprised the Allied world. The British Foreign Office obviously did not believe Doenitz and immediately reported they would demand that the Germans produce Hitler's body. But this demand was never pressed.

On the heels of the promised demand for Hitler's body, the Russians revealed that they had information contradicting Doenitz' account of the Fuehrer's death. They knew that Hitler did not die a "hero's death."

How did the Russians know?

On April 30, 1945, when all of Berlin's defenses had practically collapsed, a vital conference was held in the Reichchancellery bunker attended by Martin Bormann, Joseph Goebbels, General Hans Krebs, and General Wilhelm Burgdorf. A letter was drafted to Soviet General Gregory Zhukov asking for peace negotiations. Wireless communications were established from the bunker with the Russian officer. General Krebs was dispatched with a detailed letter outlining the peace terms. The letter informed the Russians of Hitler's alleged death and the appointment of Grand Admiral Doenitz as Commander in Chief.

General Krebs returned to the bunker the following noon

with the news that Zhukov demanded unconditional surrender and custody of everyone remaining at Nazi headquarters. Negotiations with the Russians were then cut off and a secret telegram was rushed to Admiral Doenitz advising him to announce Hitler's death and assume command.

On May 2, the day after Doenitz' announcement, President Truman declared at his press Conference that he was certain Hitler was dead and that he had this information on the best authority possible. Identity of the "authority" has never been disclosed. Later events conclusively prove that *it was impossible to make any authoritative statement regarding Hitler's death* at the time of the Truman announcement.

In fact, while Truman was declaring Hitler dead, General Dwight D. Eisenhower, at his European Headquarters, issued a communique that deepened the Hitler death mystery.

Eisenhower revealed the Allies had received authoritative information from Swedish Count Folke Bernadotte. Henrich Himmler had told him a short time before, the Count reported, that Hitler was ill and dying. Bernadotte also declared that Nazi General Walter Schellenberg had confided that Hitler was suffering from a brain hemorrhage. Both of these allegations were subsequently found to be baseless.

Winston Churchill followed President Truman's lead in giving credence to the report of Hitler's death by telling the House of Commons on May 15 that he was "of the opinion" that Hitler was dead. The Prime Minister, however, carefully avoided making such a definite and conclusive statement as that made by President Truman.

That the British Government had no evidence on which to base such an opinion is established by Richard White, Brigadier commanding the British intelligence bureau, who in September, 1945, five months after Hitler's reported death, conceded that it was still officially a mystery.

Why then did Truman and Churchill immediately give credence to the report of Hitler's death—especially at a time when every report on the mystery contradicted the other and indicated without a doubt the possibility that Hitler had escaped and invented the death myth?

One responsible American intelligence officer told the *Police Gazette* that the Truman and Churchill announcements at that time were important for the psychological impact on the Germans. Convincing the Germans that Hitler was dead created complete defeatism inside the Reich.

And it was because of these announcements by the Allies that Hitler was *never tried in absentia.*

A fragmentary report concerning the dramatic happenings in the Reichchancellery bunker first came from the Russians on May 4, when they announced the capture of Hans Fritzsche, Goebbels' deputy, who reported the suicide of Goebbels and his family. Fritzsche also declared that he had heard rumors that Hitler had committed suicide, and that his body was set on fire in the Reichchancellery garden.

The Russians discovered and identified the body of Goebbels and his family, but when it came to checking the rumors of Hitler's suicide they ran into an impregnable wall of mystery.

When the Reds entered Berlin, they set up a special guard around the Chancellery and assigned a unit of experts to search through the ruins of the building, bunker, underground passages and garden for the Fuehrer's body.

Furthermore, the Russians took into custody many of Hitler's servants and minor officials who were with the Fuehrer in the bunker.

From their testimony the following facts were determined concerning the events on the fateful day of April 30, 1945—the day Hitler disappeared: All persons in the bunker were ordered to remain out of sight and not appear in the corridors. The guards were dismissed and the supervision of all activity was taken over by Reichleiter Martin Bormann. He was assisted by Otto Guensche,

Hitler's S.S. Adjutant; Joseph Goebbels, General Wilhelm Burgdorf and Heinz Linge, Hitler's personal servant.

In the evening, the occupants were permitted free movement in the bunker and were told by Bormann, Linge and Guensche that Hitler had committed suicide and his body burned in the Chancellery Garden.

It wasn't until Erich Kempka, Hitler's chauffeur, was captured by the United States 101st Airborne Division at Berchtesgaden, that an "eye-witness" account of Hitler's alleged death and cremation was obtained. Many newspapers throughout the world published Kempka's statements as an authoritative report, thereby deceiving the public into assuming his account was official. The truth is— *Kempka's statements were subsequently discredited.*

According to Kempka, Otto Guensche telephoned him at 2:40 p.m., April 30, and ordered him to bring a large supply of gasoline to the Chancellery garden. When he arrived at the bunker he saw Bormann carrying the body of a woman whom he believed to be Eva Braun. Bormann gave the body to Kempka to deliver to Guensche who took it into the Chancellery garden.

Kempka also testified that he saw Linge and some other S.S. officers carry the corpse of a man, the upper half of whose body was wrapped in a gray blanket. Kempka said it was Hitler's body. The two bodies were placed in a ditch, drenched with gasoline, and set on fire. The mourners, who included Bormann, Burgdorf, Goebbels, Linge and Guensche, then returned to the bunker.

Kempka had no definite knowledge that the dead man was Adolf Hitler and this was conclusively established through his own words. Crossed examined by Thomas J. Dodd, chief United States trial counsel at the Nuremberg trials, here's what Kempka stated:

> MR. DODD: You are the only man who has been able to testify that Hitler is dead and the only one who has been able to testify that Bormann is dead. Is that so, so far as you know?

KEMPKA: I can state that Hitler is dead and that he died on April 30 in the afternoon between 2 and 3 o'clock.

MR. DODD: I know, but you did not see him die either, did you?

KEMPKA: No, I did not see him die.

MR. DODD: And you told the interrogators that you believe you carried his body out of the bunker and set it on fire. Are you not the man who said that?

KEMPKA: I carried out Adolf Hitler's wife, and I saw Adolf Hitler himself wrapped in a blanket.

MR. DODD: Did you actually see Hitler?

KEMPKA: I did not see all of him. The blanket in which he was wrapped was rather short, and I only saw his legs hanging out.

The body Kempka thought was Hitler's definitely was not that of Der Fuehrer. The Russians dug up a number of bodies in the Chancellery garden, all wearing clothes with Der Fuehrer's name sewed in the lining. *The important fact, conceded by every allied intelligence officer, is that Adolf Hitler's body was never found—only corpses dressed in Hitler's clothes!*

The British eventually discovered another witness to this macabre scene. His statements, upon investigation by American intelligence, exploded conclusively the myth of Hitler's suicide.

The witness was Artur Axmann, head of the Hitler Youth Movement, who arrived at the bunker after the alleged suicide of Hitler and Eva Braun. Axmann declared he saw Hitler's body lying on the sofa of his room, his face shattered and bloodstained.

Axmann later changed his story, Col. William F. Heimlich, ex-chief of the American Intelligence unit at Berlin, told the *Police Gazette*. Axmann later admitted that the body he thought was Hitler's was covered with a blanket and that he did not see the face.

"We checked every angle of Axmann's story," Col. Heimlich stated, "Remember, Axmann said he saw the body on the sofa. Well, we found blood stains on that sofa and the best technicians of our laboratory made tests of that blood. *It was not Hitler's blood type.* That's definite."

Since Col. Heimlich, who was in charge of the American Intelligence unit's investigation into Hitler's death, is the most qualified to discuss the strange case, the *Police Gazette* asked him his conclusions.

"You can state there isn't a single iota of proof that Hitler is dead. All the stories and reports of Hitler's death and suicide in the Reichchancellery are definitely untrue."

Significantly, one of the guards who was grief-stricken at hearing the news of Hitler's death, revealed that he was particularly shocked by Guensche's utter lack of concern. Strangely enough, none of the Nazis who allegedly participated in the arrangements of the suicide and funeral have ever been captured and questioned: Martin Bormann, Otto Guensche, Heinz Linge, and General Burgdorf all escaped. Their fate or whereabouts remain a mystery to this day. Only Goebbels is known to have committed suicide.

After many weeks of thorough investigation, Soviet Marshall Gregory Zhukov flatly announced in Berlin: "We have found no corpse that could be Hitler's. Hitler had good opportunities of getting away. He could have taken off at the very last moment for there was an air-field at his disposal."

Colonel General Nikolai E. Berzarin, the Soviet Berlin Commander, declared, "My personal opinion is that Hitler disappeared into Europe."

Berzarin was the Russian official who revealed that several bodies with Hitler's name sewed in the clothes were found in the Reichchancellery, but not one was that of the Fuehrer. The Russians carefully examined every body uncovered in the vicinity of the Reichchancellery. They even accounted for disjointed bones! The Soviets had conclusive means of determining Hitler's identity from intelligence data concerning him physically, including X-rays of every portion of his body—even the gold in his teeth. Thus, the burning of the body would not have been an obstacle to identifying the corpse.

Investigation by the *Police Gazette* has established that even total cremation at the highest temperatures will not destroy bones. The burning of the bodies would have charred the corpses, but couldn't have destroyed the bones. Even a British officer who wrote a report to establish Hitler's death conceded that the bodies could only have been charred and admitted that neither the body nor bones have ever been found.

Plans for Hitler's last minute escape were also uncovered by the Western Allies. At Travemuende airport, a large four-engine plane carrying 30,000 gallons of gasoline was found and the German crew captured. They admitted they were ordered, during the last weeks of the war, to keep the plane in readiness for Hitler. While at the airport, however, the plane was damaged by an R.A.F. fighter, and the crew was unable to repair it in time.

Nevertheless, it would have been simple for Hitler to escape in another plane. In fact, he did not need an airport for a getaway, since the Charlottenburger Chaussee highway, outside of the Reichchancellery, was used as an airstrip until the day of Hitler's disappearance.

British intelligence exerted every effort during the latter months of 1945 to obtain definite evidence that Hitler was dead. But the failure of their search was admitted by Hector MacNeil, British Under-Secretary of Foreign Affairs, who, on October 15, 1945, declared in the House of Commons:

"The Government has no evidence proving conclusively that Hitler is either dead or alive."

The failure of the Allied intelligence bureaus to solve the riddle of Adolf Hitler's disappearance, is a serious matter tormenting the secret services of Great Britain, France, Russia and America.

Should Hitler avoid capture and return to Germany after a peace treaty has been signed with the Western Powers and the Soviet Union, he would be a free man. The world might suddenly be confronted with a vast change in the current balance of power.

It cannot be said that Hitler's return would weigh the scales in favor of the East or of the West, but it would upset all calculations based on known political factors. *The* Police Gazette's *profound opinion is that no time should be lost before trying Hitler in absentia, and that certainly no peace treaty should be signed until the matter is settled.*

US Supreme Court Justice Robert H. Jackson, chief prosecutor at the Nuremberg trials, agreed with the *Police Gazette* that:

"If Hitler is not tried in absentia before the peace treaty with Germany is signed, then there is nothing the allied powers can do to him."

Both Thomas J. Dodd, Chief US trial counsel at Nuremberg, and General Donovan, head of the Office of Strategic Services, fought vigorously to have Hitler tried *in absentia* during the criminal trial, along with the captured Nazi leaders, but they could not obtain permission from Washington.

Why?

Today, while not one shred of evidence exists to prove that Hitler is dead, the possibility of his triumphant return cannot be lightly dismissed. Adolf Hitler did not simply disappear from the face of the earth without trace. Everything in his bloody career supports the theory that he would attempt a melodramatic return at the head of a resurgent Germany.

When?

After the Peace Treaty is signed, at which time the Allied Powers will forfeit their rights to try any more Nazis as war criminals.

THE REAL TRUTH ABOUT HITLER'S FAKE SUICIDE!

by COL. W. F. HEIMLICH

Former Chief, US Intelligence, Berlin

More light on history's great hoax—the "death" of the Fuehrer in his Berlin Bunker—by the US Intelligence officer who made investigation on the spot

Seven years ago in April, rampaging American troops, flushed with victory, smashed their way to the very gates of the Nazi capital of Berlin before they were recalled west across the Elbe River by General Dwight D. Eisenhower. To the south and east, other troops, led by gallant General George Patton had sliced their way through the crumpled resistance of the Werhmacht to Austria and deep in Czechoslovakia. The end came in May with full and unconditional surrender, a violent finale to what was to have been a "thousand year Reich".

On the first of May 1945 Radio Hamburg reported that Adolf Hitler had died a "hero's death". A few days later, Hans Fritzsche, the former aide to Nazi Propaganda Chief Paul Joseph Goebbels, said that Hitler had died a suicide.

One week after the radio report of Hitler's "hero's death," I received from the Chief of Intelligence, Supreme Headquarters, a secret letter giving data of interrogation of several former guards at the Reichschancellery, together with a sketch of the now-famous Bunker. According to information available to G-2 (Intelligence) at Supreme Headquarters, Hitler had died in the Reichschancellery in Berlin, a suicide. My mission was to prove that Hitler was dead.

In February 1945 I had been designated to plan the intelligence phase of the Berlin Operation. We were still far west of the Rhine and had only recently succeeded in straightening out the deep salient into France forced by General Von Rundstedt in the now famous Battle of the Bulge.

Upon receipt of top secret orders, I reported to Supreme Headquarters in Versailles, and together with other members of the staff selected by Supreme Headquarters to plan the Berlin Operation, I went to work in the tiny village of Jouey-en-Josas, about four kilometers out of Versailles. Our boss was Major General Paul B. Ransom. Ransom was one of the ablest staff officers in the United States Army and, personally, one of the finest gentlemen I have ever known.

A month later, our mission had been largely completed and a draft plan had been developed based on three possibilities: capture of Berlin by direct assault; capture of Berlin by "vertical envelopment" or, drop by parachute, and finally, joint capture of the city with Soviet forces. In any event, Intelligence was to have the huge job of rounding up the top war criminals, the documents, the records, the whole frightful evidence of twelve years of brutality under the Nazis. Early in March, Colonel Rufus S. Bratton, a Regular Army officer, was made acting AC of S G-2—"Plans Group G," the code name for the Berlin staff. I became his Executive Officer and later succeeded him as Chief of Intelligence in Berlin in August, 1945.

The story of how we got to Berlin is now history. The Russians captured the city on the 1st of May 1945, but the Americans were not permitted to enter the city till July 2, 1945. During that time, the Russians had thoroughly looted and visited their excesses of rape and pillage on the rubble pile of Berlin while the American troops, who could have entered the city at least two weeks in advance of the Soviet Red Army, cooled their heels west of the Elbe River. It was impossible, therefore, to begin the official investigation into the rumors of the death of Adolf Hitler until mid-July 1945. Our story must begin from that time.

were vital to our investigations because they would have conclusively identified any remains which we found.

Other investigators explored the ruins of the Reichschancellery and in the trophy room found thousands of decorations and
medals which had been stored there. Engineering assistants under
G-2 had explored the Bunker with its three levels, had donned
gas masks and hip waders to go down into the stinking third level
which was under about three feet of water. Before any examination
could be completed, that water had to be pumped out.

Preliminary investigation of the ground surrounding the Bunker in the Reichschancellery garden revealed that six feet of earth
was the total depth above the Bunker level, everything below that
being of concrete and steel. This had great bearing on the subsequent investigations.

By middle August we had collected a considerable amount of
data. Chronologically, the story began with Hamburg radio reports
of May 1 that Hitler had died. On May 8, a rumor was broadcast
that Hitler's body had been found in the Berlin ruins. But his servant said that it was not his master's body. On the 15th of May,
1945, Prime Minister Winston Churchill reported to the House of
Commons that his government accepted as true the report of Hitler's death but only three weeks later on June 9, Russian Marshall
Gregory Zhukov announced that the Russians had no definite facts
of Hitler's death or whereabouts and pointed out that the Fuehrer
might "easily have escaped by plane from the Reichschancellery
area before the fall of Berlin."

When the three leaders of state, President Truman, Marshal
Stalin, and Winston Churchill, met in Potsdam for the last conference among the Big Three, President Truman is reported to have
asked Stalin point-blank if Hitler was dead, and Stalin with characteristic bluntness and brevity replied in one word: "No."

Soon after the war ended, several people reported to have been in the Reichschancellery during the last days were captured and interrogated at great length in the American Occupied Zone of Germany. Among these were the emotional Hannah Reitsch, a German female pilot, and two officers of the SS. Their story in affect was that Hitler had committed suicide after reading his last will and designating in his political testament Admiral Doenitz (now in Spandau prison, Berlin) President and Doctor Goebbels as Chancellor of the Reich. Hitler also nominated as his executor, Martin Bormann, later tried in absentia at Nuremburg and sentenced to death.

Incidentally, Bormann has never been found although there have been many rumors of his being in various parts of the world. In connection with the investigation into Hitler's death, we definitely disproved the reported death of Martin Bormann.

This, then, we knew by early autumn of 1945. Our knowledge was pooled with that of the British and the Soviet intelligence. The Chief of British Intelligence in Berlin was Colonel E.A. Howard, not Captain Trevor-Roper as is popularly supposed because of Trevor-Roper's widely accepted book. Trevor-Roper was in no way connected with our inquiry into Hitler's "death" in Berlin except as a visitor in the early days of September, far in advance of really significant findings. The Chief of Soviet Intelligence was Major General Alexis Sidnev, Chief, NKVD (later MVD) for Berlin and Brandenburg Province.

Sidnev had copies of pictures taken immediately after fighting ceased, of Dr. Goebbels, his wife and family. Goebbels' body had also been burned by gasoline as Hitler's was supposed to have been but was clearly identifiable as the late Propaganda Chief. General Sidnev assured me that he did not have any further evidence of Hitler's demise and particularly, he did not have any idea as to what had been done with Hitler's body, despite the fact that Soviet Intelligence agents had been with the assault troops who entered the Reichschancellery on May 1, 1945!

Plane Ready for Escape

By late September, events were moving rapidly. We discovered that a transport aircraft had been found near Travamunde, a small resort city about 50 kilometers northwest of Lubeck on the North Sea. The crew of the plane had also been found and said that they were one of several such stand-by crews who had volunteered to fly the Fuehrer to some remote part of the world. Navigation maps were provided together with food and petrol supplies which would have made a non-stop flight half around the world possible.

In Berlin, a British journalist also unconvinced that Hitler had died in the Reichschancellery discussed with me the possibility of burning a body in the open air. I was highly doubtful because I had seen a US gasoline truck strafed by German aircraft during the war while fully loaded with 10,000 gallons of hundred octane gasoline. The truck burned fiercely for nearly three hours but when it was possible to approach the cab, it was found that the two men there were still clearly recognizable as human beings. The British journalist managed to acquire a 160 pound pig, borrowed 200 liters of gasoline, poured it over the pig and set it afire. At the end of an hour or so he had some thoroughly roasted pork but had not been able to consume the carcass.

A check at the Berlin Crematorium revealed that it was necessary to burn a body for three hours at 3500 to 4200 degrees in an enclosed oven at the end of which time the large bones were ground to powder. *It was therefore, reasonable to believe that Hitler's body had not been destroyed by fire in the Reichschancellery*. Nonetheless, we decided that a large-scale excavation must take place in that area.

Soviet Intelligence indicated their willingness that this should be accomplished. British Intelligence agreed that this must be done in view of the fact that the research, conducted in the Bunker itself had been fruitless. The water had been pumped out of the Bunker by engineers and a painstaking inch-by-inch search had been accomplished.

Analysis of the couch stains where Hitler reportedly killed himself revealed that the stains, while they were human blood, were not of the blood type of Hitler or Eva Braun. There were no bullet holes in the couch or in the wall behind it.

The Russian soldiers had stripped the Bunker of all small items of value and only broken furniture remained. In front of the Bunker, in the bomb-crater where Hitler was supposed to have been burned, there was only a trash pile of the debris of battle.

Meanwhile, interrogation of literally hundreds of persons who had taken shelter in the last days of war in basements, bomb-craters, and bunkers in the vicinity of the Reichschancellery had been exhaustively completed.

Naturally, none of these persons admitted to having seen either Hitler's body, or any other in the Reichschancellery proper. However, many of them had seen Goebbels' body, together with those of his family, in front of the Propaganda Ministry. Many of the stories were "tall tales," narrated deliberately in order to make the teller appear in a more dramatic light. Others could not recollect the facts because of shock which was upon them in those last days of the city and most stories were highly influenced by starvation and illness.

In the period between May 1 when the city fell and July 2 when American troops finally entered, the economic situation of the city had gone from bad to frightful. People had been reduced to the very lowest levels of human degradation in order to remain alive. The hospitals were full to overflowing, and without heat, light, drugs and medical supplies. It is a fact that 98% of all babies born in Berlin in this period died of malnutrition or dysentery.

There were stories told of hundreds of persons having been trapped in the subway which had been flooded by SS troops. Later investigation into this by the Military Government, including the pumping of the subways dry and the raising of the cars, revealed that there had been no deaths due to this action. These wild stories, together with what had been gleaned by intelligence units in Western Germany, made excavation in the Reichschancellery proper all the more important. Arrangements were therefore completed with the Soviet representatives for excavation of the Reichschancellery area around December 1, 1945.

No Trace of the Body

The American Intelligence team headed by Captain George Gabelia, one of the American officers who spoke fluent Russian, arranged for two dozen workmen to be available. At the appointed time the workmen were carried by trucks to the Reichschancellery, provided with picks, shovels and axes and the operation began.

First, all debris was cleared up, such odds and ends of war as broken machine guns, ammunition, rifles, helmets, uniforms, bits and pieces of wood, leather and metal all were examined and carefully piled in one area of the garden. The bomb-crater, located about four yards from the entrance to the Bunker was the prime target. Two screens were erected, one of wire mesh similar to chicken wire and behind it a second one much finer with half-inch holes. Every shovel full of dirt from the bomb-crater went first through the wide screen and next through the small screen in the hope that any small piece of evidence showing the presence of a human body might be quickly detected.

The X-ray photographs of Hitler's head gave us expert clues as to his dental structure and even one tooth might have been sufficient to identify his body.

As the excavation progressed, we found bits of uniform and civilian clothing including a woman's slip, a man's hat with the initials "A. H." in silver in the lining, suitcases and other pieces of clothing, books, magazines, records, diaries, recording tape and the remains of what had once been the switchboard in the Bunker.

After two days of excavation in an ever widening area we found no signs of any bodies and more significantly no evidences of burning or of fire!

On the third day of excavation I received a call at 7:00 in the morning from Captain Gabelia telling me that upon reporting at the Reichschancellery to continue the digging, he and our British allies had been met by an entire battalion of Soviet troops on guard there and had been denied access to the Reichschancellery Bunker area. I hurried to the Reichschancellery, arriving there about 7:45 in the morning. The area was indeed under guard. The Soviet major in command said that he was acting under instructions.

I proceeded to NKVD headquarters in the Luisan Strasse, in the Soviet sector of Berlin. I found that General Sidnev was "not available" and that his deputy, Colonel Tulpov was "ill." After three fruitless days, we were forced to call off further excavation in the Reichschancellery. The building and the grounds continued under guard for another six months! It was therefore necessary to send my uncompleted report of investigation into the death of Adolf Hitler to Supreme Headquarters then located at Frankfurt, Germany, together with pictures and supporting documents, with the notation that it had been impossible to complete the investigation.

In the final paragraph of that report I stated that there was no evidence beyond that of hear-say to support the theory of Hitler's suicide.

I was authorized by higher headquarters in 1945 to say that: "On the basis of present evidence, no insurance company in America would pay a death claim on Adolf Hitler."

My final report to Washington stated that no evidence was found of Hitler's death in Berlin in 1945. As a result, the "Wanted List of War Criminals," last issued in 1948, carried the cryptic notice: "Wanted: Hitler, Adolf, Reichsfuehrer."

This story has never been properly told because of the fear that it might give credence to the rumors rampant throughout the world that Hitler was indeed alive. Particularly in South America where a hard core of Nazis still exists such a theory might give rise to the belief that their Fuehrer was indeed alive in some remote part of the world awaiting a chance to return as did Napoleon from

Elba. This seems hardly credible, and it is not my place here to speculate on what actually did happen to Hitler.

More sinister than Hitler's disappearance was that of Martin Bormann, for Bormann was an organizational genius with a true passion for anonymity. Moreover, he was a true Nazi who believed passionately in that evil political system. Aside from speculation, there is no ghost in the crumbled ruins of the Reichschancellery more dangerous than that of Hitler himself and over the deliberations in Bonn as well as Washington, there still hangs the cloud of doubt: "What really happened to Hitler?"

Hitler's
Lovers & Friends

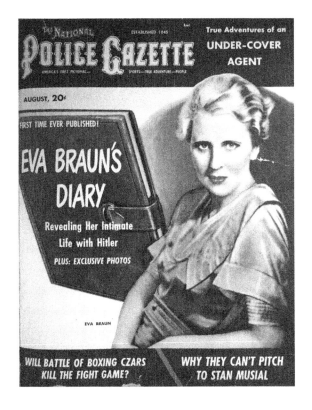

Steffi—as she was called by her fellow ladies who lunch in the Manhattan smart set of the late '40s and '50s—was actually Stephanie von Hohenlohe-Waldenburg-Schillingsfuerst, confidant of and courier for Adolph Hitler. She preferred not to talk about the old days.

The real star of this section, however, is Eva Braun and her diary. We find Eva's dear-diary entries first questioning why Adolph is always away ruling the world and doesn't have any time for her. But later entries—and pictures—reveal how when the cat's away, the mice will play. Eva did not take being second to world domination in her man's heart sitting down; she took it lying down!

But Adolph readily admits he's no Don Juan. When one woman after another falls for him, then attempts suicide, he reflects, "I do not bring women luck . . . a fact which repeats itself in a most unusual way throughout my life."

Then we get Adolph Hitler as the crime kingpin who still enjoys personally doing hits from time to time, especially when it involves his woman. One unlucky artist from Munich's Schwabing neighborhood—the "Greenwich Village of Germany"—received direct from Der Fuehrer a high-dosage lead supplement to the torso after he was discovered getting a little too Bohemian with Eva.

But in a touching moment that proved Hitler was not always cold and lacked empathy, when it came time to have his favorite dog killed—after all, the Russians were advancing and there was no way he'd let his prized German Shepherd fall into their hands—he made sure it was done as humanely and painlessly as possible.

Finally, after years of being neglected by her one true love, Eva Braun's dream comes true and she can once and for all call herself "Mrs. Adolph Hitler." Sometimes happy endings are worth waiting for.

LOVES AND INTRIGUES
OF HITLER'S GIRL CONFIDANT

By RUTH REYNOLDS

One-time secret courier of the Nazis,
now stars in US social circles

Top drawer socialities in Manhattan wag their tongues these days when, in the fashionable spots, they meet the still beautiful "Princess' Stefanie Hohenlohe-Waldenburg-Schillingsfuerst who was reported to be, for years, Hitler's personal messenger, the biggest thing since Mata Hari.

But those are fighting words with the Princess these days and no one asks her about it, or about her long fight to stay in the United States, or about her three years in an internment camp at Seagoville, Tex.

Although a woman of the world, Stefanie is still an extremely trim, attractive blonde woman, as witty and clever as ever. She has seen much of life.

As a woman of the world, she developed a repertoire of parts she could play when she found a new friend she wanted to charm. But no longer does she spice conversation with famous names as easily as one shakes pepper into soup. She is content to be Society—with a capital S—and to hope that her friends will forget about her amazing career and the suspicions that she was once a valuable lady spy for the Nazis.

Steffi, as she is called by her friends, was the daughter of a Vien-

nese family. No illustrious ancestors people her family tree—at
least not so she could claim them.

Steffi was lonely as a child. Her schoolmates at a finishing school
for the daughters of the wealthier bourgeois of Vienna were forbidden by their parents to be friends with her because her mother's
husband, a lawyer named Richter, served two years on a conviction for fraud and her mother had open liaisons with a wealthy
merchant.

Steffi burned with ambition to be somebody and learned well
her mother's teaching that there was happiness only when one was
living in the lap of luxury.

While she was still young, Steffi met her first "lap"—Arthur
Levier, a wealthy young man about town who had come from Switzerland to study at one of Vienna's technical schools—and in the
Hotel Sacher by night. Through Arthur's friends, Steffi met other
men. Many of them became infatuated with her charms and fell in
love with her. One of these was Archduke Maximilian, brother to
the heir to the throne. After love died, Max and Steffi were bound
by friendship.

Through Max, Steffi met Prince Friedrich F. Hohenloe, etc.,
who fell madly in love with her. They were married in the London
Registry office on May 12, 1914, and on Dec. 5 of that year, their
only child, Prince Franz Joseph, was born in Vienna.

Friedrich's relatives were infuriated by the marriage. In the first
place they were Catholic. Steffi was Jewish. In the second, they
could trace their ancestors back to the 12th century. Steffi couldn't
even be certain of her father. Also, they had a code of conduct for
princesses. Steffi had none.

She kept up her friendship for Archduke Maximilian and
arranged such lavish parties and revelries for him that the censure
of Emperor Franz Josef beat on Max's head and it was suggested
that Princess Stefanie might better leave Vienna for a while.

The World War was under way. Why didn't she go to the Front as a nurse?

Steffi arrived at a Polish field hospital. Here was a new world to conquer. After all, the doors of Viennese aristocrats had never been opened to her, not even after her marriage to one of them.

But her stay at the field hospital was short. Her superior, Prof. Otto Zuckerkandl said:

"She may be a princess but she is certainly no nurse."

On Nov. 21, 1916, the Emperor died. Stefanie intended to take her place among the princesses at the funeral services. But one of her husband's relatives, who was Lord Chamberlain, saw her before she reached the spot designated for mourning princesses. He told her she was, "not worthy to take a place among the mourners at the bier of this great monarch."

Stefanie was never daunted by such snubs—but they may explain why, in later years, she did the things she did and fought like a tigress to keep the place she thought she rightfully deserved.

The World War came to an end. So did the Austro-Hungarian monarchy. Stefanie, calling herself a persecuted aristocrat, went to Paris. By this time she and her husband were completely estranged. On July 29, 1920, they were divorced in Budapest. The prince married again—but Steffi kept right on using the title. She had little money but her mode of life remained unchanged.

Jeno Hermanyi-Herzman, an international banker and friend of Maximilian's days came back into her life, eased her financial burden and made it possible for her to travel. Hermanyi's friends were high government officials, political leaders and diplomats. Steffi met them. It was at this period of her life that she began to build up her political connections which have stood her in good stead.

But when economic disaster over Europe overwhelmed Hermanyi and he took his own life, Steffi was again left to her own resources—until she met a gentleman with estates in both Austria and Germany, Count Alexander Beroldingen. Her star began to rise.

She met Lord Rothermere, younger brother of the eminent British publisher, Lord Northcliffe. Rothermere had inherited the Northcliffe newspapers when his brother died in 1922.

Harold Sidney Harmsworth, Lord Rothermere, enjoyed talking international politics and, for Beroldingen's sake, Steffi tried to persuade him to back editorially the return by Poland of the Polish corridor to Germany.

But before she could get very far with that the British Lord visited Hungary, was impressed, wrote a flattering editorial about that country, and won paeans of praise from the Hungarians.

Steffi saw which way the bandwagon was going—toward Hungary, not toward Poland. She climbed aboard—and let it be known that it was she who inspired the editorial.

A popular movement started in Hungary to make Rothermere's son, Esmond, 29, King of Hungary—and Steffi did her best to keep this movement alive. But before it died, for Beroldingen's sake she had persuaded the publisher to become pro-Nazi editorially. Beroldingen next suggested that she go to Germany. Perhaps she could meet some Nazi officials and work for them. He was correct.

One of the gentlemen the Princess met in Berlin was Capt. Fritz Wiedemann, Hitler's World War company commander who was later to be German Consul General in San Francisco.

Wiedemann, impressed by Steffi's aristocratic name, her social gifts, her knowledge of politics introduced her to Hitler and to the Propaganda Chief, Josef Goebbels. The question of her non-Aryan status was settled quickly.

Steffi was made a part of the German Foreign Service in the West, with headquarters in London, not too far from her dear friend, Lord Rothermere. Her job in London was to create an atmosphere of friendliness toward the Nazi regime. She did her job well.

These were golden days for Steffi. She was being paid by the German government and also by the British publisher.

She obtained an interview with Hitler for Rothermere in 1934, arranged a meeting between Wiedemann and the British Viscount

Halifax, another between Konrad Henlein and Viscount Runci-
man and was thus, according to Wiedemann, "helpful in laying the
ground work which made the Munich agreement possible"—and
gave the Nazis more time to prepare for fight. (Steffi now says it
was another Hohenloe who arranged these meetings.)

She managed to get her finger in every pudding and some of
them had a great many plums for the little woman who had risen
above so many snubs.

Steffi, according to the publisher, was not backward about
pressing him for money. Consequently, in June, 1939, she charged
that under her agreement she was to receive $20,000 a year for life.
She lost the suit.

In October, 1939, she walked into the London Ritz for luncheon.
"Get out, dirty spy!"

Someone at a table of women said it, loud enough for all to hear
and loud enough for all to know that it was directed at Steffi. The
snubs had begun.

But in 1939, Hitler sent Steffi to the United States to discuss
some diplomatic questions with Wiedemann. She said to reporters that she would indulge in no more politics and that she had as
much to do with politics "as a rope dancer."

Nevertheless when a movement began in 1940 to deport her
she was found in San Francisco with Wiedemann. Movement after
movement to effect this deportation was begun but Steffi managed
to stave it off and in May, 1941, Attorney General Robert Jackson,
said that the movements would be dropped inasmuch as Steffi had
provided the United States with some very interesting information.
It is to be presumed that this information concerned Wiedemann
and other Nazis.

But in December, 1941, after Pearl Harbor, Steffi was caught
in an FBI roundup and in January 1942 was interned as an enemy
alien "for the duration." For her "the duration" ended in June
1945—and now she is back in New York where memories are short
and friendships quick.

EVA BRAUN'S DIARY

Here, revealed for the first time, is the only known document describing the intimate details of Hitler's secret affair with the attractive blonde who shared his Nazi life.

Hitler's favorite portrait of Eva Braun.

Of all the fanatically loyal people who attended Adolf Hitler and are still with him in his present hideout, none have known him so intimately as the young, voluptuous blonde from Munich, Eva Braun. Hitler took Eva as his mistress in the early 1930s, and she is with him as his wife today. She has been with him longer than any of his political or military advisers, or any of his personal servants.

Eva's intimate tie with Hitler was for a long time a secret, but when they heard about it, Allied Military authorities became eager to capture her. All documents describing her relationship with Hitler were of tremendous importance.

An intense search, at the end of World War II, by US Army Intelligence, turned up one of the most controversial and intimate papers of the Hitler years—Eva's diary.

Its authenticity, together with the identification of photographs from Eva's personal album, has been established by the US Army.

The *Police Gazette* publishes this historical document for the first time, with the exclusive, personal photos. It is the only existing record of the love life of Hitler.

The diary was discovered in Bavaria in Eva's treasure chest with a dozen photo albums which recorded Eva's family life and her years of amorous friendship with Hitler. The treasure included an 18th Century silver set bearing the royal emblem of the Polish Crown (the set was valued at between $500,000 and $1,000,000); a brooch worth $50,000; 50 diamonds, and thousands of dollars.

These valuables remained of the hundreds Hitler had collected all over Europe to bring back to his mistress. Authorities also found what must have been one of the most highly-prized of Eva's possessions: the blood-stained uniform Hitler wore on July 20, 1944, the day of the attempted assassination.

The uniform had been ripped off Hitler after the explosion. If US authorities had not recovered it, it would have become a shocking symbol to rally the forces of neo-Nazism and remind them of the traitors who had tried to overthrow Hitler in the past.

The fact that Eva was entrusted with this prize indicates the important role she played in Hitler's plans.

Eva Braun was attractive enough to have distracted any man, no matter how absorbed he was with the problems of his party, his country and the world. She was 5-feet-3, well-proportioned, with shapely legs, and a warm smile.

She met Hitler in the late 1920s, when she was sent by the well-known German photographer, Heinrich Hoffmann, to take pictures of the Nazi leader. She worked, at the time, as an apprentice for Hoffman, who was notorious for the beauties he kept around the shop. While taking his picture, she caught Hitler's fancy, and soon captured his affections.

A few years later, at Hitler's suggestion, she resigned from her job at the photo studio.

Eva was a natural blonde, but before she met the Fuehrer, she bleached her hair light, and had changed her hair style almost weekly in an effort to find the coiffure which suited her best. When Hitler became serious about her, all that changed. He insisted she restore her hair to its natural color, and adopt a more conservative hairdo. The new appearance didn't hide her natural charms.

From the beginning, she toured with Hitler in his small Opel as he went from one Nazi party meeting to another. As Nazism grew, and Hitler's power—measured by the booming fanatic party spirit—increased, Eva was given a Mercedes. Later she received a villa in Munich, her home town, which is only a few hours drive from the Fuehrer's Bavarian retreat—Berchtesgaden. By 1938, close friends of Hitler insisted he was about to marry Eva. He bought her an engagement ring and a wedding present. But unfortunately for Eva, the coming war and pressure of world affairs changed his plans.

Outwardly, Eva appeared well-mannered and retiring. She was always conscious of her appeal to men—Hitler and others—and constantly dieted and treated her face to maintain her good complexion. She always dressed smartly, and had a passion for extravagantly daring lingerie.

Eva was often unhappy because her status as Hitler's mistress—instead of his wife—kept her in the background. And while she was behind the scenes, the wives of Frick, Goebbels and Goering were pushing Hitler socially. They introduced him to dancers, entertainers and prominent Nazi women to get him to take a wife.

Stories were circulated, at the time, that Hitler often indulged in revels at which nude dancers performed. He always explained to Eva that his interest in them was purely artistic.

On the other hand, when Hitler wasn't in town, or when Eva wasn't traveling with him, she didn't sit home knitting. She flirted, danced, and otherwise entertained some of the SS guards at Berchtesgaden. And among her reported lovers were a number of handsome, young Bavarian Nazi party men. When Hitler was away, she threw gay parties where she displayed some of the lavish gowns from her huge Hitler-furnished wardrobe. During this time, at least three young Nazis attempted suicide because of their love for Eva.

Like many mistresses famous in history, Eva was also a schemer. Shortly after the completion of Hitler's retreat in Berchtesgaden, Eva moved in. She also managed to bring in, on practically a permanent basis, her sister Gretl, and her closest friend, Herta Ostermyer.

Some time afterwards, Gretl, who was even more flirtatious than her sister, met Hermann Fegelein, a 37-year-old former jockey who had become a minor Nazi official. After a courtship of one week, they were married. The cagey Eva persuaded Hitler to be best man, and so the blessing of the Nazi party was given to Fegelein.

So great was Eva's influence that Fegelein advanced to the rank of General in the SS (Elite Guard), even though Hitler did not personally completely approve. He didn't, however, want to act against Eva's wishes. Eventually his feelings became too great, and in his last days in the bunker, Hitler ordered Fegelein executed for traitorous dealings with Himmler in a conspiracy to overthrow the Nazi government. Not even Eva's pleas could spare Fegelein's life.

What kind of woman was the real Eva Braun, under the gay, flirtatious exterior? She was not an intellectual. She could not talk politics intelligently with anyone, let alone the Fuehrer. (She had done so poorly at school that friends nicknamed her "fathead.")

To a great extent, Eva was a frustrated woman. The lack of public recognition, plus the fact that affairs of the Nazi nation frequently took Hitler away, bothered her. She was also annoyed because he was sometimes so involved in world problems that even when he was with her, she couldn't understand him. And often he lacked affection.

So torn was she that several times she tried to commit suicide. Each attempt succeeded in bringing Hitler closer to her.

Eva's diary, which covers the most exciting days of her life between February 6 and May 28, 1935 (three years before Hitler was supposedly preparing to marry her) shows her as a childish, emotionally immature girl.

The diary covers a dramatic period in German and world history—the Germans boldly took over the Saar, and shortly afterwards Hitler openly flaunted the Versailles Treaty and created a German army. In a "free election" three weeks before Eva began her diary, workers in the Saar voted themselves back into the German Reich.

Yet Eva's writings for those days show that she was not conscious of what was happening.

FEBRUARY 6, 1935 — I guess today is the right day to begin this masterpiece.

I have happily reached my twenty-third year . . . whether I am happy is another question. At the moment I am certainly not happy. That is because I have such high expectations for such an "important" day.

If I only had a dog, then I wouldn't be quite so alone; but I guess that is asking too much.

Mrs. Schauk came with flowers and a telegram as "ambassador."

My whole office looks like a flower shop and smells like a mortuary. I am really ungrateful, but I hoped so much to get a little dachshund, and now again nothing. Perhaps next year or even after that; when it will be better suited for an incipient spinster.

Let me not give up hope. I should have learned patience by now.

I bought two lottery tickets today . . .

It seems as though I'll never get rich. Can't do anything about that. Today I would have gone to the Zugspitze (Germany's highest mountain, on the Austrian border) with Herta, Gretl, Ilse and mother and we would have lived like kings, because one always has the most fun when others share the happiness.

But the trip didn't come off.

Today I'm going to eat with Herta. What else may a simple little woman of twenty-three do? Thus, I'll bring my birthday to a close with gluttony. I believe I shall have acted in accordance with his (Hitler's) wishes.

FEBRUARY 11, 1935 — He (Hitler) was just here, but no dog and no presents. He didn't even ask me whether I had a birthday wish. Somehow I bought myself some jewelry. A necklace, earrings and a ring to match for fifty marks (about $20). Everything very pretty. I hope he likes it. If not, he may buy me something himself.

FEBRUARY 15, 1935 — It seems that the Berlin deal is really going to come off. This I won't believe until I am in the Reichschancellery.

[*Hitler was arranging an apartment for her in the Reichschancellery in Berlin*].

It is really too bad that Herta can't come along instead of Charlie (Charlotta, one of the girl friends of SS men in Munich). She would be a guarantee for a few happy days. This way there will probably be a big ado because I don't think that Bruckner (an aide in Berlin), for a change, will show his more charming side when he meets Charlie. I don't dare look forward to it yet, but it might turn out to be wonderful if everything goes well. Let's hope so.

FEBRUARY 18, 1935 — Yesterday, he (Hitler) came quite unexpectedly and it was a delightful evening.

The nicest thing was that he is thinking about taking me out of the firm and—I don't want to be too happy yet—to buy me a little house. I don't dare think of it. It would be so wonderful. I wouldn't have to open the door for our "honorable" customers and play salesgirl. Dear God, please make it come true within a reasonable period of time.

Poor Charlie is sick and can't come to Berlin with us. She's really unlucky, but maybe it is better that way. Maybe he would be very rude to her and then she would certainly be even more unhappy. I am so infinitely happy because he loves me so and pray that it will always be like this. I should never want to be to blame if once he should stop loving me.

MARCH 4, 1935 — [*Three days after the German army marched into the Saar*].

I am mortally unhappy. Since I can't write him, this diary must serve to relieve my pain.

He came Saturday for the big Munich ball. Mrs. Schwarz had

given me a loge ticket for it and so I was obliged to attend at all costs, especially since I had already accepted.

I spent a few wonderful hours with him until 12 o'clock and then went to the ball with his permission.

He promised that I could see him on Sunday. In spite of the fact that I called up and sent a message that I am waiting for him, he drove off to Feldafing (suburb of Munich). He even refused Hoffmann's invitation to tea and supper. One may look at everything from two sides; perhaps he wanted to be alone with Dr. Goebbels who was also here, but he could have let me know. I was at Hoffmann's on pins and needles, thinking all the time that he might come any minute.

We went to the train later, because he had decided to leave, but only arrived in time to see the rear lights. We (Hoffmann and the others) had again left for the train too late, and thus I couldn't even say goodbye. Probably I'm too pessimistic again, I hope, but he hasn't been here for fourteen days, and I am so unhappy and have no peace of mind. Incidentally, I don't know why he should be angry with me—perhaps because I went to the ball—but then he gave me his permission.

I am uselessly wracking my brain as to why he should be driving away without saying goodbye.

Hoffmann gave me a ticket for tonight's performance of "Venetian Nights," but I won't go. I am much too unhappy.

MARCH 11, 1935 — [*For many days, the Germans have been fighting off British attempts at a general settlement of the European armament and territorial problems. Hitler has refused to see Sir John Simon, the British Foreign Minister, who has gone to Berlin for the talks*].

I only wish that I were seriously ill and would hear nothing of him for eight days. Why doesn't something happen to me? Why do I suffer like this? I wish I had never seen him. I am desperate. I am now going to buy more sleeping tablets, at least then I'll be half-dazed and won't think about him so much.

Why doesn't the devil come and get me. I'm sure it's nicer there than here.

For three hours I stood outside the Carlton (a prominent Munich hotel) and had to watch while he brought flowers for Ondra (Annie Ondra, friend of Hitler) and invited her for supper. (Marginal note, written March 26: Just my crazy imagination) He is only using me for very definite purposes. (Marginal note, written March 26: Baloney, probably I am, too). When he says he loves me, he takes it about as seriously as his promises which he never keeps. Why does he torture me so much instead of just putting an end to the whole thing?

MARCH 16, 1935 — [*This is the day Hitler wiped out the military provisions of the Versailles Treaty, restored German universal military service, and established an army of 36 divisions. This was the crowning blow to the Allies who fought and won World War I, and wrote the peace. On this day, it was all lost*].

He went to Berlin again. If only I didn't "go off the beam" whenever I see him less than usual. Actually, it's quite natural that he shows no great interest in me at present, since there is so much going on politically (Eva's first recognition that anything else was going on in the world outside her boudoir.)

I am going to take a trip to the Zugspitze with Gertl today; then maybe my remorse will subside. Everything has always turned out alright so far, and it will be the same this time. One must have patience, that's all.

APRIL 1, 1935 — Yesterday, we were invited by him for supper at the Four Seasons (a Munich hotel famous for good food). I had to sit next to him for three hours and couldn't say a word to him. When leaving, he handed me an envelope containing money, as he had done once before. If only he had at least added a greeting or a kind word, I would have been so happy, but he never thinks of anything like that.

Why doesn't he go to Hoffmann's to eat? There, at least, I would have him to myself for a few minutes. I only wish he wouldn't come any more until his home is ready (the Eagle's Nest, in near-by Berchtesgaden).

APRIL 29, 1935 — [*Nazi party persecution of the Jews has already begun to take effect, and many of them are leaving the country*].

Things are very tough. I keep humming to myself "Things will improve," but it doesn't help much. The house is ready, but I can't go to visit him; love does not seem to be on his program at present. Now that he is back in Berlin, I feel a little better; but there were days during the last week when I did my share of crying at night, especially since I spent Easter at home by myself. I'm getting on everybody's nerves because I want to sell everything from my clothes to my cameras, and even theater tickets. Oh, well . . . things will improve. After all, my debts are not that big.

MAY 10, 1935 — [*During these days, Hitler was constantly shouting to the world that he wanted peace; but within Germany, his troops were preparing for war*].

According to Mrs. Hoffmann's kind and also tactless remarks, he (Hitler) now has a substitute for me. Her name is Walkure (which literally translated means Valkyrie, one of the mythical maidens who hover over the battlefield, choosing those to be slain), and she looks it, including her legs. But those are the shapes that appeal to him. If that is true, he will soon have annoyed her till she gets slim, unless she has Charlie's talent for thriving on worries. Worry alone seems to increase her appetite.

If Mrs. H's observations should turn out to be true, it is mean of him (Hitler) not to tell me. After all, he should know me well enough to realize that I would never stand in his way, if he should discover another romantic interest. Why should he worry about what happens to me? I'll wait till the third of June . . . I'll ask him for an explanation by mail. Now tell me again that I'm not modest.

The weather is gorgeous, and I, the mistress of Germany's and the world's greatest man, have to sit at home and look at it through the window. He has so little understanding and still makes me appear distant when his friends are around. Well, one makes one's own bed . . . I guess it really is my fault, but it is just one of those things for which one likes to blame someone else. This period of fasting won't last forever, and then it will taste much better. Too bad, though, that it just happens to be spring.

MAY 28, 1935 — I have just sent him a letter, one that is decisive, for me. Will he consider it as important as I do? Well, we'll see. If I don't get an answer by tonight, I'll take my 25 pills and lie down peacefully. Is it a sign of the terrific love of which he assures me, that he hasn't spoken a kind word to me for three months? Agreed that he's been busy with political problems, but have not things eased off?

[*Hitler had, a week before, made a "peace" speech in the Reichstag, during which he professed Germany's integrity and readiness to sign non-aggression agreements*].

And how about last year when he had lots of worries with Rohm (Ernst Rohm, Brown Shirt leader who was executed in a purge in 1934; a plot against Hitler's life had been discovered) and with Italy, and he still found time for me? True, I'm not in a position to judge whether the present situation isn't much worse, but after all a few kind words to Mrs. Hoffmann would hardly have taken much time. I fear there is some other reason. It's not my fault; certainly not. Maybe it's another woman, although I doubt that it's Walkure. What other reason could there be? I can't find any.

P.S. My God, I'm afraid I will not get an answer today. If only someone would help me; everything is so hopeless. Maybe my letter reached him at an inopportune time, or maybe I shouldn't have written at all. Whichever it is, the uncertainty is much worse than even a sudden end would be. Dear God, please make it possible that I speak to him today; tomorrow will be too late. I have decided on 35 pills to make death certain this time. If he would at least have someone call up for him. [*Eva's depression passed; she didn't take the pills.*]

WHY HITLER KILLED
HIS BEST FRIEND . . . HIS DOG

by SANFORD MERKIN

He was responsible for the murder of millions of
human beings, but Der Fuehrer wanted his dog destroyed
without pain

It was a cold, rainy spring morning in Berlin, and the rumble of Russian cannon rolled steadily over the bunker where Hitler sat planning the execution of the only real friend he had in the world.

That world had disintegrated around him rapidly within the past few weeks. The Allies were closing in from the West, and from the East the dreaded Reds were pressing closer and closer to the heart of Berlin. The mighty Third Reich was collapsing, and with it the dream of Der Fuehrer's empire.

He had retreated to the bomb-proof bunker to plot his escape. As she sat there, his friend crawled closer to him, almost as if she were trying to protect the master she loved.

Her name was Blondi and she had no way of knowing that Hitler was at that moment plotting her death. He was speaking with Dr. Haase, his personal physician, but she couldn't understand the conversation—for she was a dog.

Blondi had been with Hitler seven years, devoted and true, while around him his generals and Eva Braun, his mistress, cheated on him, lied to him, even tried to kill him.

Gift from Goebbels

Blondi was given to Hitler in 1938 by the wife of the Nazi propaganda minister, Joseph Goebbels. Der Fuehrer had been to the Goebbels' home one evening, and Mrs. Goebbels showed him a litter just born to one of their Alsatian dogs. Hitler watched the puppies frolic, admired them and asked Frau Goebbels for a blonde female that displayed particular intelligence and friendliness.

From that moment Blondi became a part of his inner circle. She grew up in his apartment in the Chancellery, went with him to Berchtesgaden, was always at his side in conferences and on trips around the Reich.

The Alsatian, better known in this country as the German Shepherd, is one of the most loyal breeds in the world. Such movies as the Rin-Tin-Tin series and others have long illustrated its courage, its willingness to die for its master.

Blondi grew to 65 pounds, and her thick coat was yellow enough to make her the perfect "Nordic" type that Hitler loved. Veterinarians checked her health periodically, prescribed the right foods. Blondi had her own room or slept in the same room with Hitler wherever they went.

Dr. von Hasselbach, one of Hitler's personal doctors, said that during the last critical years of the war, Der Fuehrer told him:

"My officers and my general staff are a bunch of traitors. They are responsible for Germany's defeat. The only ones I can trust are Eva Braun and Blondi. They'll remain faithful to me to the end."

Eva Cheated on Him

But what Hitler didn't know was that only the big yellow dog with the trusting eyes was true. Eva for years had been playing around with boyfriends both in the apartment Hitler rented for her in Berlin and at Berchtesgaden when the Nazi ruler was away.

So on the morning of April 30, 1945, Hitler took Blondi to the bunker along with Dr. Haase. As he sat stroking the dog's head, Hitler said:

"I want Blondi destroyed."

Haase nodded. "I'll have one of the S.S. men shoot her immediately."

Hitler and the only friend he trusted—
his faithful German Shepherd dog, Blondi.

"Nein! Nein!" Hitler screamed, clasping Blondi's head to his breast. "I don't want her hurt. Give her some poison that will kill her without pain. I don't want my dog to suffer."

Dr. Haase may have reflected that this was the man who had ordered the cold-blooded extermination of five million Jews, and had sent countless other millions to their death.

"Yes, Mein Fuehrer," he replied obediently.

After Hitler had fondled Blondi and given her a final embrace, Dr. Haase led her away. He mixed a poison with her food and in an hour she died peacefully.

The Russians were within a mile of the bunker, and the roar of their angry guns lit up the Berlin sky as Blondi was buried in the courtyard of the Reich Chancellery.

A few hours later Hitler and Eva Braun slipped quietly out of the bunker to make their escape. But the slumped, beaten figure of a man who once dreamed of ruling the world paused for a moment at the little mound of earth that was Blondi's last resting place.

"Goodbye, my faithful friend," Hitler muttered.

HITLER'S MISTRESS RISKED DEATH TO CHEAT ON DER FUEHRER

Adolf's Housekeeper Tells How

Adolf Hitler could dominate his Prussian generals, scare the wits out of his Storm Trooper bully boys and plunge the world into war—but he couldn't control his girlfriend, Eva Braun.

And he spent more than $1,000,000 bedecking her with jewels and finery, yet every time Der Fuehrer went off to work, little Eva kicked over the traces and made merry with her younger and more handsome boyfriends.

She risked death by cheating on one of the most powerful and ruthless men the world has ever known, but like many another Joe, Hitler never suspected. Fact is, he married the shapely blonde.

This astonishing story of Eva's unfaithfulness comes right from the hitherto secret files of Allied Military Intelligence and from Anni Winter, Hitler's housekeeper for more than 20 years.

When Frau Winter was interviewed by Intelligence officers right after the collapse of the Third Reich, she painted a different picture of the shy, retiring blonde who in Hitler's presence dressed severely and simply, didn't smoke or drink, and kept a serious, semi-refined appearance at all times.

But when Adolf hurried away from their Munich apartment, la belle Braun phoned her boyfriends, slipped into a skin-tight gown and threw wild parties. All night long sounds of revelry rolled out of the Braun apartment, mingled with the popping of champagne corks and shrieks of drunken laughter.

"She knew just what behavior Der Fuehrer expected of her," Hitler's housekeeper told Intelligence officers, "and she never gave him any chance to criticize her, for she always was on her good conduct when he was around. But when she was left alone at Berchtesgaden or at the Munich apartment, she showed her true self and did almost everything the master objected to.

Eva Flirted with Them Openly

"There were handsome young men around, and Eva flirted with them openly. She enjoyed flattery and beamed girlishly at the attention she obtained. Eva loved the outdoors and often went swimming and hiking with her Munich friends."

When Intelligence operatives went through Eva's personal belongings in the Munich apartment and at Berchtesgaden, they found plenty of documentary evidence to back up the housekeeper's statements—and a lot more.

Here for the first time you see photographs found by the Army in Eva's private albums—and it's a safe bet that Adolf never peeped into these secret pages, for there was enough evidence in these pictures to send Eva to her death, since Hitler was a jealous lover. There's no doubt, either, that the boys who posed with their arms around the dictator's mistress were off their rocker, for if Hitler suspected they were within ten miles of little Eva, they would have been target practice for the SS firing squads at dawn.

If money means anything, Hitler never had any doubts as to the faithfulness of the pretty blonde who was young enough to be his daughter. A study by Allied authorities of his financial records showed that Eva, in the 12 years she was his mistress, spent $728,000 for clothes, jewels and personal items. She also got more than $500,000 in jewels the Nazis confiscated.

When the Red Army pounded at the gates of Berlin, Eva hurriedly sent her valuables and her private papers and albums to her sister Gretl. Gretl later denied this, but Intelligence officers found the albums and Eva's diary buried in a field outside Munich.

In addition, the Army discovered Eva's cache contained a silver set with the seal of the Polish royal family valued at $500,000. The loot included a sack of American dollars and a 15-karat diamond broach with a cluster of 50 white stones.

Indicating the character of Hitler's mistress were reels of film which showed Eva and her sister Gretl swimming and doing calisthenics in the nude.

However, it was the diary that gave the Intelligence officers the proof that Eva was cheating on Adolf shortly after he started keeping the blonde Bavarian.

The diary had some interesting hints of why little Eva went on a cheating binge after a few years as Der Fuehrer's official mistress.

In 1935 Eva wrote repeatedly how much she loved Hitler. Yet even in this early period of romance, the complaints began. On May 10, she commented:

Looking Out the Window

"The weather is gorgeous and I, the mistress of Germany's and the world's great man, have to sit at home and look at it through the window. He has so little understanding and still makes me appear distant when his friends are around. This period of fasting won't last forever, and then it will taste much better. Too bad though that it just happens to be spring."

To any normal guy this would have meant that the little woman was getting restless and looking around for playmates. Eva found them.

On May 23, 1938, Eva scribbled in her diary:

"H— just had breakfast and left. He looks so handsome in his SS uniform and he has lashes like a girl's. I want him to come back, but he's afraid. He knows the penalty if Der Fuehrer finds out. But I assured him there wasn't a chance, and he said he would come back Sunday night. He's only 30 and looks much younger."

Then followed some unprintable comments.

H. was Standartenfuehrer Hoegel, head of the SS detachment of Hitler's personal bodyguards. When Adolf was away from Berchtesgaden, Eva would frequently entertain the handsome Hoegel in her rooms, and the two would go off hiking in the woods. Another "friend" who hovered around Eva when Der Fuehrer was away from the mountain retreat was Otto Guensche, Hitler's SS adjutant.

Eva took her chances at Berchtesgaden. Though surrounded by Adolf's personal bodyguards and the housekeeper who obviously didn't like her, Eva managed to steal off on mountain hikes and swimming parties.

On Aug. 14, 1939, she wrote:

"Walter and I hiked about five miles. It was wonderful high on the mountain away from all politics and war talk. We chased each other like children and then drank beer. Walter isn't like Col. —. He says he isn't frightened and would give his life for me. We took pictures and Walter said he would develop them himself."

A month later back at Munich (Sept. 12) Eva unburdened herself in her diary:

"Der Fuehrer left a few minutes ago. He gave me a lovely diamond broach and a pearl necklace and then spent 20 minutes lecturing me about using lipstick and cosmetics. He said girls of the super race didn't need such things. He also found some cigarettes, and I said they belonged to Gretl. He warned me about the evils of smoking.

"He is going back to Berlin so I think it is safe to have the party tomorrow night. I've ordered two cases of champagne. And Walter is coming."

The party must have been a big success, for later Eva noted:

"Too weak to write. The party lasted until seven this morning. I'm going to wake Walter up and make him help me clean the apartment. What a mess."

Eva Had Her Fun

So little Eva had her fun. How long it continued no one will ever know, for her diary entries stopped in 1940, probably because the war interfered with her fun, Intelligence officers said.

On the other hand Eva might have been sobered as she looked ahead to the bombings, the carnage and finally that day when Hitler married her as the Red Army swept nearer and nearer the bunker in which they hid.

But whatever the reason for the end of the diary, it's a safe bet that Eva Braun, the schoolteacher's daughter who became Hitler's mistress, knew a lot more than Der Fuehrer did about the art of cheating. He was an expert at the double-cross, but she could give him cards and spades and get away with it, and these hitherto unpublished pictures and diary secrets prove that little Eva had the last laugh on Adolf.

3 WOMEN DIED FOR HITLER'S LOVE

by JACK REICH ART

Many women loved Hitler madly—and died by their own hands . . . Here's a peek into Der Fuehrer's private life

Three women loved Adolf Hitler with a strange and awful desperation—and all three shot themselves!

These women knew that Adolf Hitler could never love them—or any other women—but they preferred death to a love that could never be fulfilled.

What was the fatal magic that drew women to his side? What was the dark secret that made him forever a stranger to them?

"My bride is Germany," Hitler would answer with an unconvincing laugh when he was asked about marriage.

And when his close friend, Heinrich Hoffman, pressed the point, Hitler delivered a response in the best Don Juan tradition. "I love flowers—but that is no reason for my becoming a gardener!"

It was the conceited, leering remark of a confirmed woman chaser, a man who wore his conquests like badges. But the Fuehrer was not that kind of man at all. Was his remark a cover-up—a vain boast to give the impression that he was not "different?"

Yet, Hitler was careful not to antagonize the female Party members. He was well aware of the value of their support. In meetings, he saw to it that they sat knitting and sewing in the front rows. Periodically they shouted enthusiastically or burst into wild applause, touching off a similar demonstration among the audience.

In modern theatrical parlance, this is known as "papering the house." And if anybody knew his theater, Hitler did.

These women were also influential in their own households. They persuaded their husbands to join Hitler, they worked tirelessly in their spare time, they gave of themselves unsparingly in their political enthusiasm.

Though he had to accept the adoration they showered on him, Hitler was embarrassed when he met them individually.

It is always better to have your workers worship you. You get more out of them. Hitler knew this and made good use of the worship, but he would not allow a woman to hold a leading position in the Third Reich.

"I allow no man to stick his finger in my political pie," he told his friend Hoffman. "And certainly no woman."

He seemed to realize that he would never be able to have a son and felt obliged to offer some sort of excuse for his failing.

"History abounds with proof that seldom, if ever, is the son of a great man also great," he said.

He felt that a son of his would never have the necessary qualities for greatness and would only be in the way. His successor, he said, had to be a man of mental stature equal to his own.

Hitler was apparently satisfied that this grand explanation let him off the hook as far as marriage was concerned. Surely nobody would question the Fuehrer's feelings on a matter that concerned the future of Germany!

Then, one day in 1927, 20-year-old Angelika Raubal—daughter of Hitler's step-sister—joined him at his table in Munich's Cafe Heck.

Geli seemed to enchant Hitler. He became devoted to her. She even persuaded him to go shopping with her, though nothing disgusted him more.

Under her spell, his social life blossomed. But whether it was to the cinema, the theater, or a drive and picnic in some out of the way spot, Hitler's attitude toward this charming girl was formal and reserved.

But when he looked at her, his eyes seemed haunted by a nameless longing. His voice was soft with a kind of helpless, groping affection.

When he moved into a house at 16 Prinzregentenstrasse, Munich, he installed her in a beautiful, lavishly furnished room. There were no strings attached. He seemed satisfied to watch her and gloat over her.

Hitler Lived with Jealous Fury

Geli chafed at this confinement. She liked lights and music and people. Sitting at the same table in the same cafe day after day listening to the same people talk politics was not her idea of a good time.

He refused to let her go to a dance. Geli begged and pleaded until he changed his mind. He agreed with a provision that his two friends, Heinrich Hoffman and Max Amman, accompany her and bring her home by 11 p.m. He even selected her dress for her—a conservative, almost prudish garment without the gaiety that Geli sought.

When Geli, flanked by her two escorts, left the ball just before 11, she was feeling far from gay. She felt like a prisoner.

Hoffman sympathized with her and told Hitler the restraint was making her unhappy. Hitler had a ready answer.

"Geli's future is so dear to my heart that I feel myself duty-bound to watch over her," he said unconvincingly. "I love Geli, and I could marry her. But I am determined to remain a bachelor."

One day Hitler's long-time chauffeur, Emile Maurice, dropped in to see Geli. Maurice was one of the oldest Party members. As he sat innocently laughing and chatting with her, the door opened and Hitler stood in the doorway, his face livid with fury.

He shouted at the terrified man, swore at him, and reached for his gun. Then he thought better of it and walked around the room, cursing the chauffeur. Maurice had never seen Hitler in such a terrible state of violent emotion.

Geli was bewildered. How could she understand a man who never unbent to her, never gave any concrete expression of love, yet felt he owned her body and soul? What did he *want* from her?

On Sept. 17, 1931, Hitler left to go on tour. As he and Hoffman went down the stairs, Geli leaned over the bannisters and called, "Au revoir, Uncle Adolf. Au revoir, Herr Hoffman."

Hitler stopped and looked up. They looked at each other for a moment, then he went back up the stairs to her. He stroked her cheek fondly, then bent and whispered something in her ear. She pulled away, angry and disappointed. Hitler left her and joined Hoffman at the door.

They drove in gloomy silence toward Nuremberg. "I don't know why," Hitler said, "but I have a most uneasy feeling."

After staying the night in Nuremberg, they set off for Bayreuth and had not gone far before a taxi caught up with them and a page boy from the Nuremberg hotel delivered a message to Hitler that Rudolph Hess wished to speak to him urgently from Munich and was holding the line.

They rushed back to the hotel. Hitler ran for the phone.

"Hitler here," he said. "Has something happened?" His face paled. "How *awful!* Hess! Answer me yes or no. Is she still alive? . . . Hess!" he screamed. *"Hess!"*

But the connection had been broken. Hitler whirled to his chauffeur. "We go back to Munich. Get every ounce you can out of the car. *I must see Geli alive again!"*

Arrived Too Late

Geli lay dead. She had found a letter to Hitler from Eva Braun— whom he had recently met—and had shut herself in her room and shot herself near the heart. She did not die at once and might have been saved—but no one had heard the shot. Young, unhappy Geli had bled to death.

After her funeral, a grim Hitler locked the door of her room and ordered no one but the housekeeper to enter it. On his orders she daily placed in the room a bouquet of fresh chrysanthemums—Geli's favorite flowers.

For two days after the suicide Hitler brooded in solitude. Then he summoned Hoffmann to his house.

"I cannot stay in this house where my Geli died," he said, desperately tired and haggard. "Mueller has offered me the use of his house in St. Quirin. Will you come with me? I want to stay there until she has been buried. Then I shall go to her grave."

Before he left the two at St. Quirin, Hitler's chauffeur stole his gun so that he should not try to kill himself.

Hitler's room was above Hoffmann's, but he did not sleep. Throughout the night he paced back and forth, back and forth. Hoffmann sat in an armchair, listening.

Dawn broke and Hoffmann wearily went upstairs to try to get him to eat. Hitler took no notice.

Another night came, and Hoffmann sat in his armchair listening to the ominous, tortured pacing in the room above. Another day . . . and Hitler's mouth was set in bitterness. Dark shadows underlined his shrunken eyes. He was haggard, drawn, and unshaved, but still he paced and still he refused food.

They reached Vienna early in the morning and went straight to the Central Cemetery. Hitler spent half an hour at Geli's grave, returned to the car and ordered the chauffeur to drive to Berchtesgaden.

"Now," he said half to himself, his eyes fixed straight ahead, "let the struggle begin—the struggle which must and shall be crowned with success."

Hitler threw himself into his speechmaking. He rushed from city to city. An almost superhuman power of persuasion seemed to come over him the moment he mounted the platform. And his speeches were fascinating.

But in unguarded moments a haunted look came over his face.

Once, at a New Year's Eve party at Hoffmann's house, an extremely pretty girl couldn't take her eyes off Hitler. She engaged him in conversation and slyly maneuvered him under the mistletoe where she threw her arms around his neck and gave him a passionate kiss.

A look of astonished horror crossed his face. The girl recoiled from it, as did the other guests. In that heavy silence he stood there under the mistletoe, biting his lip in an effort to master his anger. For the remainder of his stay, the atmosphere was icy. Eva Braun was an employee of Hoffmann and Hitler often chatted with her. But that was as far as it went. Yet Eva, the would-be *femme fatale*, told everyone Hitler was madly in love with her and that she was going to marry him.

Never, in voice, look, or gesture did Hitler suggest any deep interest in her. Perhaps his very aloofness, his mysterious inaccessibility, fired her love for him.

Then one day in the summer of 1932, Eva Braun put a pistol to her heart and pulled the trigger!

Hitler was sick with bewilderment. "Doctor," he pleaded, "do you think she shot herself simply with the object of becoming an interesting patient and of drawing my attention to herself?"

The doctor shook his head. "The shot was aimed directly at the heart," he said. "I consider it a genuine case of attempted suicide."

"You hear, Hoffmann?" he said in agitation, pacing up and down. "The girl did it for love of me. But I have given her no cause to justify such a deed. Obviously I must now look after the girl."

"I see no obligation," Hoffmann said. "No one could blame you."

"And who do you think would believe that?" he snapped. "And another thing—what guarantee is there that something of the kind might not occur again?"

And so, Eva Braun got her own way. She moved into his house and became the companion of his leisure hours. But again, that's as far as it went. There was nothing between them. It was a hollow victory for the feather-brained little shop-girl.

For years Hitler regularly attended the Bayreuth Festival of Music. There, in 1934, he met Unity Mitford, one of the six daughters of Lord Redesdale.

Unity was full of enthusiasm for Hitler's ideas. This swelled Hitler's pride. She became passionately devoted to him and toured Europe in a car decorated with the Union Jack and the swastika making speeches about him that bordered on the hysterical.

When war was declared in September, 1939, Unity was in Munich, wearing the Nazi badge that Hitler had given her. But she was followed everywhere by Gestapo agents who were not sure she was not a British spy.

Wagner, Gauleiter of Bavaria, suggested that she should leave. When she requested Hitler to come see her, the Fuehrer refused. It wasn't wise to be friendly with an Englishwoman—even a Nazi Englishwoman.

Suicide Attempt

Her dreams were shattered. In despair she shot herself through the head in a Munich park. Unity never fully recovered from her injuries, and she died in England in 1948.

Her attempted suicide haunted Hitler. "You know, Hoffmann," he said, "I'm beginning to be frightened of women. Whenever I happen to show a little personal interest—by a look or by paying some little compliment—it is always misinterpreted.

"I do not bring women luck. And that's a fact which repeats itself in a most unusual way throughout my life."

For Adolf Hitler's charm was truly fatal. Of all the strange complexities of this mysterious, brutal, driven man, none is more baffling than his unnatural relations with the opposite sex.

Women were fascinated by him, worshipped him—and fell in love with him. And then, too late, did they find that he was not capable of love? Did they see in his cold eyes the secret that Hitler hid from the world?

EVA BRAUN'S SECRET DIARY REVEALS HITLER'S STRANGE LOVE LIFE

by KENNETH PETERS

Eva Braun's own words paint an intimate portrait of Hitler as a man—and lover

Editor's Note: Diary entries for this article were reused by the Police Gazette from a previous article, "Eva Braun's Diary."

Adolf Hitler's private life was more turbulent than even his political career. He cast the same hypnotic spell over the women who shared his boudoir as he did over his fanatic Nazi followers.

As a lover, Hitler treated his women with a cold indifference that drove Geli Raubal, his first great love, to suicide and made Eva Braun, the girl he finally married, attempt suicide on several occasions. Der Fuehrer was cold, cruel and sadistic; completely devoid of any real sentimentality.

It was this total lack of romanticism in his personality that shrouded his love life in mystery. There were rumors that he was a homosexual and whispers that he was impotent. Neither was true. The truth was in between.

It was only when the personal papers and diary of Eva Braun were unearthed that the secrets of Hitler's strange love life emerged. Eva was Der Fuehrer's mistress for 11 years until he married her in his underground bunker in Berlin just before the Third Reich collapsed. What she wrote gives an intimate glimpse of the dictator as a man, statesman and lover.

The first clue to this historic record came on an autumn day soon after the fall of the Third Reich when the Munich office of the US Intelligence was thrown into excitement by an informer's tip.

Diary Discovered

Within an hour a detail of Army men, armed with picks and shovels, were tearing up a desolate field in Bavaria. Before long they struck pay-dirt—a huge treasure chest containing the diary and a dozen photo albums showing Eva's family life and her years of intimacy with the dictator.

Besides the hidden secrets the treasure included precious jewelry and thousands of dollars. This was undoubtedly the getaway hoard the two were planning to use in their escape from the ruins of Berlin.

The intelligence officers also found Hitler's blood-spattered uniform, the one he wore on July 20, 1944, the date of the assassination attempt by the generals.

That Eva was entrusted with this prize confirmed just how important she was in the life of Hitler.

Eva Braun was an eyeful that would attract any man regardless of how tightly he was wrapped in affairs that would rock the world. She was 5-foot-3, well built, with good legs and a dazzling smile.

It was in the late 1920s that the Nazi leader first met the blonde from Munich. At that time she was apprenticed to the well-known German photographer, Heinrich Hoffmann, who had a reputation for filling his staff with lush females.

Heinrich assigned Eva to take pictures of the rising politician and she immediately caught Hitler's fancy. It wasn't long before she became important to him. Several years later, she left the photo studio at Hitler's request.

Although the affair was handled with complete discretion on both sides, Eva was with the ex-corporal all through the time he was building his party and paving the way for supreme power in Germany.

At first she accompanied Hitler to bund meetings in his small Opel. As Hitler's star rose, he gave Eva a Mercedes. Later he installed her in a villa in her home town of Munich.

Close friends of the two were convinced they would marry. In 1938, he even gave her an engagement ring and bought a wedding gift. However, the pressures which later brought on the war were building up and Hitler never followed through.

Her status as Hitler's mistress made her unhappy because the Fuhrer kept her in the background. The limelight always shone on the wives of those high in the party hierarchy.

But Eva's position, nevertheless, was a privileged one. But like others of his favorites she paid for it by being subject to his petty tyrannies.

Fuhrer Made Her Behave

Hitler had a fetish on good health and, in line with this, smoking in his presence was strictly forbidden. Also something of a Puritan, the dictator frowned on dancing, too. She had to sneak her cigarettes and could only dance in secret.

Eva was a natural blonde but she used to bleach her hair lighter and experiment with her hairdo almost weekly before she met Hitler. But when their attachment became serious, he insisted that she revert to her natural shade and dress her hair conservatively.

Although when the dictator was away, Eva flirted with officers and SS guards, she was in constant anxiety that Hitler would learn of this.

The Fuhrer's anger was aroused when he heard of her being pleasant to other men.

What sort of person was this woman who shared Hitler's life?

She certainly was not intellectually stimulating—in her school days she was nicknamed "Fathead." She was gay, warm and feminine and her empty head was crammed with ideas she gleaned from movies and cheap novels. She was also interested in sports, animals, sex and clothes. She was a typical product of her lower middle class background.

Despite her outward assurance, we know from her diary that Eva was a frustrated female. She frequently confided to its chapters her loneliness and lack of recognition.

Hitler's indifference troubled her and his preoccupation with politics and world problems when he was with her annoyed Eva.

Hitler went weeks without seeing his mistress and the fear that he would desert her for another made her insecure.

Twice she attempted suicide. This did bring Hitler closer for a time but only through fear of scandal.

Eva's diary covers some of the most exciting days of her life and a time when Hitler's power was nearing its peak.

However, the entries between February 6 and May 28, 1935 show that she had little interest in the political events that absorbed her paramour.

This was the time when Germany annexed the Saar and the dictator was building his army in defiance of the Versailles Treaty.

These power plays made little impression on the Munich blonde. The pages reveal her as childish and emotionally insecure.

Never Referred to Hitler

Strangely enough, she never once mentioned Hitler by name—always using an impersonal pronoun when she referred to the lover who dominated her life.

February 6, 1935 — I guess today is the right day to begin this masterpiece.

I have happily reached my twenty-third year . . . whether I am happy is another question. At the moment I am certainly not happy. That is because I have such high expectations for such an "important" day.

If I only had a dog, then I wouldn't be quite so alone; but I guess that is asking too much.

Mrs. Schauk came with flowers and a telegram as "ambassador." My whole office looks like a flower shop and smells like a mortuary. I am really ungrateful, but I hoped so much to get a little dachshund, and now again nothing. Perhaps next year or even after that; when it will be better suited for an incipient spinster.

Let me not give up hope. I should have learned patience by now. I bought two lottery tickets today.

It seems as though I'll never get rich. Can't do anything about that. Today I would have gone to the Zugspitze with Herta, Gretl, Ilse and mother and we would have lived like kings, because one always has the most fun when others share the happiness.

But the trip didn't come off.

Today I'm going to eat with Herta. What else may a simple little woman of twenty-three do? Thus, I'll bring my birthday to a close with gluttony. I believe I shall have acted in accordance with his wishes.

February 11, 1935 — He was just here, but no dog and no presents. He didn't even ask me whether I had a birthday wish. Somehow I bought myself some jewelry. A necklace, earrings and a ring to match for fifty marks. Everything very pretty. I hope he likes it. If not, he may buy me something himself.

February 15, 1935 — It seems that the Berlin deal is really going to come off. This I won't believe until I am in the Reichschancellery.

It is really too bad that Herta can't come along instead of Charlotta. She would be a guarantee for a few happy days. This way there will probably be a big ado because I don't think that Bruckner, for a change, will show his more charming side when he meets Charlotta. I don't dare look forward to it yet, but it might turn out to be wonderful if everything goes well. Let's hope so.

(*Hitler at this time was arranging an apartment for Eva at the Chancellery in Berlin. Bruckner, mentioned above, was one of Hitler's trusted aides.*)

February 18, 1935 — Yesterday, he came quite unexpectedly and it was a delightful evening.

The nicest thing was that he is thinking about taking me out of the firm and—I don't want to be too happy yet—to buy me a little house. I don't dare think of it. It would be so wonderful. I wouldn't have to open the door for our "honorable" customers and play salesgirl. Dear God, please make it come true within a reasonable period of time.

Poor Charlotta is sick and can't come to Berlin with us. She's really unlucky, but maybe it is better that way. Maybe he would be very rude to her and then she would certainly be even more unhappy. I am so infinitely happy because he loves me so and pray that it will always be like this. I should never want to be to blame if once he should stop loving me.

Unhappy Moments

March 4, 1935 — I am mortally unhappy. Since I can't write him, this diary must serve to relieve my pain.

He came Saturday for the big Munich ball. Mrs. Schwarz had given me a loge ticket for it and so I was obliged to attend at all costs, especially since I had already accepted.

I spent a few wonderful hours with him until 12 o'clock and then went to the ball with his permission.

He promised that I could see him on Sunday. In spite of the fact that I called up and sent a message that I am waiting for him, he drove off to Feldafing. He even refused Hoffmann's invitation to tea and supper. One may look at everything from two sides; perhaps he wanted to be alone with Dr. Goebbels who was also here, but he could have let me know. I was at Hoffmann's on pins and needles, thinking all the time that he might come any minute.

We went to the train later, because he had decided to leave, but only arrived in time to see the rear lights. We had again left for the train too late, and thus I couldn't even say goodbye. Probably I'm too pessimistic again, I hope, but he hasn't been here for fourteen days, and I am so unhappy and have no peace of mind. Incidentally, I don't know why he should be so angry with me—perhaps because I went to the ball—but then he gave me his permission.

I am uselessly wracking my brain as to why he should be driving away without saying goodbye.

Hoffmann gave me a ticket for tonight's performance of "Venetian Nights," but I won't go. I am much too unhappy.

(*The dictator could spare no time then for his mistress because three days earlier he had sent the German army into the Saar and was consolidating the occupation.*)

Suicide Thoughts

March 11, 1935 — I only wish that I were seriously ill and would hear nothing of him for eight days. Why doesn't something happen to me? Why do I suffer like this? I wish I had never seen him. I am desperate. I am now going to buy more sleeping tablets, at least then I'll be half-dazed and won't think about him so much.

Why doesn't the devil come and get me. I'm sure it's nicer there than here.

For three hours I stood outside the Carlton Hotel and had to watch while he brought flowers for Annie Ondra and invited her for supper. (Marginal note, written March 26: Just my crazy imagination.) He is only using me for very definite purposes. (Marginal note, written March 26: Baloney, probably I am, too.) When he says he loves me, he takes it about as seriously as his promises which he never keeps. Why does he torture me so much instead of just putting an end to the whole thing?

(*For many days Hitler had been busy fighting off British attempts to settle arms and territory problems in Europe.*)

March 15, 1935 — He went to Berlin again. If only I didn't "go off the beam" whenever I see him less than usual. Actually, it's quite natural that he shows no great interest in me at present, since there is so much going on politically.

I am going to take a trip to the Zugspitze with Gertl today; then maybe my remorse will subside. Everything has always turned out all right so far, and it will be the same this time. One must have patience, that's all.

(*This was the day Hitler scrapped the Versailles Treaty and set up an army of 36 divisions. For the first time Eva recognized something else was going on in the world outside her boudoir.*)

April 1, 1935 — Yesterday, we were invited by him for supper at the Four Seasons. I had to sit next to him for three hours and couldn't say a word to him. When leaving, he handed me an envelope containing money, as he had done once before. If only he had at least added a greeting or a kind word. I would have been so happy, but he never thinks of anything like that.

Why doesn't he go to Hoffmann's to eat? There, at least, I would have him to myself for a few minutes. I only wish he wouldn't come any more until his home is ready.

April 29, 1935 — Things are very tough. I keep humming to myself "Things will improve," but it doesn't help much. The house is ready, but I can't go to visit him; love does not seem to be on his program at present. Now that he is back in Berlin, I feel a little better; but there were days during the last week when I did my share of crying at night, especially since I spent Easter at home by myself. I'm getting on everybody's nerves because I want to sell everything from my clothes to my cameras, and even theater tickets. Oh, well . . . things will improve. After all, my debts are not that big.

May 10, 1935 — According to Mrs. Hoffmann's kind and also tactless remarks, he now has a substitute for me. Her name is Valkyrie, and she looks it, including her legs. But those are the shapes that appeal to him. If that is true, he will soon have annoyed her till she gets slim, unless she has Charlie's talent for thriving on worries. Worry alone seems to increase her appetite.

If Mrs. H's observations should turn out to be true, it is mean of him not to tell me. After all, he should know me well enough to realize that I would never stand in his way, if he should discover another romantic interest. Why should he worry about what happens to me? I'll wait till the third of June. . . . I'll ask him of an explanation by mail. Now tell me again that I'm not modest.

The weather is gorgeous, and I, the mistress of Germany's and the world's greatest man, have to sit at home and look at it through the window. He has so little understanding and still makes me appear distant when his friends are around. Well, one makes one's own bed . . . I guess it really is my fault, but it is just one of those things for which one likes to blame someone else. This period of fasting won't last forever, and then it will taste much better. Too bad, though, that it just happens to be spring.

May 28, 1935 — I have just sent him a letter, one that is decisive, for me. Will he consider it as important as I do? Well, we'll see. If I don't get an answer by tonight, I'll take my 25 pills and lie down peacefully. Is it a sign of the terrific love of which he assures me, that he hasn't spoken a kind word to me for three months? Agreed that he's been busy with political problems, but have not things eased off?

And how about last year when he had lots of worries with Ernst Rohm and with Italy, and he still found time for me? True, I'm not in a position to judge whether the present situation isn't much worse, but after all a few kind words to Mrs. Hoffmann would hardly have taken much time. I fear there is some other reason. It's not my fault; certainly not. Maybe it's another woman, although I doubt that it's Valkyrie. What other reason could there be? I can't find any.

P.S. My God, I'm afraid I will not get an answer today. If only someone would help me; everything is so hopeless. Maybe my letter reached him at an inopportune time, or maybe I shouldn't have written at all. Whichever it is, the uncertainty in much worse than even a sudden end would be. Dear God, please make it possible that I speak to him today, tomorrow will be too late. I have decided on 35 pills to make death certain this time. If he would at least have someone call up for him.

(*During this time Hitler was proclaiming his desire for peace and trying to set up non-aggression pacts.*)

Eva, of course, didn't take the pills and she obviously adjusted to the turbulence of her emotional life with Hitler.

When the dictator built his retreat in Berchtesgaden, she stayed there with a group of her closest friends. Her relationship with Hitler was finally accepted by the top Nazis and she no longer was a dark secret in his personal life.

She was at the Fuhrer's side throughout the war. Then, in the early hours of April 29, 1945, as Berlin was under artillery fire by the Allies, Hitler married his faithful mistress in the map-room of his underground bunker.

Despite the heartaches and bitter frustrations she revealed in her diary, Eva's loyalty to Der Fuehrer was finally rewarded—she became Mrs. Adolf Hitler.

Hitler's Family

Would Henry Louis Gates touch this one with a ten-foot pole? We know Maury Povich would. But try getting DNA samples from the suspected relatives. Might as well try proving the parentage of the heirs to the British throne! After all, how many people are eager to find out they're the direct descendants of Adolph Hitler?

It is well known Hitler did not marry until the day before his "disappearance," and that he did not have any—officially recognized—children. He was too devoted to greater things. "The cheers of the mobs, the screams from the gas chambers and concentration camps drowned out the chimes of wedding bells," the *Gazette* concisely points out.

In this section, we explore the claims of those who say they are Hitler's children, or those who say they know about Hitler's children. We look at the hard road suffered by known relatives and godchildren, whose actions range from atoning for the sins of their father—as in the case of Martin Bormann the younger—to fighting legal battles over massive inheritances that would be due them under normal circumstances. Can Adolph Hitler's sister be blamed for not being content with a $4 weekly pension when her brother's fortune amounted to tens if not hundreds of millions?

Then there's some Jewish revenge. The article proving Hitler had Jewish ancestors—and knew it—pushes the concept of the self-hating Jew to it's most outrageous extreme, while Hitler's anti-Semitism, secret children, and his still being alive are brought together most poignantly by self-proclaimed daughter Gisela Fleischer Hoser. "I rather hope that my father is still alive and reads these lines to learn that his only daughter has married a Jew."

More significant to us than Gisela's conversion to Judaism—ensuring Hitler's direct descendants would be Jewish—is the image of Hitler reading the *Police Gazette*. He'd be at his secret Patagonian lair, enjoying the *Gazette*'s unique take on life. One wonders what might have been were he a regular reader during his development early in the century. Might the *Gazette* have influenced a breezier approach to life? If only, if only . . .

THE TRUTH ABOUT HITLER'S CHILDREN

By BOB HARTFORD

Sensational Discovery That Der Fuehrer Was a Father

Intelligence agents investigating reports that Adolf Hitler is still alive might well take a tip from the Bible, which advises:

"And a little child shall lead them."

Not one child but two might lead them straight to the vanished Fuehrer and solve for all time history's most baffling mystery.

For the *Police Gazette* has learned that Hitler and Eva Braun actually had two children, a boy and a girl. This was Hitler's most carefully guarded secret and it was kept so well that it has never before been made public.

Here, as a *Police Gazette* exclusive, are the inside facts and previously-unpublished photographs from Eva Braun's personal album of Der Fuehrer's family.

These are the most important clues in the mystery of Hitler's disappearance—a mystery which has baffled the best Intelligence agents of America, Britain, France and Russia.

The mystery goes back almost 12 years to the May Day when Russian troops crashed into Hitler's last known hiding place, a concrete-and-steel bunker beneath Berlin's Reichschancellery, and found the tyrant's cupboard was bare.

Outside, in the bomb-leveled garden, lay the charred remains of Propaganda Minister Paul Goebbels, his family and numerous high Nazi officials. The funeral pyre was impressive. But the bodies of Der Fuehrer and Eva Braun, his long-time mistress and bride of a few hours, were not among them.

Since then, though a German court has declared Hitler legally dead and at least a dozen of his aides have sworn they saw his body, the rumors persist that Hitler lives.

This is the true story behind those rumors—

Eva Braun was a slim, trim, blue-eyed blonde of 19 when she met Hitler at Salzburg in the early 1930s. She was then working as secretary to Heinrich Hoffman, Hitler's personal photographer.

Had Eva Investigated

Adolf was impressed with the Bavarian beauty, but before he made any advances he had her investigated—a typical Hitler precaution even in affairs of the heart.

He learned she was the daughter of a Munich school teacher, that she had two sisters and that she was a typical "girl of the people," as he liked to refer to her in later years.

He wined and dined her handsomely and she was strongly attracted to the dark, stormy man with the strange dreams of glory and the passionate power to accomplish them. Soon Eva left her job at Hoffman's studio, at Hitler's suggestion, and toured Germany with him as he went from one secret Nazi party meeting to another.

As the party grew and strutted into the open, Hitler's fortunes skyrocketed. He gave Eva jewels, furs, a Mercedes sports car, then a villa in Munich, a short drive from his palatial mountain fortress at Berchtesgaden.

Then she moved in with him, but their secret life became a public scandal that not even the clubs and guns of his goose-stepping Gestapo could suppress.

Eva got a diamond-encrusted engagement ring and wedding gifts, but no wedding. Hitler felt that the German people pre-

ferred a single man as their national idol. Besides, the creeping
shadows of war and the pressure of world affairs made him forget
Eva's wishes.

The cheers of the mobs, the screams from the gas chambers and
concentration camps drowned out the chimes of wedding bells.

Eva grew more and more depressed. In 1935, she wrote in her
diary:

*"The weather is gorgeous and I, the mistress of the world's great-
est man, have to sit at home alone, looking through a window. He
has so little understanding and still makes me appear distant when
his friends are around. Well, one makes one's own bed . . . I guess it
really is my fault, but it is just one of those things for which one likes
to blame someone else."*

Hitler also liked to look out the windows of his Berchtesgaden
retreat and the swank Berlin apartment he and Eva shared. When
he saw an attractive fraulein—or even an attractive young frau—
passing by, he often would send out his valet or one of his bodyguards to invite her in "for a cup of tea."

Eva was never invited to these intimate "tea parties." Nor did
she mention them in her diary, though she certainly knew about
them. She was content in the knowledge that amorous Adolf always
returned to her.

Another excerpt from the diary reveals a note of desperation.

*"I have just sent him a letter, one that is decisive for me," she wrote.
"Will he consider it as important as I do? Well, we'll see. If I don't get an
answer by tonight, I'll take my 25 pills and lie down peacefully.*

*"Is it a sign of the terrific love of which he assures me that he
hasn't spoken a kind word to me for three months? Agreed that he's
been busy with political problems, but have not things eased off?"*

Apparently, Eva received an answer to her letter, for she didn't
swallow the deadly pills.

She attempted suicide in 1936, however, after Hitler forced her
to submit to an abortion. She made another suicide try in 1937 fol-

lowing a similar operation. This time, she left a note saying she no longer wished to live as Hitler's mistress "without the joy of raising a family."

Apparently these incidents changed Hitler's outlook on off-spring.

He began escorting Eva to Berlin social events and parties and introduced her to his closest associates. In 1938, she vanished from public. When she again moved into the Berchtesgaden palace in 1940, she was accompanied by two small children—a girl, about 1 1/2, and a 6-month-old baby boy.

Hitler told his intimates that the children belonged to one of Eva's friends.

Outwardly, Hitler's friends pretended to believe the little boy and girl were the children of one of Eva's friends, but they couldn't miss the change which fatherhood made in Der Fuehrer.

A Proud and Loving Papa

He was with the babies constantly during his moments of relax-ation. He showered them with hugs, kisses and expensive presents. He played with them as often as he could and tucked them in bed at night.

To his credit, it can be said that the power-crazed butcher was a proud and loving papa.

When World War II erupted to full force and Hitler had little time for his tots, he invited Nazi bigwigs like Martin Bormann and Dr. Goebbels to bring their own youngsters to play with the babies in the Berchtesgaden nursery, guarded by hand-picked SS men with tommy guns.

This nursery probably was the most peaceful spot in Germany during that fateful time.

In April, 1945, while Russian tanks were forming a ring of steel and flames around Berlin, Hitler sent two of his most trusted aides to Berchtesgaden for the children. They brought the youngsters safely to a Salzburg monastery and the good monks took them in, never learning the true identities of the little fugitives.

In the days before the bright lights of glory went out forever for Adolf Hitler, his underground bunker was the scene of two gay parties.

The first was on April 20, 1945, when he celebrated his 56th birthday.

As Russian shells rocked the seven-foot thickness of steel-enforced concrete above their heads, the guests drank coffee and champagne. Hitler drank cup after cup of tea. Eva Braun proposed a birthday toast. "Faithful to the end," was the party's theme.

The end came 10 days later—and with it the second party.

At midnight on April 29, a small group of Hitler fanatics gathered in the map room of the bunker to see Eva Braun's wish finally come true. She and Hitler were married by Gauleiter Walter Wagner, who read the civil ceremony and saw that the names were properly signed on the civil register.

Witnesses included Hitler's deputy, Martin Bormann; Dr. Goebbels, Mrs. Goebbels and Hitler's personal valet, Heinz Linge.

The ceremony was over by 12:07 a.m., April 30, and the champagne corks popped a last defiance to the thunder of shells outside.

A few hours later, German General Hans Krebs was dispatched to the headquarters of Russian Field Marshal Gregory Zhukov. His mission was to attempt to negotiate the surrender of Berlin.

Krebs told the Russian commander that Hitler had married Eva Braun and that bride and groom then had committed suicide.

"What!" exclaimed Zhukov in understandable surprise. "Hitler got married and then killed himself? Why did he bother getting married if he was going to commit suicide?"

"He married Fraulein Braun so their children would be legitimate before they died," replied Gen. Krebs with a straight face.

Zhukov rejected Krebs' terms and demanded unconditional surrender. Tired and dejected, Krebs returned to the Reichschancellery bunker. Russian tanks followed within a few more hours. The first Red officers on the scene searched the empty bunker and hunted for Der Fuehrer among the bodies in the garden.

Hitler's valet, his personal pilot and several other aides were captured. All of them swore that Hitler put the muzzle of a 7.65 Walther pistol in his mouth and blew out his brains a few seconds after his bride swallowed a capsule of poison and died sitting beside him. The "witnesses" said the bodies were burned with gasoline, then buried in a shell hole in the garden. But no such corpses ever were found.

After an intensive search and investigation, Marshal Zhukov informed General Dwight D. Eisenhower, Supreme Allied Commander:

"We have found no corpse that could be Hitler's. Hitler had good opportunities of getting away. He could have taken off at the very last moment for there was an airfield at his disposal."

Also among the missing was the mystery man, Martin Bormann. Hitler's valet claimed Bormann tried to escape in a Nazi tank which was blown up by Red artillery fire but, once again, there was no proof.

Intelligence officers began unearthing reports that Adolf and Eva were parents. In a few days, Allied agents found the monastery near Salzburg. But the children were gone. No one knew where they were or who had taken them.

Then, on June 10, 1945, a British agent reported he had undisputable proof that the children were spirited out of Germany to a hideout in Sweden a week before Germany's collapse.

From Sweden, they were taken to Lisbon, Portugal, the agent said.

Portugal had been a good friend to Nazi Germany and had declared a day of nationwide mourning when Hitler's "death" was announced. Lisbon had been a nest of Nazi spies during the war and many top Nazis fled there afterwards.

On November 15, 1945, US Army intelligence agents found the family albums of Hitler and Eva Braun. The albums and a treasure in cash and gems were buried in a secluded spot on the outskirts of Frankfort-on-Main.

Photos of Children Found

As soon as they looked through the dozens of candid photos, the agents knew they had struck pay dirt. Here were the first pictures of Hitler and the children. Copies were sent to undercover agents throughout the world and the secret search shifted into high gear.

Undercover agents tracked the children through a number of towns and villages in Portugal. At times, the trail looked hot but it wound up at a dead end. The children had been taken out of Portugal, purportedly bound for Argentina.

Today, in South America and Africa, wherever friendly nations have sheltered fleeing Nazis, the hunt continues without letup though it has been 12 years from the day when Hitler "died."

For the searchers are convinced that when they finally find the missing children—a girl now about 19, a boy about 17—they'll learn what happened to Hitler and Eva Braun.

"HITLER IS MY FATHER"

by JOHN KERNEY

Shapely, blue-eyed Maria Lorento—whose Spanish-sounding name contrasts sharply with her blonde German looks—has made the sensational claim that she is Adolf Hitler's daughter.

"I am certain Hitler was my father," said Maria, who is living in a luxurious apartment in a fashionable section of Buenos Aires. "I have placed a claim at the Argentine Foreign Office to a fortune that Hitler deposited in this country. I feel that it rightly belongs to me."

The *Police Gazette* has verified the fact that more than $20,000,000 was deposited in Argentina by the Nazis in 1944. It is known that a large portion of it was Hitler's personal fortune.

Whether or not her claim is upheld, Maria's story throws new light on the once closely guarded private life of the swaggering dictator who planned to conquer the world.

Several things have convinced Maria that Hitler was her father. Certain influential Argentinians have quietly told her so. There is an amazing resemblance between her and Hitler. And then there are memories of her childhood—a period of mystery and intrigue—and a series of odd incidents and coincidences that could only be explained if her father was indeed the once all-powerful Fuehrer.

Added to this is her strong physical resemblance to Hitler.

But apart from any evidence that Maria may produce to support her claim—the claim itself is not as fantastic as it sounds.

Hitler's private life was always a closely kept secret. He believed the German people preferred a bachelor as their national idol, and so he remained single until the last fateful hours before defeat, when he married Eva Braun, his long-time mistress, in a simple, dramatic ceremony. So it was commonly believed that Hitler had no children.

But in March 1957, the *Police Gazette* obtained and published for the first time photographs and personal memoirs from Eva Braun's private album. Those pictures prove that Hitler had at least two children—a boy and a girl.

Now comes Maria Lorento's claim—and in view of the evidence in Eva's album plus other facts now known about the stormy romance between Eva and the Fuehrer, Maria may provide another link in the mysterious story of Hitler's private life.

Although there is proof that Hitler had children, their fate is as mysterious as that of the Fuehrer himself. They disappeared without trace. So did Hitler on that May Day thirteen years ago when Russian troops burst into his last known hiding place, a concrete-and-steel bunker beneath Berlin's Reichschancellery, and found the cupboard bare.

Maria Lorento bears a striking resemblance
to Hitler—the man she claims is her father.

The story that Maria now tells is typical of the mystery and intrigue that surrounded most of Hitler's private affairs in the last years of his orgy of power.

Her first clear childhood memory is of living in the household of a post office employee named Ramon Lorento, in Balboa, Spain.

"I was quite young at the time," she says. "The Lorentos treated me as one of their own children."

But Maria gradually became aware that something strange was going on. She noticed that, while the Lorentos were typically Spanish in appearance, she was not.

And then there was a mysterious Englishman named William Adams.

Adams visited the Lorento family periodically, and Maria soon realized he was something more than a casual friend. At the end of each visit he would give money to Maria's "father," and he seemed to have some kind of authority over the Spanish postal official. His financial contributions and his quietly conducted conferences with the elder Lorentos seemed to have some connection with Maria.

"Soon after the Spanish Civil War broke out in 1936," recalled Maria, "Adams made a very special and hurried visit. Soon afterwards I was told that I was being sent to live with an aunt in France."

Although she did not know it at the time, this was obviously a move by some mysterious guardian to get Maria out of the war area and into a place of safety.

Before Maria left, her "mother" handed her a bag which, says Maria, contained "a very large sum of money in silver coins and bills."

And then, with a parting hug, the Spanish woman whispered to the girl: "Someday you will learn your true identity."

Maria realized soon after reaching her "aunt" that the woman was not her aunt at all. At first the girl thought of going to the police, but then she remembered that she had been shipped out of

Spain without papers. She decided that going to the police would only involve her in more trouble.

Shortly after her arrival in France Maria was sent to the Notre Dame de la Misericorde convent in Bergerde, near the large city of Bordeaux.

Time passed uneventfully until the outbreak of World War II. Then Maria had a call from the French police, and she had to reveal the fact that she had no papers.

The gendarmes, however, showed no surprise at this. They seemed to have some secret knowledge of her parentage. They told her roughly:

"We did not expect you to have papers because we know you are a German spy."

They grilled Maria for several days, and then allowed her to return to the convent. But she was kept under strict surveillance.

The next momentous event in Maria's life was the collapse of France. The Germans swept through the country and set up regional headquarters nearby. Again the police chief at Bordeaux sent for Maria—but this time she noticed a vast change.

Again some hidden hand had moved to shield her from the perils of war.

"I was overwhelmed with courtesies. I felt that this was the result of direct instructions from the German Command," said Maria.

Maria was to return to Spain, and the police chief arranged with the Spanish Consul at Toulouse to grant her a passport. The Consul himself offered to escort Maria to Madrid. There she was introduced to a family who persuaded her to go with them to Argentina.

In Buenos Aires several people have approached Maria and told her that she is Hitler's daughter—and they have told of the large sums of money the Nazi dictator sent to Argentina for investment.

Secret documents seized by the Allies show Hitler sent $20,000,000 for deposit in South America.

Over a year ago, Maria wrote to the Argentine Foreign Office giving her life history and laying claim to Hitler's fortune.

"I was interviewed by the authorities," she says. "But nothing was done despite my legitimate claim."

One other thing has since happened that Maria believes indicates that her claim is valid.

One of her neighbors in Buenos Aires, a wealthy woman, is in the habit of throwing parties every Thursday night. At one of these parties Maria met a young English engineer named Adams who was on a brief visit to Argentina. Maria did not connect the young Englishman with the Adams of her childhood. The couple were attracted to one another, eventually fell in love, and became engaged.

Her fiancé wrote to his parents telling them of the engagement and enclosed a picture of the bride-to-be.

His mother wrote back: *Your father was delighted to hear you were engaged to be married to such a beautiful girl, but when he looked at her photo he suffered a heart attack.*

A Terrible Setback

Some weeks later Maria, whose life has been constantly subjected to the outward buffets of fate, found that her romance was over. Adams had broken the engagement without explanation. Now, more than ever she is determined to prove her birthright.

Maria is convinced that the Adams of her childhood was only interested in her in his capacity as some kind of official guardian. There was never any show of affection or any sign of a blood relationship between them. She is convinced that Adams was a special agent who was employed to look after her.

How does Maria's story fit into the pattern of Hitler's private life?

Eva Braun was a shapely, blue-eyed blonde of 19 when she first met Hitler in Salzburg in the late 1920's. Eva, who looked a lot like Maria does today, was employed as secretary to Heinrich Hoffman, official photographer for the Nazi Party and later Hitler's personal photographer.

Adolf was impressed with the young Bavarian beauty. The daughter of a Munich school teacher, Eva was a typical "girl of the people." as Hitler liked to refer to her in later years.

Eva left her job with Hoffman, at Hitler's suggestion, and toured Germany with him as he went from one secret Nazi party meeting to another. As the party grew in power, Hitler's fortunes skyrocketed and he showered Eva with furs, jewels, an expensive car and a village in Munich a short drive from his own palatial mountain fortress in Berchtesgaden. Hitler gave Eva everything, but marriage.

Because of his ambitions. Hitler was shy of marriage. Therefore, he could have no children. He was determined to maintain a facade of respectable bachelorhood.

It is known that Hitler twice forced Eva to submit to abortions. Veteran political observers believe that before she was subjected to these dangerous operations she had already borne him one child— the fruit of their early love—and had been forced to abandon it. Maria Lorento now claims to be that child.

Photographs found in Eva Braun's personal album show Hitler with two children—a boy and a girl. Hitler told his associates that the children belonged to one of Eva's friends—but obviously the Fuehrer was the father.

When Russian Field Marshal Gregory Zhukov asked German General Hans Kreb why Hitler had married Eva just before the capitulation of Berlin, the German replied:

"He married Fraulein Braun so that their children would be legitimate."

What became of the children?

It is known that the two youngest children were taken out of Portugal and that their ultimate destination was Argentina.

And that is where Maria Lorento went to live with a Spanish family who "adopted" her.

Somehow, there always seems to have been a hidden guardian looking after Maria.

What is the truth behind Maria's strange story?

Somewhere in the world, there are people who can supply the missing documentary evidence that Maria Lorento is, in fact, Hitler's daughter. Maria prays that anyone with such evidence comes forward to help her. At stake is $20 million!

THE TRUE CASE
OF ADOLF HITLER'S SISTERS

by HARVEY WILSON

Exclusively revealed! The story of Hitler's
heirs and the $20 million fortune they'll fight over!

Far across the Atlantic, in the Bavarian Alpine town of Berchtesgaden, lives a frail, little old lady who dreams of inheriting one
of the most famous fortunes in the world. Through the rear window of her tiny room she can see the Obersalzberg, the towering
mountain on whose peak her brother built his favorite retreat.
For the little old lady is Paula Wolf, her brother was Adolf Hitler,
and the fortune to which she lays claim is the 20-odd million dollars of Hitler's estate.

The 63-year-old sister of the man who was once the Master of
Europe, who boasted that his Third Reich "would endure for a 1000
years," lives in abject poverty. She is on the German equivalent of
relief, marking ends meet on a weekly check of only $4. What sus-
tains her spirit is the hope that one day the German courts will
acknowledge her as the rightful heir to Adolf Hitler's wealth.

The legal contest between Paula Wolf and the West German
government has been going on for years. The government's contention is that no positive proof of Hitler's death exists. Even though
the world believes that the German dictator shot and killed himself
in his underground bunker in Berlin shortly before the Russian
armies entered the capital, the hard-headed German courts refuse
to issue a death certificate for a corpse which they claim does not

exist. And so, in terms of strict legality, the German government takes the position that Adolf Hitler is still alive!

Austria Gets $660,000 Painting

Only once was officialdom willing to depart from this contention. At the request of the Austrian government, the Berchtesgaden courts issued a death certificate for Hitler. Their reasoning then was based on the claim of Count Jaromis Czernin-Morgan who testified that Hitler's henchmen has "liberated" a valuable painting from his castle.

The painting called "The Artist in His Studio" was an indisputable masterpiece valued at $660,000 which the fanatical Nazis presented to the Fuehrer as a love offering. Upon issuance of the *Austrian* death certificate, Count Czernin-Morgan's claim was allowed and the painting returned to him.

But whether it is justice or not, so much odium still surrounds the Hitler name, so bitterly is he execrated as a mis-leader who cost the German nation millions of lives, that Paula Wolf's suit languishes in the dust of obscure files.

Her Secret Plan

This younger sister's one real hope of gaining her brother's fortune must mark time until 1960. By that date Hitler will have been "missing" for 15 years; after such time he may be declared legally dead and her attorneys can petition that Paula be proclaimed his rightful heiress.

Meanwhile, Paula keeps to her tiny furnished room and prays that justice will be done her. She occupies herself by pecking out on a dilapidated typewriter a memoir of her notorious brother. Though they were never close (besides Eva Braun, Hitler's only intimates were his political associates), Paula insists that her brother was good to her. Once he achieved power, Hitler sent her a monthly allowance of $200, and always remembered Christmas with a gift of a Westphalian ham and a check for at least $1000. That he insisted she change her name from Hitler because "there should be only one Hitler in the world" she excuses on the grounds that it was an act of political necessity.

Ever since her brother's death, Paula has lived on the sharp edge of extreme poverty. Her home, as we said, is one room in a squalid flat in the poorer section of Berchtesgaden. The neighbors' wash is hung out to dry on the balconies of the building and the ragged children who play in the streets are often barefoot. She sighs as she remembers the days when she was pointed out with respect as the baby sister of the most powerful man in the world.

At 63, Paula Hitler is small, wrinkled and gray—a grandmotherly type to whom the past seems more real than the drab present. Her room is furnished with a bed, a large wardrobe for her clothes, a glass cabinet containing a picture of her mother Klara ("the only photograph of the family I have"), a small gas range and stove, a table with a water pitcher and a corner washstand.

Adolf as a Boy

She reminisces about her fiery brother through the rose-colored glasses of family sentiment. To her he was no monster who sought to destroy the Jewish people, who spilled more blood perhaps than any other man in history, but—"Adolf was kind to me when Father died. He took me to my first opera 'Lohengrin.' But he made me stick to my studies and keep my grades in school up.

"When we were children he would tell me that if anyone was unkind to me he would protect me. Once I told him that a boy had called me cruel names. He took me back to school to find the boy and punish him."

When asked if she ever thought her brother would become Fuehrer, Paula replied: "No. We were a poor family and that was too much to expect. But," she added with a dominant note of pride in her voice, "Adolf always had to be the leader among his boy friends. Whatever he set out to do, he wouldn't give up. And even as a boy he always knew what he wanted."

Paula never married. Perhaps her early memories of the unhappy household she and her brother were raised in affected this decision. Now, old and nearly forgotten, Paula Hitler bides her time in her tiny Berchtesgaden room, hoping that the German nation will remember that she never took any part in politics.

The secrets of Hitler's early childhood is being unfolded in the memoirs Paula is now writing. Adolf always resented his father, a Custom Official, who led a charmed life. His father Alois, was married three time, had seven children, including one illegitimate and two children born shortly after marriage. Adolf did not inherit his father's sex drive, in fact because of his father's own past, he was conditioned negatively.

Adolf's mother was the third wife of Alois and was 23 years younger than her husband. His father was 50 years old when Adolf was born. He was the third child, the two other children, Gustav and Ida, having died in infancy. His sister, Paula, was born 7 years later.

His mother was a kindly, accommodating woman, who was a domestic servant when she met and married the dashing Alois.

One question that has been asked is why Adolf never had anything social to do with his half-brother Alois (who carried the father's name) and was an issue of the second marriage. During Adolf's reign, his half-brother operated a small lunchroom in Hamburg, completely ignored by his half-brother.

The answer is simple. Adolf never actually got to know his half-brother. They went through life virtually strangers. Hitler's father died in 1903 from lung trouble and his mother supported both he and Paula on the pension paid the widow of a custom official. When Hitler was sixteen, having failed at school, he went to live with an aunt, in order to ease the burden of his mother's meager income.

In the meantime, his mother was dying of breast cancer. Paula remained at her bedside taking care of her. Adolf would return periodically to see her, but after she died in 1908, Adolf packed his bags and went to Vienna to seek an art career. He told Paula, "You will not hear from me again until I succeed!"

His Half-Sister

Once Hitler became a political figure, he became close to a half-sister, Angela, from his father's second marriage. She needed a job and Adolf employed her as his housekeeper. She had been widowed and was having a difficult time supporting herself and a pretty daughter, Geli.

Here, Adolf showed a trait inherited from his father. He fell in love with Geli, his niece, who was 18 years old, 22 years younger than he. The strain of her romance with her uncle depressed her and in 1931, when he was riding to political heights, she committed suicide in Adolf's Munich apartment.

But this didn't dim his relationship with his half-sister, Angela, who continued as his housekeeper and made a very successful marriage to a prominent doctor after Adolf came into power.

His friendship with Angela was the only close relationship he had in the family.

Paula was always in his distant past. She lived in Austria and saw him seldom. Only on two occasions was she welcomed at the Reich chancery offices of the Fuehrer, the only contact was the monthly allowance he gave her.

But now, as his only full sister she is entitled to his estate, she contends.

Paula's memoirs will cover Hitler's early life. The stern discipline his father exercised and his determined efforts to prepare Adolf for a job as a Civil Servant in the Custom Office, which he strenuously objected, the encouragement his mother gave him to become an artist, which infuriated his father.

HITLER WAS A JEW!

by HARVEY WILSON

Here, disclosed for the very first time, is fantastic proof
that Adolf Hitler, the bloodthirsty executioner of over five
million Jews, had Jewish ancestors!

How far will a man go to hide his true identity?

The answer lies above a neglected and long forgotten grave in
a small Jewish cemetery in Bucharest, Rumania. The words etched
in the cracked slab of limestone have dulled with the years, but a
finely carved Star of David remains as sharp and clear as it was that
day in 1892, when Adolf Hitler was laid to rest. Why is this tombstone, embedded in foreign earth, of any importance to the world?

It wouldn't be—if there had never been a maniacal killer who
dreamed of ruling the world by fire and hate. The tombstone is of
importance only because it proves that Germany's one-time dictator, Adolph Hitler—was a descendant of Jewish ancestors.

Hitler, the onetime paper hanger who signed the death war-
rants for more than 6 million Jews exterminated in concentration
camps, gas chambers and ovens, was obsessed with the fact that
Jewish blood flowed through his "pure," Germanic veins.

The secret that haunted Adolf Hitler was that he had inherited Jewish blood from his great, great, great grandfather, Stephan
Hiedler, who was born in Walterschlag, in Upper Austria, in 1672.

Over the years the spelling of the ancestral surname evolved from
Hiedler to *Hittler* (Germanic spelling is *Huttler*) and finally *Hitler*.

The Hitler clan was first founded in a region of Austria that lies
between Czechoslovakia and the Danube. Because of its geograph-

ical location, this part of Austria was the gateway for thousands of Jewish immigrants fleeing political and religious persecution during the 15th and 16th Centuries.

During this period both Bohemia and Moravia teemed with religious strife. In Bohemia, the Roman Catholic Church became divided with a group leaving to form a splinter group called Utraquists. The Utraquists, in turn, split among themselves with one segment compromising with the Lutherans, thus enabling Bohemian Protestantism to receive official status. From these conflicts sprang the Moravian Church.

In Silesia, the horrors of The Thirty Years War (1618–48) left the nation in famine and embroiled in religious conflict.

Settle in Austria

Under this political and religious climate many of the Jews from Bohemia, Moravia and Silesia crossed the border into Austria. And a few, like the *Hiedlers*, settled in the Waldviertal district villages in upper Austria, while others continued their 50-mile trek to Vienna.

Among the Jews who continued on to Vienna was the family of the *"Adolf Hittler"* buried in the Bucharest, Rumania, Jewish cemetery. His tombstone records the fact that he died in 1892 at the age of 60, and came originally from Austria.

Many of the Jews who settled in the Upper Austria region, soon lost their religious identity and intermarried. Stephan Heidler whose parents had settled in this region, married a Christian woman. Their son, Johann, married a Catholic who gave birth to a boy they named Martin. It was Martin who changed the spelling of the family surname to Hittler.

Martin Hittler married Anna Maria Goschl, and they had two children, both boys. One was Johann Nepomuk Hittler and the other Johann Georg Hiedler (who used the old spelling of the family name).

Johann Georg Hiedler was a miller who never stayed too long at any one place. He travelled throughout Upper and Lower Austria. In the village of Strones he became involved with a peasant girl, Maria Anna Schicklgruber, and carried on a lengthy love affair with her.

In 1837, Maria Anna Schicklgruber gave birth to an illegitimate son, Alois, who was destined to become the father of Adolf Hitler.

Five years after Alois' birth, his mother married her lover, but they did not legitimize Alois and he continued to be known by his mother's maiden name of Schicklgruber.

It wasn't until 1876, that Johann George Hiedler, then a man of 84, officially testified in the town of Weitra, in Upper Austria, that he was the father of Alois Schicklgruber. This enabled Alois, then a man close to 40, to legally change his name to that of his father. Instead of spelling it *Hiedler,* he chose to spell it as *Hitler*.

During Hitler's rise to political power, his opponents tacked a barbed reference to his background by calling him "Schicklgruber." Before Adolf was born, his father Alois had produced one son out of wedlock and married his second wife three months before a daughter was born.

Adolf's mother was the third wife of Alois and was 23 years younger than her husband. His father was 50 years old when Adolf was born at Braunau, Austria, in 1889. He was the third child of this marriage, the two other children, Gustav and Ida, having died in infancy. His sister, Paula, who is still alive and resides in the town of Berchtesgaden, was born 7 years later.

His mother, whose maiden name was Klara Polzl, was a kindly, accommodating woman, who was a domestic servant when she met and married the dashing Alois on January 7, 1885.

Hitler's father, who was a minor Customs official, died in 1903 and his mother died of breast cancer five years later.

Hitler Also Opposed Catholic Church

Adolf was raised as a Catholic. He attended the school of a Benedictine monastery at Lambach for two years, then left. Although

Hitler was vocal in his anti-Semitism, he also harbored a hatred for the Catholic Church.

His early political idol was Georg Ritter von Schoenerer, who was the founder of the Pan-German movement in Austria and came from the same district in Upper Austria where Adolf was born. Schoenerer was violently anti-Catholic and openly attacked the Catholic Church, which brought about powerful opposition against his political movement.

In later years, Hitler admitted that he was a staunch supporter of Schoenerer's and agreed with all his views. He also admitted that he learned some important political lessons from Schoenerer's failure: among them that an open attack on the Catholic Church creates too great a split to bridge.

When he came to power, Hitler quietly started a drive to diminish the influence of the Catholic Church in Germany. During the war, Hitler prepared a directive ordering the 3rd Panzergrenadier Division stationed near Rome to seize the Vatican. It took terrific pressure from his Foreign Minister, von Ribbentrop and Propaganda Minister Goebbels, for Hitler to withdraw his plan.

Why Hitler Was Anti-Semitic

Hitler grew up with a strong resentment against his father and grandfather. It was during the period when his political foes were calling him "Schicklgruber" that Hitler's anti-Semitism became most violent. A psychiatric explanation would be that Hitler attributed the passionate temperament and sex scandals in his ancestral lineage to the Jewish blood that flowed through his family tree. It became an obsession—one that was to have a nightmare effect on the entire world. To divorce himself from any identity with the Jewish blood in his veins he, turned to the practice of attempting to exterminate every Jew on earth.

One of Hitler's most infamous concentration camps was Mauthausen—where more than 2 million persons were exterminated between 1941 and 1945.

At the Auschwitz Camp in Poland, Rudolf Hoess, the Commandant, confessed: "I estimate that at least two and a half million victims were executed and exterminated at Auschwitz by gassing and burning and that at least another half million succumbed to starvation and disease, making a total of about three million dead."

Once the Fuehrer came into power, he issued orders to his family, including his sister Paula, that only he would bear the family name of Hitler—all others must change their names. To his sister he gave the surname, Wolf, a name he had used while fighting for political power with the Nazi party.

When the Nazis overran Austria, Hitler had a special S.S. squad hunt down and eliminate all families with the names of Heidler, Hittler and Hitler!

But Hitler's personal Gestapo squad never heard of the tombstone of *"Adolf Hittler"* in the obscure Jewish Cemetery in Rumania. It stands there to remind the world that Der Fuehrer was a descendant of Jewish ancestors.

THE EVIL GHOST THAT HAUNTS HITLER'S GODCHILDREN TODAY

by HARVEY WILSON

A handful of children of Hitler's top aides, who had the distinction of having Der Fuehrer as their godfather, are desperately struggling to live down the curse of the Nazi crimes.

An on-the-spot investigation in Germany by *Police Gazette* correspondents, reveals the strange twist of fate under which Hitler's famous godchildren live today.

On a bright summer day recently a crowd of 3000 men and women gathered in front of a church in Austria's Maria Kirchental. Most of them, however, had not come to that famous place of pilgrimage for religious reasons, but out of curiosity. They wanted to see Hitler's most prominent godson celebrate the sacrifice of the Holy mass.

Wearing the richly adorned vestment of a Catholic priest and skillfully handling the ornaments and utensils used in celebrating mass was young Brother Martin, son of a man who is remembered as one of the greatest anti-religionists in Nazi-Germany. SS-General Martin Bormann, the man whom Hitler appointed as his successor, had been responsible for the persecution of all churches. He was responsible for the enslavement of territories occupied by the Nazis, and for the grief of countless Jewish families.

Brother Martin, now a missionary-member of the "Heart-of-Jesus" order, says: "I want to make good what my father has done!" To fulfill this promise—a gigantic task—Martin certainly has picked a career most contrary to his father's past.

Hides Out After War

It all started during the last days of WW II, when Martin, then a 15-year-old "Pimpf" (Wolfcub) in "The Fuehrer's Hitler-Youth" found himself in the little market-town of Hintertal near Weissbach in the county of Salzburg (Austria). He did not know where his father was, nor did he know the whereabouts of his other relatives. All he realized was that anyone with the Bormann name would not be welcome anymore. He called himself Martin Bergmann and got a job as a farmhand in Maria Kirchental.

A Catholic priest, Father Franz Wimmer, started to look after the boy, and soon found out his true identity. In 1947, one year after his father (who has never been found) was sentenced in absentia to death by hanging at the Nuremburg trial, Martin Bormann was baptized.

His foster-father persuaded him to enter a monastery. Young Martin became a novice in the "Heart-of-Jesus" order.

"It was then that I started to think over and over of what my father had done. It has cost me grave inner struggles to find the way back to him whom the world still condemns. This has been possible for my only through the church."

SS-General Bormann's son is now a missionary in the Belgian Congo. He lives in the apostolic curacy of Coquilhatville. The 15 missionaries there, taking care of 15,000 souls in a province as big as Austria, live in desperate poverty.

"This poor and lonely life I have chosen as best for me—and, I hope, for others!" Martin said, shortly before his departure. But he probably will not have to work unassisted for long. One of his brothers wishes to follow and help him as a lay-brother. He, too, like the rest of the nine Bormann children alive, is now a member of the Catholic Church and is "trying to make good."

It is understandable, that most children of Hitler's former top aides do not think evil of their fathers.

Certainly the most prominent girl of former Nazi-brass is Edda, daughter of the Reichsmarschall Hermann Goering. Her teacher in Munich remembers Edda, now a young university student, as "a girl of highest intelligence. Sometimes that kid asked us (teachers) questions for which even we did not know the answer!"

Goering, once the richest man In Europe, evidently had amassed his fortune by "requisitions and confiscations" of countless masterpieces of art in foreign countries. Also sentenced to death at Nuremburg he committed suicide only hours before the execution.

His daughter Edda, celebrated during the war as "the cutest German baby," for the first time again aroused public interest in 1953. Reporters focused their cameras on the slender girl in the modest black dress, wearing a crucifix-necklace and holding a Holy Bible in her hands. She was accompanied by her mother Emmy, Goering's widow whose features show a striking similarity to those of the former "Reichsmarschall." Mother and daughter were leaving a Protestant church in Schwabing, Munich's "Greenwich Village," where Edda had been confirmed that day.

Today Edda is a determined and—many agree—beautiful young woman, knowing exactly what she wants. "I am going to study law so I can vindicate my father!" she declared recently.

Wins First Court Fight

The beginning of this career does not look discouraging. Her first battle with the courts ended with a success. After a legal fight of eight-and-a-half years the safes of the Bavarian State Bank opened and Edda received back all of the jewelry that her father had given her when she was still a little girl.

"It belongs to me, and I will see that I get back other gifts my father gave me!" friends quoted her as saying.

Though Martin Bormann and Edda Goering are the only two of Hitler's godchildren most often photographed while wearing the signs of piety (crucifixes and Bible) there are children in today's

Germany of former Nazis who were not less prominent than Goering and Bormann. These kids, too, try to do what only can be regarded as the right of every good child: vindicate, if possible, or at least help their fathers.

One of these kids even went so far as to confuse the leaders of the new West-German Army. He is Wolf Rudiger, son of notorious Rudolf Hess. The 21-year-old boy has reached the age at which thousands of other German boys have to join the "Bundeswehr" for two years of active duty. But Wolf Rudiger simply rejects the order to join his unit.

"I am not an objector to combatant service!" he says. "I would have enjoyed being a mountain-rifle," he wrote to his local draft board. "But unfortunately this is not possible because of family reasons. I am—as you should know—the son of the former deputy of the Fuehrer. My father has been sentenced in Nuremburg to a lifelong prison term. One of the reasons for the verdict was the fact, that in 1935 he signed the law for conscription."

Case of von Ribbentrop's Son

While most of Hitler's godchildren today have to fight hard to get along in this cruel world of ours, the only one who does not need to worry about his future is young, 18-year-old Barthold von Ribbentrop. This son of Hitler's former Foreign Minister (who was hanged in Nuremburg) declared during a recent stay in London:

"I do not want to enter the champagne business, like my brother. I rather drink champagne. I want to become a lawyer instead and see, if I can put the remembrance of my father into a better light. I am proud of him and I am proud of the name 'von Ribbentrop.' I do not intend to change this name!" Neither, it seems, does Barthold's brother Rudolf, now 30.

Not long ago Rudolf won a legal battle against the best-known German champagne-company in which his father had a large interest. Henkel-Sekt men had said, they would not like to include the name "von Ribbentrop" into the company name, "because it may harm business in foreign countries." A court, however, decided otherwise. Rudolf von Ribbentrop is now executive participant and as such doing pretty well.

While most of the children of former top-Nazis make or try to make the headlines once in a while in Germany, one young girl definitely does not want to arouse public interest. But if she carries out the plan she has since long in mind, she will certainly make the headlines of the world's press. She is a 25-year-old portraitist and the daughter of former Nazi youth-leader Baldur von Schirach.

Schirach, one of the three men in Spandau, has been sentenced at Nuremburg to 20 years imprisonment because of his knowledge about the deportations of Jews from Vienna. Now his daughter is determined to visit Russia's Nikita Khrushchev to ask for mercy for her father. Already she has applied at the Soviet Embassy in Bonn for a visitor's visa to Moscow.

Since Hitler's Minister of Propaganda Joseph Goebbels and his wife Magda poisoned their children and then committed suicide, Hitler's godchildren mentioned in our report are the most prominent alive today.

HITLER'S DAUGHTER
MARRIES A JEW

by LEO HEIMAN

The self-professed illegitimate daughter
of the Fuehrer says "Nazi fanatics don't scare me!"

Hitler's daughter and her husband, Philippe Marvin, son of a rabbi.
Gisela is taking instruction for conversion and plans to settle down in Israel.

The only daughter of Adolf Hitler, the late Fuehrer of the Nazi
Reich, has married the son of a rabbi and is preparing for conversion to Judaism in the Holy Land.

Twenty-five years after her father signed the "Final Solution"
decree, condemning millions of European Jews to a painful death
in execution pits and concentration camps, 29-year-old Gisela

Fleischer Hoser Marvin is studying Hebrew and seriously thinking of applying for Israeli citizenship and settling with her Jewish husband in a village near Jerusalem.

A beauteous, blue-eyed, statuesque blonde, Gisela granted me an exclusive interview at the Ledra Palace Hotel in Nicosia, Cyprus, where the young couple stayed overnight on their way back to France from a Mediterranean honeymoon.

She does not look older than 19–20 years, because of her baby-doll face and innocent eyes. Gisela whipped out her West German passport to prove her age and identity.

With a 128-lb. hourglass figure on a 5'7" frame, silk-like hair and a peaches-and-cream complexion, Hitler's daughter could have served as the advertising symbol of the perfect Aryan girl, a typical representative of the Nordic master race her father dreamed of and raved about.

But she prefers to study Hebrew and learn the laws and injunctions of Orthodox Judaism preparing for her conversion to Judaism.

My first question was whether she regards it as an irony of fate to be married to a Jew, and if she does not fear the vengeance of diehard Nazis?

She smiled sadly and fingered the gold medallion her husband bought for her in Jerusalem. The medallion, suspended from her wrist at the end of a thin gold bracelet, featured the six-cornered Star of David on one side, and the Menorah (ritual Jewish candelabra) on the obverse.

"I do not see anything ironical or funny in my marriage. It is true that I would have liked to regard it as historical justice. But let us be perfectly frank and honest about it. When my husband and I met each other, we had no idea of our identities. We fell in love as man and woman, and our strong emotional ties helped us to surmount the obstacles heaped in the path of our love.

"As to Nazis," she continued, "I fear their reaction less than what Jewish extremists or fanatics might do to me if they identified me on the street. Not that I would blame them for their spontaneous reaction.

But I do not seek an easy way out. I could have denied everything, taking refuge in anonymity and forgetfulness. Since I do not attempt to deny my blood relationship to Adolf Hitler, I guess I am motivated by some awareness of history and fate. But I am not conscious of it . . ."

She snuggled closer to her husband, and stretched out a long, shapely leg to smooth out a seamless silk stocking.

Mother Lives in Frankfurt

"Yes, I am the illegitimate daughter of Tillie Fleischer, noted German Olympic Games champion, and the late Fuehrer of the Third Reich, Adolf Hitler. My mother lives in Frankfurt, West Germany, and strongly objects both to my marriage and conversion plans. I guess she remained a Nazi at heart, still in love with the father of her child. But I am old enough to be ashamed of my parents, and to know what I want," Gisela declared.

Her husband identified himself as Philippe Marvin, 31 years old, a noted French writer and the son of Rabbi Abraham Marvin, spiritual leader of the Amoth Olam Synagogue in Lyons, who perished in a Nazi concentration camp in 1943.

Mr. Marvin is the author of "Everyone Has His Jew," a runaway bestseller in France one year ago. He met Hitler's daughter while researching background material for his book in Germany. It was love at first sight between the blonde Aryan beauty and the curly-haired rabbi's son.

"I researched some material in the archives of Frankfurt Jewish Community, when I suffered from an excruciating toothache and entered the first dental clinic I could find. There was a long line in the waiting room, but a young woman dentist treated my abscessed tooth without an appointment, and this was the unromantic way I met my Gisela," Mr. Marvin disclosed.

The toothache quickly became a heartache after he had learned who she was. But by then it was too late to prevent a stormy romance from developing into profound love.

Tillie Fleischer, Gisela's mother, was the winner of two gold medals in the 1936 Olympic Games, held in Berlin under the patronage of Adolf Hitler. Nazi Propaganda Minister Josef Goebbels produced several motion pictures starring Miss Fleischer as a "typical representative of the Aryan Master Race".

He introduced the sportswoman to the Fuehrer who promptly fell in love with her, installed her in a lakeside villa near Berlin and bought her a white Mercedes convertible. Miss Fleischer's romantic interlude with Hitler lasted exactly eight months.

When Der Fuehrer saw she was going to present him with a bundle of joy, he forced one of his aides, Dr. Fritz Hoser, to marry Miss Fleischer in the fifth month of pregnancy, and take her away to Frankfurt.

Shortly afterwards, Hitler went back to Eva Braun, his steady mistress, who was banished to Munich during Der Fuehrer's 8-month affair with Fraulein Fleischer.

Dr. Hoser, a dental surgeon attached to Hitler's medical staff, was amply rewarded for his patriotic devotion above and beyond the call of duty. He was raised to the rank of Chief Supervisor of Medical Administration in the Frankfurt area.

Learns Hitler Is Her Father

"When did you learn first that you are Adolf Hitler's daughter?" I asked Gisela.

"I was born on November 4, 1937, in the Frankfurt Maternity Hospital on Mainzer Landstrasse. My mother took me to see 'Uncle Adolf' on six consecutive birthdays. I remember the last two, in 1942 and 1943. My father, that is the man whom I regarded as my father till then, never went along.

"I remember my sixth birthday in 1943," Gisela recalled. "Because we had to travel all the way across wartime Germany to reach Hitler's headquarters near Rastenburg in East Prussia.

"As long as my father was in his command bunker beneath the

Reich Chancellery in Berlin, or in his mountain retreat Berchtesgaden on the Austrian border, reaching him was no problem even
during the war.

"But the Russian offensive in 1943 made it imperative for him
to direct military operations from the Eastern Front headquarters at Rastenburg. We had to fly and civilians were not allowed to
enter airfields, let alone board passenger planes requisitioned by
the Luftwaffe.

"My mother took me to see General Heinz Jost, the deputy
Gauleiter of the Frankfurt area. She showed him a letter in Hitler's handwriting. The General made a few calls and things started
moving right away. Two storm troopers escorted us to a black lim-
ousine and drove us to the Rhein-Main air base.

"The S.S. men went to the captain of a Lufthansa airliner,
showed him their credentials, tossed out a couple of military passengers and put us aboard, wishing us a pleasant journey.

"I was only six years old then, but I was impressed by my mother's influence and power. We landed at Koenigsberg at dusk, and
were picked up by a staff car. An army colonel kissed my mother's
hand and called her "Gnaedige Fray"—esteemed lady.

"I was just a kid and happy to ride in the colonel's lap. We
arrived late and were shown to our quarters in one of the camouflaged bungalows in the dense forest known as Wolfschanze—the
wolf's lair.

The Fuehrer's Quarters

"The next morning my mother dressed me with greater care than
usual. We crossed the road to a guard house between two mighty
oak trees. An officer came out and escorted us to the Fuehrer's
quarters. The breakfast table was set for five. Josef Goebbels and his
wife Magda already waited for us. My mother and Magda Goebbels
embraced and kissed. They were good friends from way back.

"Then the door opened and Hitler came in. I remember him

well. He was shorter than the photographs show, and had a slightly hunched back. He kissed my mother's hand and then kissed me on the cheeks and forehead, picked me up and placed me on his knees.

"He called me 'Mein Kind'—my child—but I thought nothing of it at that time because this was the usual mode of address by elderly or middle-aged persons towards children of relatives or friends.

"Breakfast was served by two waitresses, and then Hitler asked me how I liked going to school. I was in first grade then. His right arm trembled, his eyes bulged in a rather funny way, and his mustache tickled me when he kissed me again and again. 'My Gisela should have the best education German culture can provide,' Hitler told my mother when we parted three hours later.

"I think that a substantial amount of money transfer from Berlin arrived in Frankfurt a few days after our visit to Hitler's headquarters. My mother bought German industrial shares and bank securities, opening a trust fund in my name. The shares alone are worth a fortune today, but I would not touch a penny of this cursed money even if I starved to death.

"On our way back to Frankfurt, my mother cried with bitter tears. 'We could have been so happy,' she moaned. I could not understand the reason for her tears. 'Did Uncle Adolf offend you, mummy?' I wanted to know. 'He is your father, Gisela, and I love him with the purest and strongest love a woman can ever feel,' she burst out.

"I did not comprehend too much, and I frankly thought she was just hysterical. That was the last time I saw my father. Our next meeting, scheduled for November 4, 1944, was called off because he was seriously hurt in the July 20 assassination attempt and the East German headquarters were overrun by the Russians.

"In April 1945 I stood on the balcony of our Frankfurt apartment, watching American troops marching in. The Third Reich was crumbling into dust, and the war was over for us. Like any other child I was curious to see the American tanks, trucks and soldiers. Just then I heard wild shouts in the bedroom, and my mother's shouts—Hilfe, Hilfe! Help, Help!

"I thought gangsters broke into our apartment to rob and plunder, but when I entered the bedroom I saw my mother holding on to my father's picture in an ornate leather frame and a bundle of letters, while Dr. Hoser, my stepfather, was beating her with his gloves, trying to wrest the picture and letters from her.

"I gathered from their quarrel that my stepfather was scared to death of the disastrous consequences he was sure would follow if my father's letters were found in my mother's possession. 'They will hang us, they will kill us!' he kept repeating.

"When my mother saw me, she tossed the picture and letters in my direction, asking me to hide them under the pillow, then she tackled her husband with a few basic judo grips. Not for nothing was she the Olympic Games champion and winner of two gold medals for athletics. She was out of practice, but my stepfather yelped with pain as she rushed him out of the bedroom, retrieved the letters, kissed my father's picture and locked them up.

Another Family Battle

"One day later, the radio brought us news of my father's death in Berlin. My mother refused to believe that the Fuehrer committed suicide. She had another row with her husband, and accused him of treason. Dr. Hoser packed his bags, pinched me in the neck and left us for good. I never saw him again, but I heard from my mother that he is somewhere in South America. He sent her a divorce by mail in 1948.

"After finishing high school, I graduated from the Frankfurt University's Dental School and went to work in a clinic where I met my husband."

When did she learn that she was dating a Jew?

"After I treated his tooth, he asked me for a date," she told me. "Now patients tried to date me before, but I never agreed. This time, however, something clicked in my heart and I said why not tonight? We went to a night club and he took me home in his car. We arranged to meet in front of the Public Library the next afternoon. We discussed books, and then Philippe mentioned that he is the author of a book published the year before. What's the book's name? I wanted to know. He said 'Everyone Has His Jew.'

"I thought he was just kidding at first, and then when I found out he was serious, it was too late to do anything about it. I was in love with Philippe.

"In any case, I was scared to death of his reaction to my descent. Should I tell him or not?

"After two weeks of going steady, Philippe and I decided to get married. I knew all about him by then, including the fact that he was a rabbi's son and that his father was murdered in a Nazi concentration camp, on my father's orders.

"I still had not told him about myself, but when I informed my mother that I was going to marry a rabbi's son, she had a nervous breakdown. 'You can't marry a Jew!' she screamed in a tantrum. 'Why not?' I wanted to know. 'Because you are Adolf Hitler's daughter!'

"We had a big quarrel then and I ran away from home. I sobbed the story out on Philippe's shoulder, and he said he would love me and marry me even if I were the Devil's daughter!

"You are not responsible for the biological fact that Adolf Hitler was your father," Philippe reassured me, and that remains my stand now.

ADOLF HITLER'S DAUGHTER SAYS: MY FATHER IS STILL ALIVE!

by HARVEY WILSON

**Married to a rabbi's son, Gisela says that her
father would never have killed himself, and his suicide is a myth!**

"In the early days of April 1945 there was an air of gloom and despair over our apartment in Frankfurt. American troops were closing in on the city and there were radio reports that the Russians were fighting fiercely to take Berlin," Gisela Marvin, the daughter of Adolf Hitler, vividly recalled, when interviewed at the Ledra Palace Hotel in Nicosia, Cyprus.

"My mother cried for days on end, until she got a letter from Berlin. It was delivered by a special messenger in a black S.S. uniform, in a heavy manila envelope bearing the Reich Chancellery seal on both sides.

"It was my father's last message to her. He asked her to take good care of his child, meaning me, and stressed the importance of a good education.

"My mother realized right away that the end of the Third Reich was not far away and she felt that Hitler, my father, was preparing to go into exile.

"Several weeks later," Gisela continued, "The radio brought us news of my father's death in Berlin. My mother refused to believe that the Fuehrer committed suicide. 'He'd never do that!' she told me.

Hitler Had a Double

"Even years after the war, my mother maintains that he is alive and hiding somewhere. She knows some things most people have no idea about. For example, my father had a double who took over most duties exposing him to danger after the July 20, 1944 attempt on his life.

"My mother pointed out repeatedly that no coroner in the world would pronounce my father dead, for two reasons. His body has never been produced for an inquest and the people who claim to have seen him dead never were questioned in court.

"Moreover, all accounts agree that some time elapsed before he and Eva Braun closed themselves in their bedroom, swallowed the poison and fired the fatal shot. The door remained unlocked for about twenty minutes. Anyone could have entered and planted a double and smuggled my father out to a plane which waited on a nearby emergency landing strip.

'Yes," said Gisela, emphatically, "I believe Adolf Hitler, my father, is still alive."

This isn't the first time a member of Der Fuehrer's family has voiced an opinion that the man who once ruled Germany escaped from the smoldering ruins of Berlin.

Der Fuehrer's only sister, Paula, living on a pension in a small village in West Germany, is also convinced that the dictator fled from the war-torn capital of the Third Reich.

"How can anyone say he's dead, when his body was never found, and the circumstances would indicate that he could have easily escaped," she says.

Strangely, the opinions of Hitler's relatives are the same as those of the Allied officers who defeated the German armies.

Lt. General Bedell Smith, World War II Chief of Staff to General Dwight D. Eisenhower and later Director of the Central Intelligence Agency, stated on October 12, 1945:

"No human being can say conclusively that Hitler is dead."

Major General Floyd Parks, who led the first air-borne division into Berlin on July 1, 1945 and became Commanding General of the United States sector of Berlin, announced that in the light of all available evidence he had received, Hitler may very well be alive.

Major General Parks, made this revealing statement:

"I remember being present on several occasions when Marshal Zhukov, the Russian commander told how he entered Berlin two months before, and conducted the on-the-spot investigation at the Reich Chancellery bunker into the report of Hitler's death. Zhukov was strongly of the opinion that Hitler escaped. There was no evidence that Hitler died."

And, one of the most emphatic remarks came from the lips of Stalin.

During the Potsdam Conference, President Truman asked the Soviet dictator whether the thought Hitler was dead.

"He escaped," Stalin answered.

It took an official investigation conducted by Col. William Heimlich, Chief of US Intelligence, Berlin, to expose the fact that Hitler's purported suicide was a hoax.

"One thing is certain," Col. Heimlich reported, "Hitler did not commit suicide. Reports that his body was burnt are false. He had an airfield at his disposal and a plane available for his escape."

Suicide Myth

How did the myth of Hitler's dramatic suicide get started?

"The account of Hitler's suicide was circulated by his trusted Nazi aides for the sole purpose of covering up his escape," Col. Heimlich says. "I questioned them all and it was clear to me that they were pawns in perpetrating a hoax.

"Then a British historian, a fellow called Trevor-Roper wrote a book called 'Hitler's Last Days' which was based on accounts given him by Nazis. The book had a wide sale and was accepted as being authoritative. That's one of the reasons the legend of Hitler's suicide lingers on."

Allied Intelligence agents traced Hitler's whereabouts to a heavily guarded Nazi outpost in the San Carlo Bariloche region of Argentina.

Efforts to penetrate Der Fuehrer's hideout have been made by Israeli agents. But they failed. It was through these efforts that they seized Adolf Eichman in Buenos Aires in 1962.

When Gisela was interviewed at the hotel in Nicosia, Cyprus where she stayed overnight with her husband, Philippe Marvin, son of a rabbi, she concluded the interview by saying:

"I rather hope that my father is still alive and reads these lines to learn that his only daughter has married a Jew."

Yes, truth is stranger than fiction—and the case of Adolf Hitler proves it.

Hitler on
the Road

THE NATIONAL
POLICE GAZETTE

ESTABLISHED 1845

AMERICA'S FIRST PICTORIAL — SPORTS · TRUE ADVENTURE · PEOPLE

DECEMBER 20¢

EYEWITNESS
REPORTS:
*Hitler
Seen Alive!*

JERSEY JOE WALCOTT
The End of a Champion

*Beware of
Toothpaste Ballyhoo*

ADOLF HITLER

In this section we find *Police Gazette* investigative reporter George McGrath feeling his oats. He had, by far, the most bylines of the entire Hitler series, and by the fifteenth month after the *Gazette*'s first bombshell revelation, he's developed more deep-background, unnamed sources than Bob Woodward. "For the sake of brevity," McGrath writes of one source, "I shall call him 'X.'" On a roll like Ruth in the '20s, Gretzky in the '80s, or Jordan in the '90s, George McGrath—and his colleagues—give us superhuman feats of mystery solving and the skinny on exactly where Adolph Hitler and Eva Braun ended up.

As a practical consideration, could Hitler have planned an escape? The handwriting was on the wall long before April 30, 1945. You didn't need to be world's greatest medium, Madame Luce Vidi, to know where the Third Reich was heading by late 1943. And if you were keen on strategy, you knew fatal decisions were being made as early as 1941. So smart Nazis had anywhere from eighteen months to four years to plan and refine contingencies. If Hitler didn't plan an escape, therefore, one has to believe it was his intention to perpetrate the greatest murder/suicide rampage in history. And that would mean he was crazy. . . .

Where, then, would be the place most welcoming to criminals against humanity, specifically those of the German persuasion? In this section, the *Gazette* makes the case for Argentina, a contention, incidentally, disputed by no one. There was already a significant German-Argentine population—about 250,000—living there during the years of the Third Reich. Steady immigration and close ties had characterized relations between the two countries since German unification in 1871.

But any Nazi seeking a safe haven would still need a friend in high places, and that friend was Juan Perón. Vice president of Argentina in 1944 and '45, then president from 1946 onward, Perón made no secret of his willingness to offer protection to those looking to escape the fall of Germany. Adolph Eichmann and Josef Mengele were two prominent Nazis known to have taken him up on his offer.

Eichmann was not safe permanently, however. In 1960, Israeli agents kidnapped the final-solution kingpin near his home in Buenos Aires and brought him back to Israel for trial, where he was convicted and sentenced to death. Mengele, on the other hand, was never caught. Could Hitler have enjoyed the same fate? Only the *Police Gazette* has the definitive answer!

HITLER SEEN ALIVE!

by GEORGE McGRATH

US Government has photostatic copies of documents showing how Hitler and top aides landed secretly on Colombian coast.

It was midnight, April 29, 1945.

The lurid, reddish flash of artillery ran in an almost unbroken arc from the Botanical Gardens in the north, around the eastern perimeter of Berlin, to the airfield in the south.

Mingled with the whine and heavy explosion of the shells was the staccato burst of machinegun fire; the duller thud of mortars. The Russians were closing in on the doomed city.

Against the late spring night, the heavier dark bombed skeletons of the famous Reichschancellery and the Wilhelmstrasse ministries reached starkly to the sky.

German "Operation Fog" was about to begin. "Operation Fog" was the code name for Hitler's plan of escape.

On one side of the Charlottenburgerstrasse stood a small airplane, its motor idling gently, the noise drowned by the din of battle as the Russians forced their way through the suburbs of Berlin.

Three people picked their way silently across the rubble-strewn ground above Hitler's "bunker" and headed for the plane. One wore a long dustcoat and flat military hat. His eyes glittered. At his side was a woman, who shivered despite the warmth of her fur coat. Behind them was a man in the uniform of a German officer.

Marshal Ritter von Greim's heels clicked as he helped the man and woman climb aboard. Ritter von Greim was chief of the Luftwaffe. He saluted briefly and turned back. The light plane, that same model Fieseler-Storck which had snatched Mussolini from the Allies, waddled out into the middle of the wide street, its engine roared. Seconds later it was airborne.

Adolf Hitler and Eva Braun, the mistress he had married about three hours before, had fled from Berlin!

He had escaped the on sweeping Russians by a few scant hours.

This was the setting for Hitler's departure from his ruined capital, so far as I was able to piece together threads of evidence gathered by Allied intelligence agents.

I consulted official government records; I talked to many agents who had worked on the "Hitler case"; I went over official reports from the Argentine and from Colombia.

Exclusively, and for the first time, the *Police Gazette* revealed last March that Hitler and Eva Braun had made their way to a new hide-out home in the Antarctic Continent—the "impregnable fortress" Shangri-La about which Admiral Karl Doenitz had boasted as early as 1943.

At that time certain official documents were still on the "classified" list and the *Police Gazette* had been denied access to many aspects of the Fuehrer's flight.

I have now seen these documents. They categorically confirm that Hitler is alive.

These documents reveal that Hitler made an intermediary stop-over in Colombia on his way to the Antarctic Shangri-La.

I was given no explanation for this amazing stop-over. Undoubtedly, there are other documents, which still remain out of reach, and which might explain many cloudy issues. On the basis of agents' reports I deduced that the final German debacle had come too swiftly, sooner than expected, and that the Antarctic hide-out was not quite ready for Hitler's immediate occupancy.

As I shall show, these records include a report that Eva Braun,

Hitler's mistress-wife, died in the U-boat on the way to safety and freedom and was buried at sea.

I hesitate to take a stand for or against this. I shall merely present the facts and let the reader judge. Other reports confirm that no woman landed off this U-boat on Colombia shores.

But that does not mean that Eva Braun did not proceed direct to the Antarctic base. There is reason to believe that Eva was expecting a baby. Hitler might have preferred to see her in safety as well as safeguard a possible male descendant while he temporarily salvaged the Nazi party as best he could from South America.

The picture of their escape from Berlin remained confused for many years but the *Police Gazette* can now present a clear and detailed account, based on reports I saw and agents I talked to.

Der Fuehrer had left bloodshed and ruin behind him. His dreams of empire had been smashed; his country laid waste by the war he had visited upon others; his cities devastated by the air arm he had vaunted as Germany's might.

In Hitler's Reichschancellery "bunker" the stage was set for history's most fantastic and colossal deception. While the real Hitler was in full flight to Hamburg, there was a dazed and broken man resembling him in all details bidding a final goodbye to the staff of personal servants. Two hours later this man had been shot through the mouth and naptha-fed flames were licking at the half-blanketed body of the unknown "double."

"Not Hitler's Body"

Intelligence reports show that within a few hours of Hitler's departure the only two men in on the secret of this "bunker" drama—Dr. Stumpfegger and Marshal Ritter von Greim—hastily left Berlin.

Commandant Deodor Pletonov, Russian officer in command of the Berlin sector, led the first troops into the "bunker." He was explicit:

"The body was not that of Hitler. It was one of his doubles."

The hoodwinking plot was complete.

Hitler's plane set course for Hamburg, where Admiral Doenitz was still holding out behind the German front lines at Luneburg.

To this day there is no reliable eyewitness account of how Hitler and Eva Braun were taken from Hamburg to that secret U-boat base hidden in the Norwegian fjords. Although one report states he went by submarine, another believes he escaped in a flying boat.

"The Allies were blockading the entrance to the Baltic. It would have been impossible for a U-boat to have run the destroyer gauntlet through the North Sea between Germany and Norway," I was told.

Whichever way he did leave Germany, Hitler and Eva arrived at the secret port of embarkation sometime in the night of May 1.

Everything had been planned and prepared to the last detail. The flotilla of 20 U-boats (this is the closest official estimate I have been able to obtain) was fueled and victualled. Within minutes after Hitler's arrival aboard the lead submarine, the flotilla sailed. This was to be Hitler's last glimpse of the sky for nearly 50 days.

Allied naval reports show that it would have been quite possible for a U-boat flotilla to travel submerged through the Denmark Straits between Iceland and Greenland—where the Bismarck was first sighted in the naval action that led to her sinking in mid-Atlantic—and stay submerged through the entire North Atlantic until it reached the comparative safety of South Atlantic waters.

What happened aboard these U-boats; what route they followed; when and where they surfaced for the first time would be conjecture and I am dealing here solely with facts.

Until the *Police Gazette* was given access a few weeks ago to reports from Bogota, Colombia, Hitler's movements, from the time he left Norway May 2, until he was reported safe in the Antarctic Continent by our exclusive report in March this year, were an official secret.

Alive in Colombia

This new evidence was contained in a prosaic brown paper folder marked simply: "Despatch No. 418, Enclosures No. 1, 2 and 3. Date: July 2, 1948."

These enclosures are the photostatic copies of eyewitness reports of Hitler's arrival and stopover in Colombia.

I was permitted to read these documents and reveal their contents in the *Police Gazette.*

These documents comprise the stories of three men who worked to help Hitler hide in Colombia. One of them is still a self-confessed Nazi, who gives as his reason for revealing Hitler's past whereabouts:

"My only intention is to inform the world that the Savior of the West is alive, and very much so; ready to assume his leading position against Communism, which threatens to spread over the planet like an enslaving and bloody horde."

His Fascist fanaticism is self-evident. But his story is confirmed by one of the other sources—an eyewitness; a man who became disgusted with Hitler methods. This man readily corroborated this initial revelation.

I read through these reports very carefully. They vary but little and in no fundamental detail. On the contrary they substantiate one another. Only in the operational phases, where the individual was not personally present, are there differences or supplementary details. The main facts are the same. There can be only one conclusion drawn from such evidence:

Hitler arrived safely in Colombia. Hitler left Colombia in perfect health. Hitler is still alive and preparing his return.

Naturally enough, the Hitler fanatic does not reveal his name. For the sake of brevity in future reference I shall call him "X". The other two documents were signed. I may not reveal these names. For obvious reasons all sources working for the American Government must be protected.

One of these men had been concerned only in the preliminary
Nazi espionage network of pre-War days in South America and in
a very minor role, indeed, in the early stages of preparations for
Hitler's flight. His story tells us little. The other gives us specific
details including:

The dates of Hitler's arrival and departure.

The first document to be received by the government was that
of the mysterious Mr. "X".

"Hitler landed from the submarine 1048 at Bahia Honda,
Colombian coast of Guajira, early in the morning of July 19, 1945.
He was accompanied by six men: two radio and precision instru-
ment experts; two lieutenant-colonels, one an infantryman the
other an artilleryman; a Luftwaffe major and a naval U-boat expert.

"All were dressed in civilian clothes, disguised as local Colombians.
One of the pieces of baggage contained 3,000,000 American dollars.

"After landing on a bend of the wide and beautiful bay of Bahia
Honda, they were met by two coordinating agents and four strong
rustic Indians, who waited to carry baggage for them. Everything
had been prepared. Horses were waiting nearby and a little further
away stood a tarpaulin-covered truck."

Mr. "X" Reveals

The former Hitler collaborator, who had decided to abandon his
Fuehrer and turn to the Allies even at this late date, was shown
Mr. "X's" statement. To safeguard this new informant's anonymity I
shall refer to him as "E.I.S."

E.I.S. was one of the masterminds behind the preparations for
Hitler's arrival. His full statement concerning Hitler's stop-over
in Colombia is contained in Enclosure No. I of Despatch 418. He
stated:

"I am a Colombian, a well-off man, educated in Europe. I first
met Hitler during the 1936 Olympics in Berlin. A former school-
mate, the friend of the German Minister of War, managed to get

me an interview with Der Fuehrer. I was enormously impressed by his brilliant and genial personality. I had always thought Hitler scorned the Latin races and the Spanish-Americans especially. The way he received me, his manner toward me and the long conversation we had, changed my viewpoint entirely.

"Every time I visited Germany I saw the Fuehrer and our friendship grew. More than once I helped him with South American diplomats. I obtained his consent to a German-sponsored industrialization experiment I wished to put into effect on land I possessed in the Narino area of Colombia.

"I spent the greater part of the War in Europe. Once I was persecuted in a European country (name withheld) by agents of Moscow. I managed to escape into Germany and then to Switzerland."

E.I.S. traced how he became an agent for Hitler in Colombia.

"Jan. 12, 1945, I was visited by a German agent. He asked me to report on the safest place in South America, in my opinion, for a temporary refuge for Hitler and a group of German scientists and officials, in case they should have to 'disappear temporarily from the world scene.'

U-Boat Escape Decided

"I recommended my fatherland, Colombia. Its immense uninhabited territories lend themselves to complete seclusion. Furthermore, I owned isolated lands where absolute secrecy could be maintained. I informed the German agent that the group could easily enter the country either on the Pacific coast of Narino or on the barren shore of Guajira. I advised Bahia Honda on the coast of Guajira.

"January 15, I was asked to prepare a travel itinerary with details of a possible plan. I did so.

"January 30, I was informed that the voyage from Germany would be made by U-boat and my suggestion for a landing at Bahia Honda had been adopted. I was instructed to go to Colombia and arrange all details. German agents there would be at my complete disposal. The Nazi added:

"'The Fuehrer has full confidence in you.'"

E.I.S. gave additional details:

"Once in Colombia I chose my collaborators with care. Two of them were faithful family retainers; the third was a high official in the Colombian army. I needed three more. I picked an Antioquian conservation chief, who knew the land and the natives better than anyone in the country; a liberal, violently anti-Communist newspaper editor and, finally, the sixth was a woman, an intelligent and enormously wealthy export heiress of the Valle de Cauca. She was one of Hitler's best agents in Colombia."

"I Met Hitler on Beach"

Here E.I.S. confirmed the Hitler fanatic's report of the U-boat landing in Bahia Honda. He altered a few minor details, however, making it apparent, in the opinion of intelligence experts, that Mr. "X" was not present at the beach when Hitler arrived although a member of the party at Hitler's hideaway ranch.

"Effectively," says E.I.S., "Hitler and his group disembarked in Bahia Honda July 19, 1945. But the 'rustic' Indians mentioned by Mr. 'X' were none other than four of my accomplices. They were wearing peasant garb for ease in traveling and so as not to excite undue comment. We could not take the chance of hiring real 'Guajiras' to handle the baggage. They might have sold us out to the Allies.

"The two 'coordinating agents' were the heiress and myself. She was in man's clothes, even to the sombrero."

E.I.S. revealed to the American authorities that he believed he knew the Hitler agent but had never known his name—and at that time personal questions would not be appreciated.

"I think he is a tall and slender Dutchman, who was part of the group at the ranch-house to which he went finally and which was occupied exclusively by Hitler and his immediate henchmen. This Dutchman had been taken to the ranch by agents before Hitler's arrival. He can only have gained his information about the Bahia Honda landing second-hand, which would account for the few discrepancies. But, factually and fundamentally, his story is correct about Hitler's arrival and seclusion at the ranch."

E.I.S.'s story of the cross-country flight to the ranch shows the wealth of attention to planning and the inherent suspiciousness of Hitler's followers.

"Hitler and his group spent six days on horseback, riding only by night, from Bahia Honda to an airplane landing strip at La Loma. I and three of my accomplices had gone ahead and we waited there at the rendezvous hour. We had procured two small Stinson four-seat planes to ferry the party to my ranch at Narino.

"Then I was suddenly informed that Hitler had changed his mind. He would not hide out at my ranch. Instead, his agents had picked a destination unknown to me at the time. So secretive were all the moves Hitler made that even I did not know of the other two ranches which had been readied for him.

"Hitler and five others boarded these planes and flew off. With them went the plans of several German secret weapons, which they would never leave out of their sight for an instant. We and the remainder of the group would travel with the baggage and equipment in trucks towards La Jagua.

"It was a month later before I saw Hitler again in his ranch-house in the Bogota 'savanna' and learned details of the flight.

"They had landed at dawn on July 26 after a hazardous flight by night across the mountains without radio help. At the ranch three persons, one of them the Colombian ranch owner, waited for Hitler. I had not known that these men were involved in the plot before. Apparently, Hitler's right arm must not know what the left is doing. Nevertheless, I continued to be a member of his personal staff."

Where's Eva Braun?

E.I.S. then throws a verbal bombshell in his report.

"After our arrival at the ranch, I asked a member of Hitler's U-boat group—'What about Eva Braun?'

"He replied: 'She died aboard the U-boat. It was cerebral hemorrhage. We buried her at sea.'

"I cannot vouch for the truth of this record. I was not aboard the U-boat. But it might have accounted for the Fuehrer's unsociable, silent and apathetic attitude. The only enthusiasm I saw him show was during discussions of a worldwide crusade against Communism."

E.I.S. revealed that only once, at the beginning of 1946, did Hitler fear his hide-out had been discovered.

"The Russian Embassy in Bogota suddenly expanded its staff. We thought the Russians had heard of our ranch-house. But they had not. The M.V.D. had heard Hitler 'might be' in Colombia. They were making a routine check. That was the reason for the influx of Red spies. Hitler had an agent in the Embassy and we soon knew their secrets."

Additional details came from Mr. "X".

"Hitler visited three different ranches in the Bogota 'savannas'. He received all the newspapers and the *New York Times* was translated for him daily. He had three clandestine radio stations on mobile vans and was in constant communication with his agents.

"Hitler was not known by his own name, nor did his employees ever call him 'Fuehrer'. Only his closest German servants knew his real identity. The ranch hands thought him a mine operator, fond of rural tranquility and of hunting. He wore a heavy beard and eyeglasses. It was a complete disguise."

As mysteriously as he had arrived, Adolf Hitler and his group of scientists, military men and advisors, left Colombia.

"I have not seen Hitler since April 5, 1946," states E.I.S. in the document held by the US

"When I returned to the ranch ten days later on April 15, I found it deserted. The laboratory, all equipment, personal effects had gone. Everyone had faded into thin air. Not a sign of his presence remained. The retreat had been perfect."

Hitler had quietly embarked on a U-boat and had gone to his Antarctic hide-out.

Exclusive details of his Antarctic retreat were given by the *Police Gazette*, in the March, 1952, issue.

A document in the possession of a government agency in Washington categorically reveals:

"Hitler has four submarine bases at his disposal, each with six U-boats. Strategically placed along the Antarctic and South American Continents are dumps of fuel, food and medicaments. U-boats can make the longest cruises and return to base without risking discovery.

"Among the persons with Hitler in his hideaway is an eminent German physician, whose 200-bed hospital is equipped with the latest medical developments in drugs and surgical therapy."

Adolf Hitler may be a remote criminal but so long as he lives, he will be a danger to world peace. He is perfecting his weapons and they may well prove more destructive and further advanced, even in the domain of nuclear development, than those possessed by the Allies.

IS PERON HIDING HITLER?

by GEORGE McGRATH
Police Gazette Staff Investigator

Ex-US Ambassador to Argentina Spruille Braden
told *Police Gazette*: "Hitler could very well be hiding
somewhere in South America."

The springboard for a renewed Nazi attempt at domination of the world lies in the Argentine. More than 75,000 Germans, many of them "wanted" by the Allied Intelligence Services, are living openly under Col. Juan Peron's protection, preparing for the "triumphant" return of their Fuehrer Adolf Hitler.

Is Hitler himself at their head in the Argentine?

Has the defeated Fuehrer moved his headquarters from the Shangri-La he had established in the Antarctic, to the Argentine?

Is fascist dictator Juan Peron hiding the onetime overlord of the Third Reich and deliberately hoodwinking the Allies? And—Does this Argentine disciple of Hitler and Franco plan to help Hitler engineer his return to Germany from this South American base?

These questions are uppermost today in the minds of anxious politicians who are well aware of the dangerous potentialities of such a situation and who are convinced that Hitler is not dead; that he succeeded in escaping from Berlin, and is *ALIVE* today.

Evidence in the hands of American and British Intelligence Services points damningly to the fact that Col. Juan Peron, the Argentine military attache who marched behind Hitler during the Fuehrer's entry into conquered Paris in 1940, is giving the deposed German Nazis his personal protection.

There is absolute proof that many of Hitler's immediate aides, a number of his trusted lieutenants in the dread Gestapo, and his evil genius and close confidant Martin Bormann, sought refuge in the Argentine from Allied courts of justice and the hangman's noose.

There is absolute proof that these men form the backbone of the new *Nazi International*, and are at the root of all the neo-Nazi parties now operating in Germany, where they are undermining Premier Konrad Adenauer's efforts to establish a sound democratic government.

These men will stop at nothing; they are preparing to overthrow the Bonn government while secretly negotiating with the Russians in the Eastern Soviet-controlled Germany. The blueprint of asylum in the Argentine had been drawn up by Martin Bormann, as exclusively revealed by the *Police Gazette*. Bormann had actively encouraged General Farrell and Colonel Peron in their successful rise to power and had "loaned" them Nazi money for their campaign.

A grateful Peron opened wide the doors of the South American fascist state. Germany's interest in the Argentine became paramount; they took precedence over all other foreign interests, including those of the United States. Nazis took over control of nearly every important industry in the nation. This is not hearsay. It is established and unassailable fact. The American government knew it and was powerless to act.

Assistant Secretary of State William L. Clayton, testifying before the sub-committee of the Senate Military Committee on June 25, 1945—only a few days after the surrender of Germany—stated that 108 *major* Nazi economic enterprises were operating in the Argentine as Nazi spearheads for a future comeback.

Even before the end of the War, at a time when the Allied invasion of Hitler's Fortress of Europe was an accomplished fact and the defeat of the Germans but a question of a few months, President Franklin D. Roosevelt knew that Hitler and his top aides would try to seek refuge in the Argentine, which was rapidly becoming the new world center of fascism. On September 29, 1944, the President publicly referred to:

"The extraordinary paradox of the growth of Nazi-fascist influence and the increasing use of Nazi-fascist methods in the Argentine."

German money had bought a huge slice of Argentine territory—nearly 100,000 square miles of ranchland in the hinterland provinces of Rio Negro and Chubut, in Patagonia. These ranches, which surpassed even the vast holdings of the richest Texas cattlemen, were policed by Germans. Allied agents never succeeded in penetrating their confines.

IS PERON HIDING HITLER?

HITLER GOES SIGHTSEEING IN PARIS — The famed Eiffel Tower, symbol of the City of Paris, stands in background as Hitler and his party tour the conquered capital of France on July 15, 1940. Col. Juan Peron, dictator of Argentina, was among the foreign military dignitaries who greeted Hitler's entry.

Mr. Spruille Braden, who was American Ambassador to the Argentine at the time of the German surrender, and who later became Assistant Secretary of State, immediately recognized the danger of Peron's open support and covering up of former Nazi leaders.

"Unless the Nazi element in the Argentine can be extirpated it will remain a serious threat for the future," said the Ambassador.

Mr. Braden, who is now chairman of the New York City Anti-

Crime Committee, has never ceased to denounce these Nazis in the Argentine. He has repeatedly stressed that these men will be free to return to their own country and reorganize neo-Nazi parties, despite their wartime record of atrocities, once a peace treaty has been signed between the Allies and the Bonn government.

One of the most notorious Hitler agents in a key position in the Nazi underground movement in the Argentine is Ludwig Freude. Freude figures high up on the blacklist of the United States Intelligence Service and of M.I.5 (the British Military counter-espionage organization).

Careful investigation by the *Police Gazette* disclosed startling facts, hitherto dormant in State Department files. One report stated baldly:

"Facts which have developed since the opening up of sources of information in Germany point to the conclusion that Freude is properly described as the leader of the 'stay-behind' organization, which was set up when German official diplomats were compelled to leave Argentina owing to Allied, and particularly American, pressure."

Germans Ordered Out

At this time Peron was playing safe. Ostensibly heeding Allied demands, he ordered the Germans out of the country and issued orders seizing German owned property. In reality, he allowed the few Germans who were forced out of the country, to appoint successors and he left their property untouched and their successors' operations unrestricted.

The State Department records referred many times to Freude: "When Counsellor of the Nazi Embassy Wilhelm von Pochhammer was repatriated July 6, 1944, he gave Freude a power of attorney to act on behalf of the Embassy and handed him 45,280 pesos of his own money for 'safe-keeping.'

"At this time General Wolf, chief of armed forces in the German

Embassy, left the military attache's fund of 200,000 pesos to Freude for 'intelligence purposes.'"

According to State Department records, documents seized in the German Foreign Office, and interrogation of Wilhelmstrasse personnel revealed that Freude had played an important role in handling the "M" funds of the German Reich. These funds were a secret reserve for financing intelligence activities and other concealed Nazi enterprises.

Cover Up

As Ambassador Braden told the *Police Gazette*:

"We have never been able to ascertain fully the complete scope of Nazi infiltration into the Argentine. Our Intelligence and economic officers traced $400 million of Nazi funds into that country. These were known as 'M' funds. The Argentine government flatly refused to cooperate with us in developing further information of Freude's Nazi activities and took every precaution to cover him up and protect him from our intelligence investigation. Freude's son," stressed the Ambassador, "was Peron's personal secretary."

In 1945, when Edelmiro Farrell was still head of the State, Peron halted all investigation into Freude's activities by the Argentine Committee for Vigilance and Liquidation of Enemy Property. Peron personally vouched for Freude's integrity and Gen. Farrell ordered Committee Secretary Dr. Carlos Adroque to cease his investigations of this shady Nazi agent, who was a devoted follower of Martin Bormann.

After Hitler's escape from Berlin and flight to Colombia, first, and, finally, to his secret Shangri-La in the Antarctic, as revealed exclusively by the *Police Gazette*, Nazi agents were given almost free access to the Argentine. The doors were opened wide and all pretense thrown to the winds when Peron assumed complete and absolute power.

The *Police Gazette* investigator uncovered startling facts which reveal how the Nazis in a few years virtually took over the reins of power in this South American country.

Dr. H. Theiss, a former Gestapo organizer and official, became special adviser to the Argentine Federal Police and immediately appointed three other Germans as his aides. They were Dr. F. Adam, Herr H. Richner and Herr J. Paecht.

Men in Power

Dr. Hans Koch, a notorious Nazi, the behind-the-scenes boss of the Instituto de Promocion de Intercambia, which holds a monopoly over all imports and exports, is another leading Nazi put into power by Martin Bormann through his friend Peron. Still others were Colonel Hans Ulrich Rudel, of the Nazi wartime air force, who became a technical adviser to the Argentine government's military aviation industry; Rudel went back to Germany, where he now heads a Nazi underground movement; and Otto Skorzeny, the German S.S. pilot who snatched Mussolini from his prison and brought him to Germany.

These facts are highly significant and fraught with danger for the democratic world. They represent an open renunciation of the Allies and flagrant approval of Hitler and his methods.

It is no secret in the Argentine that the Nazi spies, Paul Wutke and Kathe Muller, who had been expelled in July, 1946, on the insistence of the US Government, have been allowed to return and live quite openly in the Argentine.

In the Argentine capital itself, a Nazi newspaper, the *Freie Presse*, extolls the merits of the fascism. A prime mover on this paper is Robert Kessler, of the German Gestapo. On his staff is Herr Freisler, notorious Hitler agent who worked for some time in Franco's Foreign Ministry before being ordered to the Argentine.

There is absolutely no denying the salient facts:

When the War ended in Hitler's ignominious fake suicide, there were 60,000 of the finest German brain-trusters and organized by Martin Bormann in the Argentine to form a basis for Hitler's underground activities and springboard for his return to power.

Today there are more than 75,000 of these picked men and (this is well known to our State Department) the majority of these post-War arrivals are Nazis who are wanted in the Allied zones of Germany, fled to this Nazi South American refuge.

How did they elude the American, British and French Intelligence officers?

It may be comparatively simple for one or even a dozen men to flee to freedom. But for more than 15,000 to have done so shows clearly the existence of a well-organized Nazi pipeline to freedom and, more sinister yet, obvious collusion from the Nazi sympathizers among the personnel among Allied officials.

Allied secret service agents in Germany and in the Argentine have reported suspicious incidents indicating that Adolf Hitler himself has abandoned his icy Antarctic retreat and moved his entire headquarters to the Patagonian hinterland, probably to the area of Bariluche.

"It is a vast Nazi stronghold," Ambassador Braden reported to the State Department some time before. "I sent agents there to check. They were detained and ordered to leave the area. We have never been permitted free movement in this part of the Argentine. We don't know what is going on there."

The Time Is Ripe

In Germany, General Hermann Bernhard (Papa) Ramcke, 63-year-old Nazi paratrooper, a few months ago considered the time ripe to launch a vicious attack on the "real war criminals"—the Allies. Shouting that President-elect Eisenhower was a *Schweinhund,*" he worked himself into a frenzy.

"Our beloved Fuehrer will return to Germany soon," he vowed.

Two Nazi generals, who had organized the meeting—S.S. General Herbert Gills and S.S. General Felix Steiner—passed him frantic notes and he clammed up.

Again, Heribert von Strempel, former secretary of Hitler's Embassy in Washington, D.C., and one of the organizers of the Bund 5th column in the United States, has been openly accused in the Bonn Parliament of "reporting to Nazi authorities *overseas* concerning the situation in Germany."

Who are these Nazi "authorities" overseas but Adolf Hitler and his staff?

Meanwhile, Hitler's trusted confidant Martin Bormann has been active in Germany itself within recent months.

Maj.-General Partridge, Chief of US Military Intelligence, said as recently as a few months ago to this reporter:

"It is entirely possible that Hitler escaped. We have never received any definite and final proof that he isn't alive."

There is a little doubt that a guiding hand lies behind the carefully coordinated Nazi demonstrations occurring throughout Western Germany.

Ambassador Braden, among others with inside knowledge of State Department reports, firmly believe that the fountain head of Nazism now lies in the Argentine and that the supposed Nazi leaders in Germany are no more than puppets obeying orders given from the South American stronghold.

INSIDE HITLER'S SECRET HIDEOUT

by GEORGE McGRATH

Police Gazette reveals inside story of Der Fuehrer's hidden Shangri-La in vast wilderness of the Antarctic.

Editor's Note: Hitler is alive! Hitler is plotting to return! These are facts the Police Gazette *has investigated and fearlessly revealed during recent months. The* Police Gazette *has produced evidence to support these facts from important Allied leaders and politicians, from American diplomats, and even from the US Army Intelligence colonel charged with investigating Hitler's death.*

Why doesn't the United States Government take immediate action to use our information—track down Hitler, arrest him, and bring him to trial? That is a question we are asked several times daily. The answer is this: Our government's hands are tied. We are a democratic nation and we cannot trespass upon, invade, or interfere with the territorial integrity of another country.

Adolf Hitler has been hiding in the Argentine. Our former ambassador to Argentina, Spruille Braden, tracked down seventy-one Nazi war criminals. He asked the Argentine Government to arrest these men and deport them. He asked the Argentine Government to pursue Hitler and his henchman, Martin Bormann. But Juan Peron, dictator of Argentina and fascist admirer of the Fuehrer, refuses to take action. He is the protector of Hitler and his Nazi supporters.

That is why the US Government is powerless to act.

Adolf Hitler, defeated Fuehrer of the Third Reich, has once again retreated to his secret Shangri-La in the vast wilderness of the Antarctic Continent—whose existence was first revealed in the

Police Gazette in February, 1952. The Fuehrer and his beetle-browed, ruthless henchman, Martin Bormann, have been forced to temporarily abandon their carefully prepared plot to seize power in Germany.

As revealed exclusively in the *Police Gazette*, Hitler, using Bormann as his go-between, had reached a sinister agreement with the Red dictator, Joseph Stalin—whose armies were to place the Fuehrer in absolute control of a unified West and East Germany in defiance of the Allies and at the risk of war. Early this year the Hitler-Stalin plans had been completed, and with Stalin's knowledge and approval Hitler left his Antarctic hideout for the immense Patagonian ranch which the Argentine dictator, Juan Person, had permitted the Nazis to use as a postwar base.

Then came disaster. Dr. Walter Naumann and his ring of Nazi agents in the Western Zone of Germany were arrested by British Intelligence agents who had heard of the plot to restore Nazism. That setback could have been overcome—but then Stalin died.

Bormann, who had been in Moscow, flew back to the Argentine and told his Fuehrer that the Kremlin was likely to become the theater for one of the bloodiest "palace revolutions" the world has ever seen. The struggle for Stalin's crown, he said, would rage between Georgi Malenkov, Lavrenti Beria, Marshal Nicolai Bulganin, and Vyacheslav Molotov, until one emerged as the new tyrant.

A Change of Plans

Hitler's foresight showed him that he could not make his bid for power until he and Bormann could again deal with a Soviet leader who would be the undisputed master of all Russia. Basically, nothing had changed but the time element. At a solemn cabinet meeting, held in the main headquarters building of the Patagonia ranch, Hitler decided to again retreat to that South Polar Shangri-La which had served him so well as a hideaway after the fateful days of April and May. 1945—when he was reported an "ignominious suicide" and Germany finally surrendered in a little schoolroom outside Rheims.

In the past two years, the *Police Gazette* spared neither time nor expense in tracing the Fuehrer's movements from the moment he escaped from shell-rocked Berlin before dawn on April 30. We have sifted hundreds of reports dealing with the Fuehrer's secret hiding place. Grand Admiral Karl Doenitz first revealed Germany's plan to save the Nazi superlord from victorious Allied vengeance as far back as 1943, when he publicly announced:

"The German submarine fleet is proud of having built for the Fuehrer, in another part of the world, a Shangri-La on land—an impregnable fortress."

The *Police Gazette* traced Hitler's flight with Eva Braun, his newly married wife, and Martin Bormann by U-boat to Colombia and then to Antarctica. But no real description of this Polar hide-out could be obtained at that time.

Now, however, since the Fuehrer has postponed his plan to reconquer Germany, a disgruntled Nazi agent in the Argentine has produced new and detailed information. The *Police Gazette* checked part of this information with the Hydrographic Office of the United States Navy Department. The Navy confirmed that knowledge of such particular geographic phenomena could be possessed *only by someone with personal experience in that area*. It could not be faked.

The Birth of Shangri-La

A Shangri-La for the Fuehrer was first conceived by Marshal Hermann Goering, obese and lascivious Nazi Minister for Air, and the limping, immoral Josef Goebbels, the Fuehrer's Minister for Propaganda—who originated the Nazi slogan: "The bigger the lie, the more people will believe it."

Only one place in the world still remained ninety percent unexplored, and at that time it was considered almost wholly inaccessible. This was the Antarctic Continent—the sixth and largest continent in the world. Approximately five million square miles in area, it is as large as Europe and North America combined.

Admiral Doenitz was called in for his naval know-how and asked: "Where in this gigantic continent—the largest, highest, and coldest in the world, surrounded by the stormiest seas in the world—is the best location for a new and last Berchtesgaden Shangri-La?"

Admiral Doenitz consulted Germany's leading Arctic navigator, Captain Alfred Rithscher. Together they picked that part of Queen Maud Land which lies off the Atlantic-Indian Antarctic Basin to the south of the Weddell Sea and astride the Greenwich meridian. Only the coastline of this part of Antarctica had been charted from the sea by Norwegian sailors, who had named the unexplored coastal strips Ragnild Coast, Princess Astrid Coast, and Princess Martha Coast. But its formidable ice cliffs had daunted even these intrepid Norwegians. They had been seeking peaceful exploration only—not a hideaway.

The German Naval Command—Admiral Doenitz's command—placed Captain Rithscher in charge of a special expedition. The members of the expedition were reticent and secretive to an unusual degree. No announcement was made at all until Captain Rithscher returned to Germany from the South Pole. Then a singularly terse statement was issued:

"The *Schwabenland*, Captain Rithscher in command, sailed from Hamburg on December 17, 1938, and reached the Antarctic Continent in the vicinity of the Greenwich Meridian in January, 1939. A series of aircraft flights were made and the coast was photographed from twenty degrees east to ten degrees west. The vessel retired northward on February 6 and reached Cuxhaven, Germany, on April 11, 1939."

New details of this important voyage have fallen into the hands of *Police Gazette* investigators. The Germans had planned well. The

Antarctic area they picked for the Shangri-La lay between seventy and seventy-five degrees south—the farthest "inaccessible" land from the South Pole and unlikely to attract postwar explorers trying to reach the Pole itself. It also offered the best climatic conditions—once the shore had been reached.

This part of the Antarctic is the most hazardous area in the world. Shipwrecked seamen on pack ice have little hope of escape. In the Arctic, the pack ice moves around or across a comparatively open sea which is shore-bound except for several open straits, where contact with the shore is invariably made. The Arctic pack may be safely traveled upon, and the abundant life in that region has enabled shipwrecked seamen to reach civilization again even after long journeys.

In the Antarctic, on the contrary, the drift of the pack ice is around and outwards from a central land mass toward the stormiest seas in the world. The wind averages forty-three miles and hour all year round, and gales of eighty to a hundred miles an hour are common.

Secret Mission Is Successful

The expedition was well conceived. The *Schwabenland* reached Queen Maud Land as the shore became ice-free. By February and March, ships have little difficulty in reaching the area, and the water usually remains clear until September. Before the ice closed in again for the winter, Captain Rithscher had completed his surveys and made his secret reports to Admiral Doenitz by air courier from the nearest German consulate in the Argentine. Most important, the Nazi supply ships, with construction materials, supplies, and laborers, were able to sail in.

Captain Rithscher found few natural harbors. He only sought one. For the most part, he moored to ice floes by sea anchors and kept steam up in readiness to move.

Ostensibly, the *Schwabenland* was combining a modicum of

exploration with a search for the best whaling areas. Germany needed whale oil, and the Antarctic seas have been famous since the first days of sailing ships for their number and variety of whales—ranging from the thirty-ton "babies" to giant 150-tonners.

The *Schwabenland's* true mission was far different. Specially designed airplanes, launched by new catapult devices that could throw a much heavier and longer-range plane into the air than any ever before carried aboard ship, flew over the area all day. They surveyed and photographed the entire area, and they landed and took off again from the huge natural runways lying along the 2,000-foot-high "foothill plains" to which Captain Rithscher gave his name—the Rithscher Uplands. These Uplands stretched in steadily but gently rising slopes, from the 2,000-foot plateau to the 12,000-foot Kottas Mountains in the west and the Muhlig-Hoffman Mountains in the east and north.

Somewhere off this Rithscher Upland the *Police Gazette* was told, in one of the Neumayer group of mountains, Adolf Hitler's Shangri-La was ordered built. The area was given a new name—New Schwabenland.

The *Schwabenland* crew found brilliant sunshine there even in February, with cloudless skies and light air. They found that men could work comfortably outdoors, stripped to the waist, although the climate was always cold—never rising above thirty-two degrees Fahrenheit. But because of the dry cold, it was a healthy climate, and disease would be virtually unknown. Few bacteria could live in that extreme cold.

Apart from the cold—an obstacle man's ingenuity could overcome—conditions were ideal for an inaccessible hideout. Unlimited supplies of fresh water existed the year round; during the summer, seals and penguins were plentiful; birds of all kinds were everywhere; and there were tremendous quantities of edible fish—mainly a small rock cod—apart from the whales, which could keep the settlement supplied with fuel oil.

According to reports given to the *Police Gazette* by the Nazi informant in the Argentine, Captain Rithscher even chose the Shangri-La mountain hideout. A snow-free rocky spur that lay at the base of one of the higher mountains, it was honeycombed with natural caves, which made it virtually a hollow hill. It was within a few miles of one of the finest natural airfields in the world, and was within easy reach of a land-locked bay that needed little of man's improvements.

Work on the Shangri-La was commenced in the summer of 1939. During that first summer, a fleet of between ten and twelve ships carried several hundred laborers (the picked product of the concentration camps) to the Polar region, together with heavy hauling and clearing machinery.

Building a dock and raising all supplies from the coastal harbor to the 2,000-foot plateau atop the ice cliffs wasn't an insurmountable task for the German engineers. Within two months, skillful dynamiting and interior shoring with special cold-resistant steel made in the Ruhr enabled the engineers and construction foremen to seal up the mountain into comfortable living accommodations.

Long before the war ended so disastrously for Hitler, the Fuehrer's hideout had been completed. German ingenuity and know-how had been exploited to the utmost. The hollowed-out mountain had been transformed into a fabulous retreat, lacking no luxury. Between three hundred and five hundred workmen had labored constantly over a period of five years to build this Antarctic Berchtesgaden designed to maintain one hundred persons in autonomous comfort for a minimum of ten years.

Entrance to the mountain retreat is gained via a series of three canal-lock-type double doors set in concrete flush in the mountainside. These insure that a minimum of cold air enters and hot air emerges during normal comings and goings. The factory-like interior, according to our Nazi informant from Patagonia, consists of two shells separated by air spaces. The outer shell is made of a special cold-resistant battleship steel, which will take temperatures of eighty degrees below zero Fahrenheit. The inner shell is made of reinforced concrete, lined mostly with pressed panels of fiber insulation.

Only a scant half-dozen of the one hundred Germans in this Shangri-La are permitted to visit the Fuehrer's personal headquarters, reportedly situated in the rear of the "factory." These headquarters have been copied, lavishly and almost exactly (although in miniature), from the Chancellery in Berlin, where Hitler used to live. There are certain basic differences in the furnishings. Steel has replaced wood; indirect lighting had replaced the huge crystal chandeliers; and plastic floors have replaced marble.

The *Police Gazette* was told that nothing is lacking in this hideout. Green vegetables are grown fresh in soil that previously knew only the primitive sparse and coarse Polar grass and the lower-life lichen and fungus. Specially constructed and heated "stables" hold domestic animals of various types, mainly fowl.

A most interesting aspect of this mountain retreat was revealed by the Nazi agent. An entire block has been set aside as laboratories for German scientists. These scientists are reportedly continuing their research into phases of atomic and radar research, guided missiles, and other "secret" war weapons—although the physical testing grounds for these weapons lie in the Argentine.

One detail the *Police Gazette* was unable to obtain from this source: "I do not know whether Eva Braun is with the Fuehrer in this Shangri-La. I haven't seen her. But I do know she boarded the escape U-boat with him in the Norwegian fjords that day early in May. I heard rumors she died during the voyage to Colombia, but I just don't know."

Whether his wife is with him or not, Adolf Hitler has the physical means to lie hidden until the time is ripe, join forces with the new Soviet dictator, and then, once more, strike to win Germany.

HITLER IS ALIVE

By JAMES ROGERS

An isolated, mysterious fortress in
South America hides Fuehrer's secret fortune

Hidden from civilization and under heavy 24-hour guard, a string of modern ranch buildings near Lake Viedma in the remote plateau region of Argentina shelters two of the world's best-kept secrets—

The mystery of Adolf Hitler's vanished two-billion dollar fortune, and the even-more mysterious disappearance of Der Fuehrer himself.

For more than eleven years a group of heavily-armed men in this barren and unexplored region of South America have turned back occasional visitors to the ranch, and the native population long has been aware that this territory is forbidden ground.

But from authoritative Washington and Buenos Aires sources the *Police Gazette* has learned that this Patagonian territory of 10,000 sq. miles is the purported hideout of Hitler and his aides, who escaped before the fall of Berlin with his two-billion-dollar loot.

Long before Berlin fell in April, 1945, the Lake Viedma ranch had been prepared for Der Fuehrer's coming. And from many spots on the continent—and even from the United States—millions of dollars had been cleverly siphoned into Argentina to await the dictator's exile.

How It Was Done

These preparations were started in 1938 by Ludwig Freude, a close friend of Hitler and a key figure in the Nazi worldwide network. To assure cooperation from Argentina, Freude became an intimate of Juan Peron, the South American bully-boy, and through the war, Freude's son was Peron's personal secretary.

Although Freude's old buddy, Peron, has been overthrown and is in exile, the present Argentina regime has given no indication that it intends to root out the nest of Nazis near Lake Viedma. Plenty of Third Reich money is still in industries in the Argentine and Hitler's stronghold has not been molested. Land purchases in the isolated Patagonian plateau were made by the Nazis in 1938 and soon the region was buzzing with Nazi officials, SS guards and Berlin businessman, rushed there by plane on mysterious errands.

Former US Ambassador Spruille Braden reported these activities to the State Department.

"We have never been able to ascertain fully the complete scope of Nazi Infiltration into the Argentine." Braden said. "Our intelligence and economic officers traced $400,000,000 of Nazi funds into the country. The Argentine government flatly refused to cooperate with us in developing further information of Freude's Nazi activities and took every effort to cover him up and protect him from our intelligence investigation."

What Braden—and the State Department—didn't know until now is that the four hundred million dollars was only a drop in the bucket! Millions more were being smuggled to the Lake Viedma ranch under the Nazi code "Operation M Fund!"

A few top Hitler aides believed that this fund was for espionage in the Americas. But only Freude and another Hitler henchman Martin Bormann, knew that "Operation M Fund" was really Hitler's own secret fortune, his insurance against the collapse of the Third Reich.

Another indication of how this fortune was handled can be gathered from a secret State Department record which the *Police Gazette* has obtained. According to this report, "When Counsellor of the Nazi Embassy Wilhelm von Pochhammer was repatriated

July 6, 1944, he gave Freude power of attorney to act on behalf of the Embassy and handed him 45,280 pesos of his own money for safe-keeping . . . At the time General Wolf, chief of armed forces in the German Embassy, left, the military attache's fund of 200,000 pesos was turned over to Freude."

Freude converted most of the cash to gold, and had it buried near the ranch. But another part of the fortune was invested in various Argentine projects, not only as long-range capital investment, but as a form of bribery to Peron, who it is also believed, cashed in on the secret. The vast amount of these investments was indicated in testimony of Assistant Secretary of State William L. Clayton, who told the Senate Armed Services committee June 25, 1945, that 108 *major Argentina economic enterprises were under control of the Nazis.*

Hitler's Fortune

Meanwhile, Martin Bormann (reported by British Intelligence as "dead or missing," now believed living in the Lake Viedma area) was handling Hitler's secret fortune in Europe. More than $100,000,000 was channeled through Swiss banks to Argentina, and Allied intelligence agents traced the transactions to Bormann. They found his trail—but not the money.

Hitler's personal treasures, including gold and silverware, rare paintings and other *objet d' art*, were flown out of Germany by the Luftwaffe to the Balearic Islands, where Nazi sympathizers removed them to a hiding place in Palencia in northern Spain. From there the treasure, estimated to be worth at least twenty million dollars, was taken piecemeal to Argentina.

Hitler, in his book "Mein Kampf" and throughout his career, kept telling the German people that he was a poor man, but American agents discovered after the war that this was another of his "big lies." They found that he truly was one of the world's richest men.

Secret Financial Records

Secret Reich accounting records show that Hitler from 1935 to 1945 received a salary of from $2,640,000 to $6,000,000 a year, including expenses. He received $100,000 annually as president of the Reich, the same amount as Chancellor, and drew unlimited funds out of six different expense accounts which ran into millions.

In addition, Hitler had another scheme that netted him more than twenty million dollars. This was the issuance of commemorative postage stamps which were sold to stamp collectors throughout the world. These issues were called semi-postals—a stamp sold for a higher value than its value for postage, the difference going to the so-called National Cultural Fund. But this fund was Hitler's own private financial baby, so the money went right into his bank account! It, too, was transferred by Bormann to Lake Viedma.

Another lucrative source of income was the book "Mein Kampf." It earned more than seven million dollars in royalties throughout the world, while inside Germany, it brought Hitler nearly $15,000,000!

An idea of the vast extent of Hitler's hidden fortune can be gained by what was confiscated at the end of the war—when the Allies were able to grab only a fraction of the loot. The US government found $3,000,000 in American currency hidden in the German Embassy in Washington. This was in 1945 after Germany had surrendered. Until that time, the Swiss government had looked after German property. Under international law the United States could seize the Embassy only after surrender, and since Switzerland had handled so much of the transferring of Nazi money, it could have been more than a coincidence that some of the cash was stashed there.

Hitler also got away with another fortune he had order Stored at Neuschwanstein Castle on the Austrian border. From October, 1940, Martin Bormann acting under Der Fuehrer's instructions, used the castle to store priceless art collections stolen from France, the Netherlands, Belgium, Poland and other conquered nations. After the war Dr. Gunther Schiedlausky of the Berlin State Museum appraised the "remains" of the collection at more than fifty million dollars.

Also in the castle US Army officers found a three-quarter mile long tunnel in which was stored gold-encrusted, diamond-studded vessels, collections of precious stones and other jewels of untold value.

Near Hitler's Berchtesgaden retreat, Allied intelligence officers, found $33,000,000 in gold bullion stolen from Hungary. In the retreat itself, Lt. Col. W. P. Machemehl, chief finance officer of the 101st Airborne Division unearthed a $2,642,000 hoard of currency from 26 nations. But evidence was found that at least ten million more in paper currency and gold had been removed form Berchtesgaden by Bormann prior to the entrance of the American forces.

After careful checking, the Allies took an inventory of the money, jewelry, art collections and other valuables stolen by Hitler. The total figures are:

Poland	.... $280,000,000
Czechoslovakia	.... $ 40,000,000
France	.... $470,000,000
Belgium	.... $180,000,000
Netherlands	.... $ 80,000,000
Hungary	.... $140,000,000
Roumania	.... $100,000,000
Norway	.... $ 50,000,000

This loot reached a staggering total of $1,340,000,000. Some of it was recovered and returned to the plundered nations, but thanks to Hitler's two aides, Freude and Bormann, most of this huge fortune was transferred to the Argentine, where it still remains.

The above figures do not include the vast amounts taken

directly from the Third Reich and also sent to the ranch hideout in South America.

The exact total of Hitler's mighty fortune will never be known. His worldwide financial operation was a closely-guarded secret, as carefully hidden from the world as his escape by submarine to Argentina.

Guarded by Storm Troopers

US Intelligence officials feel certain that the entire plot was part of Hitler's long-range plan to finance another Nazi offensive from South America if he lost World War II. And they are convinced that Hitler is still alive on that heavily guarded ranch, but so far no American secret agent has been able to penetrate the curtain of veteran Storm Troopers who watch every road and entrance night and day.

Until the curtain of sub-machine guns is penetrated, the world must assume that one of the world's richest men is guarding his two-billion dollar fortune in a remote retreat in South America, biding his time to strike again.

And that man is Adolf Hitler.

World's Greatest Medium . . .

LUCE VIDI SEES HITLER ALIVE

by KENNETH PETERS

**Her prediction of President Kennedy's
assassination amazed the whole world!**

Madame Luce Vidi, the world-famous medium who had seen in
her crystal ball the assassination of President Kennedy and had
predicted the time of the tragedy, and had also seen the death
of French boxer Marcel Cerdan, the former middleweight champion, in a plane crash, has now revealed that she came face-to-
face with Adolf Hitler.

It was five o'clock in the afternoon, on September 1, 1964, that
the image of a man, tired and shrunken appeared in her crystal ball
while she was sitting in the study of her Paris apartment.

The Face of Hitler

At first it was only a dark silhouette, but bit by bit the face bright-
ened. It was the face of an old man. It was creased and wrinkled,
but there was no gentleness in the lined face, and the eyes had a
fixed, frightening and piercing gaze.

It was the face that had haunted her nightmares ever since
1945, when reports of Hitler's suicide in his Berlin bunker were
blazoned across the front pages of the world's newspapers at that
time. Madame Vidi was overwhelmed with a strange inner percep-
tion that Hitler's presence still hung over Europe.

This is the way Adolf Hitler may look today,
his mustache gone, his hair thinned with age.

The face of the former dictator lingered in Madame Vidi's mind the whole night long. At 5 a.m. the next morning, she consulted the crystal ball again. After 20 minutes of intense concentration, the face reappeared, this time in even clearer detail; and as she stared into the ball, the image grew until Hitler's whole body was revealed.

He looked completely exhausted. He walked with a slight limp, shuffling awkwardly like a senile old man of 76. Yet a quality of ferocity still emanated from the ruined body. Behind smoked glasses, his gaze burned with demented madness and unrelenting hatred.

Hitler was clean-shaven and only a few wisps of white hair straggled over his forehead. There was an ugly scar, probably a souvenir of a previous assassination attempt on the left side of his chin.

The most noteworthy details of the face in the crystal ball, however, were the ears, which stuck out from the skull. The medium explained that the type of ears Hitler had indicate a violent temperament, with dangerous and uncontrollable passions. Hitler's double, the man Luce Vidi believes died in the Berlin bunker in the dictator's place—had ears that were set close to his head.

This would bear out a statement made by Col. W. F. Heimlich, former chief of US Army Intelligence in Berlin, who has said that the blood stains found on the couch in the bunker where Hitler supposedly committed suicide, were *not* the dictator's blood type.

Luce Vidi has one more contribution to make to the Hitler mystery. Where is he hiding?

"All I can tell you," she said to the French press, "is that I saw something behind him when his image appeared in the crystal ball. At first, I thought it was a rock. Then I recognized a large, immobile turtle sleeping on sand, under a blinding sun. So, I was able to identify the place as a tropical country, possibly South America."

Luce Vidi's remarkable revelations confirm the investigations of Jack Comben, correspondent of the *London Daily Express* who, in January, 1964, journeyed to an area in the remote provinces of Rio Negro and Chubut, to investigate reports that, before Germany's defeat, hundreds of hard-core Nazis had purchased 10,000 square miles of land. It had been turned into an impregnable fortress for "very high-placed Nazi war criminals and their followers."

According to Comben, and reported in the May, 1964 issue of the *Police Gazette*, the huge, sprawling, heavily guarded complex is located at Paso Flores, 100 miles north of San Carlos de Bariloche. Is Hitler one of those Nazi war criminals? It seems extremely likely.

The *Police Gazette* has been told from unimpeachable sources that Adolf Hitler, accompanied by a woman, flew out of Berlin on the night of April 30, 1945. They proceeded to a secret Nazi submarine base in Norway, where a U-boat was ready for immediate departure.

On July 10 of that same year, the U-boat put into a port in Argentina and unloaded tons of cargo, including millions in treasure.

The submarine also carried 36 passengers. Neither the German Commander or the Argentine authorities would release any statement concerning the mysterious craft, its cargo, or passengers, except to say that the U-boat was on a routine cruise. This, in spite of the fact that the commander and crew should have surrendered the sub to the Allies on May 2, when Germany surrendered.

US Intelligence agents quickly started their own investigation of the incident but were consistently frustrated in their efforts by the Argentine Government. The mysterious passengers of the submarine were protected by officials and any information concerning them was withheld from our agents.

Later, it was reported to Washington that the Nazis had built an impregnable fortress in the San Carlos de Bariloche area as an escape haven for Adolf Hitler.

So that tropical country which formed the background for the image of Adolf Hitler in Luce Vidi's crystal ball may be Argentina—where the aged despot—his heart brimming with hatred, and his mind full of the days when the sound of his voice shook the world, lives out his time in misery.

Israeli Agent Reveals

EVA BRAUN SEEN ALIVE

by HARVEY WILSON

Eichmann informer spots Hitler's mistress near Fuehrer's hideout in Argentina!

"Eva Braun is alive!" These are the words of one of the Israeli undercover agents, who captured Adolf Eichmann in Argentina.

"The last we knew, she was living in a well-guarded hideout near Paso Flores in the Rio Negro Province of Argentina," the agent told me during an interview in the lobby of the King David Hotel in Jerusalem.

And how does the Israeli secret service agent know this startling fact?

"The same informer, who put the finger on Eichmann for us, told us," the Israeli agent revealed.

Adolf Hitler's mistress being alive confirms the findings of Col. W. F. Heimlich, former Chief of US Army Intelligence, Berlin, who was in charge of the official investigation into the disappearance of Hitler and Eva Braun.

Although much has been written about Hitler, very little has been said about Eva Braun.

Yet, the facts surrounding her disappearance, tell the whole dramatic story of the greatest hoax in history—the purported suicide of Der Fuehrer and his mistress!

Eva Braun, whom Hitler befriended when she was a secretary

in the photographic studio of Heinrich Hoffmann, the Nazi Party's official photographer, and whom Der Fuehrer later made his mistress in 1933, when she was 21, was a frivolous, self-centered girl.

She had no interest in politics and cared less for affairs of state. Of all the people in Hitler's entourage, she was the least likely to commit suicide.

Yet, soon after the Nazi dictator disappeared, reports were circulated that he had married her in his underground bunker—as Allied troops were closing in on Berlin—and that they then both committed suicide.

This theory has been disproved by Allied intelligence.

If Hitler was so insistent that everybody near him commit suicide, how was it that none of his personal secretaries who were closer to him than Eva Braun, and his adjutants who were with him constantly, were never asked to make the supreme sacrifice?

Bodies Never Found

It is a well-known fact that neither Der Fuehrer's nor Eva Braun's body was ever found. It has also been established that it would have been impossible to burn and cremate the corpses in the Reichancellery courtyard.

Yet, the most important clue which Allied intelligence uncovered, indicating that Eva Braun and her dictator-lover had escaped from Berlin, was the telltale fact that *none of Eva's possessions could be found in her bunker*!

Furthermore, every one of Hitler's staff who had remained behind and had been captured, admitted that Eva Braun appeared in "good spirits."

"She never worried about anything. I can't see her taking poison," Heinz Linge, Der Fuehrer's chauffeur, said.

Although Hitler allegedly shot himself to death, while Eva reputedly ended her life by swallowing poison, neither the bottle from which she allegedly drank the poison, nor drops of the drug which might have stained the floor or furniture were ever found.

Furthermore, significant analysis by Allied Intelligence of the blood stains on the couch upon which the Nazi dictator died revealed *they were not of Hitler's blood type!*

There were no bullet holes in the couch—or in the wall behind it!

The best indication that Eva Braun had fled cropped up a few months after the Third Reich collapsed.

A report from Munich, Eva's home town, reached Army intelligence that at Eva Braun's direction, her personal belongings were hidden away in a chosen site in Bavaria.

Treasure Chest Found

Army Intelligence agents, taken to the site by an informer, dug up in an open field a huge treasure chest, containing Eva Braun's personal diary, along with a dozen photo albums, depicting her intimate years with Hitler.

In addition to these hidden secrets were found jewels, as well as thousands of American dollars.

Intelligence agents surmised that the presence of American dollars among Eva Braun's possessions from her Munich apartment, clearly indicated her intention to use the money as a getaway hoard.

Another indication that Eva Braun had fled came from her family, who lived in Munich. Her mother, father (a minor civil servant) and her sisters, Gretel and Ilsa, displayed not the slightest grief, over her reported "death."

Herta Ostermyer, who was Eva's best friend, expressed doubt that Eva would ever swallow poison.

"She loved life too much. She had no interest in governmental affairs Eva loved sports—she was an excellent swimmer—and had a fond ness for animals, the movies and clothes," said Herta.

What subject did Eva like to discuss most?

According to Herta, whenever the girls got together, Eva would gossip about the personal relationships of their friends, the various flatteries of men, and sex.

"In Eva's world," her friend confided, "she separated men into two categories. Either they were attractive or unattractive.

"If she weren't so fearful and loyal to Der Fuehrer, she would have been a real flapper, carrying on affairs with numerous men. She was in love with the pleasures of life!"

How did Eva Braun get to Argentina?

Allied Intelligence sources have long suspected that Hitler flew out of Berlin the night of April 30, 1945. He fled with Eva, and they made their departure in a Flieseler-Storch plane.

They reportedly carried several suitcases and proceeded to a secluded Nazi submarine base in Norway. There, a fully-stocked U-Boat was awaiting them.

It is significant that two German U-Boats arrived a few months later at Mar del Plata, Argentina.

This area in Argentina is easily accessible to the Nazi outpost which Israeli agents found north of San Carlos de Bariloche.

"Before and after the collapse of the Third Reich, top Nazis had purchased thousands of miles of ranchlands in the Rio Negro and Chubut Provinces of Argentina," said an Israeli agent, who spent many years working undercover in this region.

"They virtually bought out all the luxurious hotels in the San Carlos de Bariloche area, which has the same natural beauty as Bavaria.

"Little Nazi Germany"

"This territory in Argentina is known as 'Little Nazi Germany' and is not far from the Chilean border," the Israeli agent continued. "Over $400,000,000 of Nazi funds were transferred to Argentine banks, through Switzerland, in the last days of Hitler's rule.

"It was with this money that Hitler's top aides, who escaped, purchased this land."

It was in this area that Israeli agents infiltrated into the German communities and learned the whereabouts of Eichmann, Eva Braun, and other top Nazis.

The Israelis, picked for the mission because they spoke German fluently, looked like Aryan Germans. They affected a Prussian military bearing and operated from San Carlos de Bariloche.

"We picked San Carlos de Bariloche as our permanent base," the Israeli agent said, "because it is a well-known luxury resort for wealthy Germans.

"They come to this place from all over the world. Visitors include many dignitaries from Europe. Besides beautiful hotels, there are also estates and ranches in this area. Our presence there didn't arouse any suspicion.

"And it was here," the Israeli agent confided, "that we made contact with a man high in Nazi circles, who put the finger on Eichmann, enabling us to capture the former chief of the Gestapo unit who was responsible for killing 6,000,000 Jews.

"It was from this same source that we learned Eva Braun was alive—living in a Nazi fortress near Paso Flores with other top Nazis. According to our informant, she hasn't changed much," the Israeli said.

"Her blonde hair is now streaked with gray, but otherwise she's still trim and shapely. She was 33 years old when she disappeared. Now she's 54, and clearly recognizable."

Israeli Intelligence believes that Eva Braun is living in a Nazi settlement on the bank of the swift flowing Limsy River, 100 miles north of San Carlos de Bariloche, where the Nazis have created the most extraordinary surviving outpost of Hitler's Germany in the world today.

German men and women pursue a secret existence under strict discipline. Strangers cannot penetrate into the immediate region of the Nazi fortress.

The men wear Afrika Korps-style uniforms, with the same type caps that Field Marshal Rommel's elite army wore in the desert campaigns.

"This Nazi camp is protected by armed guards," the Israeli agent revealed. "No one can get within five miles of it."

"And the man who is the commandant of this Nazi fortress is Walthar Ochaner, former top officer of Hitler's personal communications unit.

"On several occasions," the agent related, "When we drove up the highway leading toward Paso Flores, we were stopped by armed guards when we tried to detour on private roads leading to the Nazi encampment. As a result, we had no choice but to turn back."

After the Israeli agents seized Eichmann while he was walking down a Buenos Aires street and flew him to Israel, all agents were recalled from Argentina because of the international crisis that resulted.

Today, undoubtedly, the armed guard around the Nazi fortress where Eva Braun reportedly lives in her own Nazi world, has been strengthened.

POSITIVE PROOF: HITLER IN ARGENTINA

by GEORGE McGRATH

Argentina shields Nazi wealth—and Hitler . . . Allies fear Der Fuehrer's capture could cause international complications . . .

Indisputable evidence that Adolf Hitler is alive and living in the Argentine has been uncovered by the *Police Gazette*. Although this new information is in the hands of Government intelligence chiefs, the United States and its allies are not lifting a finger to catch the runaway Nazi dictator.

A Government official has told us the reason. He says Hitler would be the biggest global hot potato in history if caught. The governments of the world, in fact, wouldn't know what to do with him.

The *Police Gazette* in 1951 dug up and published absolute proof that Hitler's purported suicide was a fake. This magazine also produced overwhelming evidence that the deposed tyrant was hiding in Argentina.

Incontrovertible new information now backs up our exclusive reports in every detail. Documents in the files of Allied intelligence authorities have been examined by this reporter and the facts verified by the highest counter-espionage sources.

American officials possess sensational reports telling how the Nazis moved thousands of men and women and close to a billion dollars from Germany to South America. More important, these papers describe the Nazis' strategy for the future.

Capture Would Divide Free World

What, then, is blocking a concerted effort to round up the Hitlerite plotters?

First, according to one of the highest ranking intelligence officials in Washington, the major World War II Allies fear the effects of Hitler's capture on the current international picture. They are afraid it would reopen the 15-year-old scars of the war.

The capture would divide the nations of the free world. The Kremlin would undoubtedly twist and distort these squabbles in an attempt to prolong them.

The effects within Germany could be even more serious. The West is trying to unite the German population on our side in the struggle against Red tyranny. But Hitler's return would create unprecedented division and controversy among the Germans.

Some Germans would insist that Hitler be executed. Others would want to leave him alone. Fanatics might even be impelled to try to return him to power through a putsch.

The eagerness of the Allies to let sleeping dogs lie was illustrated unexpectedly only this fall. A man first identified as Martin Bormann, Hitler's evil genius and trusted deputy, was seized in Argentina. The man denied he was Bormann.

Before any detailed investigation could be made—and without even allowing time for the flying of anti-Nazi witnesses from Europe—Argentine officials accepted the man's claim.

Was the suspect really Bormann?

Washington officials are sure of this much: Bormann definitely did go to Argentina after Nazi hopes of victory flickered out in 1945. Also, Bormann was a key figure in the organizing of Nazi colonies in South America.

If the powers that be were so determined to back away from Bormann—or his double—imagine their reaction to the apprehension of Hitler.

At the heart of the Argentine hands-off attitude is the tremendous political and economic power wielded in Argentina by the Germans, including many wanted Nazis. The Germans are particularly strong in the vast, sparsely settled areas of Patagonia. Using funds funneled from Germany late in the war, the Nazis bought thousands of square miles of ranchland. Armed Germans keep strangers from even entering these sprawling holdings.

The information which follows—like the new revelations about Hitler—has been obtained from official files and previously unrevealed official documents.

Nazi Haven in Argentina

In November, 1943, eighteen months before the war ended, the Nazi high command chose Argentina as a prospective haven in case of defeat. Argentina was already a virtual ally of Germany. German officers were in high positions in the army and German industrialists controlled a big segment of the economy.

Key figures in the Argentine government were Nazi sympathizers. Juan Peron, later Argentina's dictator, had even marched into Paris with Hitler when the Nazis crushed France.

Immediately after the decision of November, 1943, Hitler ordered Willie Koehn, chief of the Latin American section of the German foreign office, to travel to Argentina by U-boat. Koehn slipped through the Allied blockade with 40 large crates.

The boxes contained Der Fuehrer's personal valuables, as well as millions of dollars worth of jewels, paintings and other items which the Nazis had seized in occupied countries. The submarine surfaced off the coast of the Mar Del Plata. A tugboat operated by Buenos Aires' Defino Line—then Axis-controlled—brought the crates ashore.

Allied intelligence agents verified this information by grilling Koehn after the war. More details came from seized foreign office documents.

Hitler's Suicide a Hoax

New pieces in the jigsaw have been added year by year ever since. Much of the freshest information comes from former German agents now working for other countries.

American intelligence officers determined soon after the war that the Hitler suicide story was a hoax. US experts made exhaustive chemical tests in Hitler's bunker, where he was supposed to have died of bullet wounds. They found bloodstains, but not of Hitler's type. Outside the bunker, where the bodies of Hitler and Eva Braun, his mistress, were supposedly burned and buried, our technicians found not so much as a single human tooth.

In tracing the flight of the top Nazis, Allied intelligence has established that $750 million in Nazi wealth was transferred from Germany to the Argentine in the war's waning days.

Hermann Goering shipped out $25 million in cash.

Admiral Karl Doenitz, named by Hitler as his successor, sent a fortune to a relative, Edmundo Wagenknecht, owner of a big import-export firm in Buenos Aires.

Joachim von Ribbentrop sent $500,000 to the Argentine firm "Securitas" in the name of his cousin, Martin, a Buenos Aires businessman. Von Ribbentrop also had $10 million deposited in Argentina in the name of Pedro Rodriguez Panchino.

But the most vital currency transfer came when $200 million was forwarded to top Hitler aides in the German embassy. This money, believed earmarked for Hitler and his personal entourage, was used to buy a tremendous slice of Patagonia.

Nazi Wealth

Allied intelligence agents now know that all the currency transfers went from the Dresdener Bank of Berlin to the Schweizerischer Bankverein in Switzerland. From Switzerland the money went to the Argentine.

Once the funds arrived in Argentina, they were shifted around with typical German efficiency. Some cash was used to acquire control of blue chip industrial firms in various Latin American republics.

Other millions were diverted to the Nazi underground transportation network. This secret network enabled thousands of Nazis to flee Germany. By circuitous routes they traveled from Germany to Spain, then to Argentina. Karl Adolf Eichmann, captured in Argentina early this year by Israeli agents, reached South America this way.

In 1944 General Arturo Rawson, leader of the Argentine coup which ousted the civilian government, told a US embassy official confidentially that many top Nazi technicians and party bigwigs were already in his country.

On January 22, 1945, on the letterhead of the German Ministry of War, Heinrich Himmler notified Nazi gauleiters in Europe that certain party leaders would be sent abroad on a top secret mission. The next month 340 Nazi stalwarts received orders to leave. All were traced to Argentina.

Six weeks after Germany collapsed, a number of Nazi submarines sought refuge in the Argentine. The Argentine government acknowledged that some had arrived. But the most significant arrivals were kept secret.

Allied intelligence knows that in the summer of 1945 Hitler and Eva Braun disembarked from a U-boat off the Argentine coast in the vicinity of San Clemente del Tuya. Eva was wearing masculine attire. One source of this information is a top Nazi who had also been landed by submarine. This man, nabbed long afterwards in Montevideo, Uruguay, received immunity from prosecution when he turned informer.

Spruille Braden, then US ambassador to Argentina, received the San Clemente del Tuya report and asked the Argentine government for an explanation. Argentine officials insisted the report was false, but refused to give any further information. Braden thereupon sent US intelligence operatives into the San Clemente del Tuya area.

They received nearly 100 eyewitness reports from natives who said two submarines off the coast had delivered a large number of persons to rowboats. The boats headed for a remote section of the shore. Natives who got too close to the landing site were turned back by armed guards described as Germans.

Shortly after Braden started his investigation, a respected democratic newspaper, *Critica*, published in Buenos Aires, reported from an authoritative government source that Hitler and his top Nazi aides had been transported to South America. The publisher immediately received this threat:

"Stop the presses and suppress that story."

Critica did not yield. A band of armed Nazis, shouting "Heil Hitler" and "Long Live Germany," stormed the paper and tried to burn down its building. Truckloads of newspapers were burned in the streets. Before the siege ended, two persons had been killed.

The Intense search for Hitler by the Allies immediately after the war was stymied by the lack of Argentine cooperation. Braden has told the *Police Gazette*:

"If the Argentine government had cooperated with us we could have captured the top Nazis. We had information from the best informed and most authoritative sources that Hitler as well as Martin Bormann was hiding out in Patagonia.

"When I sent my agents there to investigate, they were ordered out of the region by armed guards who were Germans. Without the cooperation of the Argentine government, we were powerless to capture anyone there."

Government Shields Dictator

It remains up to the Argentine government today to decide whether Hitler will ever be captured. As Braden put it: "Unless the Nazi element in the Argentine can be extirpated, it will remain a serious threat for the future."

In 1949, British intelligence, in rounding up a Nazi underground cell in Berlin, discovered documents which linked Bormann with the rebirth of Nazism there. And, significantly, the correspondence of top Nazi leaders in Argentina still closes with "Heil Hitler."

Over the years since the war Argentine governments have come and gone. Dictator Peron has long since been booted into exile. But the Nazi element is so well heeled and firmly entrenched in Argentina that the ups and downs of one regime or another have no effect on it. No matter who is in power in Buenos Aires, he must play ball with the Germans.

And the future?

Although the Allies have lost interest in Hitler, the Nazis have not lost interest in the conquest of the world. Top-secret documents confirm that the Nazis are biding their time patiently, maintaining ties with sympathizers in Germany and dickering sporadically with the East German Communists—just as Hitler once dickered with Stalin.

The Nazis are waiting for the right moment for a new power grab. With their tremendous buildup of strength in Argentina, the "right moment" for the Nazis might come sooner than either Americans or Europeans expect.

The Ever-Looming Threat of the Nazi Party

You know that friend you had when you were younger who would tell these outlandish stories about what he'd done or witnessed in his life? The one you thought was making it all up, until one day you found out at least some of it was actually true? And from that point on you opened up to the possibility that maybe, just maybe, everything he said was true? In this section, your friend the *Police Gazette* gives you that moment.

The *Gazette* claims the Socialist Reich Party, the successor to the Nazi party in post-war Germany, was getting support and direction from both former Nazis and the Soviet Union. Think of it, Hitler—assuming he's alive—and Stalin working together to bring Nazis back to power in Germany. But it gets better; the *Gazette* claims that not only did the Soviets give support to the SRP, but that the SRP was also getting more support than the West German Communist Party! The reader would be within reason to declare "Ridiculous! This could never happen." But do a little research, then come back and tell the *Police Gazette* it's wrong. We'll wait. . . .

The *Police Gazette* goes in depth into the very real issue of a resurgence of right-wing extremism in Germany. Because most top Nazis either fled or were brought to justice at Nuremberg doesn't mean there weren't still tens of thousands of true believers left behind from the rank and file who'd gone through twelve years of indoctrination plus the embarrassment of a lost war. These were the kind with violent tendencies and chips on their shoulders looking for something to do, the kind that almost made mince meat out of Paul McCartney during the Beatles' tenure in Hamburg in 1960. And the *Gazette* correctly points out how the West German government struggled to keep this burbling underground in check for at least twenty years after the war.

So, you're a Nazi—with a very particular skill set—who decides Germany is not the place to practice your craft anymore.

Could a freelance consultancy be in your future? "Have swastika, will travel?" The *Police Gazette* lets us know Juan Perón wasn't the only one hiring. Gamal Abdel Nasser of Egypt also found a need for experienced professionals in the fields of eliminating enemies and creating empires. When one door closes, another opens. Indeed.

HITLER'S AIDES ARE SHAPING THE NEW GERMANY

by GEORGE McGRATH

WANTED: Martin Bormann, Hitler's secret ambassador.
The Allies are looking for him.

Though Adolf Hitler is hidden away in the Antarctic, there is good reason to believe his presence is felt very strongly in Germany today. How is this possible? It is possible because the image of Hitler still serves for countless Germans as a reminder of the good old days. It is also possible because agents of Hitler's dreams and ideas are fanning the flames of Nazism in Germany and wherever persons of Nazi sympathies live throughout the world today. Chief among these agents is Martin Bormann.

In Hitler's last will (*Police Gazette*, January, 1951) Bormann was named Minister of the Nazi Party. Observers of the German political scene feel sure Bormann is acting in that capacity today. Though other Nazis of record—including Major General Otto Ernst Remer of the Socialist Reich Party—are the nominal leaders of the new Nazi movements, there is conclusive evidence that Bormann is the behind-the-scenes force directing the entire organization.

How strong is the Nazi movement in Germany today? According to reports on Western Germany by John J. McCloy, US High Commissioner, the neo-Nazis, represented by the SRP are a resurging political threat. "They invent scandal and rumors about the democratic parties and parliamentary leaders and dub anyone who opposed Hitler a traitor. They vilify the Allies and seek to distort Allied policy and the genuine desire of the Western Powers to bring Germany back into the community of nations as a democratic partner."

Last year, McCloy's report continues, the SRP garnered 11 percent of the total vote in the state elections in lower Saxony. In Bavaria, for example, 15,000 of the 35,000 government employees are former Nazis. The same is true throughout Western Germany.

Clever former party members are, in most cases, directing the new Nazi movement. But one-time Nazis who knew him in the old days feel sure that even the cleverest are taking orders from Hitler through Martin Bormann.

Bormann, they indicate, is not only rallying Nazi sympathies in Germany, he is rounding up would-be members of the new movement all over the world. Since the end of World War II, reliable reports have indicated Bormann has been, at one time or another, in Russia, Italy, Spain, Chile, and in various parts of the Russian, American and British zones of Germany. And wherever he has appeared, he has left his mark.

Whether luck, or fate, Hitler chose Bormann for the role he now plays, it was a strategic choice. A veteran of two world wars, he was a fanatic Nazi up until the surrender of Germany, Even then, with Russian forces almost smothering Berlin, he made a frantic attempt to rally the German people in a last-ditch fight.

Bormann is 52 years old. He was born in Halberstadt, in Eastern Germany. At an early age, he acquired a taste for war, violence and struggle. After serving the German forces in World War I, he joined a volunteer group in the Baltic states to fight the Russians. A few years later he was active with the effervescing ultra-nationalist groups that were a part of the German political scene in the early twenties. He was involved in some political assassinations perpetrated by one of the groups, and in March, 1924, was convicted as an accomplice and sent to prison for a year.

Less than two years after leaving prison, he joined the Nazi party. Like a number of others who were later to gain prominent posts, Bormann started with the Nazi party press. He worked up to a position of importance in the SA, and when Hitler came to power, he was named chief of staff to Rudolph Hess. By 1942, he had become secretary to Hitler, an honorary official of the SS, and he had pledged to give his life for the Fuehrer.

When Berlin fell on May 2, 1945, and the Chancellery was in ruins, rumors said that Bormann, as well as Hitler, had died. It soon became obvious that both men were very much alive. Four months after the end of the war, American intelligence picked up a report from Scandinavia to the effect that "Martin Bormann made a 22-minute speech yesterday (August 21) on a secret radio station. This speech was heard in Stockholm. The secret radio reported that 'Hitler is alive and in good health and that loyal Nazis will once more make themselves conspicuous as soon as proceedings against Goering and other Nazis end.'"

Party fanatics didn't have long to wait. During the next few years Bormann was reported at various places in the American and French zones of occupation. Military police and constabulary forces of the occupation armies were called out on short notice to blanket, block off, and search large areas of the country. Their tips, forwarded from otherwise reliable sources, always came too late. Bormann was never uncovered.

About this time the story was circulated that Bormann had escaped to Russia, or at least had access to the Russian zone and to Russia. This was stated flatly, in May 26, 1948, by former SS Obergruppenfuehrer Gottlob Berger, while he was testifying in the Wilhelmstrasse trial.

Berger explained that Bormann, to his knowledge, was a secret confidant of the Kremlin and had escaped to Russia when the collapse came. He added that he had noticed Hitler's orders concerning the treatment of Western powers had become more severe towards the end of the war, and that this was undoubtedly due to the influence of Bormann to the fuehrer. Already the sinister mind of Hitler's crafty lieutenant was shaping the pattern of things to come in the German post-war scheme.

The testimony of Berger was expanded, outside the court, by Dr. Froeschmann, his counsel, who stated that Berger was firmly convinced Bormann was in Russia and would appear as Commissar General for Germany "when Russia is able to gather all of Germany into her sphere of influence."

Saw Bormann with Russians

Subsequent developments indicated that Berger may have known only half the story. Early in 1949, the *Marburger Presse* interviewed Vassilie Vassilevsky, a Soviet officer who had fled to Western Germany. Vassilevsky declared he had substantial information on the activities of Martin Bormann in the Russian zone, based on material accessible to him in his capacity as political officer of the Red Army. He claimed to have seen Bormann behind Russian lines.

Vassilevsky called attention to a speech in 1947 by the chief of the political section of a Soviet guard division who stated "A leading NSDP (Nazi party) politician and personal friend of Hitler's helped the USSR in its struggle against Hitler's Germany to its victorious end."

The ex-Soviet officer also pointed out that Bormann's name had rarely been mentioned by Soviet war propaganda and that, in contrast to other leading figures, Bormann had maintained an attitude of positive self-assurance in the fuehrer's bunker up to the end. Subsequent events have indicated good reason for this assurance.

More recent reports have quoted a Russian major in Berlin who described Bormann as "our best technician in civil war." Traveling under false papers provided by the Soviet secret police, sometimes using an alias, sometimes not, Bormann has moved all over the world, encouraging, coordinating and stimulating the underground movement which—financed by Russia—is attempting to mold a striking force around a core of former SS officers.

The pivotal force, which has enabled Bormann to work for the Communists while conveying Hitler's orders as well, is an effort to undermine and destroy the influence of Great Britain and the United States, and restore to Germany its unity—under a Nazi regime. Hitler's genius—as executed through Bormann—perceives that the most direct and effective way to that goal is through the Russians.

Bormann started playing the Russian game in short order. It has been revealed that, early in 1946, he had so completely sold himself to the Russians that they dispatched him—accompanied by a former Gestapo official named Wilhelm Koener—to China where the instructed Mao Tsetung in the organizing of a secret police force which would have the ruthless, fascistic effectiveness of the Gestapo.

Between trips for the Russians, Bormann returned to rally forces in Germany. On February 7, 1949, the editorial office of a weekly Munich news magazine received—following publication of an article entitled "Martin Bormann—Stalin's Gauleiter"—a letter signed "M.B." and posted in nearby Wurzburg. It protested statements made in the article. Handwriting experts established the fact that the letter was written in the same hand as a letter of Bormann to Admiral Doenitz, dated April 29, 1945.

During this time, intelligence sources had received reports from Chile, Spain, and Turkey, indicated Martin Bormann had been seen in each of these places, Rumors have indicated he was also in Argentina, a hotbed of Nazi activity and for a long time a haven for fascists who fled Europe at the end of World War II. Four prominent Germans now in Argentina, according to reports, are General Adolf Galland, the Luftwaffe's leading tactician; Kurt

Tank, the Focke-Wulf designer; Guido Beck, Czech atomic scientist who aided Nazi experiments; and Hans Ulrich Rudel, the Luftwaffe's fighter ace.

Heads Ring of Smugglers

One of the most recent corroborated reports indicated Bormann has been in Italy. The report, picked up by American intelligence officials in 1950, indicated a young smuggler, arrested near Levanto, had stated that Bormann was alive and living on the Italian Riviera. He had entered Italy, the report continues, thanks to a clandestine organization for the expatriation of German war criminals to South America via Genoa. The young smuggler named Bormann as head of the organization. He also added that Bormann had changed his name to Becker and had undergone operations to change his appearance.

But, Bormann's chief role has been in Germany itself, where, since 1948, a host of political parties under the ultra-nationalistic banner have cropped up to plague the government of chancellor Konrad Adenauer. For the most part, these parties have directed their appeal to former Nazis, refugees, landed aristocracy, professional soldiers, and other dissatisfied elements in Germany. Most of these appeals have been ineffective, at best.

One exception to the generally weak extreme-rightists however, is the Socialist Reich Party (SRP), which seems to have high-level masterminding, reminiscent of the old Nazi Party itself. In a recent Lower Saxony election the SRP polled some 367,000 votes, enough to seat 16 SRP candidates in the state legislature.

It's almost impossible to distinguish the philosophy and tactics of the SRP from those of the Nazi Party, Military music plays throughout the meetings, and strong-arm squads, insignia, and violently emotional appeals all are mindful of the Nazi regime of old.

The SRP speakers have revived the "stab in the back" legend to explain the defeat of the Third Reich. All Germans who opposed

Hitler are termed traitors. Significantly, the SRP, favors the creation of Europe as a "Third Force" between East and West.

It is this "Third Force" lure that points up the relationship of communism to Hitler's orders for the revival of the Nazis in Germany. The Communists, too, have baited their line with talk of a "Third Force." And there are other signs of the close kinship that Bormann apparently has brought about by working for the Communists and Hitler at the same time.

Obvious Appeal to Communists

At neutralist conferences, such as the so-called German Congress in Frankfurt last year, Communists and Communist stooges openly rubbed shoulders with SRP delegates. More significantly, the Communists and their youth auxiliaries, no longer interfere with SRP meetings. During the Lower Saxony elections, even Communist hecklers stayed away from SRP rallies. Bormann's spadework in setting up a mutual admiration society between the interests of Hitler and Stalin seems to be paying off. Hitler, in his Antarctic hideout, can well afford to gloat.

Even the Communist press in Germany all but ignored the SRP showing in Lower Saxony. This was in spite of the fact that the SRP has an obvious tie with the Communist line which shouts to the German voters that Western Germany is definitely on the high road to fascism again.

In mid-1951, Commissioner McCloy's pungent observations on the SRP-Communist kinship were strengthened by reports from competent German observers. Federal Chancellor Konrad Adenauer, voicing the view of many of his countrymen, stated that close connections existed between certain radicals of the right and the Communists, with both groups deriving financial support from the same source. This support is now estimated at hundreds of thousands of dollars.

If anything Adenauer's statement seems mild. But it does bear out the fact that Hitler, in dispatching Bormann to set up an alliance with the Russians in 1946, had lost none of his canny sense of timing. In short order, the Communists were so sold by Bormann that they now dip from the same larder as the neo-Nazis in order to influence Germans with their propaganda lines which are now a blend of Communist and fascist doctrine.

So far, any attempts to outlaw the Socialist Reich Party have been ineffective. Bormann has seen to that, through methods known only to a selected few, high in the party's brain-trust. The SRP continues, in spite of the fact that it is the successor organization of the Nazi Party by its very origin, its leaders, its internal organization, its program, its propaganda and the conduct of its followers, Its aim is to impair the democratic systems of Germany's Federal Republic. To do this, Bormann and other leaders of the SRP have recalled to use the guile which helped establish the Nazi Party in years past. The activities of the democratic parties are systematically defamed. Rumor-mills are rampant. Officials are accused of treason. And everyone who has negotiated with the Allies has been warned that he may have to face future court action. A growing feeling of uneasiness and insecurity threatens the Germans who cross the SRP. The terror of midnight raids, brutal interruption of privacy, and a feeling that life—once again, as in the Hitler days—is cheap, and dispensable, crowds the German horizon. Most Germans don't have to tax their imaginations to know what is coming.

So far, the SRP has a standard answer whenever legal measures are suggested, in an effort to combat their activities. They call this "terrorism," and say that it must be countered with terrorism, thus offering an excuse for the continuation of their insidious work.

Neo Nazis Follow Hitler

Meanwhile, the Socialist Reich Party is growing. Bormann, acting as the go-between, advises party spokesmen of the line that Hitler has formulated in an effort to spread the party's influence throughout Germany and the world.

Such a party spokesman is tall, fiery Otto Remer, whose normally steady eyes take on a glassy glow when he addresses large audiences, much the same as Hitler's when he used to speak. Some members of Germany's democratic parties dismiss Remer's political addresses contemptuously. But Remer says things the German people want to hear.

"Within two years, we shall be marching again," he once said. Later, he added, "Once we are in power we shall soon right matters." The words are ominously reminiscent of the rumbling past. They could have been written again by Hitler himself.

WILL STALIN BOMB U.S. WITH HITLER'S SECRET WEAPON?

by GEORGE McGRATH

The Fuehrer's plans to rain death on American cities are in Stalin's hands. Will he use them?

Are the most fearsome and deadly weapons yet devised by mankind poised today for the destruction of the United States? Will pilotless, radar-controlled bombs of hitherto unimaginable power be launched with devastating effect against every major city in America at the push of a button?

The safety of these cities, and the lives of their millions of inhabitants, depends upon the unpredictable whimsey of one of the most bloodthirsty, callous, and soulless dictators ever recorded in the history of the human race—Joseph Stalin.

Stalin's threat to the United States lies not in the distant future. It is ever-present, immediate and MOST URGENT.

For it is now known to American military leaders in the Pentagon that Stalin possesses the secret of Hitler's most potent and secret weapons—ones which were being tested and which would have been used against New York if the Allied armies had not advanced faster than anticipated by German scientists.

Hitler's weapons were rudimentary in 1945 but they were still capable of immense destruction both materially and psychologically. Yet the most important factor was that Hitler's scientists had blueprints on their boards depicting the tremendous aerial monsters of the future—and how to build them.

Scientists Made Prisoner

If the War had lasted a few more months these drawing-board weapons would have been launched across more than 4,000 miles of land and ocean to strike directly at the Nazis' principle opponent in the war—the United States.

As Germany's agony drew to an end in April 1945, a three-pronged drive was launched by the United States, Britain and Russia to capture German scientists and their secret weapon development. At the same time, Hitler and Martin Bormann planned the evacuation of many of the Nazis' top-flight research engineers and scientists, who escaped by U-boat through the Allied Atlantic blockade.

Stalin's secret police failed to seize any atomic secrets or German experimentation on heavy water potentialities in Norway. But they did capture several of Germany's leading scientists, laboratory technicians and construction experts, as well as an important number of blueprints.

For the past seven years these German scientists and technicians have been working under close guard hand in hand with Soviet scientists. They are not treated as prisoners but as collaborators for, to these men there was only one master—science. They had exchanged one Fuehrer for another but scientific research continued unabated.

They worked well and they worked hard. Today Stalin's weapons are ready; his bases prepared. The giant jet-rockets lie on their launching ramps aimed at their targets—the chief cities of the United States and Canada. Only the warheads of atomic explosive, paralyzing gas or some, as yet, undisclosed weapon have not yet been rammed into place—the work of but a few hours.

The threat is imminent but let us assess calmly the origin and potentialities of these secret weapons that Stalin stole from Hitler. Let us coolly evaluate this race to conquer the world between Stalin, with his immense Soviet springboard, and Hitler, who has hitched his hopes for return to power, as the leader of an anti-Communist Western crusade, upon the retorts and laboratory equipment of the scientists who are in hiding with him in his Antarctic Shangri-La.

For arrogantly concealed in his Antarctic Shangri-La, Adolf Hitler disdainfully watched the Allies go through the farce of pronouncing him dead and partially cremated. He must have laughed when he saw reports of his suicide and chuckled in his singularly mirthless manner when he read that his body had never been found. He knew he was alive. He also knew that the men in Allied governments know he was alive. But he know, too, that these men would never admit he had escaped their impenetrable mesh and flown to a new haven, from which he was preparing a new blood-bath.

Let us also evaluate the strength of ourselves and our Allies in this field of scientific atomic and supersonic destruction and what resources we have to deter or parry the will to war of two mad-dog enemies:

Hitler's reversal at the hand of the Russians in 1942 had precipitated a change in his war plans. No longer could he rely upon German industry to produce an unending stream of tanks, planes and the thousand and one other weapons needed by an army in modern warfare. Every day that passed saw the United States' war potentiality augmenting as more factories came into full war production. It was but a matter of time before the preponderance of power inevitably would swing to the Allies.

He made the decision to switch his Number One priority to the laboratories of his scientists, Secret bases were established in Norway, Holland and Germany. Orders were given that the scientists "must" produce new and powerful weapons with which the Allies could be beaten.

I knew more of Hitler's development of "secret weapons" than the average man in those days of wartime hush-hush because I was part of an Air Force team which flew photographic reconnaissance over these hide-away laboratories and testing grounds. Day after day, our fast twin-engined Mosquito airplanes would force through to Peenemunde or over the Norwegian testing grounds with automatic cameras churning as we flew at 40,000 or more feet. We were unarmed since the weight of photographic equipment precluded guns, and we relied on our speed to escape the Messerschmidt interceptors.

These photographs were interpreted by experts. We followed closely the development of his two major secret weapons—the V-1, irreverently called the "doodlebug" by the British, because it chug-chugged its way over London with the noise of a motorcycle, approximating a self-propelled 1,000 pound bomb, and the V-2, a stratospheric rocket-bomb, which arrived without warning due to its faster-than-sound speed.

Apart from photographic reconnaissance the Allies had a spy track into Germany's war plans and Hitler's switch-over to the laboratories after his failure to cross either the English Channel or the steppes of Russia. Britain's Number One Intelligence agent was an anonymous person, obviously highly placed in the secret councils of Hitler's Reich, and his identity became known only in the latter days of the war, after his murder.

The "Yellow Bird"

It was Admiral Wilhelm Canaris, Chief of Germany's Counter-Intelligence Service.

Nothing could happen in Germany without the Admiral knowing it . . . while he lived.

Admiral Canaris was the mysterious "Yellow Bird," who sent the Allies vital information. He even told the British Staff of Hitler's 1940 invasion of France and the Lowlands nearly three months before the event. Suspicious, they disregarded it. The Maginot Line was "impregnable."

According to his own lights, Admiral Canaris was no traitor. He and his friends were old-vintage Junkers. They hated this village upstart, Hitler. They despised his domineering and ill-bred fascists.

They were willing to play ball while he re-armed Germany; moved back into the Rhineland; regained the Saar and seized Austria. All this belonged to the Fatherland, they considered. But when, by his rape of Czechoslovakia, he showed his lust for power had no limit, they turned against him. Wisely, they foresaw the danger to Germany of a World War.

Canaris made six attempts to kill Hitler. His sixth and last was the bomb-plot in Hitler's Russian headquarters. The Fuehrer had left the room a few seconds before the bomb exploded. Canaris had overstepped the mark. The plot was traced back to him. He was arrested, sent to jail, tortured horrendously and then executed. A Nazi butcher strangled him with a wire noose as Allied troops approached. The "Yellow Bird"—the "Mr. X" of all mystery stories and plots—was dead. But he had opened the Allies' eyes to Nazi secret weapons.

German military scientists began experimenting with these V-2 rockets before the war but it was only in 1943 that this bomb was ordered for mass construction by Hitler.

Dr. Walter Dornberger, former German expert on the development of flying bombs and one of the "brains" behind the V-1 and V-2, who is now a resident of the United States, has stated categorically that the World War would have taken a different course if Hitler had supported the project earlier, instead of waiting until "two years too late."

"The bomb could have been in production by 1942," says Dr. Dornberger, "but Hitler had not removed his opposition."

Dr. Dornberger said that experiments with these big rockets started several years before the War and that the famed V-2, which fell noiselessly out of the blue on London workers just after the invasion of Normandy, was "the outcome of 60,000 changes made to the first trial model."

Dr. Dornberger gave a slight indication as to the lines upon which Hitler's scientists are now working when he told a recent International Astronautical conference, that space travel to Mars today was "technically feasible" but there was little point in concentrating on it until such time as scientists had developed new fuels which would shorten such a voyage to four months instead of the present four-year estimated period.

Hitler is undoubtedly working on new fuels. But his goal is not the conquest of space for man but the conquest of the earth for himself.

There is no doubt today but that both Hitler's scientists, and those working on the plans Stalin stole in Germany, have succeeded in perfecting this death-dealing robot to the point where it can be guided or directed to vulnerable targets with almost pin-point accuracy.

No scientist, or even a Washington Pentagon general, will deny today that it is more than "just possible" for such a robot weapon to be accurately aimed at a city target *more than 3,000 miles away.*

There would be no warning. These stratospheric rockets travel many times faster than the speed of sound. They would blast into the target before the noise of their passage was near the ground— just as their much slower counterparts did in the London blitzkrieg days of 1944. Again there would be no time for radar warnings. And if such a warning were given, there is no weapon in our possession *today* which could intercept the target and destroy it before it blasted our cities.

According to information leaking out of Russia, the Soviets have constructed and are busily rushing additional construction of launching sites for these supersonic rockets. These sites are located within striking distance of the leading American and Canadian cities and industrial plants. The deadly robot missiles would streak far above the North Pole on their way to the target areas.

Hitler's Three Weapons

In his secret Antarctic laboratories, Hitler has established some of the most elaborate scientific equipment known to the world today. Around him are gathered, according to reports from Argentina and Colombia, a select handful of top-ranking Germany "brains" and a great number of the younger men who once served their apprenticeship during the early days of the war.

In this lonely hide-away, Adolf Hitler and his scientists are pressing to completion at least three secret weapons with which they hope one day to gain a final, complete and devastating victory

A few details have leaked out concerning the scientists' experiments and work. Through South American sources, Allied agents have learned that Der Fuehrer's technicians have perfected a nerve gas more powerful than anything the Allies possess; that they have pushed development of stratospheric bomb-head rockets to a point where both great range and precision bombing have been attained, and that they have evolved a type of bomb more closely resembling our hydrogen bomb than the atom bomb.

These three weapons alone, used ruthlessly and without warning, could ensure victory for any one nation.

It is in the nerve gas that the German scientists in hiding are reported to be furthest advanced. Both the United States and England have been developing this gas with the help of Hitler's wartime German scientists captured at the close of hostilities. England recently announced that her nerve gas would destroy the nervous systems of any who breathed it and might bring death.

But Hitler's scientists are reported to have already gone far beyond that stage. Agents in South America return with reports that they have developed a gas which can be used effectively over an area of several miles and that the effects of this gas will paralyze the enemy's nerves ONLY for a few hours. During this time, the gas-using troops will push forward, occupy the terrain, disarm the paralyzed victims, sit down and wait for them to recover and then march them off as prisoners. Not a shot would have been fired and there would be no casualties. It would be a total and bloodless victory.

Nevertheless, Stalin, working on the sound basis of the plans he stole from Hitler and using the brains of many of Hitler's leading scientists, has a tremendous advantage.

He has the whole industrial and military resources of Russia to fall back upon while Hitler lacks all but the technical know-how to build a limited number of these weapons.

Stalin is probably not so far advanced in either atom bomb or hydrogen bomb research as the United States. But he has atom bombs. The destructive power of these bombs may be only half that of the American bombs; they may have only the power of the "lightweight" bomb which tore the heart out of Hiroshima.

But Stalin has the initiative of all dictators when they go to war. And scores of these "lightweight" atom bombs, falling suddenly on our cities, could well spell the destruction and conquest of this country of ours.

What have we with which to parry such weapons and to deter dictators from using them?

The United States' stockpile of atom bombs is the greatest in the world and the thought of the vast retaliation devastation might well deter an aggressor.

Again both England and the United States have made great progress with wholly automatic aggressor-destroying guided missiles. These self-guided missiles pilot themselves towards the enemy in the air. Unlike the hit-and-miss land artillery, their mechanism leads them inevitably to an explosive point of contact with the enemy. These missiles, when perfected, would shoot down even the fastest supersonic and stratospheric robot rocket-bombs launched against this country. But to ensure 100 percent reliability there would have to be at least three such interceptor missiles for every robot or piloted aggressor.

Against the paralyzing gas, the British have evolved a gas-mask, which is now being made in several armament factories. But again, the surest Allied defense against any of these Stalin and Hitler secret weapons lies in the reliability of the self-guided interceptor missile to destroy the aggressor in the air and upon our potential to launch swift retaliatory war.

This alone will deter the would-be conquerors of the world and ensure "peace in our time."

HITLER'S *SECRET* AGENT

by GEORGE McGRATH

The sudden rebirth of the Nazi movement in Germany foretells the awaited return of Hitler. Who but Martin Bormann could be the secret plotter of that world-shaking event. . . .

Adolf Hitler, whose sensational escape to freedom from the Allied forces closing in on Berlin was first revealed by the *Police Gazette* last March, has now set in motion the initial moves of his plan to recapture control of Germany and launch a new attempt at world domination.

The sinister pattern of the Fuehrer's plan has been thrown into sharp relief by recent events in the Bonn capital of the Western Zone of this defeated and divided nation, which came so close to imposing ruthless dictatorship upon Europe.

Nazis, who had gone underground and were operating under-cover since the unconditional surrender of The Fatherland and the official "death" of Hitler, have received new instructions from their Fuehrer's hiding place in the Antarctic. These orders, the *Police Gazette* is convinced after careful investigation, were relayed through Martin Bormann, Hitler's personal secretary and confidant, who was named by the dictator as executor of his personal Last Will and Testament, and who escaped from Berlin after staging the mock suicide of the Fuehrer.

These Nazis are now running openly for office in Parliament or other offices under various party labels. Invariably, somewhere in their political campaigns, is a scarcely disguised glorification of Hitler and the new Reich of which he dreams.

The Military Intelligence Service of the United States Army has taken official note of the rebirth of Nazism in Western Germany. Seated at his desk in the Pentagon, beside a huge map of the Western Zone of Germany, Major-General Richard C. Partridge, Chief of the US Intelligence Branch, told the *Police Gazette:*

"We have had complete reports on the revival of Nazism in Germany. We have heard about the way these former Hitler followers are running for office once again."

Once more Major-General Partridge took a positive stand on the question of Hitler's "suicide" and assured the *Police Gazette:*

"We have never received any definite proof that Hitler is dead."

He confirmed that no country held this proof.

The facts concerning Hitler's impending bid once again for the leadership of the German people are simple and self-evident. They fall into two distinct categories—two stages of a plot to put Adolf Hitler, Fuehrer of the Third Reich, back into power as the Fuehrer of the *Fourth* Reich!

To begin, there is the story of Martin Bormann. It is the sordid, despicable tale of Hitler's brutish, murderous henchman and "successor"; of how he escaped from Berlin; how he faithfully carried out the Fuehrer's orders and secretly prepared the first steps of the Nazi movement.

The Inseparable Link

On top of that, there is that rebirth of the Nazi spirit in Germany itself; the mysterious electioneering programs that have recently put so many former Nazis into office under the present democratic Bonn government and in municipalities throughout the Western Zone.

These two stages may appear poles apart but, in reality, they are inseparably linked. Without Martin Bormann's amazing plan to cover the Fuehrer's escape and his own flight from Berlin as Russian troops closed in—without his single-minded ruthless and fanatic devotion and utter loyalty to the Nazi cause, Hitler would have been captured and executed ignominiously, and the entire Nazi movement, with its tremendous force for destruction and evil, would not at present be stirring in resurrection!

Martin Bormann is responsible, more than any other person, including Hitler himself, for this Nazi revival. Inextricably inter-woven with Hitler's attempt to seize power again is the story of his evil genius and secret agent, Martin Bormann.

Martin Bormann bludgeoned his way to the top ranks of the Nazi party. A bloated, bullnecked, scar-faced thug, with receding hairline, swarthy complexion, cold, penetrating eyes, and the man-ners of a pig, Bormann is one of the most cold-blooded killers ever to have belonged to a party of lustful executioners. Nazi officials who thought they could criticize Bormann's dirty fingernails or his Chinese-type table manners, found themselves lucky to be merely in jail or in a concentration camp.

Wanted by the Allies as a war criminal, with a price on his head, Martin Bormann is a comparatively young 53. He is a confirmed Red-hater from the time when he joined a group of war veterans in the Baltic.

Back in Germany, Bormann became a blackmailer, back-alley thug and petty mobster. His powerful, stocky frame and "mugging" operations brought him favorable recognition by the Rossbach "Free Corps" group in Mecklenburg in 1922. In 1924 he escaped the gallows when convicted of complicity in one of the political assassinations common to German politics of that era and only drew one year in jail.

It was after this that Bormann joined Hitler's newly-formed Nazi group, taking part in the ill-fated *putsch*, before becoming assistant to Rudolf Hess, then Hitler's white-haired boy. Even in those early days of Hitler's rise to power Bormann played cannily. Nazi officials whispered quite openly that Bormann had betrayed S.S. leader Roehm to Hitler, resulting in his "execution" and the shooting of thousands of Nazi storm troopers.

Becomes Hitler's Aide

From strong-arm thug to a personal friend of Hitler, Martin Bormann played every angle with cunning. As assistant to Hess from 1933 on, he soon made himself useful to the Fuehrer.

When Hitler wanted to build his famous Eagle's Eyrie at Berchtesgaden, Martin Bormann undertook to clear the local farmers and inhabitants from the neighborhood. Half-a-dozen of the more important Nazi officials such as Field Marshal Hermann Goering wanted villas near Hitler. That was arranged, but by this "arranging" Bormann became a multimillionaire in real estate. He "acquired" the only respectable inn in Berchtesgaden by the simple expedient of arresting and executing the owner.

When Rudolf Hess fled to England at the beginning of the War, Bormann became Hitler's personal secretary. The one-time thug and murderer had come a long way, further than anyone had thought possible even when in 1927 he had been Nazi press chief in Thuringia.

Prepared Fuehrer's Escape

Martin Bormann had no friends or confidants. His schemes were in his head. As the war news worsened for the Germans, Bormann became Hitler's only confidant. It was Bormann who evolved and prepared the entire plan for Hitler's escape; it was Bormann who staged the final flight to the Antarctic hide-out.

The German Volksturm, a Home Guard of old and disabled, was placed under the direct personal orders of Martin Bormann. He ran it for the protection of the Fuehrer.

In 1945 the situation became desperate. In Hitler's "bunker" shelter in Berlin, Bormann saw that the end was near and that it was time for the Fuehrer to escape. The plans had been prepared. Now they were to be carried through.

Hitler's personal will was signed with Martin Bormann

named executor. Then his official Last Will and Testament was prepared and signed. Within minutes of signing his will, Hitler was speeding away to Norway in a small plane while Bormann carried through the plan. News that Goering was attempting to negotiate with the Russians reached Bormann and he flew into almost an insane rage, according to eyewitness reports brought out at the Nuremberg trial of the Nazi leaders. He rushed off an urgent coded signal to the Gestapo officials at Berchtesgaden, where Goering was staying, that the Marshall should be executed on the spot. Bormann had overreached himself in this one partic-ular. A reply came back that the officers could not shoot Goering unless ordered personally by Hitler. Bormann had already "sui-cided" Hitler; he could not bring him back to life again without exposing the whole plan of escape.

Within minutes after Hitler's sudden departure, Martin Bor-mann sent a message to Grand Admiral Doenitz:

Dear Grand Admiral:
  Since all our divisions failed to appear our situation seems to be beyond hope.
  The Fuehrer dictated last night the attached political Testament.
                              Heil Hitler, yours,
                                          (signed) Martin Bormann.

This was followed within a few hours by the announcement by Doenitz of Hitler's "suicide."

Bormann had only one task to carry out before he could make his own escape. It was a task on which the entire escape plot rested.

Carrying the body of a Hitler double, Bormann held an impromptu funeral pyre in the grounds of the Chancellery. A few witnesses later testified that Hitler had been cremated. They had not seen Hitler's face; they had not seen his body. The Russians, who found this partly cremated body, formally declared that the body was not that of Hitler.

"The teeth did not match dental charts of Hitler's teeth," they informed President Truman, Prime Minister Churchill, and Premier Stalin at the Potsdam meeting.

As Major-General Partridge confirmed in the Pentagon a few weeks ago:

"We have never received any definite proof of Hitler's death."

Martin Bormann was now ready to leave. To the world, Hitler had committed suicide.

Bormann Disappears

The *Police Gazette* talked to numerous soldiers, German civilians and war correspondents who were on the Berlin scene within hours of Bormann's flight. Painstakingly, the story was pieced together. It is a dramatic tale, worthy of some greater cause.

Taking two of Hitler's servants with him, Bormann left the bunker by the exit near the main Chancellery door. He had waited until May 2, when his short-wave radio picked up a coded message telling him the Fuehrer was safe in Norway and about to board a U-boat for Colombia, which Bormann had picked as the first hide away for his Fuehrer.

Bent almost double, Bormann and the two servants ran a zigzag course across the Wilhelmstrasse and the open ground leading to the Kaiserhof about a 100 yards away. The ground was swept by intermittent shellfire and Russian snipers were shooting wildly.

In front of the Kaiserhof, he ducked into the U-bahn (subway) entrance and once again was back underground in comparative safety.

Walking down the deserted, rusting subway tracks, Bormann came to the end of the line—an abrupt end caused by a British bomb which had split open the tube and flooded the subway system from that point on. Several thousand Germans, who had been sheltering from the bombs in this part of the subway, had been killed outright or drowned and trampled by water or the ensuing panic. Allied observers later reported the "stench as terrifying."

At this point, according to Allied reports, Bormann climbed up an emergency exit ladder at the side of the tunnel. He came out above ground near the Admiralpalast.

He was now on the last lap of his escape route. Near the outskirts of the city he had to cross the bridge over the canal leading to the main road west. Only this one danger spot faced him—the bridge. Russian snipers were shooting at every sign of life on this main thoroughfare.

It was six o'clock in the morning. Day had broken. Off to one side, in the shelter of a building, stood a German tank. Bormann showed his Hitler Secretary pass and his Reichleiter's authority to commandeer any unit of the German armed forces at any time. Orders passed and the German tank moved slowly off, Bormann trotting alongside in its lee, while one of Hitler's chauffeurs and the other servant strode along the opposite side.

The tank revved up. The tank rolled across the bridge. Within two yards of the end, a bazooka shell exploded with devastating effect against the side of the tank, which burst into flames. A MAN WALKING ON THE SIDE NEAREST THE ENEMY WAS KILLED; HIS BODY DECAPITATED.

That man, say the Germans, was Martin Bormann. Yet two independent witnesses, the tank commander and one of the machine gunners, state that Bormann was walking on the side *opposite* the enemy.

The Russian bazooka corporal, too, afterwards stated that he saw two men running from the tank, fired at them with his rifle and missed. One of them was a squat, heavy-set man . . .

Months in Hiding

That man was Bormann. Bormann did not die on the bridge, as was afterwards proved when he showed up at the Swiss border, crossed and spent several months hiding as an unsuspected alien in that neutral country before visiting his Fuehrer in Colombia. Bormann had escaped.

Seen fleetingly in various countries, the last reports stated that Martin Bormann had been contacting various Nazi supporters in Italy. The *Police Gazette* questioned Major-General Partridge about these reports.

"It is quite true, he said. "We received exactly the same reports."

THE SECRET BEHIND NAZI PLOT TO REGAIN POWER

by GEORGE McGRATH

Police Gazette gives facts that prove the sinister hand of Hitler moves behind the shocking alliance of Nazis and Reds in Germany today.

It is a sinister, brutal, but damningly true fact that Adolf Hitler, defeated Nazi dictator of the Third Reich, and Joseph Stalin, his Communist archenemy of World War II, have now joined forces and together are completing their plans for the domination of the entire world.

Almost eight years to the day after the Western powers, in unwilling but necessary alliance with Russia, defeated Germany and brought an end to the bloodiest conflict in the history of the world, these two dictators, with cynical disregard for civilized morality, are now preparing to resume their brief, world-shocking alliance of 1939. They are determined to crush all freedom-loving peoples under the jackboot of Nazi autocracy and the knout of Soviet imperialism.

The facts are clear. The holocaust these Nazi and Communist leaders seek to precipitate has been evident, but officialdom in Washington and London remained blind and deaf to the danger until a few weeks ago, when British Intelligence agents followed the trail pointed months before in the *Police Gazette* and swooped down on a small but important band of Soviet-financed Nazi ringleaders in Western Germany.

Although the British Intelligence Service has refused to make public any of the facts bared by the arrest of these seven top leaders of the Nazi underground, Mr. Ivonne Kirkpatrick, British High Commissioner in Germany, is known to have disclosed to Chancellor Konrad Adenauer that its ramifications assumed "extremely dangerous proportions for the future safety of the democratic world."

The *Police Gazette* has warned of this danger repeatedly. As far back as September, 1951, the *Police Gazette* was the first to force an admission from American and British intelligence officials that *they had no proof* Adolf Hitler had committed suicide.

Ferreting out facts and interviewing reliable and informed personalities such as Col. W. F. Heimlich, former Chief of US Intelligence in Berlin, who conducted the official investigation of the Hitler death reports; Major-General Richard C. Partridge, Chief of US Intelligence in the Pentagon, and Mr. Spruille Braden, US Ambassador to the Argentine at the end of the War, among others, the *Police Gazette* drew the inevitable conclusion:

Adolf Hitler was alive and had escaped from Germany; Martin Bormann, Hitler's henchman and trusted confidant, had escaped also and was acting as liaison agent between the Fuehrer and the neo-Nazis in Germany, and—

Many of the leading Nazi industrialists, politicians and military brains were living openly in the Argentine, where they plotted Hitler's return and the rebirth of a new and victorious Germany.

Now, from confidential sources in Western Germany and from refugees who have just escaped from behind the Iron Curtain, the *Police Gazette* has been able to piece together the horrifying details of a gigantic and calamitous Nazi-Soviet mutual assistance pact, which aims at the eventual conquest of the globe. This world-domination was to be achieved in four stages:

The Four Stages

1. The Nazi party would climb to power within the confines of Western Germany. They would be aided by Soviet financing in

the final stages and, in view of universal German resentment at the continued presence of occupying forces, could expect the withdrawal of these Allied troops within "a reasonable length of time," after the ratification of the Peace Treaties;

2. Hitler would return in person. With Soviet approval and support he would declare the whole of Germany united once again into a single and powerful Reich under his authority. Poland would probably be sacrificed as a separate entity and be absorbed within Russia proper;

3. The build-up period. Once again butter would be discarded for guns; German heavy industry would work night and day producing arms and machines of war; huge training programs would be launched and Germany would become an armed camp. In 1933 it took Hitler less than six years to transform an unarmed Germany into the most powerful single nation in the world. This time it would not take him so long.

4. Acting in concert with Russia, the Nazis and the Communists would launch a war of aggression upon their two major enemies, the United States and England. As in all wars precipitated by soulless dictators, the democracies would be at a disadvantage; the enemy could choose his day and hope to offset America's superior power of the atom and hydrogen bombs by the impact of the initial onslaught.

Despite apparent astonishment in Washington and London at this disclosure of Communist support for the neo-Nazi party in Western Germany, the *Police Gazette* warned several months ago that Hitler was rebuilding his political machine from the sanctuary of his Shangri-La hide-out and would without doubt use Stalin's obvious might and powerful political situation as a stepping-stone. With the British arrest of these seven Nazis, Hitler's plan becomes clear.

Acting under Hitler's guidance, Martin Bormann held the reins of what remained of the Nazi party, whose leading members had been hanged, imprisoned, dispersed or had fled. His task was to form once again a band of determined, ruthless fanatics who would serve as the nucleus of an eventual return to power.

Until the time of the Berlin blockade by the Russians, when the Western powers showed the Soviets they would not surrender to threats, the Nazis in West Germany remained dormant. They held aloof from contact with fellow Nazis in East Germany, who were very much underground at this stage; from the German military staffs in captivity in Russia and from the Communists themselves.

With the lifting of the Berlin blockade when it was broken by the air lift, the Soviets virtually admitted they had been stalemated by the Allies. When the Western powers then announced their intention of rearming Western Germany and making her an integral part of the anti-Communist defense front, Hitler saw his chance.

Martin Bormann was given orders to activate the Nazi movement in Western Germany. It was essential for Der Fuehrer to have a "going concern" before he made his approach to Stalin. Bormann, whom Hitler in his Political Testament called his "trusted friend," had laid his plans well.

The New Nazi Spirit

Berchtesgaden, shrine of the Nazi party, became the birthplace of the new "Nazi spirit." A youth movement, the *Deutsche Jugend*, was established there and spread throughout the Western Zone. A clandestine Nazi newspaper called the *Deutschland Brief* was circulated by the scores of thousands and openly attacked the occupation forces while advocating friendlier relations with Russia. It was edited by one "Hek Rau," whose real name was discovered by Allied Intelligence agents to be Heinz Erich Krause, a young, rabble-rousing Hitler admirer.

"The Soviets alone," asserted the *Deutsche Brief*, "could help unite Germany." This Nazi underground newsletter once again trumpeted the excuse used after World War I and raised the old Hitler cry of "the real culprits are the Jews."

By the spring of 1952, Hitler felt his movement was well under way. No longer were the Nazis an underground movement except in name. They now called themselves the SRP—the Socialist Republican Party. They were a recognized and important political element. When, in 1932, Hitler was moving towards power, the Nazis had exactly eleven seats in the Reichstag; today the SRP has thirteen seats in the Bundestag. Hitler knows it does not take many rabble-rousers to steer a successful movement.

In the West German Social-Democrat government of Konrad Adenauer, Martin Bormann had deployed a very large number of Nazis. Last year, the Bavarian Socialist radio station charged that the West German Foreign Office was a "rat's nest of Nazis" and accused Adenauer of giving 85 percent of the government jobs to former Nazis. Adenauer's reply was significant and revealing. Denying the charges he said:

"The figure is incorrect. *The true percentage is sixty-five.*"

Adenauer's hands had been tied by Bormann. The Chancellor set up a Bundestag (Parliamentary) Committee of Investigation, which queried 21 of the key men but decided only four had records meriting dismissal and took this decision only upon the insistence of the Allies, for Hitler's 13 representatives in Parliament blocked action in the other cases.

These four men who were thrown out of public office into the Nazi underground were Curt Heinburg, economic counselor and chief of the political division of the Foreign Office under von Ribbentrop, who had worked out "a solution of the Jewish problem in Serbia," meaning slave labor, concentration camps or death; Werner von Grundheer, Nazi Ambassador to Greece, who had been in control of the "Jewish problem" in Denmark; Herbert Dittmann, Chief of von Ribbentrop's personnel department, and Werner von Bargen, responsible for the persecution of Jews in Brussels and Paris.

The Committee's investigation, although it was hushed up by the Nazis and given little attention by the Allies, revealed startling facts.

In the Political Department of the Bonn Government, the entire executive staff of ten were Nazis;

In the Landes (Federal States—equivalent to our States), seven out of eight top officials were veteran Nazi Party card holders;

In the Commerce Department, all five key men were Party members;

In the Culture Department, three out of four executives were Party veterans, and

In the Personnel Department, 18 out of 19 executives were Hitler regime office holders and 14 of them were Nazi Party veterans.

Martin Bormann had succeeded in placing in the Bonn Foreign Office such dangerous Nazis as Legation Counsellor von Keller, former top assistant to Woermann, Hitler's Secretary of State who was tried at Nuremberg; L. C. Melchers, war criminal and Jew baiter, an expert on the Middle East and Hitler's negotiator with the Grand Mufti of the Arab world; Heribert von Strempel, former Secretary in the German Embassy in Washington and one of the organizers of the Nazi Fifth Column in the United States.

Most significant of all, Bormann had once again brought into being the nucleus of a new German General Staff. With the Allied decision to rearm Germany, official permission was given German generals to set up headquarters in converted barracks on the Argelanderstrasse in Bonn. While apparently obeying all Allied orders for the reorganization of infantry divisions *only*, this new German General Staff has openly created staff schools embracing all branches of *theoretical* military instruction. The emphasis is on the theoretical because Germany today has no tanks, heavy artillery or warplanes. This General Staff issued an official order *Einheitliche Politische, Wirtschaftliche, und Technische Ausbildung* (unified political, economic, and technical training) which strangely resembled orders in the Third Reich training manuals. This order was hastily withdrawn when a copy fell into Allied hands and drew a sharp reprimand from British Army Headquarters.

This was the situation of the Nazi move towards regaining power in West Germany in the late spring, last year, when Hitler made his first approach to the Soviets. Details of who made the ini-

tial contact and where it was effected are not known but the immediate sequence of events is significant and startling.

Pavlov's Secret Mission

In August, 1952, according to a Jewish refugee who had held an
executive position in the East German Communist government and
who only escaped last January during the wave of anti-Semitism
sweeping Iron Curtain countries, a burly, six-foot, 220-pound
Russian, Ivan Mihailovitch Pavlov, who was first assistant to the
dreaded Soviet Secret Police Chief Beria, flew in a Russian military
transport plane to the Argentine to confer with the Nazis in exile.
He is known to have spent ten days in the Argentine and to have
visited the remote hinterland of Bariluche, where Adolf Hitler was
last reported.

When Pavlov returned to Moscow aboard the same plane—the
Soviets use their own planes for all diplomatic purposes, trusting
their couriers, personnel and pouches to no one—he was accompanied by a "trusted and important Nazi agent." This agent, says
this refugee source, was Martin Bormann.

Details pieced together from these Iron Curtain refugee sources
indicate that, less than a week after his return to Moscow, Pavlov
flew to Magdebourg, in East Germany, with Bormann.

In Magdebourg, home of the Prussian General Staff and foster-
home of the German spirit of militarism, jackboot and brutality,
Pavlov and Bormann held secret conferences with Field-Marshal
von Paulus and his ranking staff officers, who had been captured
by the Russians during the War and whom Stalin had carefully
nurtured for just such an opportunity.

In September, according to refugees from East Germany, Martin Bormann traveled into Western Germany to consult with Dr.
Naumann and Dr. Scheel. Adolf Hitler, in his Political Testament
to the German people, had named Dr. Naumann to replace Josef
Goebbels as Minister of Propaganda in his last-ditch cabinet and

had appointed Dr. Scheel as Minister of Church and Education. *Both of these men were among the seven top-ranking Nazi underground leaders arrested recently by the British Intelligence agents.*

Martin Bormann called Major-General Hermann Bernhard Ramcke, Nazi paratroop general, into conference with the top brass of the reconstituted Western Bonn General Staff. Ramcke was sent, according to refugee sources, on a mission to von Paulus' staff headquarters. This mission, apparently, was to coordinate, with the entire approval of the Soviets, a general training program for *ALL* German officers and men. The program would adhere closely to the pre-war Nazi training manuals and would be "paralleled by the Bonn training program."

The effects of the August agreement between Stalin and Hitler became apparent almost immediately. In October last year, two highly significant events occurred, one in the East, the other in the West zones of Germany.

In the East, 25,000 East Germans paraded in the rebirth of a German army. Stalin sent Nikolai M. Shvernik, President of the Presidum of the Supreme Soviet, to attend. In the parade were Air Police, the nucleus of the new German Air Force, wearing embroidered wings on blue lapel tabs, and Sea Police, the nucleus of a revitalized German Navy.

"More than half the men marching in these air and sea contingents," say refugees who watched the parade, "were men from West Germany. They were being trained in weapons they could not use under Allied occupation." It is now no secret that the Soviets are training both East and West Germans in U-boat warfare.

Hitler's Aides Meet

In the West, two former S.S. generals organized a rally of former blackshirts in Verden, Lower Saxony. Generals Herbert Gille and Felix Steiner sent orders for 5,000 of the one-time dreaded S.S. butchers of the Hitler regime, to attend. They lacked their sinister black uniforms which had struck terror into all, but their jackboots were highly polished and the measured cadence of their faultless goose-step left a chill in the hearts of Allied onlookers.

Asked why these 5,000 had all registered with full names and addresses, the generals stated they merely wished to form a veterans' association of veteran blackshirts. But it was at this rally that General Ramcke got out of hand. He seemed to see Hitler back in power and disclosed too soon that the Nazi movement was not dead, that it had been re-activated and that the Germans were but awaiting a new "Der Tag."

"I am proud to have been on the Allied black list," he shouted to the gathering. "One day it will be the list of honor."

While the entire rally shouted in chorus and the two frantic generals tried to shut him up, he led a chant of: "Eisenhower *Schweinhund* (pig-dog)."

Red-Nazi Alliance

In coordination with the German side of the new mutual assistance pact, Soviet Russia struck too. This time, as a preliminary step, she launched a wave of anti-Semitism, starting with the satellite nations. Using an anti-Jewish battle-cry, both Stalin and Hitler have hopes of cementing their alliance and of bringing to their support the entire Moslem Arab world, embracing North Africa, the Near East and India.

Despite the astonishment of the Western World and the open disbelief that Stalin and Hitler could again reach an agreement, history supports the warnings carried to the democratic world by refugees fleeing in fear from the Red terror at the rate of more than 1,000 a day.

The German General Staff has a 200-year old tradition of friendship and alliance with the Russians. Frederick the Great, with the help of the Czar, defeated the French in the war of 1756 to 1763; Bismarck laid down a doctrine of German policy towards the East which he called "Russian reinsurance." When Kaiser Wilhelm violated this unwritten code, he lost the first World War; when Hitler violated it again in 1941, he lost the second World War.

In exile, Hitler has had much time to realize the truth of an adage formulated a century ago by the Prussian military genius, General Clausewitz:

"With Russia, Germany can conquer the world; against Russia, Germany cannot prevail."

HITLER IS ALIVE—
PREPARES TO RETURN!

by GEORGE McGRATH

Police Gazette reveals for the first time the actual details of
the Nazi conspiracy to restore Der Fuehrer to power in Germany
and pave the way for world revival of Hitlerism.

From his hiding place in the Argentine, Adolf Hitler has organized a widespread Nazi International whose roots are firmly laid
in Germany and whose tentacle-like branches of intrigue extend
to Cairo, Madrid, Rome, and the United States—where former
members of the Nazi Bund lurk as a potential Fifth Column.

In this article, the *Police Gazette* is able to reveal for the first
time the true facts about this *Nazi International*. Step by step,
through the tangled morass of post-war German political parties,
phony veterans associations, and underground movements, the
Police Gazette has traced the clear-cut pattern of Hitler's conspiracy
to return to power as Fuehrer of the Reich.

Although the sudden arrest of seven Nazi ringleaders by
British Military Intelligence agents last January forced the Bonn
Government, against its will, to act on the evidence placed under
its nose, the lid to this cesspool of Nazi chicanery was never
lifted. A few bare facts were allowed to escape. They were very
bare. They did not mention how Hitler and his infamous henchman, Martin Bormann, had organized this core of Nazism and
had appointed, as *Gauleiter*, Dr. Werner Naumann—another of
the war criminals supposed to have died with Hitler and Bor-

mann in Berlin. (Dr. Naumann is very much alive and is now in a British army jail.)

Bonn's discreet handling of this plot did not disclose to the German people that this underground movement was part of the *Nazi International*; that it consisted of approximately 5,000 of the most rabid Nazis; that it coordinated the efforts and policies of all the right-wing political parties in Western Germany; and that it was in constant liaison with the Communist underground and banned Red movements. Nor did Bonn disclose to the Germans that this neo-Nazi movement had access to the secret files and documents of the democratic Adenauer cabinet—and that the full details of the NATO plans for West European defense against the Reds in Germany were in the possession of the Nazis and, therefore, in the hands of the Soviets.

Above all, no mention was made of the fact that Fuehrer Adolf Hitler's return to Germany is fixed tentatively for 1957.

The *Police Gazette* has regularly published the facts about the Hitler conspiracy ever since it produced irrefutable evidence in September 1951 that the three major allies of 1945 (United States, Britain, and Russia) had never obtained proof of the Fuehrer's death—and that not one of the leading government officials in the US or Britain would say for the record that Hitler committed suicide in his famous bunker beneath the bomb-torn, shell-ruined Reichskanlei. However, the full picture of the Nazis' post-war plot became clear only after the British swoop on seven ringleaders of the *Nazi International* in the British Zone of Germany, and the subsequent arrests by Bonn police of nearly 50 neo-Nazi and Communist co-schemers.

Documents seized by British Military Intelligence agents show that the *Nazi International* was organized by far-sighted Germans several years before the Nazis' last stand in Berlin.

Bormann's first move after he escaped from Berlin (according to British M.I.5, which received reports of his arrival in Switzerland) was to contact the Nazi Party's numerous financial agents in

Zurich, where colossal unseizable bank accounts had been cached in various currencies. He then contacted Nazis in Italy (where he lived as a monk under the name of Brother Martin) before going to Madrid. Whether Bormann personally visited Cairo, where a strong *Nazi International* cell was established, or whether he sent an emissary to contact the Nazis there, is not clearly shown in the documents.

John J. McCloy, former US High Commissioner in Germany, was informed by a Munich source of the existence of the *Nazi International* in Madrid, Rome, and Cairo, and transmitted his information to the Allied secret services.

Bormann was next seen in the Argentine, where (as revealed previously by the *Police Gazette*) he reported to Hitler. The Fuehrer was being hidden in the wilds of Patagonia by a strong Nazi organization with the active support of Argentine dictator Juan Peron.

Hitler and Bormann decided to make Dr. Werner Naumann chief of the neo-Nazi movement in Western Germany as the representative of the *Nazi International*. Naumann was one of the Fuehrer's most trusted followers (he was appointed by Hitler in his last will and testament as Minister of Propaganda to replace Dr. Josef Goebbels in the surrender cabinet of Grand Admiral Karl Doenitz). Even more important to the Fuehrer and his *Nazi International* of those days, Naumann was believed dead. He was living under an assumed name near Hamburg.

The Truth About Dr. Naumann

The sensational truth, published here for the first time, is that Allied Intelligence agents reported that Naumann died in the bunker with Hitler. One of the judges at Nuremberg, Michael Musmanmo, as late as 1950 wrote a book in which he dismissed Naumann as "reported killed in Berlin", which is why Naumann was never brought to trial. Actually, while the Allies were writing him off as "dead", Naumann, together with Bormann, was the last to escape from the bunker. Both men safely crossed the Weidedammer Bridge, on which Bormann was later reported to have been killed by a bazooka shell.

Dr. Naumann, who today is only 43 years old, was a rabid Hitler follower from the start. The son of an *Amtsgerichtsrat* (Police Court magistrate) of Silesia, he joined Dr. Josef Goebbels in the Propaganda Ministry and soon rose to become permanent secretary of the Ministry. He made his last public speech when he ranted over the Berlin radio a few days before the Fuehrer "committed suicide." He said:

"At the head of the defense of Berlin stands our Fuehrer, and this alone characterizes the struggle for Berlin as unique and decisive. Never has he been so close to the hearts of his soldiers than in this grave hour. We are not shaken by our recent military reverses. National Socialism has made Germany strong and flourishing."

From the time he escaped from the bunker until he was arrested by the British last January, Naumann remained hidden from Allied intelligence agents. Only once was he mentioned briefly, by the Communist East German news agency, as having attended a meeting of the neo-Nazi and pro-Red *Bruderschaft* (now banned, but certainly not defunct) veterans' brotherhood in Bielefeld in November 1950. It was this short paragraph in a Red paper that led to his arrest.

British M.I.5 agents have since traced the permanent liaison that was established between Hitler's Shangri-La headquarters, the *Nazi International* cells in various countries, Dr. Naumann's top-secret role in the Nazi revival in Western Germany, and the various neo-Nazi and Red groups in that country. This liaison operated chiefly through the United States, where former members of the Nazi Bund remained unswerving adherents of the Fuehrer. It was through the undercover activities of the American cell of the *Nazi International* that fascist representatives from all countries arranged a secret meeting in Sweden in 1951. The slogan at that meeting was: *"Fascists of the world—unite!"*

As chief of the *Nazi International* in Germany, Dr. Naumann was the hidden hand behind the organization of the *Freikorps Deutschland* (German Free Corps) as the neo-Nazi centralizing agency. The *Freikorps* was pledged to restore the Fuehrer to power over a "united and unified" Germany. It boasted a 25-point program featuring such inseparable Nazi ideals as militarism, the pre-ordained superiority of the German people, and their right to world power. Naturally, all members were sworn to absolute obedience in this secret anti-Jewish, anti-Jesuit, anti-Masonic group.

Documents seized by British Intelligence agents last January prove that while the *Freikorps* was founded as a legitimate right-wing political party of between 1,000 and 2,000 members, Dr. Naumann had arranged for this political "front" to conceal the real nature of the organization—which consisted of approximately 5,000 carefully chosen and highly-trained Nazi men and women.

Nazi-Communist Plot Exposed

It was British M.I.5 agents from this headquarters who, investigating the one-paragraph mention of Dr. Naumann in an East German newspaper, exposed the Nazi-Communist plot and arrested Dr. Naumann and his six top assistants.

Evidence of the plot was then handed to Chancellor Konrad Adenauer by the British High Commissioner, Sir Ivone Kirkpatrick, a former Foreign Office expert and adviser on Germany and Hitlerism. Sir Ivone *demanded* that the Bonn Government pursue the investigations.

Reluctantly, Bonn's police arrested four members of the *Freikorps*. Then papers found at their homes spurred Chancellor Adenauer and his Minister of the Interior, Robert Lehr, who at first had pooh-poohed the plot as "British propaganda," into feverish action. Eleven more members of the *Freikorps* were held for questioning and the *Korps* was officially dissolved. Four members of the National Front, 10 members of the Socialist Action, and 28 members of the Free German Youth (all Communist organizations) were arrested and their parties also were dissolved.

A dragnet search was made by British and German police at the homes of these 50-odd leaders of the *Nazi International*, neo-Nazi agencies, and collaborating Communist parties. It revealed the sinister web of intrigue that Dr. Naumann and his assistant, Dr. Gustav Scheel (who also was mentioned in Hitler's last will as Minister for Church and Education) had woven into every phase of German activity—including the Bonn Government itself.

How the Freikorps Operated

The *Freikorps* was a dangerous spider. As the central governing agency of the neo-Nazi movement in Germany, it knit into its executive committee the leaders of the Hamburg Truth and Justice League, the S.S. Aid Association, and the remnants of the Socialist Reich Partei—all extreme, right-wing political groups.

Freikorps leaders assumed control of the Free Democratic Party—the second largest political party in Chancellor Adenauer's ruling coalition—and thus infiltrated the government's highest posts. Democratic in name only, this party's chairman is deputy Chancellor to Adenauer. Its strongly nationalistic platform was written by Dr. Friedrich Middlehauve, deputy chairman of the party and, at the same time, a member of the *Freikorps*. Dr. Ernst Achenbach, another member of the party's Foreign Policy Committee, is legal adviser to Dr. Scheel.

The *Freikorps* collaborated with West German Communist organizations—mainly the *Bruderschaft*, which originally was founded as a violently anti-Western powers war veterans' group and was financed by the Russians. Herr Helmuth Beck-Broichsitter, chairman of the now-banned *Bruderschaft*, is a top member of the *Freikorps*. He is now under arrest in Bonn.

British military police arrived too late to be completely successful when they raided the headquarters of West Germany's new

Hitler Front youth movement, also organized by the *Freikorps*. The secret files and membership lists of this movement, reportedly numbering more than 80,000 potential reserves for the *Freikorps* para-military formations, had disappeared. Only empty filing cabinets remained.

German heavy industry plays an important role in neo-Nazi plans for the rearmament of Germany. Shortly before Christmas last year it was reported from Munich that Alfred Krupp, the German armaments king of Hitler days, who was pardoned and released from jail, had returned to Munich. Documents seized by the Bonn Government reveal that Krupp, Naumann, and Scheel held an important conference there.

The *Freikorps* deceptive "Trojan Horse" was situated well inside the Bonn Government's military staff, according to British agents. They say that top-secret NATO plans for an Allied and West German defense of West Europe are now in the hands of the Russians—undoubtedly given to the Reds by the neo-Nazi undercover organization.

Sir Ivone Kirkpatrick bluntly told Chancellor Adenauer that some 200 highly secret neo-Nazi and *Nazi International* documents, many of which were seized in the tiny Hamburg hospital room occupied by Dr. Scheel (he is no invalid, but the hospital is managed by Frau Inge Doenitz, wife of the Grand Admiral), bared the dangerous and widespread nature of this plot to overthrow democracy in Germany and establish a Soviet-backed Nazi plan to restore Hitler to power.

The British charged that Dr. Naumann had made minute plans to create a new Nazi Germany within four years—united and unified in a single party. They told Adenauer that papers seized on Karl Kaufman, former Hamburg Gestapo chief and assistant to Dr. Naumann in the *Freikorps*, showed that Naumann had access to the secret files of the Bonn Government, had constant contact with many former generals of the *Wehrmacht* (both in the West and in the Russian-dominated East zones of Germany), and had planned to seize political power by swinging all of the right-wing parties, particularly the German Party and the all-German Bloc, into their orbit.

These papers showed that the *Freikorps* was looking towards Soviet Russia for direct help in unifying Germany into a strong, single state in return for a Nazi promise to weld a Nazi-Government alliance against the rest of the world.

Under the time-table laid down for returning Hitler to Germany and for reestablishing a new and stronger Reich, the *Freikorps* planned to seize power in 1956. Arrangements had been made for the coup d'état to coincide with the release that same year of Grand Admiral Karl Doenitz from the Spandau prison upon completion of his ten-year Nuremberg jail sentence.

Doenitz would assume control of the new Nazi Government under the mandate of Hitler's last will and testament—and within one year, the *Freikorps* believed, Germany would be strong enough for Hitler to return without fear of Allied reprisals.

Dr. Naumann's Plan

Dr. Naumann's plan was simple and logical, say the British. He reasoned that the Allies would not dare march against Germany if the Nazis first obtained the support of the Soviets.

The *Freikorps* believed that in the United States, the Nazi Bund would have bolstered Germany's value as a bastion in the East against a Russian invasion of France or the Lowlands. The Bund would have succeeded, they felt, in turning American public opinion against Britain and France.

Meanwhile, *Nazi International* agents in the Middle East and North Africa would have created unrest by linking these nations with a Nazi anti-Semitic movement. Britain and the Lowlands, they thought, would not attempt a demonstration against Germany, even though her initial twelve divisions were weak, for fear of Russian intervention. France might protest, but she could not act alone.

In the United Nations, they were confident, the pro-Arab and Asian blocs would frustrate any attempt at more than superficial condemnation, and the Soviet could be counted upon to veto any motion in the Security Council.

Hitler would have won the day. Within weeks his heavy armaments industry would be churning out war materials. It would then be too late for intervention of any kind, and the arms race that leads inevitably to war—to World War III—would be on once again.

This is the pattern for Hitler's return. What action will the Allies take, now that they know?

HITLER'S HAND
REACHES BACK INTO GERMANY

by BILL DAVIS

"We will hold our meetings, even over your dead bodies," is the threat made to German officials by Nazi leaders. Here's the first authoritative account of the new menace . . .

The blood-soaked hand of Hitler is reaching back into modern Germany. Brutal and menacing, it is stirring up a brand-new hotbed of Nazis.

Less than a decade and a half after Allied power completed the annihilation of the dictator's regime, Germany today again echoes to the ominous sound of "Heil Hitler." It appears at the foot of letters to newspapers. It has been heard at meetings of former Nazis. It is linked to a campaign to "whitewash" German war atrocities—even to claim that they were never committed.

And as the pro-Nazi faction grows in strength, West Germans and foreign observers recall with black misgivings the pattern of the Hitler rise to power.

For the neo-Nazi movement of today has much in common with that begun by the power-crazed housepainter it seeks to imitate.

Already Nazi-hating West Germans, protesting a meeting of an organization formed of former S.S. members, have been threatened with "reprisals."

Already, a Nazi-minded editor—Robert Kramer, of "Die Anklage," (The Accusation)—has demanded in his columns "the founding of the old party again."

Already, through Kramer, pro-Nazis have discovered that the way of the transgressor is not always too hard to take. For Kramer escaped with a remarkably light sentence—two years in Jail (perhaps less with parole). And as Nazi victims have been quick to point out, the judge who handed it to him—Senat-President Kanter, presiding over the Third Criminal Senat of the Criminal Court—himself stands accused of responsibility for killing more than 100 members of the Danish underground movement. Kanter has not yet refuted the charge.

Five major factors flash danger signals at those West Germans who dread the prospect of a return to Third Reich horror. They are:

1. *The letters written to neo-Nazi publications by former S.S. men, openly signed "Heil Hitler," "German Salutation," and "Long Live Liberty."* They are eagerly read by former Nazi officers and high-ranking officials of the Hitler regime, many of whom now hold well-paid jobs and prominent positions in the political, economic, and social life of West Germany.

Outcry Against "Hitler's Bloodhounds"

2. *The newly-formed organizations of former Nazi fanatics.* These are numerous and varied in size. They exist to weld together and help sympathizers of the Nazi cause—such men as editor Kramer, who will be sure of many a helping hand on his release from Jail. When one such group, composed of former S.S. men (known as "Hitler's Bloodhounds" by their victims), planned a meeting in the town of Arolsen, the public outcry was so great that eventually the meeting was held elsewhere. But not before a spokesman of the organization threatened: "The meeting will be held one way or the other, even over your dead bodies." Other similar organizations, though not so blatant, are known to be increasing their membership by every means possible.

3. *The "whitewashing" or denials of war atrocities.* Typical of Nazi efforts to erase memories of war crimes were statements made

at the meeting described above by ex-S.S. General "Panzer" Meyer. The war crimes, he said, were nothing but stories, and those that circulated them "dirty swine." Amid thunderous approval, Meyer declared: "Let us take care that these germ-carriers of mental decay find no propagation. The crimes of Mazzabotto and Lidice are only fairy tales."

(Lidice, a mining village in Czechoslovakia, was "eliminated" as a reprisal for the assassination of S.S. General Reinhard Heydrich).

4. *The important positions held by men known to have been Nazis.* Under the headline "Law Scandal in Mannheim" a West German newspaper has reported that several former Nazi judges again hold responsible positions in the Mannheim law administration. Public prosecutor Rehder-Knospel, for instance, used to be first public prosecutor at one of the so called "special courts" (Sondergerichte) in Prague.

A facsimile of a sentence, condemning 15 Czechs on the grounds of alleged sabotage to death and bearing, among others, the signature of Rehder-Knospel, has just been published.

Rehder-Knospel is not the only Nazi-jurist to hold a high post in the Mannheim law-administration. There are others: Busse-jahn, former county court judge on a special court in Danzig and Graudenz, today acts as county court judge in Mannheim; Lohrey, former district judge on a special court in Mannheim, today is a director at the Mannheim county court; Von Muhlenfels, another former county court judge at a Nazi special court in Mannheim, today is attorney general in the same town; Dr. Heinrich, former attorney-general at the special court in Mannheim, today is director of the county court in Mannheim.

At least three more judges in the law administration of Mannheim alone (a city of 290,000) are known to have held high posts during the Nazi regime. Their names are no secret: Drs. Brauns, Muhlenberg, and Hoffrichter.

5. *Lack of action against former Nazis or Nazi supporters.* Many ex-Nazis have reached retirement age. But they still manage, some-

times with the help of institutions like the SS's "Organization for Mutual Help" or with the aid of some still-active, influential former party-friends, to receive an old age pension. The merits they "earned" themselves during the Third Reich pay off well in West Germany of 1959.

Ex-Nazis Draw Fat Pensions

A Frankfurt administration court sentenced the town of Offenbach to pay its former Nazi-mayor Schranz, retroactive as of April 1, 1951, a transition salary and after his 65th birthday a monthly pension. Schranz became a member of the Nazi party as early as 1925 and acted as mayor of Offenbach from 1934 until the end of the war in 1945.

Pensions men like Schranz and other former members of the Nazi party receive today sometimes run to almost incredible amounts. The former Secretary of State in the Nazi Ministry of Justice, Dr. Kurt Rothenberger, was sentenced during the Nuremberg trial of war criminals to a long prison term. He was released in October 1951.

Since that date Rothenberger has received 190,726 German Marks (about 47,000 dollars). His monthly pension thus amounts to 2073.19 German Marks, equivalent to the monthly salary of a West Germany company president.

Rothenberger was succeeded by Franz Schleglberger in the Ministry of Justice. Together with Nazi-leader Kaltenbrunner he inspected concentration camps during the war, and found "everything in order."

With his assistance the notorious 13th decree was prepared, under which Jews were no longer subordinate to the courts but to the SS.

Schleglberger receives a monthly pension only slightly less than that of his predecessor.

Former Nazi-lawyer Lautz still receives a monthly government pay-check of 750 German Marks, roughly two-and-a-half times as much as the average West German income.

Firms Loyal to Hitler Still Flourish

Business firms which today contribute to the Economic Recovery of West Germany showed exactly the same loyalty to the Nazi Government. But no steps have ever been taken against them.

The neo-Nazis of today are tarred with the same brush as the thugs who rose to power with Hitler. By uncovering their organizations whenever possible, the West German Government and democratically-minded citizens, are fighting them tooth and nail. Only recently, lectures dealing with the dark days of the Hitler era have been made obligatory in West German High Schools. And it is more than a gesture of goodwill that the West German Government wants to extend reparation rights to former victims of the Nazi regime now living in East Germany.

But West Germans know only too well the Hitler threat is real. Even the government has no doubt that the neo-Nazis have found fanatical supporters among disgruntled veterans of World War II and easily-influenced youths who think of Hitler as a martyred hero.

HITLER'S TOP AIDE IS ALIVE!

by HARVEY WILSON

Martin Bormann directs world wide anti-Jewish campaign from hideout

Today, throughout West Germany 30,000 Jews, the remnant of the half-million who lived there before Hitler's purges got going, are lying low again, wondering just how far the clock is slipping back for them.

In Cologne, West Germany, a synagogue was smeared with a Nazi swastika and daubed with the dictum "Juden Raus" ("Jews get out").

In Berlin's Glienicke Park, 25 German students dressed with the old trimmings—brown shirts, breeches, jackboots and armbands emblazoned with swastikas, chanted Nazi songs and tramped with a Nazi flag.

In New York two teenagers and a mail clerk of 21, were discovered with swastika armbands, a recording of Adolf Hitler's maniacal rantings and membership cards in a hate-inspired National American Renaissance Party.

In Cleveland four high school boys of "superior intelligence" organized themselves into the "Fourth Reich," dedicated to extermination of "all Jews and Communists."

This wasn't a quarter century ago when Hitler was whipping Germany into World War II. This was 1960.

It was happening in far flung parts of the world—in London and Rome, in Cincinnati and Chicago. Churches have been desecrated, public buildings vandalized. Even tombstones have been violated by painted swastikas.

Martin Bormann was fulfilling his destiny—Martin Bormann, the man who seized leadership of the ruthless SS (Elite Guard) when Der Fuehrer foresaw his doom as Russian artillery battered Berlin on April 29, 1945—nine days before Germany's unconditional surrender. Martin Bormann was executing his heritage of hate.

Bormann was the No. 2 Nazi in 1945, Hitler's first deputy.

For 15 years he has flitted from city to city, nation to nation, continent to continent. He has never been caught—but now the *Police Gazette* can reveal that he has been seen, stamped as the mastermind plotting a world-wide rebirth of anti-Semitism. That's the way Hitler willed it that night of April 29, 1945, in the momentary security of a bomb shelter under the Reichschancellory.

Bormann has been playing an international game of hide-and-seek with intelligence officers. But last August an Italian secret service agent came face-to-face with him in Argentina.

The agent waited three years, and his patience was rewarded. During those three years he gained the confidence of the Fascist units in Italy working closely with Bormann's Nazi cells.

Infiltrating the Fascist underground in Italy, the agent became a courier to and from Bormann's contact man in Munich, operating under the undercover name of "Max Wagner," one of the cruelest characters to cross from Germany to Northern Italy during the Hitler-Mussolini war alliance.

The courier, having established himself in the trust of Wagner, was sent to Argentina with documents for one Kurt Keppler. He was given an address in Buenos Aires.

INSIDE THE *NEW* HITLER NAZI EMPIRE!

by HARVEY WILSON

Ex-henchmen of Hitler from Nazi Germany now work for Nasser and are changing the United Arab Republic into another gory Third Reich

Today, while the memory of the chaotic empire once ruled by Adolf Hitler is dimming in a world threatened by nuclear war and communist aggression, that very same chaotic empire is being recreated step by step in the Middle East.

Gamel Abdel Nasser, self-appointed Fuhrer of the Arabs, has gathered about him hundreds of Hitler's ex-henchmen and embarked on an ambitious program to make the United Arab Republic identical to the Third Reich.

Nazi Pattern Followed

Following "Mein Kampf" with fanatical slavishness, every phase of life under Nasser is in strict adherence to the pattern set by Nazi Germany.

For example, Nasser has realized, as did Hitler before him, the importance of controlling the youth of the nation. The new generation in Egypt has been formed into the Arab version of the Hitler Jugend, complete with the uniforms, the marching and the teachings of state supremacy over the individual.

The organization is identical, with the basic unit of 15 youths, boys or girls, being grouped into larger and larger units along military lines. Only one thing has changed, the Nazi swastika has been replaced by the crescent of the Muslims.

In charge of this nation-wide regimentation of youth is a staff composed *entirely* of former Hitler Jugend leaders, imported especially for that purpose. They do as they did for Hitler.

Names Are Changed

Heading this staff are two ex-SS Generals. In overall command is Colonel Hassan Suleiman, formerly SS Gruppenfuhrer Moser of Sudenten-German origin. Moser is assisted by Lt. Colonel Amman, who in actuality is the onetime SS Gruppenfuhrer Buble.

Under their able guidance, little has been changed from the German pattern. The Egyptian youth today goose-step and salute much as did their predecessors of 30 years ago.

Nor has the older generation of Egypt been overlooked. Following Hitler's lead, Nasser has attempted to win over as much of the population as possible by propaganda, while the unruly rest are dealt with by his Arab SS and Gestapo. As is every other organization within the U.A.R. Nasser's Secret Police and Elite Guard are patterned directly after the original Nazi Conception and staffed by ex-Nazis.

Nasser's security forces are divided into two major organizations, as in Germany, the Secret Police and the Elite Guard. The Egyptian equivalent to the Nazi SS is the State Security Cadre, the SSC. It is an extremely well organized body of Arab storm troopers, 70,000 strong.

It is identical in every way to Hitler's Elite SS Guard. In fact, while Nasser uses former Nazis only in advisory or supervisory capacities, the SSC contains many ex-storm troopers within its rank and file.

The SSC Headquarters are located on Liberation Square in Cairo, in a building reminiscent of the old Gestapo Headquarters at Prinz Albrech Strasse in Berlin. It is staffed entirely with old-guard Nazis, with overall command in the hands of Leopold Gleim.

Now calling himself Lt. Colonel Al-Nasher, Gleim was once head of Hitler's personal bodyguard and formerly commanded all Gestapo units in German-occupied Poland.

As in Nazi Germany, Nasser has called for nationwide regimentation of youth trained by staff of former goose-stepping Hitler Jugend leaders.

Following Germany's collapse in 1945, Gleim escaped to Egypt. He was tried in absentia as a war criminal by the Allies and sentenced to death for atrocities his units committed under his orders.

Far from being a hunted, dogged refugee as was Adolf Eichmann, he sits securely in his Arab office, once again directing the arrest of enemies of the state.

Nasser's Gestapo, like Hitler's, has several departments whose combined aim is to eliminate all opposition to the regime by the use of terror, arrest and extermination.

Former Gestapo Chief in Charge

One of these is the Secret Police, organized and run by Joachim Damling. Damling comes well-equipped for his post, having been the head of the Gestapo in Dusseldorf under Hitler. Under his command, the Secret Police has become every bit the efficient terror weapon that the Nazi Gestapo once was.

His nominal title, Advisor on Special Activities, belies Damling's real role as Nasser's Heindrich Himmler!

Another department under Damling's control concerns itself with the operation of concentration camps. There are five major concentration camps in Egypt.

Concentration Camps Active

As in the early days of Hitler's regime, they are used primarily for the imprisonment and liquidation of political prisoners. Two of these, El-Kanater and Abu-Sabal, are located outside of Cairo. The rest are situated away from the populated areas, with one at Maharik in upper Egypt, one at Qena and El-Kharga in the desert, and the fifth at Samara, 200 kilometers southwest of Alexandria.

This last is typical of the extent to which the Nasser government is imitating the Third Reich. It was built as an exact duplicate of Dachau by use of old blueprints and photographs. Dachau was not designed for detention of prisoners, but for their extermination. Nasser's Dachau at Samara is being used for the same sinister purpose. The likeness is almost incredible.

Hitler Experts Hired

In overall command of the concentration camp system, working directly under Damling, are two experienced ex-SS officers, well versed in their jobs. Dr. Hans Eisele was once chief physician at the Nazi concentration camp at Buchenwald. Heinrich Willermann was at one time medical director at Dachau. Willermann, formerly a SS Hauptstabsarzt, is now known as Lt. Colonel Naim Fahum.

The control of the nation's regular prisons is also in the

hands of former SS personnel. Supervision of these prisons is the responsibility of the Egyptian Security Police, which in turn is directed by Colonel Ben Salem. Salem, under his former name of SS Oberfuhrer Bernhardt Bender, once headed the Intelligence Service of the Nazi Secret Police in the Ukraine during the war. His SS training has helped him immeasurably in his present work, that of reorganizing all Egyptian prisons according to Gestapo concepts.

The economy of the United Arab Republic is also being reorganized along Nazi patterns. This includes the building of a powerful military machine paid for by increased taxes and contributions from other neo-Nazi circles. The U.A.R. is also pushing a program of heavy industrialization and an increase in agricultural production in a method recalling the five-year plan carried out by Hermann Goering in the late 1930's.

The economic planning of the U.A.R. is largely in the hands of Hjalmar Schacht, Hitler's former Reichbank president and Minister of Economics. Operating from his headquarters in Dusseldorf, where he presides over a bank, Schacht has established a vast network of German-Arab trade to help Nasser's economic policy.

One aspect of this trade, the "import" of ex-Nazis into the U.A.R. for the exclusive use of Nassar's government, is handled quite effectively by Schacht's son-in-law, ex-SS Colonel Otto Skorzeny.

During the war, Skorzeny commanded the Special Services branch of the Waffen-SS. His unit carried out such missions as the rescue of Mussolini, the kidnapping of the Hungarian regent Admiral Horthy, and the placing of 150 storm troopers behind Allied lines in the early days of the Battle of the Bulge.

At the end of the war, Skorzeny escaped to Spain, where he carried on a fight to clear himself of war crime charges which lasted several years. Once cleared, by means of a long legal battle with the West German government, Skorzeny set about the establishment of a world-wide organization whose purpose was to keep the ideals of Naziism alive.

Possible Bormann Link

It is quite possible that he is acting under orders from Martin Bormann, once No. 2 Nazi under Hitler and who now lives in the Argentine. However, no definite connection between the two has ever been uncovered. From his headquarters outside Dublin, Ireland, Skorzeny directs this vast network of neo-Nazis in their attempt to propagate the Nazi faith. Since Nasser assumed power in 1952, Skorzeny has been one of his chief henchmen in the Nazification of the U.A.R.

Working under the innocent guise of an import-export firm in Cairo, and using the unlimited resources placed at his disposal by Nasser, Skorzeny imports items of a very special nature. For the exclusive use of the U.A.R. government, he smuggles in former Nazi officials.

Through his hands pass ex-Gestapo agents for Nasser's police, former Hitler Jugend leaders for the Egyptian youth movement, SS generals and propaganda officials, Luftwaffe parachutists and Afrikakorps officers; in short, every kind of Hitlerian lieutenant who fulfills certain basic requirements.

These requirements are simple: A fanatic belief in Naziism, acceptance of Nasser as the new Fuehrer, hatred of America, France, Britain and Israel, and some special skill for use by the U.A.R. Day-by-day and month-by-month more Nazis arrive in Egypt to help Nasser re-establish the Third Reich.

The influence of Naziism in Egypt is not new. It had its beginnings in the years before World War II. Egyptian Nationalists saw in Hitler's Germany a force which would break the British Empire, and thus liberate Egypt from English rule. With the defeat of Rommel in 1943, this dream did not end, but instead the mutual enemies of Germany and Egypt tended to draw the two closer together.

Even after the collapse of Germany in 1945, the Egyptians admired Hitler's accomplishments, and many fleeing Nazis found a better home in the Nile valley than did others in Argentina. The almost hero-worship which Egyptians had for the Nazis grew until it culminated in the successful seizure of power by the pro-Nazi forces under Nasser.

Not only are the men around Nasser, and indeed Nasser himself, aware that the Nazis are gaining more and more control of the U.A.R., they heartily approve it. As General Naguib said of the Germans in 1954, "They are the only ones in whom we have confidence."

In 1952, following the revolt which put Nasser into power, one of the new Fuhrer's ministers, Dr. Noureddine Tarraf, said: "Hitler is the man of my life. The German dictator had been an ideal leader. I have always wished to live like him."

Even the rank and file of the U.A.R. refer to Hitler affectionately as "Abu Ali."

The U.A.R. has also gained many of its Nazi personnel by offering unconditional protection to war criminals. Such men as ex-SS Major Otto Remer, who is wanted by the West German government for his neo Nazi activities after the war, have been welcomed in the U.A.R. with open arms. While such men as Adolf Eichmann found seclusion and secrecy in the Argentine, others have found employment and open approval of their Nazi beliefs in Nasser's Egypt.

What *Would* Happen to Germany and the Jews

IF HITLER CAME BACK TODAY!

by HARVEY WILSON

Der Fuehrer is far from forgotten in today's Germany.
The rest of world may shrink from the memory of the
Nazi terror, but an authoritative public opinion poll reveals
that Hitlerism is still alive . . .

Facts revealing the true feelings of the German people toward Hitler, and which are of tremendous significance to the Free World, have just been uncovered because a high German official was indiscreet in an interview.

Asked this question by a reporter: "Would Adolf Hitler have an easy job taking the German people in if he came back today?" Dr. Fritz Bauer, Attorney General of the powerful state of Hesse, replied:

"If I am to be honest, *yes!* If Hitler appeared in Germany today, he would not be rejected by the German people. I do not believe that the young German democracy would be strong enough to show him the door. Just the fact that the Germans would not turn their backs on him at once, would have the effect that Hitler and his ideas would find a good soil for growth in the Germany of 1963."

These opinions caused such a storm of protest that Dr. Bauer was threatened with removal from office by his party; and the Federal Government was wild.

The official German pollsters (Institut fur Demoskopie in

Allensbach) sent out interviewers to different parts of West Germany to question representative citizens. Newspapers and magazines got into the act and took polls on their own.

The facts brought in by these opinion-takers will greatly surprise the American public.

It was found, for instance, that Hitler is higher in public opinion today than Erhard, the popular Minister of National Economy, and heir-designate of Chancellor Adenauer. Hitler is higher even than Frederick the Great and Bismarck, the two national idols of the German people.

Five percent of the population over 16 in West Germany—that is, every twentieth person—considers Hitler to be the greatest statesman in German history.

Allensbach asked: "Would you say that without the war, Hitler would have been one of the greatest German statesmen?"

Yes! answered 36 percent of those asked. This is the answer of Germans in Germany today—18 years after Hitler's defeat. In 1955, 48 percent answered *Yes* to the same question.

Grim Facts About Poll

A particularly grim fact that was brought out by these recent polls is that more than one-third of the Germans today are satisfied with Hitler as he was up to 1939; this was the Hitler who had long before muzzled the press, wiped out political parties, persecuted the Jews, and set up the concentration camps.

When the questioners dug a bit deeper for reasons, it was brought out that Hitler had incorporated Austria, the Sudeten country, the Memel region and half of Czechoslovakia into Germany, and seemed to be going on to new triumphs, they said. In other words, Hitler without war and above all without a lost war, was all right. No one seemed to remember the price that had been paid by the German people and by other nations for Hitler's so-called successes up till the spring of 1939.

Politicians, trade unionist, publicists, students, school teachers, secretaries, office workers were all asked for their opinions.

An Important Question

Interestingly enough, there was one question to which their answers were almost a uniform *No*. A politician like Hitler would have no chance today.

Eugen Kogon, professor of political science at the Darmstadt Institute of Technology, and author of the well-known book, "The SS State", states his opinions thus:

"Would the people of the Federal Republic, with the political knowledge and political morality of those days, but in the changed national and international conditions of today, be victims of Hitlerism? I say: *No*. Except for a couple of idiots, maybe. Particularly the modern, young people find the Hitler hysteria both revolting and comical.

"Also, today Hitler would have far fewer reasons and excuses to get excited than then: no Versailles, no reparations, no unemployment, no many-party system, no continual change of governments. . . . Everybody knows that."

NO VERSAILLES, Kogon says; and strangely enough, he is right. Actually, Germany lost much more in 1945 than in 1918. And yet from 1919 to 1939 the German people suffered under the "shame of Versailles"—while today the partition of Germany into three parts, a Polish Communist strip, a German Communist strip, and a democratic strip is accepted philosophically by the inhabitants of the democratic strip.

Although the separation of the Eastern regions of Germany is still the subject of stormy demonstrations now and then, the great majority in the West seems to be more or less reconciled to the separation of the Soviet Zone.

NO REPARATIONS: There were some; Krupp was dismantled until 1951. But at the same time the Marshall Plan, that pumped

13 billion dollars into Europe, sent billions into Germany too. But the Young Plan of 1930 provided that Germany should at first pay 1.6 billion marks a year and in 1966, 48 years after the end of the first World War, would have to pay 2.4 billion marks in reparations! A certain amount of foreign illusions certainly helped Hitler a great deal.

No Revolt in Sight

NO UNEMPLOYMENT: In 1932 there were 5.6 million unemployed in Germany. Thirty percent of those who wanted to work could not. Thousands of them hung around in the city parks, playing cards, arguing, or sleeping with a newspaper over their faces. Today there are jobs for everyone who wants to work.

NO MANY-PARTY SYSTEM: In January 1933 there were twelve parties represented in the Reichstag, seven of them with less than twenty deputies. In the fourteen years of the Weimar Republic there were twelve different Chancellors, three in 1932 alone. In the fourteen years of the Federal Republic the West Germans have been blessed with a single inexhaustible Chancellor and a permanent Minister of Economics. Only three parties are represented in the Bundestag, since the election law keeps splinter parties out of Parliament.

In 1932 street fighting between the parties, above all between Nazis and Communists, caused 140 deaths and thousands of wounded. Many voters who did not have Nazi ideas felt that it was vitally important to get rid of the dangerous radical *left* party, the Communists, by means of the apparently less dangerous radical *right* party—to drive the devil out with Beelzebub in order to save the state. Today the German Communist Party is forbidden.

And so the economic and political conditions have changed basically in Germany. Instead of the universal despair of 1932, universal plenty reigns in 1963. People that are satisfied do not want revolutions. Since Hitler's rise is unthinkable without the dangerous conditions of the Weimar period, a Hitler has no practical chance *today*.

Many Would Support Nazis

And what about tomorrow? Could a Hitler have a chance *tomorrow*? There is no simple answer. "I would not shrink at a political murder!" was one student's opinion. "I would join at once, if the new man was clean!" admitted a retired detective.

One of the questions that the Allensbach public opinion researchers asked was, "Supposing that a new Nazi party tried to come to power, what would your stand be?"

"I would welcome it and support such a party," said five percent of the adult Federal citizens.

"I would welcome it, but not help it along," said another five percent. These two groups together form the genuine Nazis: seven percent of the Germans today (Ten years ago, it was 13 percent.)

"I would do everything I could to prevent it," declared 34 percent. One-third of the adult population in West Germany today are active opponents of a new dictatorship: not a bad result.

But: According to the positions taken, it is "indifferent" to almost one out of five West Germans (over 16) whether a new Nazi party came to power, and 12 percent had no opinion at all to express. People with that reaction make perfect fellow-travelers. Together they make 30 percent of those asked, and combined with the declared Nazis, 37 percent. If you add to this the 29 percent that would be against having the power taken over by a new Nazi party, but would not do anything to prevent it—a deceiver of the people who of course fears only active opponents, could count on pretty good chances. A sad state of affairs.

The students that were asked what they would do if a new Nazi party arose today can be broken up into three groups:

THE BRAVE: "To the barricades! If that does not help, work in the underground. In little groups, giving out leaflets."

THE PRUDENT: "Put a toothbrush in my pocket and beat it."

THE SHREWD ONES (A small minority): "I'd support the man, to make the best of the situation."

In order to weigh the chances of a "new Hitler," it would be best to examine three points:

What are the old Nazis doing?

How many new Nazis are there, and how organized are they?

What influence among apparently harmless citizens do the teachings of the talented Dr. Goebbels, "Reichsminister for Public Education and Propaganda," still have?

As we know, the old Nazis are doing all right for themselves: former Ministers (Oberlander), present Secretaries of State (Globke), former Federal Attorneys General (Frankel) and numerous judges and high police officials.

Unknown Nazis

Along with the old Nazis that have been known for a long time, or at least since a short time ago, there are those that are still unknown. On that subject Attorney General Bauer said in his interview:

"I don't think we shall ever see the end of our work. One war criminal trial brings five other crimes out. It is an avalanche that never comes to an end. I don't know how we are ever going to be able to get our hands on all these whole, half and quarter Nazis that there still are in Germany. The latest disgraceful affair in Wurzburg, where a young doctor unmasked five prominent citizens as old first-class Nazis and as a result had to leave the state, is a typical one.

"It is no cheerful task that my attorneys and I have taken on ourselves. We have a whole desk drawer full of anonymous threatening letters to prove it. Here and there our efforts are greeted with joy, but if you ask me whether we are popular among the population, the answer must be no. The Germans don't want any more old Nazis and their deeds to be brought out into the open."

And what about the new Nazis? On March 7, 1963 the Federal Ministry of the Interior published an extensive report on "Radical Right and Anti-Semitic Tendencies in 1962". Of the many details given in it, the following are the most interesting:

There were fifteen right radical parties in 1962, as against twenty-two in 1959.

The total membership of these parties has gone down from 17,200 to 11,500 in the last three years. (Enrolled members in the Nazi Party; in 1931: 806,000). All the right radical youth organizations had a total of only 1000 members in 1932 (Hitler Youth 1932: about 100,000).

The Office for the Protection of the Constitution took up 205 "Nazi and anti-Semitic actions" in 1962: anti-Semitic statements, painting of swastikas, desecration of cemeteries and illegal pamphlets. In 1960 there were almost six times as many (predominantly in connection with the kidnapping of Eichmann in Argentina)

Almost half of those committing the actions were under thirty. In one-fourth of the cases the Ministry of the Interior lists them as mere "disorderly conduct."

The Federal Minister of the Interior comes to the following conclusion:

"Radicalism of the right in the Federal Republic is in a state of continuing splitting and isolation.

"On the whole, there is no acute danger to constitutional order in the territory of the Federal Republic under existing political and economic conditions."

This is a question that is challenged by those who do not believe that the poisonous Hitler-Goebbels heritage can be dismissed so easily.

Dr. Thomas Denier, Vice-president of the Bundestag, expresses an entirely different opinion. He believes that political parties have given up their spiritual and political goals. "Political thinking has adapted itself to the feeling of prosperity," he says. "They (the parties) boast of being 'people's parties.' Actually they have given up any and all clearcut goals, and promise all things to all men . . . Basic political questions—to say nothing of ideals—play a smaller and smaller part, and group interests a larger and larger part.

"These politically washed-out Germans are not at all resistant to a 'strong man,'" he continued. "The glorification of De Gaulle on his triumphal journey through Germany was also in large part the glorification of a 'Fuehrer' with the great imperial gesture, regardless of the fact that he has wiped out democracy in his country.

Hitler's Admirers

"In point of fact, we find everywhere the admirers of Hitler's 'accomplishments.'

"In six years Hitler built 3700 kilometers of superhighways," they say. "The Federal Government has just got up to 970 kilometers in fourteen years." Under Hitler, they tell us, there was no adolescent problem and no juvenile delinquency, but instead girls doing their year of service, enough nurses, Strength through Joy cruises and subways for every big city.

In some respects these people are right. But they are wrong or they lie when they act as though there were no reverse side to the coin. If you are ready to accept galloping inflation, to sacrifice freedom of speech and gradually all freedoms, to put barbed wire around innocent men and exterminate Jews with gas, then for that you can certainly have superhighways and girls doing a year of service. A competent dictator can do some things. But it calls for a Price. And the price is too high.

So far as the Jews are concerned, Attorney General Bauer said:

"You cannot get a German today to give his honest opinion about the Jews. To foreigners he will always bewail what happened to the Jews during the war, but under this thin surface coating there lurks a red-hot anti-Semitism, even though there is no Jewish problem in Germany." (Bauer later denied the word "red-hot."

A spokesman for the Federal Government explained on February 28, 1963 that as early as 1960, in connection with the Eichmann incident, the Government had shown in a White Book that there were no points of support for "any considerable portion of the German people holding anti-Semitic attitudes."

The writer, James A. Huebschmann, wrote a letter to the Danish newspaper on this matter:

"Just who writes the White Book that is so often quoted? Where do they get their information? The White Book looks to me like calling the accused man up in court to testify against himself. Only an international, independent commission can cast light on this."

In its report of March 7, 1963, on right-radical and anti-Semitic tendencies, the Federal Ministry of the Interior concedes that although the number of anti-Semitic actions has decreased—because of criminal prosecutions—still:

"Undoubtedly the decrease in publicly manifested anti-Semitism is not as a rule due to any change in the opinions of its supporters."

If we put side by side the Government report made in March of this year, the less cheering results of the public opinion questionnaires, and the statistically imponderable, but deeply-rooted popular admiration for Hitler's partial accomplishments, we get the impression:

There may not be a very great deal of Nazism in circulation in the body of the German people, but it is not so very little either. All the experts seem to agree that as long as the people have plenty to eat and plenty of jobs, Naziism is no danger.

But suppose that food gets a bit short? Suppose there is a depression, unemployment, banks close, the employment offices are crowded and the TV set goes back for non-payment. Even a Nazi party that turned up *today*, we found, would receive seven percent of members and thirty percent of fellow-travelers. What would happen after a crash?

Of the students asked, about half gave a man like Hitler a big chance in the event of a serious depression, a quarter gave him slight chances, and the last quarter gave him no chance, even with a depression and certainly none at all without a depression.

What should be done then? The only sure means, obviously, is to avoid a depression. And for the long run, to try to anchor democratic feelings deeper in all Germans than they have gone so far. We can see some hopeful signs.

Recent Report of Hitler's Death Is False!

Recent newspaper reports from the Soviet Union have created the misleading impression that the Russians officially regard Hitler as dead.

THIS IS NOT TRUE!

The *Police Gazette* asked the Soviet Government to confirm the recent reports and learned that the minor Red Army officer who expressed this opinion to an American author, who was writing a book, was speaking only for himself and had no first-hand knowledge of the facts.

The Soviet position was clearly spelled out by the official statements made by Marshal Georgi Zhukov, Chief of Operations during the Battle of Berlin; Colonel-General Nikolai E. Berzarin, the Soviet Berlin Commander; Major-General Alexis Sidnev, who was Chief of Soviet Intelligence for Berlin; and Stalin himself.

Three weeks after the Russians occupied Berlin, Marshal Zhukov announced: "We have found no body that could be Hitler's. Hitler had a good opportunity of getting away."

Colonel-General Berzarin revealed that several bodies with Hitler's name sewed in the clothes were found in the Reichschancellery, but not one was that of Hitler. In a radio broadcast, Berzarin stated: "My opinion is that Hitler disappeared into Europe."

Major-General Sidnev, who, as the Red Intelligence officer conducted the on-the-spot investigation into reports that Hitler had committed suicide in the bunker, said: "No clue to support the theory of Hitler's suicide was uncovered by Soviet intelligence."

And when Marshal Stalin was asked point blank by a US official at the Potsdam Conference if Hitler was dead, Stalin with characteristic bluntness and brevity replied in one word: "NO!"

Another myth that has been given wide circulation is that Hitler's dentures were found. This is not so! Colonel W. F. Heimlich, former Chief, US Intelligence, Berlin, reported to Washington: "No evidence has been found of Hitler's death in Berlin . . . We had X-ray photographs of Hitler's head which gave us expert clues as to his dental structure and even one tooth might have been sufficient to identify his body. None were found."

After 20 Years in Hiding . . .

HITLER CAN NOW RETURN

How He Escaped and Has Eluded Capture

by HARVEY WILSON

It was 20 years ago, on April, 30, 1945, that Adolf Hitler mysteriously disappeared from his underground bunker in the Reich chancellery in war torn Berlin. He vanished, as Allied forces were encircling the city.

Rumors soon circulated that Der Fuehrer had committed suicide and his body burned in the Reich chancellery courtyard. But the truth, as Allied intelligence agents were to discover later, was that Hitler and his top aides had escaped. Reports of his death were a hoax.

An on-the-spot investigation conducted by Col. W. C. Heimlich, Chief of US Intelligence in Berlin, disproved the theory that Hitler had committed suicide. He reported to Washington that there was no evidence of Hitler's death.

Just recently newspaper reports from unnamed European sources have stated that the Reds had found and removed Hitler's body. These reports have no basis of fact and intelligence officials suspect that they are being circulated by Nazi agents to frustrate any world-wide search for Der Fuehrer.

It was Col. Gen. Nicholai F. Berzarin, Soviet Berlin Commander, who declared after he entered Berlin, "My personal opinion is that Hitler disappeared into Europe!" And he was the first Allied official to urge an immediate world-wide hunt for the missing dictator.

If the Reds had found Hitler's body, Col. Gen. Berzarin would have been the first to know it!

Why Hitler Can Return

Today, top officials in the West German Justice Ministry concede that Hitler might be alive. They were prepared for it as they announced that the 20-year constitutional statute of limitations will expire May 8. After that date, *no more Nazi war criminals will be brought to trial.* Hitler, and his top aides, such as the notorious Martin Bormann, can then come out of hiding and safely return to Germany if they wish.

Apparently anticipating the protests, Heinrich Thiesmeyer, spokesman for the West German Justice Ministry, called on Intelligence services all over the world to deliver before May 8, Hitler and his chief aide, Martin Bormann, and 2,000 other Nazi fugitives still at large.

After that date, war criminals would not only be saved from prosecution in West Germany but would no longer be subject to extradition should they show themselves in foreign lands.

A top ministry official told the *Police Gazette*:

"The West German government is fully aware that no evidence of Hitler's purported suicide was ever found.

"We also know that Col. W. F. Heimlich, chief of United States intelligence in Berlin at end of the war, and who conducted the official American army investigation, reported to Washington that Hitler had 'every opportunity to escape.'

"And we have received reports from diplomatic and intelligence sources that Hitler and top aides, such as Martin Bormann, are alive and hiding out in South America.

"Under these circumstances, we wanted to officially state far in advance that the statute of limitations covering all Nazi war crimes expire May 8 of this year—so we could not be accused of having minimized or kept the date a secret."

The West German official showed considerable annoyance over implications that the Bonn Government should be expected to find the Nazi fugitives.

"People seem to forget that after the war the United States, Britain, France, and the Soviet Union each had their own military government ruling German territory," this official pointed out.

"The Federal Republic of Germany didn't come into being until Sept. 1, 1949, four years after end of the war," he added.

"If the Allies were unable to round up all the fugitive Nazis that escaped through their fingers in the years they ruled Germany, how can we be expected to find them now?" he asked.

"We have done everything in our power to find and prosecute Nazi war criminals," this spokesman said. "The West German courts have convicted 5,445 persons for such crimes."

Of these 818 were sentenced to death; 486 have been executed.

"There are 750 cases still pending that will occupy the German courts for years," he said.

"We are anxious to prosecute every case that is brought to our attention before the May 8 deadline," the German official concluded.

Vigorous Protests

But that very May 8 date is vigorously protested. Gerhart H. Seger, now living in New York and a former German Reichstag member from 1930 to 1933, argues:

"The statute of limitations, in this case 20 years, is being applied on the date of Germany's surrender, May 8, 1945.

"There is no reason to use that date. From 1945 to 1949 all Nazi criminals were tried by Allied Occupation courts, and the German sovereignty did not begin until the German Constitution became effective, May 23, 1949.

"It would be far more logical to count the 20 years of limitations from that date Instead of May 8, 1945.

"This would give the Federal Republic of Germany four more years of possible prosecution of Nazi criminals without changing or violating the constitution."

Another outspoken critic of the move is Kurt Grossmann, spokesman for the major Jewish organizations in the United States on German Matters.

He charged bitterly that the decision "must shock anyone interested in the cause of Justice and also in the democratic development of the Bundes Republic."

Grossmann pointed out that Dr. Robert M. W. Kempner, former United States War Crimes Prosecutor in Nuremberg, estimates there are about 10,000 Nazi murderers not yet prosecuted.

"These would benefit by the incomprehensible decision of the Bundes Cabinet," Grossmann declared.

He contends that thousands of unknown "Nazi murderers" are still free because they have not yet been identified in war crime cases.

"The experience has been that when a Nazi is brought to trial, in defending his position he names the superiors, or other Nazis, that directed him to commit the atrocities." Grossmann stated.

"In the 750 cases pending, most of which won't be tried until after the statute of limitations expires, Nazis named by defendants as actual murderers will escape punishment."

And this includes Hitler, Bormann and other top Nazis.

Are there mysterious forces at work behind the Bonn Government's decision?

No less a personage than German Chancellor Ludwig Erhard himself favors extension of the statute. He said it is not bearable to let perpetrators of the most atrocious crimes go scot-free.

Dr. Erhard assured Dr. Nahum Goldmann, president of the World Jewish Congress which also protests the decision, that he, Erhard, would like to see the statute extended for 10 years.

"But I am bound by the decision of my cabinet," he told Dr. Goldman recently.

Nazi Influence

Of the more than 2,000 known Nazi war criminals still at large, many of them hiding in South America, some exert considerable influence inside West Germany today.

It is believed that the powerful friends of these fugitive Nazis influenced the decision of the Bonn Government.

This becomes more apparent with admissions in recent months of high German officials that many top Nazis believed to have perished in the flaming ruins of defeated Germany have actually escaped.

Fritz Bauer, prosecutor in Frankfurt, publicly declared that the German Republic has reliable information that Deputy Fuhrer Bormann is in South America.

Gerhard Schroeder, German foreign minister, told friends that Dr. Joseph Mengele, author of Hitler's plan of genocide, is living "somewhere in Paraguay."

These men slipped away during the collapse of the Nazi war machine. Many believe Hitler did also.

Marshal Georgi Zhukov, supreme Soviet commander in 1945, announced flatly in Berlin:

"We have found no corpse that could be Hitler's. Hitler had good opportunity of getting away.

"He could have taken off at the very last moment for there was an airfield at his disposal." (The "airfield" was an autobon adjacent to the Reich Chancellery where Hitler was staying.)

Major Gen. Floyd Parks, who led the first US airborne division into Berlin on July 1, 1945, told the *Police Gazette* that in the light of all available evidence he had received "Hitler may very well be alive."

What were the facts of the time?

The bloodstains on the couch where Hitler was supposed to have shot himself were analyzed by US Military Intelligence during Col. Heimlich's exhaustive probe.

They were not of the blood type Hitler was known to have. Nor were they of Eva Braun's type.

Hitler reportedly shot himself on that couch. But there were no bullet holes in the couch or in the wall behind it.

Reports that Hitler's body was drenched with gasoline and burned in the Reich Chancellery courtyard and his ashes strewn about the garden were disproved by US Intelligence agents.

They doused a 160-pound pig with 200 liters of gasoline and set fire to the dead animal. All they got was roast pork. The carcass remained.

A check with the Berlin Crematorium revealed that it was necessary to burn a body for three hours at 3,500 to 4,200 degree heat in an enclosed oven in order to reduce the body, including the large bones, to powder.

An inch-by-inch search of the entire courtyard was made under Col. Heimlich's direction.

First, all debris was cleared up, such odds and ends of war as broken machine guns, ammunition, rifles, helmets, uniforms and bits of wood, leather and metal.

All were examined and piled in one corner of the courtyard.

Then, two screens were erected—one with mesh the size of chicken wire and, behind this, one with half-inch holes.

No Clue Discovered

Every shovelful of dirt in that yard went first through the wide screen and then through the narrower one. There was not the faintest sign of any part of a human body.

Col. Heimlich reported.

"After two days of excavation in an ever widening area we found no signs of any bodies and, more significantly, no evidence of burning or fire!" This was conclusive; the report that Hitler's body had been burned in the courtyard was a hoax.

High United States officials authorized Col. Heimlich to publicly state afterwards:

"On the basis of present evidence, no insurance company in America would pay a death claim on Adolf Hitler."

It was the decision of the Allied Powers, however, to keep the report of Col. Heimlich confidential. Authorities feared that anything promoting the belief that Hitler had escaped alive from Berlin would be disruptive in occupying Germany.

With the belief that Hitler was dead, the psychological defeat of Germany would be complete, they reasoned. It wasn't until years later that the *Police Gazette* brought the Heimlich report into the open.

It is interesting to note that the last published list of "wanted war criminals" issued by the Allies, in 1948, included this cryptic notice:

"Wanted: Hitler, Adolf—Reichsfuhrer."

Now, time is running out on the search for Hitler. Once the statute of limitations expires, on May 8, he can come out of hiding from his remote, guarded hideout in South America and breathe the air as a free man.

Hitler & Mussolini: Pen Pals

This section presents letters between Adolph Hitler and Benito Mussolini written from May 9, 1940, to December 31, 1940. The *Police Gazette* claims it's the first mass-circulation magazine or newspaper to print them, which is not surprising. Along with the fun, irony, and nonsense, the *Gazette* at its best always included well-reported, serious news you might not get anywhere else.

The first letter is dated the day before Germany began its blitz-krieg against western Europe. Within six weeks, France, Belgium, the Netherlands, and Luxembourg were all conquered, and British forces had been pushed back into the Channel. Italy joined the war on June 10, and by the end of the month, the two countries controlled all of continental Europe, not counting a few neutral nations. These were the salad days for Hitler and Mussolini. And their giddiness is infectious. You almost start rooting for Hitler to win . . . until you remind yourself he was a psychopathic mass murderer.

Hitler's irrational hatred for Jews and Communists, among others, would be his downfall. By summer of 1940, only Britain stood in the way of total victory. But Hitler knew if he wanted to deal with Communism at its fountainhead, there was only one place to be. In Mussolini's return letters, his puzzlement at Hitler's dithering over how and when to attack Great Britain is evident. When Hitler writes him on December 31, 1940—the last letter printed by the *Police Gazette*—he looks forward to 1941 being the year they wrap things up, but never reveals the real reason he didn't throw a full assault against Britain. His hatred for Communists had trumped his strategic vision, and he'd already begun preparations to attack the Soviet Union. The move meant complete suicide—figuratively, if not literally. But in the letters we see him luring Mussolini into following his lead without telling him his primary intent. He is a duped Duce, and would pay the ultimate price within five years.

Another thing these letters show is Hitler during lucid moments. There are no rants against the groups mentioned above. He is kind, courteous, thoughtful, articulate. Without the psychosis, Hitler is Napoleon. Just another in a long line of European strongmen who want to unify the continent by force. In France, to this day, Napoleon is a hero. Without the systematic torture and genocide, might Hitler have been viewed that way as well?

THE SECRET LETTERS BETWEEN HITLER AND MUSSOLINI

How they plotted to rule the world—told in their own words!

For Adolph Hitler, the Spring of 1940 marked the peak of his world-shaking career. The seeds of destiny, planted long ago, had grown, blossomed and burst into full bloom like the roses in the gardens behind the Reichschancellery.

He could see the roses from the office where he sat down on May 9 to write a letter to his friend Il Duce, who had the face of a bull dog, the voice of a lion, and the heart of a chicken. Roses as red as the blood that bathed Norway and Denmark, red as the poppy fields of Holland, Luxemburg, Belgium, and France that soon would be crushed by the German war machine.

The time for a massive attack on the Western Front was only hours away as the little man with the Charlie Chaplin mustache bent over his massive mahogany desk and scrawled a page of history, wooing Mussolini with a word bouquet from Der Fuehrer's garden of destiny. These are the words in which he announced the beginning of the Nazi attack on the West:

Adolf Hitler to Benito Mussolini

Berlin, May 9, 1940

Duce:

When you receive this letter I shall already have crossed the Rubicon.

The information which we received some days ago about the conversation between Chamberlain and Reynaud is undoubtedly exact. It emanates from the first concrete information about the impending operation by the British against Norway. I can therefore personally vouch for the exactness of the contents.

In spite of this the conviction within me has been reinforced that just as in the case of Norway a grandiose false maneuver is involved here too which is certainly aimed at inducing me to withdraw troops from the decisive front.

In the last few days there has been an increase in the number of reports that England, having learned from her experiences in Norway, is now resolved to carry out a surprise occupation of a certain number of important military bases in Holland. For this purpose England has demanded of the Dutch Government that it agree to the landing of British troops on its territory and to the occupation of airfields. The attitude of the Netherlands Government is uncertain. In any case they will not offer serious resistance. Their ties with British interests are too strong as is also the influence exerted by British money.

Halifax's speech yesterday suddenly let us know that the Norwegian adventure was to be regarded as having been abandoned in order to continue the struggle in another place. Troops have already been embarked or are being embarked at numerous places on the English coast. It is absolutely out of the question that their destination is the Mediterranean.

You can see for yourself, Duce, the true sentiments and attitude of Holland and Belgium, from the documents which I am enclosing for you herewith. The records of the threatening events of the last few days are still required to make them complete. The military situation is clear.

It will be impossible in future to cut Germany off from the north and deprive her of supplies of ores.

An attempt to attack the German Western Front from the Rhine to the frontier of Luxembourg is likewise out of the question. Any attempt would be drowned in a sea of blood.

Nor would it be possible to end the war in the Allies' favor by cutting Germany off from her sources of petroleum supplies since, as a result of our domestic measures directed toward autonomy and our Four-Year Plan, we shall already be in a position to supply our own requirements in the course of this year.

The only possibility for France and England to hope for a success would be to destroy the Ruhr or at least paralyze production there. From the beginning, all Anglo-French military plans have been directed toward this objective.

As, judging from the situation, we have been threatened since yesterday by immediate danger, I have therefore decided today to give the order to attack on the Western Front at 5:35 a.m. tomorrow to ensure the neutrality of Belgium and Holland, above all by military measures.

I beg you, Duce, apart from any feelings, to understand the force of the circumstances which compel me to act. It is a question of life or death for my people and the Reich for the next 500 or 1,000 years.

I should be failing in my duty if I did not fulfill what my judgment and necessity demand of me.

I hope that I shall be successful in creating shortly that situation to which I referred at our last meeting.

I will keep you informed as to the operations and you will thus be in a position to consider in complete freedom the decisions for which you deem it advisable to assume responsibility in the interests of your people.

With the greetings of an old comrade,

Yours,

(Signed) *A. Hitler*

Hitler's letter was a stirring call to arms but Mussolini, ever cautious, wasn't quite ready to embrace the grim Goddess of War. His reply was a careful one, offering congratulations and hope for success, but not yet naming the date when Italy would start shooting.

He added little to the faint, half-hearted promises made on his last meeting with Hitler two months before at the Brenner Pass. Then he said Italy soon would be ready to back up Germany's military offensive, but he pointed out that "financial limitations" would prevent his country from sustaining any long-drawn-out war effort. The heavy-jawed dictator wanted a quick knockout, not a close decision after 10 rounds.

Benito Mussolini to Adolf Hitler

Rome, May 10, 1940

Fuhrer:

I thank you for the message you sent at the moment when your troops were receiving the order to march to the west. As in the case of the campaign in Norway, the press and action of the Party will guide the mind of the Italian people toward understanding the necessity with which you were faced.

I feel that time is pressing for Italy, too, and I am deeply grateful for your promise to keep me informed of developments in the operations in order to put me in a position to make my decisions.

As for the Italian armed forces, the navy is ready and by the end of May two army groups in the east and west and also the air force and the anti-aircraft formations will be ready.

It is superfluous for me to tell you that I am following the progress of your troops with confidence and in a spirit of comradeship.

(Signed) *Mussolini*

The defenses of Holland, Belgium and Luxemburg were cracked like egg shells. On May 10, 1940, the first day of the Western Front campaign, Luxemburg fell. On the second, Holland was overrun by Germany troops. On the third, demoralized French troops began pulling out of Belgium. The skies poured down a steady black rain of bombs, bullets and paratroopers. German tanks ruled the roads,

German planes ruled the airways, Germany guns smashed all oppo-
sition. Frightened France clung to the desperate hope that the Magi-
not Line would hold, but Hitler knew the Swastika flag soon would
fly over Paris.

Flushed with victory, Der Fuehrer detailed his conquests in a new
dispatch to Mussolini. And his enthusiasm infected the Roman dictator.

Adolf Hitler to Benito Mussolini
The Fuhrer's Headquarters, May 13, 1940

Duce:

Pray accept first of all my grateful thanks for the understanding
which you showed for the pressure under which were forced to act.
Your personal attitude, which, as I know, is also that of your party,
press and public opinion is a factor which is operating greatly to
our advantage.

Today, I can give you, Duce, a general survey of the results of
our initial operations. I should like to preface it with the assurance that here, just as in Poland or Norway, our opponents, lacking
direct successes, will naturally have recourse to the most nonsensi-
cal lying reports. I consider this policy stupid, for it will be repudi-
ated by the reality in the shortest possible time.

The following are the events of the last few days: The attack
began on the front between Groningen and the southern tip of
Luxembourg, This is therefore an air line of about 450 km. Since
yesterday morning advance troops have also been working their
way forward in turn toward the Maginot Line at various places on
the front between the Moselle and the Rhine.

Paratroopers in Action

The first three days' offensive on the abovementioned 450 km.
front resulted in a breakthrough at all the frontier and fortified positions. Parts of these were extremely strong installations whose pow-

ers of resistance were greatly strengthened by the integrated system of rivers and canals. In spite of this, the whole of northern Holland, that is the province of Groningen, has already been occupied, the Issel position breached or opened up, and gaps made in the Grebbe Line at several important points. Independently of these, however, paratrooper, and airborne troops have also been dropped between The Hague, Rotterdam, Dordrecht and Norddeich. These formations, planted some 120–130 km. in front of our lines, have fought with unprecedented bravery; they safeguarded the bridges which they occupied, gained ground and repulsed all attacks by the Dutch and probably by several smaller English units also.

Since last night they have been joined by the vanguard of the first armored and motorized units, who had overcome great obstacles and resistance. Infantry divisions are proceeding by the same route by forced marches. Contact has thus been established and the fortress Holland breached from within. South of this the Juliana Canal, the Meuse, the Willems Canal, the Meuse and Scheldt Canals and the Albert Canal have been crossed. German units are here converging on Antwerp.

Difficulties Slow Advance

The most difficult problem, Duce, was the crossing of the Meuse and the Albert Canal near Maastricht. This sector is covered on its flanks by the fortress of Liege which was greatly strengthened and enlarged after the World War. Already the Meuse is a difficult obstacle. But west of this the Albert Canal provides an absolutely first-class artificial reinforcement. All the bridges over it had been prepared for demolition. The bridges, moreover, were under fire from the Eben-Emael fort, the strongest defensive works on the whole of the western front. The Maginot Line has no fort similar to this in extent and armor. This fort and the bridges over the Albert Canal, which actually cannot be replaced in a short time, were subjected to a lightning attack at 5:30 a.m. on May 10. The fort was silenced a few minutes later. Of the three bridges over the Albert Canal, two are completely undamaged and the Belgians were able to damage the third only slightly. Only the Dutch succeeded in blowing up the bridges in Maastricht as the result of an unfortunate failure on our part. However this was less important, for these could at once be replaced by military bridges. The attack on the fortress of Liege itself began simultaneously with this. It was broken into, block by block and fort by fort, and I have just received the report that the Swastika flag is flying over the citadel at Liege. The divisions which had meanwhile been thrown across the Meuse and the Albert Canal hurled back the Belgian units and repulsed French counterattacks. They will begin an offensive in a westerly direction immediately on being brought up to strength.

South of Liege thickly wooded country, which was extremely strongly fortified and prepared for demolition by months of work, had to be broken through. The area through which we had to fight our way has a depth of 100 km, in the air line from the German frontier to the Meuse south of Namur. This area was so penetrated in the fighting that last night sections of the spear heads reached the Meuse, and were encamped a few kilometers away. Since this morning the bulk of the divisions have been linking up everywhere. Luxembourg was overrun on the first day. French advance posts in the southern part of Luxembourg and Belgium were attacked and thrust back to the Maginot Line. In this way, the necessary cover has been created for the further operations by the northern wing against the Dutch and Belgian coasts.

These are the territorial results of the first 3 days! The material results: A large number of Dutch and Belgian divisions were attacked, partly overrun and partly destroyed. French attempts to delay or hinder developments in the situation by sending forward their armored and motorized units were repulsed everywhere. The number of prisoners already runs into tens of thousands.

In the air: On the morning of May 10, 72 French airfields were attacked, some being damaged and some destroyed. Since then our *Luftwaffe* has been striking at the deployment of many troops in uninterrupted sorties, has destroyed more and more airfields and already gained complete mastery in the air during the first day. Apart from aimless bombing attacks at night it is no longer possible for the French or English air forces to be employed effectively—especially in the daytime. I may give you an example: The moment the bridges outside Maastricht were rebuilt, an enormous stream of German troops began to move forward across them and the bridges over the Albert Canal.

Destructive Air Attacks

The English and French air forces really began destructive attacks and indeed twice: the first time with 16 aircraft; all 16 were shot down, eight by fighters and eight by anti-aircraft fire. The enemy air force was not able to hinder or interfere with the deployment or advance of our troops in any way. Isolated attacks on German cities and also on the Ruhr—which incidentally are denied by the English because of their cowardly fear of our reprisals—were grievous for individual victims but were completely unimportant from the economic or military point of view. The losses sustained by the French, English and Belgian air forces in the first three days of the fighting amount to at least between 1,100 and 1,400 aircraft. Numerous airfields have been destroyed and their hangers wrecked.

At sea: Here above all our aircraft have inflicted further heavy losses on the English in continuous attacks. The ranks of the British Navy have been visibly thinned particularly in destroyers and cruisers.

So far our own losses on land and in the air are extraordinarily slight. There is no comparison between them and those of the enemy.

This, Duce, is the situation, as it stands today. Pray accept my thanks for the letter which you addressed to me in these historic days and comradely greetings from.

Yours,

(Signed) *Adolf Hitler*

Five days later, another glowing victory report. Holland was completely occupied. The Belgium campaign was almost over. Brussels was surrounded by a ring of fire and steel. Antwerp was collapsing. Blitzkrieg lightning bolts had pierced the Maginot Line on a wide front and the French forces were scrambling wildly to set up new defenses.

Each letter from Hitler now encouraged Mussolini to get into the act fast before it was all over. Each letter made the Duce more anxious to grab some of the glory before Hitler owned the world.

Though his days were so busy he had little time to eat or sleep, Hitler set aside precious minutes for long, detailed reports to his brother dictator. For he wanted Italy's help badly, little realizing how bad that help would be.

> *Adolf Hitler to Benito Mussolini*
> *The Fuhrer's Headquarters, May 18, 1940*

Duce:

A week has now elapsed since the beginning of the offensive. I will give you quite briefly a picture of the situation as it appears today:

1) The offensive which was launched between Luxembourg and Groningen in Holland is now piercing all the essential systems of fortifications and fieldworks on the whole of the front except for that section lying between Maubeuge and Dunkirk.

This last section is however unimportant, because it is already completely cut off.

2) Holland is completely occupied by German troops. The islands of Zeeland are almost completely in our hands, the island of Walcheren, which is the last one before Antwerp, offered to surrender last night.

3) Belgium. Belgium has lost the whole of her canal system; the Dyle position which lies in front of Brussels and connects Antwerp with Namur has completely collapsed; the English and

French are withdrawing in disorder everywhere; advance troops reached Brussels last night; the city is already surrounded on a wide front toward the south; the fall of Antwerp is imminent. The southeastern fortifications of Antwerp were penetrated in the course of yesterday, a number of forts are already in our hands. Three forts in Liege are still holding out but are not hampering us and we are having them watched by a few companies. I am not using time or material to deal with this any further. The same applies to Namur. West of Namur we have already thrust forward as far as Charleroi and have surrounded it on the north and south.

4) The Belgian territory situated to the south of Charleroi and Liege is completely occupied by us, as in Luxembourg. French troops were thrown as far as the Maginot Line everywhere.

5) The Maginot Line itself in its extension from south of Garignan to near Maubeuge has been pierced on a front of over 100 km. and left far behind us.

6) The *Luftwaffe* has gained complete mastery in the air. There is now hardly any interference by enemy aircraft in the daytime. There are scattered incursions at night with a small number of bombs dropped. The military or economic damage done is nil. Except for the victims of a French air raid on Freiburg in Breisgau, the number killed by enemy air attacks on the territory in our rear still does not amount to 40 people.

7) The Dutch Army has ceased to exist. The Belgian Army has been largely smashed.

Many French and English divisions have been most heavily hit and partly reduced to disorder, so that they no longer represent any serious fighting force.

8) As far as the damage to their rear transport system permits, the French are endeavoring to establish a new defensive or offensive front as the case may be. I am keeping an eye on this. The miracle of the Marne of 1914 will not be repeated!

Our losses, Duce, are extraordinarily slight when set against the successes obtained.

This is briefly the situation at the moment, the result of 8 days' fighting. The spirit of the Army and the *Luftwaffe*, their courage in face of death and their discipline are outstanding.

Pray accept the cordial greetings of a comrade.

Yours,

(Signed) *A. Hitler*

Dunkirk convinced Mussolini that he couldn't lose by siding with Germany.

Though he had not yet received Hitler's report of the great retreat across the English Channel, Mussolini knew by June 30 that the British had given up France. The Dunkirk withdrawal began on May 26 and continued to June 4. Nine hundred ships, many of them tiny fishing boats, carried 338,226 troops over the Channel to England, including 26,175 French soldiers and marines. The valiant rescue fleet worked night and day, pounded constantly by shells and bombs from the sky and shore.

Before history's most heroic retreat was over, Mussolini decided to commit Italy to all-out war. He lost no time then in relaying the news to Hitler.

Il Duce was sure the next stop would be England, and he wanted to be with pal Adolf when London's bridges came tumbling down.

Benito Mussolini to Adolf Hitler

Rome, May 19, 1940

Fuhrer:

I thank you for having found time during a pause in the tremendous victorious battle to send me a communication on the progress of the operations. I repeat that these operations have been followed not only with interest but with enthusiasm by the Italian people who are now convinced that the period of non-belligerency cannot last much longer. I intend to give you important news on this subject in the next few days.

I assume that your Foreign Minister has already informed you of the messages which were sent to me by Roosevelt and Churchill recently and of my replies; but all this is only of relative importance now.

I send you my most comradely greetings.

(Signed) *Mussolini*

In this letter, written on the eve of the Dunkirk withdrawal, Hitler appraises the fighting troops—gives his opinions of the Dutch, Belgian, English, and French soldiers, and of his own German warriors. With the fall of France assured and English troops preparing to pull out for home, Der Fuehrer allows himself the luxury of relaxing and expressing his innermost views on men and war. This is a contemplative, even philosophical letter, unlike the achievement reports that preceded it. Through his written thoughts, Hitler gives the reader an insight to his own complex character.

Adolf Hitler to Benito Mussolini
The Fuhrer's Headquarters, May 25, 1940

Duce:

Days of great historic moment have passed since my last letter to you. I have not written to you about this yet since such weighty decisions and measures, as have now become possible, always ran the risk of setbacks. But this danger has now definitely passed. The numbers of the infantry units pouring in through the breaches made by the armored and motorized divisions are now so great—and are increasing hourly—that any attempt to bring about a turn of fate would only lead to further and even greater setbacks for the English and French commands. Before I gave the order for the final breakthrough toward the Channel, I was of the opinion that even at the risk of the evacuation or withdrawal of some Anglo-French forces there would nevertheless have to be a lull in our advance. In the two days thus gained, we succeeded in repairing the roads, which were in part terribly devastated, to such an extent that thanks to the formation of large transport groups there is no more fear of any supply difficulties. Similarly, the infantry divisions which were striving onward in forced marches were now able to link up again with the armored and motorized units which were surging forward. The military dilettantes of the press of our Western Powers of course saw this at once as a slackening in German pressure. Duce, only a fraction of the number of German infantry divisions has so far made contact with the enemy. Of the armored units, three divisions have so far only had slight skirmishes, two further armored divisions have as yet had virtually no contact with the enemy. Of the motorized divisions a number of crack units have also made no contact with the enemy. They will not be sent into action until today or tomorrow. Furthermore, the success gained has justified the measures which have been taken. At the moment the front toward the south is very strongly reinforced while in the north we have already advanced beyond Calais.

Air superiority has been completely achieved in so far as the French air force is concerned; as regards the English air force, it is so far secured that protection of the continent against English air attacks is guaranteed at all times.

Opinion of Enemy

As for the morale of our enemies, Duce, the following may be said:

1) THE DUTCH: They offered much stronger resistance than we first expected. Many of their units fought very bravely. However, they had not the appropriate training or any experience of war. Thus they could generally be overcome by German forces which were often numerically greatly inferior.

2) BELGIUM: The Belgian soldier on the whole also fought very bravely. His experience of war is to be rated as considerably greater than that of the Dutch. At the start his tenacity was amazing. It is now failing visibly, now that he realizes that his function is essentially to cover, if at all possible, the English withdrawal.

3) THE ENGLISH SOLDIER: The English soldier has the qualities which were typical of him during the World War. Very brave and dogged in defense, clumsy in attack, miserably led. Arms and equipment are first rate, the organization on the whole is bad.

4) THE FRENCHMAN: Very marked differences become apparent in the French when their military ability is evaluated. There are very bad units side by side with excellent ones. On the whole the difference in quality between the active and non-active divisions is extraordinarily noticeable. Many of the active units have fought desperately, the reserve units are for the most part obviously not equal to the impact of battle on morale. For the French, just as for the Dutch and Belgians, there is of course in addition the realization that they are fighting to no purpose for objectives which have hardly anything in common with their own real interests. In the same way, their morale was very adversely affected by experiencing that wherever possible the English were striving in the main to spare their own units, preferring to leave critical spots to their allies.

As far as the German armed forces are concerned, Duce, the successes gained justify the favorable opinion I have always held of them. This applies in striking fashion to our *Luftwaffe*, to the excellent armored units, but especially to a valiant and always reliable infantry. The artillery, too, has fulfilled expectations.

The German Army and the German *Luftwaffe* are emerging from this fighting completely unimpaired as regards material and personnel. They have, however, been enriched by additional experience and an extraordinarily feeling of confidence.

In this connection I should like to point out that a small band of heroes has been fighting in Narvik since April 9 under the most difficult conditions in snow and ice and on the most meager rations and in addition hampered by being forced to go carefully with every cartridge against a vastly superior enemy. But we have now succeeded in pushing forward the construction of our northern advanced air bases to such an extent that it will shortly be possible to help this valiant little band of warriors by means of uninterrupted air attacks. We intend to see that these fiords gradually become more and more a graveyard for British ships. On land, too, these men will then receive support from the most modern dive bombers.

It is not possible to say how long Allied resistance will last in the encircled zone. The mass of our heavy and heaviest artillery which has been brought up, the guarantee of abundant supplies of ammunition, and also the employment of fresh infantry divisions will now permit us to proceed with brutal force on this front. It will probably collapse in a few days under the weight of the attacks now beginning.

Bitter at French

General Weygand will not be able to do anything about it. But he will receive the same thanks from the degenerate parliamentary rascals as did his predecessor, Gamelin. When I think, Duce, that precisely M. Reynaud is one of the chief culprits in this catastrophe, and when on the other hand I keep in mind the treatment and the fate meted out by these parliamentary Democrats to those who are nevertheless still patriotic soldiers, and the fate in store for them in the future, then I am filled with immeasurable contempt for a system and an era which hands over the fate of great nations to these inferior products of nature The arrest and shooting of true patriots in these countries can lead to nothing but their collapse. I can understand opposition being resisted in one's own country. But the thought of patriotic members of one's own opposition, who have proved by their previous conduct their boundless love for their own people, being delivered up to a foreign power from a desire to be rid of them, and with tacit consent that they are to be shot by Senega-

lese, is so repulsive, that I have a profound feeling of spiritual solidarity with these victims, although reason is bound to tell me that
by robbing themselves of their most valuable blood these nations
are anyhow only destroying themselves. It seemed that Degrelle
and Mussert have also been shot, one in the citadel at the other at
Abbeville, along with many others. If this proves to be true, it will
only be proof that the fall of this regime is at hand, just as the murder of Codreanu meant more to Rumania than the mere extinction
of a member of the opposition.

Duce, you will understand my feelings, for somewhere above
the community of the mediocre there is a solidarity or at least a
feeling of sympathy, between exceptional men.

Accept, Duce, my most sincere and comradely greetings.

Yours,

(Signed) A. Hitler

Benito Mussolini to Adolf Hitler

Rome, May 30, 1940

Fuhrer:

I thank you once more for the message which you sent me and
in which I found the information concerning the courage of the
soldiers of the different armies particularly interesting.

In the meantime I have received news of the capitulation of Belgium and I congratulate you on this.

I have delayed my reply to you for some days because I wanted
to announce to you my decision to enter the war as of June 5.
Should you consider that I ought to wait a few days longer for the
sake of better coordination with your plans, you will tell me so; the
Italian people are however impatient to be at the side of the German people in the struggle against the common foe.

During these nine months the efforts made in the field of military preparations have been significant. Today there are 70 divisions
whose striking power is good; of these, 12 are overseas (220,000

men in Libia, 100,000 in Albania). Italian East Africa has 350,000 men available—Italians and natives—who are not included in the figures given.

As I have told you earlier, the Navy and Air Force are already on a wartime footing.

I shall assume supreme command of all the armed forces. If I had the means I could form another 70 divisions, for there is no lack of manpower.

From the political point of view I consider it necessary not to extend the conflict to the Danube Basin and the Balkans, from which Italy too must draw those supplies which she will no longer be able to obtain from beyond Gibraltar.

I think that a statement on these lines which I shall make at an appropriate moment will have a reassuring effect on those nations and will render them impervious to any possible moves by the Allies.

Once this is established, our General Staffs will take the requisite steps for the development of the operations.

While awaiting a reply from you, pray accept, Fuhrer, the expression of my comradely friendship.

(Signed) *Mussolini*

Editor's Note: With Italy on his side, Hitler felt the struggle for Europe would soon be over. But now that Mussolini finally set the long-awaited date for an Italian declaration of war, a strange thing happened. Hitler asked him to wait a bit longer!

THE SECRET LETTERS BETWEEN HITLER AND MUSSOLINI

Second Installment

On May 31, 1940, Western Europe lay broken and bleeding beneath the marching boots of German armies. The Dunkirk retreat was at its height. The British Expeditionary Force was pulling out of France as fast as 900 ships could shuttle across the English Channel.

It was Adolf Hitler's greatest hour of triumph; it was England's most valiant hour of defeat. And Mussolini was straining at the leash to get into the war, now that he saw Hitler's successes. But Der Fuehrer asked Il Duce to withhold his official declaration a few more days— or to make it any time but Friday, June 7. As he explains, many Germans believe that Friday is a bad day to begin ventures. And Hitler was never a man to risk the wrath of the gods.

Adolf Hitler to Benito Mussolini
The Fuhrer's Headquarters, May 31, 1940.

Duce:

The information which you have just imparted to me in your letter has moved me most profoundly. If there could still be anything which could strengthen my unshakable belief in the victorious outcome of this war, it was your statement. Our two regimes will not only set the pat tern of the new Europe, but above all they will together be strong enough to safeguard and preserve the results of their struggle for a long time to come.

You wish me, Duce, to give you my views on the intended date for your entry into the war and whether its postponement for a few days might be in our common interest.

In this connection I should first of all like to give you a conclusive picture of the state of the operations at the moment.

The battle against the British Expeditionary Force and the remnants of the French 1st, 9th, and 7th Armies will be over today, tomorrow, or the day after tomorrow at the latest. Apart from the Dutch and Belgian Armies at least 52 French and English divisions have been hit by the catastrophe. Of the English Expeditionary Force one division was not in this zone at all; but had been installed with small detachments north of Saarbrucken along the Maginot Line. It had been withdrawn from there and is now probably the only British division in France which is anywhere near complete. Part of a British armored division which was in Flanders has escaped and is at present also south of the Aisne or the Somme. Everything else which England sent to the Continent has been defeated and destroyed. For some days they have been attempting to save what men can be saved with every conceivable kind of ship.

Of the French divisions in this zone some part may perhaps have escaped right at the beginning of the fighting. But all in all by far the bulk of all active French divisions can be regarded as completely wiped out, and the same applies to a large number of reserve divisions.

It is not possible at present to form any idea of the numbers of prisoners or the extent of the captured war material. It may give you some idea, Duce, when you hear that five complete infantry divisions had to be detailed by us to move this immense mass of prisoners.

There is no need for me to assure you, Duce, that further operations will follow in the shortest possible time, but in view of the vast area covered several days will be required for organization.

If, Duce, you can postpone your date for three days at the most, this would have the following advantages: Our *Luftwaffe* has now reconnoitered new operational airfields of the French Air Force pretty accurately and ascertained the strength of these forces. In conjunction with other measures they will again attack these French air bases during the next few days and if possible, utterly smash them. If, as a result of action already embarked upon by Italy or for fear of such action being imminent, France should transfer her Air Force at the last minute, then this might nullify our operation while you, Duce, would not be able to obtain immediate information about the new operational air fields to which some of the remnants of the French Air Force are certainly still being transferred. Otherwise I am hoping at any rate to be able to put the French Air Force out of action once and for all in the course of next week. But once they had fled it requires days of searching to find out their new hiding places.

These are the reasons why I would request you to consider whether it might be possible to postpone your entry into the war until about the end of next week, say until June sixth or eight. The seventh would of course do as well, but it is a Friday and may perhaps be regarded by many—at any rate there are such among the German people—as an unlucky day on which to begin. But, Duce, no matter which way you decide, even the mere fact of your, entering the war is an element calculated to deal the front of our enemies a staggering blow.

In this connection I should like to assure you that I am happy that you yourself are assuming supreme command of your armed forces. On the basis of my own large experience I regard this as an important prerequisite for success.

Didn't Want Balkan Conflict

Similarly, I fully endorse your view that it cannot but be desirable for us to keep the Danube Basin and the Balkans out of the conflict, if this is at all possible. I am likewise of the opinion that such a declaration by you, Duce, will remove this element of danger. The crushing defeat of France—and this seems to me to be the most decisive factor of all—is of necessity bound to secure for you, Duce, and for your country political hegemony as a power in the Mediterranean—a hegemony which already exists by force of geography.

Please inform me, Duce, of the final date you have chosen and which I will keep as a strict secret known to only a few. I can then give my General Staff instructions at once—apart from sending the *Luftwaffe* into action—to take further steps and establish liaison with your officers immediately.

I should however point out to you once more, Duce, that if for any particular reason—say the keeping of the date secret, ect.—you think you would prefer to go into action on the fifth, this date too will, of course, be acceptable to me.

Should you, Duce, find it necessary or even expedient for you, yourself, to see me and speak to me personally at any time, I am, of course, prepared to arrange a meeting with you immediately.

I now greet you, Duce, in loyal comradeship secure in the consciousness of great joint success.

Yours,

(Signed) *Hitler*

Hitler's troops had done the bloody work of battle, but Mussolini wanted to make sure his unsoiled soldiers would share in the glory. So his letter announcing when Italy would declare war and begin hostilities also carried a request that Hitler include "a representative contingent of the Italian army" in the goose-stepping victory parade through France.

Benito Mussolini to Adolf Hitler
Rome-Berlin, June 2, 1940

Message from the Duce:

I thank you most sincerely for the message which you sent me in answer to mine, which was delivered by Ambassador Alfieri. The

victorious conclusion of the first phase of the war in Flanders has
. . . ignited the enthusiasm of the whole Italian people. Regarding
the date of Italy's entry into the war I fully appreciate the advantage
of delay which allows your *Luftwaffe* to identify and destroy the
French Air Force. This brief delay permits me . . . to take still better
defensive precautions and . . . in all spheres. My program is as follows: On Monday, June tenth, declaration of war and on the morning of June eleventh the commencement of hostilities. Regarding a
meeting, I thank you for having proposed one, but I think it would
be better for it to take place after Italy's entrance into the war. In the
speech which I shall make a few hours after the declaration of war,
I shall say that true to her policy Italy does not intend to extend the
theatre of war; and I shall name the Danube and Balkan countries
including Greece and Turkey. Now I will express to you my wish to
see at least a representative contingent of the Italian Army fighting
side by side with your soldiers, in order to demonstrate in the field
the affinity of arms and the comradeship between our revolutions.
If you accept my offer I will send you a few regiments . . . consisting
of courageous soldiers capable of offering resistance. Meanwhile I
send you my most heartfelt greetings and best wishes for the success of our armed forces.

(Signed) *Mussolini*

*Hitler, of course, replied that he would welcome a few Italian regi-
ments. And he proposed that Mussolini accept a like number of German regiments "as a token of our comradeship in arms."*

*But his offer was not made out of generosity or friendship for Il
Duce. Hitler had nothing but contempt, for Italy's fighting forces. He
didn't trust them and wanted to make sure Mussolini's troops had
German reinforcements to keep them in line when the Italians moved
against France.*

*For this tricky maneuver, Hitler chose crack Alpine troops who
could fight alone if necessary. It was his war, and he was taking no
chances on Mussolini losing it for him.*

Adolf Hitler to Benito Mussolini
The Fuhrer's Headquarters, June 9, 1940

Duce:

I would now like to thank you by this means for your last communication. I have already had you informed of my approval of everything you proposed. Today, in addition to a brief report on the situation I must tell you how glad I am to have the opportunity of welcoming Italian comrades on our front. I know that those regiments of *Bersaglieri* are extremely good soldiers. Now, I should also like to give you, Duce, a few German regiments as a token of our comradeship in arms, and for this I actually had in mind Alpine troops, provided you can employ them on your front against France. Some have already distinguished themselves in Norway, others are fighting on the western front. There they have proved their mettle also. I should therefore be glad, Duce, if you thought it possible to employ them on your Alpine front, and would accept this as a token of our comradeship.

Since I did not know whether it would be possible for you further to postpone your operations for military reasons, I endeavored to bring ours forward by a few days. This we succeeded in doing. The air attacks on the big airfields in the Paris area and on the aircraft awaiting completion in the factories were a very great success. The French Air Force is now scarcely in evidence (apart from a few aircraft at night).

Hope For Quick Victory

The big attack, which was designed first of all to bring up a concentration of French reserves, fulfilled its purpose. We succeeded in exploiting our initial successes to such an extent that I was able to supplement these operations by giving orders for another and even bigger attack. Fighting has been going on since this morning on a front of about 300 km. While writing this letter I have so far no reports on the results of today's attack, but our pressure is so strong that the whole of the French front will collapse in a few days' time. This is already the case in the first sector of the battle.

Meanwhile operations seem finally to have come to an end in Norway. The King of Norway and his Government have left the country. It is not known where they have gone. The Commander in Chief of the Norwegian forces in the Narvik area has asked for a truce and has ordered his units to stop fighting. For the last two days my little band of heroes up there have themselves been making attacks again and despite their numerical and other inferiority have driven back the enemy. The *Luftwaffe* has again damaged a cruiser. Part of the fleet penetrated to the Lofotens and closed in on the English aircraft carrier *Glorious*. It was sunk together with a destroyer, a submarine-chaser, a 22,000 ton transport and a 9,500 ton tanker and a few smaller vessels.

When this fighting around Narvik is finished, a small band of the bravest men under the leadership of a heroic officers whom I have known for many years will have achieved something rare in military history. Their personal efforts were just as great as their conquest of hardship, hunger, frost, and all the sufferings connected with this. At times, this detachment was almost 1,000 km. away from the nearest main body of German troops. The only means of communication with them was by air. While I am writing this, the spearhead of the operational troops, advancing in snowstorms over terrain which can only be negotiated with difficulty by a few mountaineers, is now barely 100 km. from Narvik as the crow flies. It is indeed only spirit and will power, Duce, which make men and which at the same time are their strongest weapon.

I greet you in comradeship.

(Signed) *Adolf Hitler*

On June 10, Mussolini shoved Italy over the brink of war, as he had promised pal Adolf he would do. Hitler sent a telegram of con-

gratulations, delivered while crowds in the streets of Rome were still cheering Mussolini's declaration.

Stirring as the roll of drums, the crash of cannon, the roaring flight of fighting planes were the words in which Hitler gave his solemn pledge:

Adolf Hitler to Benito Mussolini

Telegram
The Fuhrer's Headquarters, June 10, 1940—9:40 p.m.

Duce:

The historic decision which you announced today has moved me most profoundly. The whole German people is thinking of you and your country at this moment. The German *Wehrmacht* is glad to be able to stand at the side of its Italian comrades in battle.

Last September the rulers of Britain and France declared war on the German Reich without any reason. They turned down every offer of a peaceful settlement. Your proposal for mediation, Duce, was also received at the time with a brusque "No." While we have always been very closely linked together ideologically by our two revolutions and politically by treaties, the increasing disregard shown by the rulers in London and Paris for Italy's vital national rights struggle for the freedom and future of our peoples.

Duce of Fascist Italy, accept the assurance of the indestructible community of arms between the German and the Italian peoples.

I myself send you as always in loyal comradeship my greetings.

Yours,

(Signed) *Adolf Hitler*

THE SECRET LETTERS BETWEEN HITLER AND MUSSOLINI

Part III

HOW ENGLAND ESCAPED THE TERROR OF NAZI INVASION!

The *Police Gazette* is the first publication ever to present the most important and dramatic letters in history—the personal correspondence between Hitler and Mussolini.

In this third installment of their letters the two dictators reveal in their own words their hopes and plans for conquering the world, and their deep respect for the fighting spirit of England. Driven back across the Channel, Britain alone in the Summer of 1940 faced the victorious Nazi armies and grimly awaited the cross-Channel invasion which the world expected Hitler would start at any moment.

In midsummer of 1940, with the Allied armies on the continent defeated and German troops in Paris, an eager Mussolini was more than anxious to participate in Hitler's victories. He wanted to share in the spoils and offered Italian troops to aid in the assault on England.

Benito Mussolini to Adolph Hitler

Rome, June 26, 1940

Fuhrer:

Now that the problem is to conquer Great Britain, I remind you of what I said to you at Munich about the direct participation of

Italy in the assault on the Island. I am ready to contribute ground forces and air forces and you know how much I desire to do so.

I ask you to answer me in such a way that will be possible for me to pass to the phase of execution.

In this expectation I send you the most comradely greetings.

(Signed) *Adolf Hitler*

Hitler cleverly dodges Mussolini's offer of troops and sets forth his reasons in detail in the letter of July 13, 1940.

It offers remarkable insight into Hitler's devious thoughts and the way he went about putting them into action.

Adolph Hitler to Benito Mussolini
Fuhrer's Headquarters, July 13, 1940

Duce!

After your departure from Munich I received report that your train was held up by an air-raid alarm. I became conscious of the fact how greatly your life, too, is endangered. I should like therefore to ask you kindly to accept two railroad cars with antiaircraft equipment as a personal gift from me. . . . Field Marshal Goering's train, when attacked, promptly shot down an English plane with those four-barreled antiaircraft guns. To a height of at least 1500–2000 meters their effectiveness is excellent.

Mussolini and Hitler during conference on how to invade England.
Their masterminding backfired.

Please regard this gift simply as a token of concern from a friend.

At the moment I am in the midst of the preparations for the second phase of the struggle. These preparations are very extensive.

A landing by German troops in England is an undertaking whose success appears certain only if all the preparations are made with the most painstaking care. Such thorough preparation is also in full accord with the character of my General Staff. It requires so precise a co-ordination among command, troops, material, transport facilities, supply services, etc., that the success of the first assault is assured only if it is possible to calculate exclusively with known factors. That applies not only to the troops and to material but also—as already stressed—to the command.

Next there is the special fitness of the commanders to be selected for the tasks assigned to them. We have learned extraordinary lessons in Norway and have seen there, just as during the first strikes in the West, how much success of such very hold undertakings depends on the fitness of individuals. Even within the ranks of our own *Wehrmacht* mistakes did occur and had unfortunate consequences. Thus, for example, the task force dispatched to take hold of the Maastricht bridges failed, while on the other hand the task force to which had been assigned the more difficult objectives of taking Fort Eben-Emael and the canal bridges near Maastricht was able to carry out its assignments splendidly. Yet, Duce, these assignments had been previously practiced on models almost four months, and tested on objectives in similar locations again and again.

The attack on England has now also been discussed and studied in all its numerous details by the units in question or by the commanders. Contrary to the methods of the World War the principle of it is attaining a maximum of effect with a minimum of men.

Hitler Tells Invasion Plans

This can be achieved only by the most intense study of the task and equipping of men, after thorough deliberations, with the only suitable weapons. My responsible advisers are convinced that it would no longer be possible today to replace any of the units intended for those first assaults even with another German unit, without giving the latter another four to six months time for preparation. But there is also another factor, namely that at the landing operation, which is extremely dangerous, a certain percentage of material losses must be expected. For replacement purposes it is therefore important to use uniform weapons and ammunition as for as possible. . . .

Beyond that there are numerous other reasons—especially those connected purely with the exercise of command—that make it seem impossible to operate with two different armies in a theatre which is anyhow so limited. At least in the first stage that seems out of the question. Only after a firm foothold has been permanently established and the area of operations secured could this question be taken up again.

However much, Duce, I appreciated your offer—of making a substantial number of Italian divisions available for the attack on England—as an act of comradeship and kindness—at the same time we must give consideration to everything that is likely to secure a successful outcome for this bold decision. With my advisers I have also gone fully into your further offers, Duce, to provide ships or aircraft. Here it will probably be easier to find a possibility for cooperation between our units. However, Duce, the decisive point seems to be this: We are confronted with a foe who still represents an enormous World Power.

I have made to Britain so many offers of agreement, even of cooperation, and have been treated so shabbily that I am even now convinced that any new appeal to reason would meet with a similar rejection. For in that country at present it is not reason that rules, but probably the smallest portion of wisdom in history. I believe, however, that for this reason we must all the more put our struggle on the broadest possible basis and neglect nothing in any way likely to hurt this powerful adversary and help in our cause.

It therefore does not matter in the least, Duce, where these various blows fall. They all will help to shake that State, remove that unscrupulous gang of warmongers and finally make the country ready for peace.

Count Ciano has informed me that Italy is getting ready for an attack on Egypt and the Suez Canal. Any such strike, Duce, is an enormous gain.

Praises Italian Attacks

I was therefore delighted to hear that your navy has succeeded in holding firm with such distinction and was especially glad of the attacks of your air force on British convoys and warships.

Permit me to tell you therefore that I follow your own struggle with an ardent heart and ardent wishes. I shall do my best to assist, in order to share your burden as soon as this is in any way possible. In this I wage an eternal struggle against time, which is unfortunately needed to prepare the operations which one would prefer to launch this every moment.

With cordial and comradely greetings,

(Signed) *Adolf Hitler*

Though disappointed by Hitler's refusal to allow him to participate directly in the planned assault on Britain, Mussolini offers grandiose plans for a large-scale attack on Egypt. Though cast in a second-class role, Il Duce writes as though he were a full-fledged partner.

Benito Mussolini to Adolf Hitler
Rome, July 17, 1940

Fuhrer!

Permit me first of all to thank you for the mobile antiaircraft guns which you kindly presented to me. This is an attention on your part which testifies to comradely courtesy and whose full significance I know how to value. As soon as time permits I shall visit the battery and have it put into action.

I fully understand your response to my offer of Italian units for the landing in England. As I see it, this should mainly be of symbolic value, that is, express in visible for our comradeship in arms. I understand perfectly what you have told me, and will not insist further—all the less since our aim is the same, even though we fight on different sectors. If you see a possibility for direct intervention by the Italian Air Force please tell me. We now possess units of new, very fast and efficient machines. The preparation for a largescale attack on Egypt is not completed. . . . I hope I can begin the offensive at the same time as your attack on England.

On the ninth, tenth, eleventh and twelfth the English fleet in the Mediterranean was very badly hit. The denials of the English Admiralty are grotesque. I need not tell you that Italian Army reports tell the truth, even when this does not seem entirely necessary.

Your Ambassador in Rome will have informed you of my complete agreement with your letter to King Carol. If he is wise he will not miss this opportunity of reaching a compromise which Teleki himself desires.

French policy, which is not clear, is being followed here with much attention, especially in the colonial possessions.

But the most important thing is to strike the decisive blow at Great Britain.

No doubt whatsoever bothers me: the Revolution will be victorious!

Please accept, Fuhrer, my always friendly and comradely greetings,

(Signed) *Adolf Hitler*

Mussolini, determined to enter into Hitler's grand strategy, despite the fact that his offer of troops has been politely refused, offers his analysis of the unfolding battle for the world. Here he astutely sizes up the possibility of American entry into the war.

Benito Mussolini to Adolf Hitler
Il Duce del Fascismo-Capo del Governo,
Rome, August 24, 1940

Fuhrer:

We have not had an opportunity for an exchange of ideas since our discussion of June 18.

I consider it opportune to tell you what I think of the situation at this moment. To begin with, as regards the Danube Basin and the Balkans, which is to keep that zone outside the conflict. The measures of a military character at the Greek and Yugoslav borders are simply of a precautionary character, prompted by the fact that both countries are deeply hostile to the Axis and ready to stab it in the back if a favorable occasion should offer itself.

The Italian police have discovered in the environs of Trieste no less than five large arms caches, hidden by Serbian partisans. It is not unknown to you, furthermore, that both Greece and Yugoslavia have almost completely mobilized their armed forces, and there can be no doubt concerning the effective, continuous, and verified complicity of Greece with Great Britain. All Greek ports are bases against us. But for all of that, and barring unforeseen developments, it is not in this direction but toward Egypt that I intend to direct the Italian efforts within the near future. The preparations are now completed and we are approaching a season more favorable for combat and for the march across the desert.

Blasts the French

Marshal Graziani has already received the order to attack on the same day when your Army attacks Great Britain. Despite the difficulties of terrain and climate, I believe we will defeat the English forces as well as the Egyptian forces if—as seems likely—they should Join the English, And now permit me *tour d'horizon.*

France. I feel sure that you cannot have failed to not the extraordinary psychological phenomenon, so typical for the indomitable pride of the French, that France does not consider herself conquered. Vichy-France is counting on English resistance and American intervention. What is happening in North Africa indicates the intentions of the French Government. It is therefore necessary to watch and impose such peace as will render it innocuous for several generations at least.

United States. Barring a complete reversal—always possible in a country of such genuine hysterics as are the American politicians—the possibility of American intervention ought to be calculated as a reality, especially if Roosevelt is reelected, as seems probable. Roosevelt will be unable to make a contribution in men but he will give greater material assistance, especially aircraft. This is happening already and so even that possibility cannot prevent Great Britain's defeat.

Pressure on U.S.A.

Japan. I have not yet seen the results of the new "course" of Japan's police. The Japanese, although they are most clear in their aims, are very slow and mysterious in their methods. I think that the policy of the Axis in Tokyo ought to be to "ease tension" in Russo-Japanese relations and on the other hand to "increase tension" to the maximum between the United States and Japan.

Returning again to military matters, it is superfluous for me to tell you with what joy Italian sailors and aviators are preparing themselves to act, alongside their German comrades, against Great Britain.

Accept, Fuhrer, my always cordial and comradely greetings.

(Signed) *Adolf Hitler*

P.S. As regards the harvest in Italy: the harvest has yielded 700,000 tons less bread grain, but was extraordinarily good in regard to corn, rice, potatoes, beans, sugar beets, fruit and green fodder. We are therefore not unduly concerned about our food supply.

Mus.

Hitler's greatest disappointment is shown in this letter of September 17, 1940, where the real reason why the Nazis didn't invade England is revealed.

It is actually the turning point of Der Fuehrer's career, though it was to be some time later before the Nazis leader was to realize it.

Adolf Hitler to Benito Mussolini
September 17, 1940

Duce!

In the first place please accept my most cordial thanks for your last letter. I read it with great interest and can only endorse your general views on the situation.

The fact that a relatively long interval lies between my last letter and today's is due not only to the tremendous amount of preparatory work but also to the uncertainty of a situation that makes it difficult to prognosticate even for the very near future. . . .

The attack on England, upon which all our work and preparations are centered, has suffered the worst kind of delay so far owing to the weather; our meteorologists are at a loss to explain this or find parallels for it. For a month and a half we have been waiting for a few clear days in the west, for we absolutely must have that much time to justify the really large-scale commitment of our *Luft-waffe*. Since we unfortunately do not possess supremacy at sea, the absolute mastery of the air is the most decisive prerequisite for the success of the invasion operation.

For weeks now we have been carrying on aggressive warfare of progressive intensity with our air forces against the British Island. The character of these attacks, however, is still one of more or less severe reprisal raids. Unfortunately we have not had the weather needed for the really large-scale attacks. Nevertheless we have certainly already had notable successes even with our present attacks.

As in Norway, our pilots are fighting under the most unfavorable conditions imaginable with really admirable heroism. And so extraordinary progress has been made in attrition of the British Air Force that, to the extent of the radius of our fighter planes, we can already talk of real control of the air. I am waiting, as I did last year, for weather that will make it possible for me to have the final, annihilating blows dealt, and with me—I can assure you of this, Duce—is waiting the entire German *Wehrmacht*!

I have observed your own successes with great pleasure, Duce; the successful attacks in North Africa. The German people are with you in these battles, and every success which you achieve, Duce, whether on land or sea or in the air, is felt here exactly as if it were our own.

Since circumstances do not allow us to foresee when hostilities will cease, we are, I believe, forced to act farsightedly in making all possible preparations so that no matter what is still possible this fall we can in any case continue to prosecute the war successfully in the winter. I am, therefore, convinced that it can be important to make it possible for Spain to enter the war. The Spanish Government has applied in this sense to Germany with a number of military and economic requests. The military requests can be filled very easily, for they involve in the main only the detachment of some artillery and a number of special, troops.

France as such is finished. There is still danger of a secession movement in her northern colonies. There is no assurance that such secession might not even occur in secret agreement with the French Government. If, however—whether with or without the knowledge or desire of the Vichy Government—North Africa should join up with the British, this might give new impetus to the British cause, at least for a certain period. But as soon as there is a reliable bridge to North Africa via Spain I would no longer consider this danger to be very great. For Spain, too, a clear decision in this direction means increased security. This is one point.

Plots to Keep US Out of War

The other point is our relations with Japan. My Foreign Minister will give you the reports, Duce, that we have received regarding the possibility of a new development in the east. I believe in principle that in spite of all other misgivings a close cooperation with Japan is the best way either to keep America entirely out of the picture or to render her entry into the war ineffective.

If you should consider it advisable, Duce, for us to confer once again, I would gladly come either to the border or to a North Italian city so as to return in this way your last visit, which I recall so vividly.

Moreover, my Foreign Minister is familiar with everything and can speak with you on all problems, Duce.

Once more, please accept my thanks for your last letter, and my cordial regards,

In loyal comradeship. . . .

(Signed) *Adolf Hitler*

HITLER–MUSSOLINI LETTERS
REVEAL THE REAL REASON
HITLER LOST THE WAR

Hitler warmly greeted Franco in October 1940 while German
staff officer looked on. Franco was friendly but he planned a double-cross.

*A gamble that failed . . . this was one of the most decisive factors in
the history of World War II.*

*The time was October 1940. Two men bestrode the world. Hitler
and Mussolini, arrogant, swaggering, cocksure.*

*The gamble they made—and how their trump card turned out to be
a dud—is revealed for the first time in these secret letters between them.*

*They were outwitted by a third dictator, a wily little man named
Franco. Upon the greedy bargaining of the Spanish Claudillo the history of the free world turned.*

*The German Naval Staff was urging Hitler to concentrate his attack
on Gibraltar and the Suez Canal. To do this Hitler was advised to woo
Franco and bring Spain into the war on the Axis side without delay.*

But this letter from Mussolini to Hitler shows that the Duce regarded Franco as a trump card to be played when they were ready.

Benito Mussolini to Adolf Hitler,
Rome, October 19, 1940

Fuhrer:

I should now like to say a word with respect to Spain. The taking over of the conduct of foreign affairs by Suner affords us assurances that the tendencies hostile to the Axis are eliminated or at least neutralized. On the other hand I do not feel that the internal economic situation has improved.

Again, I express my conviction that Spanish non-belligerence is more advantageous to us than her intervention. We ought to keep intervention as a reserve: it is a card that we ought to play at the most opportune moment in accordance with the given circumstances, such as prolongation of the war through 1941 or an overt intervention of the United States.

Meantime Spain will have the time necessary to prepare herself.

The Duce couldn't have been more wrong. Sitting on the fence, Franco was becoming less and less certain that the Axis powers were going to win the war—and more and more determined to stay out of it.

Hitler, against the warnings of his advisors, was planning to attack Russia rather than strike a killing blow at the British by going through Spain to take Gibraltar from the rear. Both Admiral Raeder and Goering were for the Spanish campaign.

If Gibraltar and Suez were taken Raeder said "it is doubtful whether an advance against Russia in the north will be necessary."

A Shock for Hitler

Two months later, when Hitler decided to bring Spain into the war and to provide a small German force to help Franco take Gibraltar, it was too late. Franco stalled and finally refused flatly to attack the British stronghold.

At this show of "ingratitude," Hitler wailed miserably in a letter to Mussolini dated December 31, 1940.

Here is an extract of his comments on Spain:

Spain, under the impression of what Franco considers to be the changed situation, has for the time being refused to cooperate with the two Axis powers. I fear that Franco is committing here the greatest mistake of his life. I consider the idea of his receiving grain and other raw materials from the democracies as thanks for his aloofness to be unrealistic naiveté. They will put him off with promises until the last kilogram of grain in the country has been used up, and then the fight of the democratic powers against him personally will start. I regret this, for we had made all the preparations for crossing the Spanish border on January 10 and attacking Gibraltar at the beginning of February.

In my opinion that attack would have led to success in a relatively short time. The troops for this were excellently selected and trained, and the weapons were especially designed and readied for the purpose.

From the moment in which the Strait of Gibraltar was in our hands the danger of any kind of untoward behavior on behalf of French North and West Africa would have been eliminated. For this reason I am very sad about this decision of Franco's, which does not take account of the help which we—you, Duce, and I— once gave him in his hour of need.

I have only a faint hope left that possibly at the last minute he will become aware of the catastrophic nature of his own actions and he will after all—even though late—find his way to the camp of the front whose victory will also decide his own fate.

Even Hitler's personal magnetism, his bombastic role of "world historical genius" and master of Europe, failed to impress Franco.

When they met the crafty Spanish dictator skillfully avoided every attempt to lure him into the war and he left the arrogant Fuhrer almost bursting with suppressed rage.

Meanwhile, Hitler was still going ahead with operation Barbarossa—his wild plan to invade Russia. But he revealed nothing of this in that letter of December 31 to the Duce. He was apparently still on friendly terms with the Soviet Union.

Wrote Hitler:

I do not believe in any Russian step in our disfavor as long as Stalin lives and no very special crisis occurs on our side . . . However, it is the soldier's function to anticipate the unexpected in wartime and take it into account. Therefore, Duce, I consider as a prerequisite for any sure conclusion of this war the existence of a German *Wehrmacht* that is strong enough to oppose any conceivable eastern eventuality. The more obviously strong this power is, the smaller will be the probability that it will have to come forward for such unanticipated contingencies.

Soviet Friendship

I wish to state at the same time that the present relationship with the Soviet Union is very good, that we are on the point of concluding a trade agreement satisfactory to both parties and that therefore the hope is justified that the difficult points still open can also be solved in a reasonable manner. Really it is only the questions of Finland and Constantinople that are separating us.

Regarding Finland I do not see any problem at all, since we consider Finland as basically not belonging to our sphere of interest and only do not wish to have a new war break out there.

Regarding Constantinople and the Straits it cannot be to our interest to deliver up Bulgaria or the Straits themselves to Bolshevism. Here, too, however, it will be possible with a little goodwill to find a solution that avoids the intolerable and helps what is just and desirable to win out.

The solution will be all the more certain of success, however, the more it is realized in Moscow, too, that we are by no means under compulsion to take any step that does not suit us.

Although he doesn't mention it to Mussolini, it is a fact that some months before he wrote this letter Hitler had already made up his mind to launch his attack on Russia—whether or not he had first brought Britain to terms. In fact, Hitler's conception of the war at this point seems to have been that it was already won in the west, and that only the east menaced his grandiloquent plans for world domination.

In this same letter of December 31 to Mussolini, Hitler says:

The war in the west has actually been decided. A tremendous final thrust will be necessary to force England under, in so far as England does not break down under the increased effect of our air and submarine warfare. Therefore strong German forces are none the less necessary in order, when the conditions are right for success, to proceed directly against England for the last decisive attack.

The massing of these formations, and particularly of the tremendous stocks of material, requires anti-air-craft protection that goes beyond what could be estimated hitherto.

The British, in fact, could wait until Hitler was ready to deliver his final crushing blow—just as Hitler and Mussolini had thought that Franco would wait until they whistled for him.

These revealing letters show how one of the greatest gambles in history failed. If the depraved dictator and his paunchy comrade had wooed Franco months earlier, they might have struck at Gibraltar through Spain and brought Britain to her knees.

The man who played the slickest hand in this historic game was Franco, who smiled and blandly bluffed his fellow dictators—but never sided with them.

When Franco sat on the fence he had the destiny of the world sitting right beside him.

HITLER–MUSSOLINI LETTERS REVEAL THE SECRET FEAR THAT HAUNTED HITLER

The time was December 1940. Hitler stood at the peak of power, with all of Europe crushed or trembling beneath his heel . . . but he was haunted by a secret fear.

It was not a fear that he might lose the war. He considered that as good as won.

Hitler feared his enemies within the German Reich.

This fact is revealed in a wartime letter written by Hitler to Mussolini.

The letter, which was among secret Nazi documents captured by the US Army, has been obtained exclusively by the Police Gazette. *It throws a new light on the two dictators who tried to dominate the world.*

It shows that Mussolini, too, was haunted by the fear of being overthrown or assassinated—that he was afraid even to leave Rome.

The letter is written by one frightened, lonely man to another.

Hitler admits that he knows the loneliness that goes with supreme power.

He tries to reassure the Duce that the "watchful waiters" who are out to destroy him can be out-smarted and silenced. Then, in a rare disclosure of his inner fears, the Fuhrer admits: "I have these people, too."

As well as disclosing the internal conflicts that seethed around the two dictators, this letter gives Hitler's evaluation of the first year and three months of World War II.

Adolf Hitler to Benito Mussolini

December 31, 1940

Duce!

At the end of this year I feel impelled from the depths of my heart to express to you my good wishes for the coming year. I do so with feelings of friendship that are all the warmer since I can imagine that the recent events will have made you more lonesome, in relation to many people who are in themselves insignificant, but in return also more receptive to the sincere comradeship of a man who feels that he has thrown in his lot with you for better or for worse.

Let me make a statement at the start of this letter: namely that there are innumerable examples in the history of wars and nations of the events that are affecting all of us today. In the majority of these cases great powers have almost always reached too low an estimate of strength in the attack on smaller countries at the beginning, and have then very often suffered reverses in the initial stages of these fights.

German history possesses quite a number of examples of this. I therefore consider it necessary in every case of this sort to attack with superior forces if in any way possible, even when there is danger of losing the sympathies of those who consider a balance of forces to be necessary for a fair victory.

Since the occurrences in Greece and Albania and in North Africa I have been pondering without letup the really effective countermeasures which could be undertaken, on my part particularly.

As regards the direct help to Italy, your wishes are known to me, Duce. They shall be fulfilled—in so far as this lies in our power. In some areas it will not be possible. However, it will be possible to find expedients that will lead to the desired result after all.

Now let me consider the general situation, Duce:

Distrusts the French

The French Government has dismissed Laval. The reasons communicated to me officially are untrue. I no longer doubt for a second that the reason is that General Weygand is sending extortionist demands from North Africa to the Vichy Government and the latter does not feel able to proceed against General Weygand without incurring the danger of losing North Africa. I consider it possible that in Vichy itself quite a number of persons are covering the Weygand policy, at least secretly. I do not believe that General Petain personally commits disloyalty. However, one cannot be sure of that, either. This forces us to maintain a sharp scrutiny of what is going on.

Discusses Rumania

General Antonescu has recognized that the future of his regime and also his person depends on our victory. He has drawn clear and unequivocal conclusions from this which, in my eyes, has greatly increased his stature as a soldier. My personal impression of him in general was that of a fanatical Rumanian protagonist and resolute officer.

North African Situation

Duce. I do not believe that any large-scale counter attacks can be made in North Africa now. The preparation of such operations requires a period of at least three to four months. Then, however, will be the beginning of the season in which German units, at any rate, cannot function successfully there at all. Moreover, the tanks, which are not equipped with special cooling devices, can hardly be of any service in such heat. At any rate, not far-reaching operations that require this commitment for days at a time.

The decisive thing there seems to me to be to bring about a

reinforcement of anti-tank defenses even at the risk of thereby divesting other Italian units of them for the time being.

I know, Duce, that all commanders object to giving up the weapons and units allotted to them. However, I have intervened in this way in my own *Wehrmacht* numerous times. In the face of the opposition of individual corps or army leaders, I have taken out units, withdrawn weapons, and committed them at places where I considered they would be more useful.

In particular I believe, as I recently emphasized, that we must try with all possible means to weaken the British naval position by using the air force. Aside from this, Duce, no decisive measures can be taken anywhere before the month of March.

Transports that have not been in preparation for a long time require a very long time to get under way, even with the greatest utilization of all workers. Furthermore, many railroads are so overloaded at the present time that any new transports can be undertaken only at the price of present ones.

In spite of all this I regard the future with calm assurance. Your people, Duce, will only emerge hardened from the first reverses. The British attempt to separate the Italian people from you will lead to their being bound to you more strongly than ever before. The few persons who regards such an attempt with hopeful sympathy are not to be identified with your people in any case, and by no means represent any sort of valuable factor of national resistance.

In the most favorable case they are always only watchful waiters and never hot-blooded fighters. If they are uncovered prematurely it can always be considered to the advantage of a leadership that can all too easily let itself be deceived about the fact of their existence by the temporary silencing of these persons. *I have these people, too!*

I can understand, Duce, that you do not have much time now, and in particular that you do not like to leave Rome, As soon as you believe you can take it upon yourself, however, I cordially request that you have me notified. I will then be at your disposal at all times, Duce, and will be happy to see you again.

Perhaps I can also give you more information then about the progress of operations that are now in the planning stage.

Now please accept once again my most cordial wishes for success in the coming year.

Everything that is in my power and in the power of my people will be done to make this the year of final victory, that is the best wish that I can express at the turning point of this historical time.

In loyal comradeship,

Yours,

(Signed) *Adolf Hitler*

Thus concludes a remarkable letter from the German dictator. Hitler's references to internal enemies were almost prophetic, for nearly four years after the letter was written an attempt was made on the Fuhrer's life when a time bomb exploded during a conference at his headquarters in East Prussia. Mussolini was shot by the Italian Partisans and his body strung up as a public spectacle.

Odds & Ends

In this section we wrap up some "Hitler Is Alive!" odds and ends.

George McGrath gets back on the job in one big hurry when Hitler's valet, Heinz Linge, is released from a Soviet prison after serving ten years and goes around telling the press he saw Hitler's dead body in the bunker and saw him cremated.

The tracking and capture of Final Solution showrunner Adolf Eichmann is given a straight and in-depth treatment, while in another story we're told of the claim that Joseph Stalin's favorite ashtray was made from the top of Hitler's skull.

The last original *Police Gazette* reporting on the Hitler subject appears in May 1972, prompted by the appearance of Dr. Erwin Giesing, one of Hitler's physicians, on German television. The good doctor blasts Soviet claims of Der Fuehrer's death, while also taking time to refute the vicious Soviet assertion that Hitler only had one testicle. Dr. Giesing admits it was possible Hitler had escaped Berlin alive.

With renewed vigor, the *Police Gazette* concludes the article by saying it is "sending one of its top investigative reporters to find out" if Hitler is still at his "heavily guarded fortress . . . in a remote region of Patagonia" and to "be on the lookout for this important article." The reporter was never heard from again.

Then, on December 7, 1972, when the bodies of Martin Bormann and Dr. Ludwig Stumpfegger—of "silk-cord operation" fame—were discovered in Berlin, it took significant juice out of the *Gazette's* main assertions. Bormann, too—the *Gazette* had always said—was still alive and causing trouble. It turned out Bormann and Stumpfegger had never made it past May 1945.

The *Police Gazette* concluded its 132-year run with the January 1977 issue, an issue devoted entirely to "Hitler Is Alive!" reprints. If alive, Hitler would have been eighty-seven, which is a good age for any self-respecting Fuehrer to finally retire. Together, he and the *Police Gazette's* "top investigative reporter"—now with him à la

Lieutenant Colby in *Apocalypse Now*—rode off into the sunset of a Patagonian heart of darkness.

If the reader hadn't already figured it out by now, alive or dead, Hitler stood in as a metaphor for all surviving Nazis, as well as any group holding fascist ideologies around the world. As long as the threat of right-wing extremism exists, Adolph Hitler will always be alive. As for the *National Police Gazette*, scholar Guy Reel has likewise observed, "As a reflection of the modern American male, the *Gazette* still lives, and it may be a very long time before it ever really dies."

EICHMANN'S CAPTURE
SPOTLIGHTS HITLER'S HIDEOUT

by GEORGE McGRATH

**Israeli commandos are convinced that
somewhere in Argentina hides Adolf Hitler—very much alive!**

A fantastic cloak-and-dagger operation costing more than $100,000 led to the capture of Adolf Eichmann—killer of millions of Jews—by Israeli secret agents. It took them six months to find his hideout in Argentina.

Five secret agents were sent on the mission to capture Eichmann—one time head of the Nazi Gestapo Bureau which ordered the killing of six million Jews.

At the time this article is being written, Karl Adolf Eichmann sits in his lonely cell in Jerusalem awaiting trial.

Among the personalities of the third Reich, Hitler, Himmler, Goring, Goebbels, the name of Eichmann will not be listed nor known to the average person. He led a secluded life, not sharing a love of pomp, pageantry, and public notoriety with Goring and the others. Yet this former Lieutenant Colonel of the SS was responsible for more deaths than any other Nazi save Himmler and Reinhard Heydrich. As head of the Jewish resettlement program it was his job to personally order the mass extermination of Jews throughout the territories controlled by Germany, a job which he did with ruthless efficiency.

Eichmann was an Austrian like Hitler, and came from Linz, the same city where Hitler attended secondary school. He was born in 1906, 17 years after Hitler, but both men grew up in identical surroundings. As a boy, Eichmann saw the Austro-Hungarian Empire, crumbling from corruption within, suffer defeat after defeat on the battlefields of World War I.

In a post-war Austria, its lands divided into many small nations, its government torn by conflicts between left, center, and right, and its economy ravaged by alternating inflation and depression, Eichmann found his first hatreds of the Jews. Seeing in the Jew the cause of all misery, all corruption as did Hitler before him, Eichmann went to Germany to study and to escape the "Jewish-ridden state" which he felt was Austria.

Vents Wrath Against Jews

Once in Germany, his studies were forgotten in the struggle for National Socialism, which he discovered shortly after his arrival. He became a party man, he joined the SA, and in his brown uniform fought for the Nazis in the streets. By the time Hitler was made Chancellor in 1933, Eichmann had become an officer in the SA; transferred to the nucleus SS elite corps under Himmler. When the Gestapo came under Himmler's control in 1934, he saw in it a further chance to vent the wrath of his anti-Semitism and quickly joined it, retaining his SS rank and position.

As the powers granted to Himmler grew, so did Eichmann with it. The culmination of his efforts was his appointment to head the newly created section 4A 4B of the RSHA, or the bureau in charge of

Jewish resettlement of the Reich main security bureau. By the end of the war in 1945, this section was to be known as Dienststelle Eichmann, or Eichmann authority, in his honor. This post was created for him shortly after the anschluss with Austria in 1938, when the SS, having completed the elimination of other enemies to the new order, could turn its attention more completely on the Jewish question.

Eichmann's first assignment in Vienna, was the expulsion of Austrian Jews from the Reich.

The word expulsion to Eichmann meant in reality the application of what Hitler called "the final solution to the Jewish problem," in short: extermination. Eichmann had only two superiors in the SS; Heydrich and Himmler, both of whom also wanted the application of the final solution. Adolf set about his task with a vengeance, and before long his organization was herding Jews into concentration camps throughout Germany, Austria and the other annexed territories.

Murdered Jews En Masse

By the autumn of 1941, Dienststelle Eichmann was exterminating Jews in Poland, Czechoslovakia, and occupied Russia; in addition to importing more victims from France, Norway, and the rest of the conquered lands to the west of Germany. The Jews in Stettin and Schneidemumuehl were wiped out en masse, while 30,000 Jewish gypsies living throughout eastern Germany were rounded up within a week, never to be heard from again.

Some attempts were actually made at resettlement, primarily in lands in eastern Poland. Through deft planning, trainloads of refugees would arrive east of the Vistula with over half of the Jews nothing but frozen corpses. The Warsaw ghetto was established by walling up a section of the city; and then filling it with Jews. They lived in filth; food provided was usually rotten, with a meal for one having to feed ten. They lived 5 to a room, with inadequate plumbing, no sanitation precautions taken, and no medical facilities. As a crowning touch, Eichmann authorized the use of the ghetto as a marksmanship training ground for the Hitler Youth; young Nazis would be turned loose in the ghetto streets with rifles and any Jew was fair game.

There were other facets to Jewish resettlement which Eichmann employed. One was the establishment of Auschwitz, which was not a concentration camp in the usual sense of the word, but an extermination camp. It was designed not to hold prisoners, but to first gas them and then cremate them. One of the most efficient men in Eichmann's organization, Roudolph Roess, commanded Auschwitz in the 4 years of its existence, and managed to murder over 3 million Jews in that period.

After the invasion of Russia, Eichmann found transportation a problem which he solved by sending the exterminators to the Jews instead of bringing the Jews to established sites. Four Einsatzkommandos were formed, and were roving units designed to exterminate Jews town by town, burn the bodies in any convenient manner, usually in a large pit, and move on to the next slaughter as quickly as possible.

For smaller jobs, special trucks resembling moving vans were designed especially for Eichmann. Once loaded with Jews, carbon monoxide from the truck motor was piped into the van, killing those inside. At home in the Reich, Jews from the Balkans were dying by the thousands in camps such as Bergen-Belsen; Dachau; Buchenwald.

In the east, to deal with the increasing number of Jews coming from Russia as transportation improved, camps such as Treblinka were built, while the ovens at Auschwitz were enlarged to a capacity of 6 thousand a day. But the Nazi tides of fortune were turning, at Stalingrad and El Alamein. Hitler's armies were first stopped, then pushed back, then destroyed. Eichmann, in his office on Kurfuerstenstrasse in Berlin continued the mass murders, using methods which had become routine.

By spring of 1944 the Russian armies had reached Romania and

Hungary, and Hitler ordered the removal of all Jews from Hungary before it became a front-line combat zone. Eichmann was chosen as the perfect man for the job, promoted to commander of all security police in Hungary, and moved into a suite at the Hotel Majestic in Budapest where he could direct operations more easily.

As Russian troops entered a section of the Carpathians, on the 8th of April, 1944, the round-up began. By the 15th of May, over 300,000 Jews were in ghettos, coming from surrounding territories in Czechoslovakia and Yugoslavia as well as Hungary. Before the round-up had been finished, the first shipments had already left for Auschwitz with 90 men, women and children to one cattle car, without food. A total of over 400,000 Jews were deported from that one area alone before the round-up was over. At Auschwitz the ovens worked 24 hours a day, while supplementary burning-pits were dug to help with the surplus Jews.

Eichmann offered to "sell" 70,000 Jews to the allies in exchange for 10,000 trucks, the exchange to be made in neutral Turkey. The deal was not accepted, but it didn't matter to Eichmann as he had already executed the Jews which he had promised in return for the trucks. In his opinion, he could always find 70,000 Jews when he needed them.

He sold 2,784 Jews to Hungary for 5 million Swiss francs; Jews which had been taken in Hungary to make them more valuable. But Hitler had heard about the transaction and consequently gave Himmler a verbal thrashing which put an end to the sale of concentration camp inmates.

On July 20, 1944, Hitler was almost killed in the bomb plot against him by a group of army officers. As a result of this, Himmler was given more power, including the command of army group vistula, and Eichmann also was given more authority.

He returned to Berlin; Hungary being almost entirely in Soviet hands by now, and also because Hitler, as a result of the sale of the Hungarian Jews, had ordered that "no concentration camp inmate must fall into allied hands alive!"

With his new-found authority, Eichmann began to sharpen his attacks on the Jews; now they were no longer arrested and packed off to some remote extermination camp, they were hunted down in the streets and machine gunned on the spot.

But as the Reich crumbled, Eichmann didn't commit suicide. As did Himmler and many other top Nazis, he tried to escape. Captured by the Americans while wearing the uniform of a Luftwaffe private, he was interned as a common soldier. He escaped in 1946, and spent the next three years hiding out in various parts of Germany. Then, by way of Spain, he escaped to Argentina.

With plastic surgery hiding his once childlike face, he was joined by his wife and three children. But the Jews, of whom so many had died at his hands, were hunting him.

In 1958, when his wife returned to Linz to renew a passport, Israeli agents picked up the trail which led them to the mass-murderer. Eichmann was fond of women. An Israeli agent got in touch with one of them. She, fortunately, had the only picture of Eichmann as he looks today. This led to his capture. Near the end of May, of this year, Eichmann was captured by Israeli agents in Buenos Aires as he walked down the street towards his home.

Hitler's Hideout

But Karl Adolf Eichmann, Hitler's mass murderer of six million Jews was only one of many top Nazi war criminals who escaped and sought refuge in Argentina. His capture has now put the spotlight on the secret hideout of Adolf Hitler and his henchmen in a desolate area of Patagonia.

It is definitely known that hundreds of Nazi war criminals are now living there; among them Martin Bormann, deputy Fuhrer. This was confirmed by former US Ambassador, Spruille Braden, who tracked down seventy-one wanted top Nazis and urged the Argentine Government to arrest and deport them. But the Nazi influence was so powerful that no action was taken. Even the personal secretary and confidant of Dictator Juan Peron was the son of Ludwig Freude, Hitler's chief agent in South America. Freude was entrusted with $400,000,000 in transferred Nazi funds from Germany, according to the US State Department.

These Nazi funds bought a huge slice of Argentine territory; many thousand square miles of ranchland in the provinces of Rio Negro and Chubut, a part of Patagonia. These ranches, surpassing even the vast Texas holdings of the richest cattlemen in the United States, were settled by leading Nazis who had been secretly landed at Mar Del Plata by U-boats immediately after the war and who are still there.

The landing base was so heavily guarded, Allied Intelligence agents reported, that they were unable to learn the identity of all the important Nazis who disembarked.

Whether Hitler and Eva Braun were among them has never been determined, but it is evident that Hitler did not commit suicide.

If Eichmann could have escaped, Hitler could easily have done the same since he had greater means at his disposal.

The reports of Hitler's death was a complete hoax to cover up his escape and prevent a world-wide manhunt for him. Eyewitness accounts of his purported death and fake photos of Der Fuehrer's corpse were circulated to confuse the investigators. It is a known fact that Hitler had several doubles.

"We found absolutely no evidence of Hitler's death in Berlin" said Col. W. F. Heimlich chief of US Intelligence in Berlin, who had conducted the official investigation. "He could easily have made his get-a-way by plane from outside the Reichchancellery area before the fall of Berlin," Col. Heimlich explained.

"Analysis of the couch stains where Hitler reportedly killed himself revealed that the stains, while they were human blood, was not of the blood type of Hitler. There were no bullet holes in the couch or in the wall behind it."

Col. Heimlich further discounted the rumors that Hitler's body was burned in the courtyard outside his bunker.

"We dug up everything in the courtyard. Two screens were erected, one of wire mesh similar to chicken wire and behind it a second one much finer with half inch holes. Every shovel full of dirt from the bomb-crater went first through the wide screen and next through the small screen in the hope that any small piece of evidence showing the presence of a human body might be quickly detected.

"The X-ray photographs of Hitler's head gave us expert clues as to his dental structure and even one tooth might have been sufficient to identify his body. But nothing was unearthed that gave us any evidence that Hitler had been burned or buried there."

Like Eichmann, it is reasonable to assume that Hitler escaped and also had plastic surgery to make him unrecognizable. But Israeli secret agents with their fanatic cloak-and-dagger operation and unlimited funds may someday shock the world by finding Hitler's Hideout and probably the Fuhrer himself.

ADOLF HITLER'S FAKE SUICIDE!

by HARVEY WILSON

There is a deep and significant motive
behind the Soviet's sudden interest in trying to convince
the world of Adolf Hitler's death . . .

Today the Kremlin is making desperate efforts to erase from the world's memory their own previous announcements that "Hitler is alive."

Close on the heels of the announcement that Israeli agents had finally brought the mass-murderer Adolf Eichmann to justice came a flood of not-so-cleverly disguised Communist propaganda designed to "prove" that Adolf Hitler was dead. But their hasty, slipshod attempts have failed. Another big Soviet lie has been disproved and the reasons for their clumsy cover-up of Hitler's escape revealed.

This propaganda took many forms, as devious as they were numerous, but in spite of all the items of "conclusive proof" suddenly brought forward by Red leaders, it remained nothing more than propaganda. There is, for example, the now-famous photograph purporting to show Hitler's body shortly after his suicide, as it lay in the garden of the Reichschancellery in Berlin. With it came the incredible story that lay behind this photograph.

The Communist leaders would have us believe that the Russian news agency, Tass, discovered the photograph when it was printed by chance in an obscure local Soviet newspaper, *Kazakhstan Pravda*.

Tass then claimed that the editors of this small-town journal "just happened" to discover the photo among the effects of a local citizen who had recently died.

This Soviet citizen was supposed to have been an ex-soldier named Ilya Sianow. Tass asserted that Sianow had been a private in the 176th Soviet Guard Division, the outfit which captured Berlin in May, 1945.

On the way to Berlin, Sianow's division passed through Liepsig. There Sianow "liberated" a motion picture camera and carried it with him to the Reich capital.

Phony Photo

On the evening of May 1, Sianow's platoon was ordered to attack the Germans defending the garden at the rear of the Reichschancellery where the entrance to Hitler's underground bunker was located. Sianow was the first soldier to enter the garden, and—so the Soviets allege—he took time from the battle to shoot some pictures of the Fuehrer's body, and only then did he continue in the attack.

After the war the camera and its pictures accompanied Sianow back to his peasant hut somewhere in the interior of the USSR, and there the prints lay forgotten for 15 years. By some remarkable coincidence, these photos were discovered shortly after Eichmann's capture, and offered to the world as positive proof of the dictator's death. Only one thing went wrong with the Red lie: it didn't work.

First, the photo directly contradicted the official Nazi version of Hitler's death, so much so in fact that Eric Kempka, Hitler's chauffeur who was with him in those last Berlin days, branded the photograph a "downright fake."

For one thing, the body was supposed to have been burned with 180 liters of gasoline, yet the corpse in the photograph clearly shows no burns.

Hitler was supposed to have shot himself through the mouth, yet the photo clearly shows the bullet hole in the forehead.

Hitler was supposed to have been cremated and buried in the garden of the chancellery, yet when Sianow took his photograph 24 hours later, the body had somehow gotten back into the bunker, as the background of the photo shows.

Confronted with this unanimous rejection, even from those old-guard Nazis who wish to keep Hitler's escape a secret, the Reds dropped the subject. But that was not the last they heard of it.

It seems that someone in Tass didn't get the word from above to forget about the photo, and disastrously released the news that the picture was indeed a forgery, and in reality was taken from a semi-documentary film made by the Soviet movie industry in 1950, on direct orders from Stalin. This film used actors and stage settings instead of newsreel clippings. The government of the USSR has not mentioned this photograph since, for even if the incredible story about Private Sianow were accepted, the overwhelming proof of forgery could not be overlooked, not even by the Communists.

Besides, the Reds now had more tricks ready up their sleeve.

One was the testimony of Marshal Zhukov, conqueror of Berlin in 1945, who flatly stated on June 10 of that year:

"We have found no corpse that could be Hitler's. Hitler had good opportunities for getting away. He could have taken off at the very last moment, for there was a plane ready and an airfield at his disposal."

Colonel General Nikolai E. Berzarin, the Soviet Berlin commander who conducted the on-the-spot investigation into Hitler's reported death at the Reichschancellery bunker, was emphatic that Hitler had escaped from the smoldering rubble of Berlin. He declared:

"My personal opinion is that Hitler disappeared into Europe."

This opinion was supported by Stalin himself. At the Potsdam Conference in August, 1945, President Truman was reported to have asked one important question of Stalin: Was Hitler Dead?

Stalin replied with characteristic bluntness: "No."

A Tower of Lies

But since then the Communists' line changed as it always does when they find it convenient to evade the truth. Directly after Eichmann's capture last year, Zhukov started singing a different tune. Now, he declared, Hitler is dead. No evidence, no motive for the about-face; just the plain statement of "fact." This sudden, unexplained switch caused Zhukov a loss of face within the Soviet Union. It was done on the express orders of Zhukov's superiors, and for no other reason.

Another attempt to prove that Hitler no longer lives was made when the Russian government "allowed" a certain story to filter out of the country, once again shortly after the arrest of Eichmann. This story asserts that as Stalin lay on his deathbed in the Kremlin in 1953, he informed his doctors that his beloved yellow ashtray—a yellow, shallow bowl about 5 inches across that he always kept at his bedside—was actually made from the top of Hitler's skull. This rumor, which was really spread by Communist agents throughout the world on orders from Moscow, was supposed to have traveled through the Russian medical circles, and then siphoned out into the free world by way of international medical conventions. Few people if any accepted the tale, and then it too was quietly dropped by the Reds.

Another closely related story was circulated in much the same manner and concerns a personal museum which Stalin kept hidden somewhere in the sub-basement of the Kremlin. This museum, where Stalin was supposed to have spent many hours gloating over his conquest of the Third Reich, was reported to contain articles from Hitler's last days in Berlin, including the remains of the dictator himself, all neatly encased in a pressurized glass coffin. Investigation of this particular story shows several interesting facts: namely, that Stalin never mentioned anything about the existence of such a museum, that no one ever saw it while Stalin was alive, or since his death.

Cunning Purpose

Many of the other less spectacular attempts by the Communists to cover the escape of Adolf Hitler serve a definite and cunning purpose. While the West German government, when they officially declared Hitler dead on October 25, 1956, were primarily concerned with stopping the growth of new Nazism within West Germany itself, the Reds are thinking in terms of their puppet state of East Germany.

The definite connection and timing of this sudden onset of Soviet propaganda with Eichmann's capture cannot be overlooked. Before Eichmann was found hiding in Argentina, very few people believed it possible that a high-ranking Nazi official could have escaped from the closing ring of allied might in Europe.

Then, on December 20, 1960, came the startling revelation that another big Nazi war criminal had been discovered in a small town near Hamburg, Germany.

He was Richard Baer, former major in the SS Corps, wanted on charges of mass murder. As last commandant of the infamous Auschwitz concentration camp, he was supposed to have sent thousands of Jews to their deaths in the gas ovens. Nazis who had preceded him as heads of the camp, including the notorious Rudolph Hoess, had already been executed on the same charge.

Like Eichmann, his former boss, Baer has been presumed dead. Unlike Eichmann, he didn't hunt cover in a foreign country, but stayed put in Germany. It was not until October of last year that authorities learned that Baer might be alive.

How Top Nazi Was Caught

In answer to a reward of nearly $2500 for information leading to his capture, the German state attorney was tipped off that a master lumberjack called Neumann, living with his wife in a hut on the Prince Bismarck estate in Dassendorf, might really be Baer.

Samples of the lumberman's handwriting were obtained and compared with those of Baer's. They checked. Police with drawn guns crept up on the cabin.

Facing the authorities, "Neumann" at first denied that he was Baer, but when his wife came out of the cabin and asked, "Oh, daddy, what's happened?" he broke.

"All right, I'm Baer," he admitted. He was taken into custody. For 15 long years, this man had successfully evaded capture, though he was hunted as a fugitive by an entire nation.

The long-delayed discovery and capture of Eichmann in the Argentine and Baer in Germany gave the world convincing evidence that other high-ranking Nazis, formerly checked off as dead, have also escaped.

If these relatively minor cogs of the once-powerful Nazi machine could have avoided recognition and capture for 15 years, then surely Hitler and Martin Bormann, with their greater power and influence, have done the same. They must be alive today. All evidence points to that fact.

No one realizes this more than the hierarchy of the Communist world. For several important reasons, the fate of Hitler is giving the Soviets great concern.

Naturally they want revenge for the damage and suffering caused by Hitler's legions during the war. But there is a much deeper, much more significant motive behind this sudden interest. That is the cold war.

As long as Hitler remains hidden, he constitutes a potential threat to the Communist as well as the free world. Those nations under Communist domination are a sterile breeding ground for any effective Nazi movement because of the strict political control by the Communist party, the Red Army, and the ever-watchful MVD. The reason the Soviets want to prove that Hitler is dead, is to destroy the hopes and dreams of the Nazis still remaining in East Germany, of ever returning to power.

While the sudden reappearance of Hitler might not seriously disturb the internal situation of these countries, the Soviet propaganda machine then would accuse the free nations of conspiring to harbor the No. 1 Nazi war criminal. The Soviet Union, in short, has nothing to lose and very much to gain by covering up and "authenticating" Hitler's death.

The free world, on the other hand, has much to lose by allowing

Hitler to remain free. For one thing, many of the Fuhrer's followers are still around, waiting for his return. These men still dream of the power they had under the Nazi empire Hitler once ruled. Granted that they live in the past, and yet if Hitler were to reappear they would once again swear their loyalty to him unto death.

Naturally such people have little chance to regain the power they once had, but they are numerous enough and fanatical enough to cause a serious threat to the stability of the free world. This is not only what the Communists know, but what they hope for. If the free world were to be put off-balance because of such a sudden resurgence of Nazism, the Communist bloc might be able to gain an over-powering superiority.

Hitler's Bunker Destroyed

It is primarily for this reason that Hitler's bunker, containing possible evidence of his escape, was ordered blown up by the Russian government. This is why Zhukov was ordered publicly to change his mind concerning Hitler's death, in spite of a tremendous loss of face, and this is the reason that the Communists have tried to conceal the escape of Adolf Hitler.

The free nations cannot afford to allow Hitler to remain at large any longer. The world is now faced with factual proof that Hitler not only could have, but probably did escape, along with others such as Bormann and Eichmann. All that remains necessary is his capture and trial, not only in the name of justice, but to defeat the Russian war lords in their attempts to protect this greatest of all criminals. If they succeed, then they'll be a step closer to their goal of world domination.

EICHMANN'S LAST WORDS REVEAL HITLER IS ALIVE!

UNTOLD STORY OF THE NAZI HIDEOUT IN ARGENTINA

by HARVEY WILSON

Deep in South America's "Little Germany," big shot Hitlerites are hatching plans for a violent comeback

A political volcano is ready to erupt in Argentina. The Nazi underground is emerging, and with it the world will soon learn that Hitler is still alive.

It is no longer a secret among the Nazi hierarchy that Der Fuehrer and his top aides have been hatching the Fourth Reich from their hideout in the vast, sparsely populated Patagonia region of Argentina.

In Adolf Eichmann's march to the gallows in the courtyard of Ramla Prison, in Tel Aviv's outskirts, he kept bellowing: "Long live Hitler! Long live Germany!"

These words—his last before the noose tightened around his scrawny neck—not only expressed sentiment. They also reflected his subconscious admission that Hitler was still at large.

Allied intelligence agents report that Hitler's existence is now being publicly acknowledged by Argentine Nazis.

Any evening in the swanky Cabana Restaurant in Buenos Aires, a rendezvous for the wealthy German colony, dozens of Germans rise, lift glasses of champagne and cry: "To Hitler! To The Fatherland!"

There is no longer any question in the minds of Israeli Intelligence agents that Hitler and his top aides are secure in an Argentine hideout.

The agents have personally seen such fugitives as Martin Bormann, Deputy Fuehrer under Hitler; Johann von Leers, a high-powered Hitler propaganda man; Hans Rudel, Hitler's personal pilot, and Dr. Joseph Mengele, whose inhuman experiments upon Jewish children and women shocked the world.

So bitter is Israeli hatred of Mengele that his capture, next to Hitler himself, would be considered a major triumph.

Ironically, it was the Israeli agents' hunt for Mengele that brought them to Eichmann. Their decision to grab Eichmann on the streets of Buenos Aires and secretly fly him to Israel stemmed from the failure of the West Germany Government to effect the extradition of Mengele from Argentina.

The story behind this strange episode has never been told before.

The *Police Gazette* can now reveal that, in the spring of 1959, Israeli agents tracked the infamous doctor to Argentina.

Extradition Blocked

At that time, it was the policy of the Israeli Intelligence Service to inform the West German Government of the whereabouts of escaped war criminals. The Bonn Government would then move for their extradition and trial.

Bonn followed through after Mengele was "fingered." But Argentina refused the request on the ground that the charges against Mengele were of a political character.

Also turned down was a request for the extradition of Dr. Karl Klingenfuss, a former counselor to the Nazi Foreign Ministry, who was wanted for mass murder. It was obvious that the Nazis were so firmly entrenched that they had official protection.

Under these circumstances, the Israelis decided to take matters into their own hands. But the two Nazis promptly fled to new hideouts after getting wind of the extradition requests.

In hunting down new leads, the Israelis got hot on the trail of a really big fish—the High Executioner of the gas chambers, Eichmann.

Having been burned once, the Jewish agents were not going to risk losing a prize catch of such magnitude. So, in a daring move, they pounced on Eichmann and spirited him out of Argentina.

Fuming over the kidnapping, the Argentine Nazis consolidated their forces for a broadscale attack on the Jews.

Two neo-fascist groups—Tacuara and Mazorca—plotted a violent Hitlerite campaign to wipe out Jewish communities.

Groups of Nazi thugs seized Jewish youths and branded them with swastikas. They harassed Jewish families in a diabolical campaign of terror.

After Eichmann's execution, the outbreaks became so widespread that one hotbed of violence, Buenos Aires University, closed for a day to avoid further "incidents."

Soon afterward, a shocking report came from a high Argentine police official. He charged that neo-fascists, egged on by the Nazis, had been operating with police protection.

The official, Raul Angelini, blew the whistle on the Nazis after resigning as chief of Federal Coordination (Argentina's FBI).

Angelini accused his superior, Enrique Green, head of the federal police, of closing his eyes or taking "inadequate measures" against the vehemently pro-Nazi Tacuara Society.

The startling story of Nazi infiltration in Argentina dates back to pre-World War II days. German financial interests were deeply entrenched in the country's economy. At the outbreak of war, Argentina's sympathies were flagrantly pro-Nazi, though it professed to be "neutral."

When Hitler marched into Paris after the Germans overran France, Argentine dictator Juan Peron was right there with him.

Nazis occupied top positions in the Peron government.

George Mann, a German financial expert, was special adviser to the Argentine Ministry of Finance.

Col. Walter Osterkamp, former head of the Luftwaffe school in Werneuchen, Germany, was confidential adviser to the Argentine Air Force.

And Gen. Carlos von der Becke, Chief of Staff of the Argentine Army, had close relatives on the German General Staff.

Guiding spirit of the Argentine Nazis was Ludwig Freude, an old-time Hitler crony, who was the mysterious power behind the scenes in the German Embassy. Freude's son was Peron's confidential aide.

With the imminent collapse of the Third Reich, top Nazi officials transferred $400,000,000 of German funds to Argentina. Allied Intelligence traced the personal fortunes of such Nazi stalwarts as Luftwaffe chief Hermann Goering and von Ribbentrop to Buenos Aires.

These millions bought a huge slice of Argentine territory, including thousands of square miles of ranchland in the provinces of Rio Negro, and Chubut in Patagonia. The methodical "super men" turned this vast area into a Little Nazi Germany, policed by armed guards.

This is where the top Nazis fled when the Third Reich was destroyed. It was a perfect setup for a hide out.

After the German surrender in 1945, Nazi war criminals filtered into Argentina by submarine, plane and cargo vessel. During the closing days of the war, Bormann had established an escape route through Spain.

Eichmann followed this underground route. Ironically, Eichmann's version of his escape has been verified by an ex-Nazi agent who was Bormann's chief lieutenant in the underground.

Plastic Surgery

A few days after Eichmann's execution, this agent, Angel Alcarzar de Velasco, came out of hiding in Paris and admitted his part in the Nazi underground.

Velasco revealed that the last time he conferred with Bormann was in 1958 in a mountain village in the Andes. By that time, Deputy Fuehrer Bormann's appearance had been changed radically. He had undergone three plastic surgery operations on his face. He was also much thinner and was practically bald.

On several occasions, Israeli Intelligence agents had come within an arm's reach of Bormann. He was observed drinking beer in the A.B.C. German Restaurant in Lavalle St. in the heart of Buenos Aires. But he was surrounded by bodyguards. A few months before Eichmann was captured, he slipped away and is now reported hiding in Patagonia.

Before Bormann left Spain, he confided to Velasco that "Europe will see Hitler again before long, leading a new and more powerful Germany."

Velasco's disclosures were nothing new to Allied Intelligence agents, who have known that Bormann, Hitler and his key aides escaped from the smoldering ruins of Berlin.

Soon after Soviet Marshal Zhukov entered Berlin, he announced: "We have found no corpse that could be Hitler's. Hitler had a good opportunity to get away. He could have taken off at the very last moment, for there was an airfield at his disposal."

Six months after Germany's collapse, Gen, Eisenhower said: "The Russians have been unable to unearth one bit of tangible evidence of Hitler's death."

And Lt. Gen. Bedell Smith, who headed the Central Intelligence Agency right after the war, bluntly reported: "No human being can say that Hitler is dead."

The most important clue to the whereabouts of Hitler has been supplied by high-ranking Nazis during bouts of heavy drinking in Buenos Aires cafes. They openly discussed having met Der Fuehrer, who is 73 now, in Bariluche, a quiet town in Rio Negro province.

The new outbreaks of Hitlerism reveal the hand of the fanatic old master at work.

Brutal Beatings

Just as in Germany, during the heyday of Nazism, hardly a day passes without some anti-Semitic incident in Argentina's larger cities. Jewish students have been brutally beaten, some of them severely disfigured. Walls have been scribbled with Nazi slogans. Windows of Jewish-owned stores, have been smashed and synagogues desecrated.

In this climate of violence, Israeli commandos, sworn to avenge the murder of six million Jews by bringing Nazi war criminals to justice, are themselves being sought by Argentine authorities.

But nothing will deter these commandos from stalking Hitler and Bormann. They have sworn to "follow them to their graves."

Meanwhile, Argentina boils with political unrest as the Nazi Underground starts to emerge from the shadows.

HITLER IS ALIVE: SUICIDE A FAKE!

by BILL DAVIS

The plan of Major Kainitsch provided for Der Fuehrer and all the Nazi leaders to escape on two planes—plan also provided for a Sgt. Schmidt to be found burned, in Hitler's uniform and a bullet in his head . . .

An attractive German woman—the daughter of Adolf Hitler's top personal aide, Martin Bormann—has finally broken her silence on the most daring cloak-and-dagger exploit of World War II, Hitler's escape from Berlin.

The woman, Frau Ute Eva Bormann Riedmann, is the one person who has the inside, first-hand knowledge of Hitler's flight.

For years she refused to discuss the matter. But recently Bormann's daughter went to Italy to be married to Gerhard Riedmann. They tried to keep the engagement secret, but Italian reporters spotted the advance wedding notice in a small newspaper in Bolzano.

When Ute and Gerhard arrived in Bolzano, reporters and columnists swarmed around them. But they refused to be interviewed. Finally, four days before the marriage, one enterprising newsman got to see them alone. He left a visiting card, asking for an interview.

"I don't know how it happened," the reporter said later, "but three days before the marriage Gerhard Riedmann telephoned me, making an appointment. He came right on time with his fiancé, and we drove out to a restaurant outside the city."

For hours Bormann's daughter and her fiancé sat with the reporter, sipping beer and chatting. Her disclosures being printed here for the first time in the United States provide dramatic details of Hitler's faked suicide and confirm and shed additional light on the *Police Gazette's* exclusive revelation in 1951 that the dictator had escaped.

The woman spoke softly as she recalled called how Hitler had called his general staff to a top-secret meeting in battered Berlin in April of 1945. Bombs were exploding outside. The Fuehrer's dreams of conquest were going up in flames. While Bormann's daughter was not at the meeting, she had heard full details of it from members of her family who later escaped from Berlin.

Plans for Escape

"The Allied divisions were already on the point of occupying Berlin when the general staff assembled." she said. "Hitler was there, very excited and very much afraid. Goebbels was there, and many others. My father was there, too. They were laboring on a plan to escape.

"Major Kainitsch prepared everything. Hitler was supposed to escape on a light plane. My father was to stay to the end and spread the news of the Fuehrer's suicide, communicate it to Admiral Doenitz and have his will recognized. Then he could make his getaway in turn on another aircraft.

"The second plane never arrived, and my father was left in the bunker. When the Americans and Russians occupied Berlin, they found charred bodies in the cellar of the Chancellery. Although a body was found dressed like Hitler, It was not the Fuehrer. He had gotten away to South America."

Frau Riedmann lit a cigarette before continuing.

Hitler and aide Martin Bormann, who helped formulate plan for escape. He stayed behind to spread news of Fuehrer's suicide.

"Kainitsch's plan," she said, "provided for a deception. There was to be a stand-in for Hitler in the final climax. It was to be an SS sergeant, a man named Schmidt, dressed in the Fuehrer's clothes. A bullet in his head would make things look like suicide, and a can of gasoline would destroy the body for identification."

Frau Riedmann's account fits in perfectly with Independent proof—unearthed by the US Army and the *Police Gazette*—of Hitler's successful flight.

When the first Russians burst into Hitler's bunker, several bodies were found. Hitler's uniform was on one charred corpse. But Allied intelligence agents obtained X-rays of Hitler's teeth from the dictator's personal dentist and established that the body was that of someone else.

Colonel W. F. Heimlich, former chief of US Army Intelligence in Berlin, reported these results of his investigation:

"I could find no evidence of Hitler's death. He had ample opportunity to escape. There was an airfield and planes available at his disposal."

Hitler Wasn't Depressed

Interviews with Heinz Linge, Hitler's chauffeur, and other members of his staff who saw him a few minutes before his alleged death supported Heimlich. One after another, they said Hitler did not appear despondent or depressed when he called them in to say goodbye.

"He seemed more like a man about to take a trip than a man who was going to die," said one.

All of the members of Hitler's staff conceded that they had not seen Hitler die.

Heimlich used a scientific approach to completely demolish the myth that Hitler was a suicide.

"Analysis of the couch stains where Hitler reportedly killed himself," said Heimlich, "revealed that the stains, while they were human blood, were not of the blood type of Hitler or Eva Braun. There were no bullet holes in the couch or in the wall behind it."

Heimlich was determined to leave no stone unturned in his investigation. After proving positively that none of the corpses in or near Hitler's bunker was the dictator's, Heimlich had the entire area dug up to see whether Hitler's body still lay buried.

Ute Bormann talks to reporter in exclusive interview, telling of how Hitler made escape to South America.

"I arranged for an American intelligence team to undertake a careful examination and excavation of the Reichschancellery area," said Heimlich. "First, all debris was cleared up. Such odds and ends of war as broken machine guns, ammunition, rifles, helmets, uniforms, bits and pieces of wood were examined.

"The bomb crater, located about four yards from the entrance to the bunker was the prime target. Two screens were erected, one of wire mesh similar to chicken wire and behind it a second one much finer with half-inch holes. Every shovelful of dirt from the bomb crater went through the wide screen and next through the small screen in the hope that any small piece of evidence showing the presence of a human body might be quickly detected.

"The X-ray photographs of Hitler's head gave us expert clues as to his dental structure and even one tooth might have been sufficient to identify his body.

"As the excavation progressed, we found bits of uniform and civilian clothing including a woman's slip, a man's hat with the initials 'A.H.' in silver in the lining, suitcases and other pieces of clothing, hooks, magazines, records, diaries, recording tape and the remains of what had once been the switchboard in the bunker.

"After days of excavation in an ever-widening area, we found no signs of any bodies, and more significantly, no evidence of burning or of fire.

"On the basis of this on-the-spot investigation, I sent my report to Supreme Headquarters at Frankfurt, together with pictures and supporting evidence, stating that there was nothing to support the theory of Hitler's death."

Escaped on Plane

Fray Riedmann revealed that Hitler flew out of Berlin the night of April 30, 1945, "on a littler Fieseler-Storch plane that landed on the Unter den Linden during the night and which he boarded with a woman and some suitcases."

Once again, this jibes with evidence uncovered by Allied agents. Their confidential conclusion was that Hitler flew to a secluded Nazi submarine base, where a fully-stocked U-boat was waiting for him.

The submarine took Hitler and Eva Braun to the Argentine coast in the vicinity of San Clemente del Tuya. Accompanied by armed guards, Hitler and Eva went to a pre-arranged retreat in the wilds of Patagonia. US intelligence agents are convinced that Hitler is still there.

Frau Riedmann was no more than a child at the time of Hitler's flight. She has never seen Bormann since the end of the war, she said in the interview, and she is sure he is dead.

"His image still lives in my memory, though," she confided. "I have a fond memory of that sturdy man with the strong neck, the eyes a little cold, that only lit up when he was surrounded by the tribe of his children, in the villa at Obersalzberg in Bavaria.

"My brothers and I were almost always alone there with our mother. Papa was always away. Sometimes he didn't come home for months. I always saw him with gentlemen, in uniforms like his, that often came to visit us.

"One of them, especially in the last months we lived in Obersalzberg, was very attentive to us and brought us presents. I think, but I can't be sure, that he was the Fuehrer."

The woman gazed off into space as she offered this insight into the Bormanns' home life of nearly 20 years ago:

"My father was good, perhaps the best father that a girl would want to have. He showered me with presents and talked to me for a long time about things that I couldn't understand at that time, of course.

"With my oldest brother, Martin Jr., who was then in the Hitler youth movement, his relations were cooler, as if more official, although cordial. They thought of themselves as both in the same army and there was no room for anything else.

Father Was Worried

"Mama was sick already by then. She was never in good health. Papa was very worried, although he tried to hide it. But he didn't have much time for us. Nazism had him so full of the idea of Greater Germany that everything else was pushed into the background.

"I realized this much later, when everything was finished, and I also realized that my father was a great idealist, maybe the only one among all the leaders that Hitler had surrounded himself with.

"He had an idea—it was not for me to judge whether it was right or wrong—and he followed it out to the end, like a man, taking all the consequences. That is one more reason why I can't have a bad memory of my father."

Frau Riedmann's reference to Hitler's "will" is another element of her story that fits in with the jigsaw puzzle assembled by Allied investigators. Besides naming gaunt, grimfaced Karl Doenitz as his successor, Hitler's will was designed to keep the fires of hate burning in the hearts of his followers. The will was a blueprint for the perpetuation of the Nazi Ideology after Hitler himself had gone under cover.

Part of the tirade went this way:

"It is not true that I or anybody else in Germany wanted the war in the year 1939. It was desired and provoked entirely by those international statesmen who were either of Jewish origin or who worked in the Jewish interest . . . Centuries may pass, but out of the ruins of our cities and art monuments the hatred will arise and be constantly renewed against the people who are alone ultimately responsible: International Jewry and Its assistants.

"As late as three days before the outbreak of the German-Polish war, I proposed to the British ambassador in Berlin a solution of the German-Polish problem—similar to the case of the Saar area, under international control. This offer cannot be explained away, either. It was only rejected because the responsible circles in English politics wanted war, partly because of the expected business, partly driven by a propaganda arranged by international Jewry.

"But I left no doubt about the fact that the real culprit in this murderous struggle, Jewry, would also have to pay for it, if the people of Europe were again to be treated as so many packages of shares by these international money and finance conspirators.

"Furthermore, I left no doubt that it would not be tolerated this time that millions of European children of the Aryan people should starve to death, that millions of grown-up men should suffer death, and that hundreds of thousands of women and children should be burned and bombed to death in the cities, without the real culprit suffering his due punishment, even through more humane methods. . . .

"Above all, I obligate the leadership of the nation and its followers to the most minute observation of the racial laws and to pitiless resistance against the universal poisoner of all people, international Judaism."

Hitler left this blueprint behind in hopes it would pave the way for a Nazi comeback.

He has never been able to stage this comeback, but as long as he is alive he remains one of the most dangerous men in the world. Riedmann's disclosures again show that Hitler escaped from the flaming ruins of Berlin.

HITLER IS ALIVE!

New Eyewitness Report of Nazi Hideout . . .

by HARVEY WILSON

Reporter confirms *Police Gazette* articles revealing
existence of secret Nazi outpost in Argentina

For the first time, an outsider has seen Adolf Hitler's super-secret
hideout in the wilds of Argentina.

His eyewitness account of the impenetrable Nazi stronghold,
confirms the startling facts first unearthed and published by the
Police Gazette, twelve years ago.

Traveling through the mountainous region of Rio Negro province—a sprawling wilderness of lakes, waterfalls, gigantic glacier
caves and forested Islands—Jack Comben, correspondent of the
London Daily Express, discovered the last secret outpost of Hitler's
Germany, 100 miles north of San Carlos de Bariloche.

It was in 1952 that the *Police Gazette*, after having obtained
top secret Allied Intelligence reports and information based on
Interviews with former members of the Wehrmacht, revealed that
Hitler and his mistress, Eva Braun, had escaped from the ruins of
Berlin.

When the defeat of the Third Reich loomed imminent, plans
for Hitler's escape were drawn up by Martin Bormann, the Dictator's closest confident. The project was entrusted to Admiral Karl
Doenitz, Nazi U-boat specialist and Commander-in-Chief of the
German Navy, who was later to boast:

"The German submarine fleet is proud of having built for Der

Fuehrer in another part of the world a Shangri-La on Land—an impregnable fortress."

This "impregnable fortress" to which Admiral Doenitz had alluded was in the heart of a huge slice of Argentina territory that had been purchased by Nazi agents in South America. This "Little Nazi Germany" covered over 10,000 square miles of ranchland (the size of the state of Massachusetts) in the provinces of Rio Negro and Chubut. And the armed camp, that was to become Hitler's hideout, was in a region north of San Carlos de Bariloche.

Visits Nazi Outpost

Recently, in January, 1964, correspondent Jack Comben, journeyed to Bariloche to investigate reports of the Nazi outpost. Here is his report:

"I have come back from visiting the most extraordinary surviving outpost of Hitler's Germany in the world today.

"In a camp on the bank of the swift-flowing Limay River, 2,500 miles south of the Equator, in the heart of the Argentine, German men, women and children are living a strange and secret existence under steely discipline.

"Local people cannot penetrate into the camp, which lies at Paso Flores, 100 miles north of San Carlos de Bariloche. The inmates of the camp are forbidden to talk to strangers. All men in the camp wear Afrika Korps-style uniforms, with the same peaked caps that Field Marshal Rommel's elite army wore in the Western desert."

The camp is sealed off to all non-Nazis. No person without the proper credentials can set foot in it. Armed guards make sure of that. To further ensure secrecy, every piece of mail entering or leaving the camp is subjected to the most rigorous censorship.

"The camp," reported Comben, "seems to be completely under the control of the camp commandant, a gray-haired man called Walther Ochner, who is known as Der Hauptmann. I have been able to establish that Ochner was a high official in Hitler's communications organization. His right-hand man is Edgar Fiess, a former SS officer."

Fake Suicide

When victorious Allied troops took over Berlin, the first reports out of the beleaguered city were that Hitler had killed himself in his bunker beneath the Reichchancellory. These reports said that Hitler and Eva Braun, whom he had married just before the fall of Berlin, took their lives in a suicide pact and that their bodies were then removed by trusted friends to the courtyard, drenched with gasoline and burned.

This version of what happened to Hitler and Eva was circulated throughout the entire world—but Allied Intelligence soon disclosed that the "suicide" was a hoax.

Members of Hitler's staff, who saw him a few minutes before his alleged death, contradicted each other as far as the suicide report was concerned. They all pointed out that Hitler, when he called them in to say "goodbye," didn't act like a man about to take his own life.

"He seemed more like a man about to take a trip than a man who was going to die," declared one.

And all members of Hitler's staff conceded that they hadn't *actually* seen their Fuehrer die.

Col. W. F. Heimlich, former Chief of US Army Intelligence in Berlin, who was in charge of the official investigation into Hitler's disappearance, in an exclusive interview told the *Police Gazette*:

"I could find no evidence of Hitler's death. He had ample opportunity to escape. There was an airfield and many planes available at his disposal."

Scientific Tests

Furthermore, scientific tests made by Col. Heimlich and his probers proved that the suicide story was a hoax.

"Analysis of the blood stains on the couch where Hitler reportedly killed himself," said Heimlich, "revealed that the stains were not the blood type of Hitler, or Eva Braun. There were no bullet holes in the couch, or in the wall behind it."

What's more, Col. Heimlich had obtained X-ray photographs of Hitler's teeth from the Dictator's personal dentist. These would establish beyond doubt if any teeth found at the burning site were that of Hitler's. But no such evidence could be found.

Determined to leave no stone unturned in his quest to learn Hitler's fate, Col. Heimlich had a crack US Intelligence team make a needle-in-the-haystack search of the Reichchancellory area. "First," he said, "all debris was cleared up. Such items as broken machine guns, ammunition, helmets, uniforms and bits of wood were examined."

No Clues Found

"A bomb crater, located about four yards from the entrance to the bunker, was the prime target," Col. Heimlich explained. "Two screens were erected, one of wire mesh similar to chicken wire and behind it a second one much finer with half inch holes. Every shovelful of dirt from the bomb crater went through the small screen in the hope that any small piece of evidence showing the presence of a human body might be quickly detected.

"The X-ray photographs of Hitler's head gave us expert clues as to his dental structure and even one tooth might have been sufficient to identify his body. But after days of excavation in an ever-widening area, we found no signs of any bodies and—more significantly—no evidence of burning.

"On the basis of this on-the-spot investigation, I sent my report to Supreme Headquarters at Frankfurt, together with pictures and supporting evidence, stating that there was nothing to support the theory of Hitler's death."

And furthermore, no corpse of a female was found in the ruins, although Eva Braun was supposed to have died with Hitler and their bodies burned side by side in the courtyard.

How Hitler Escaped

The *Police Gazette*, was told by unimpeachable sources, that Hitler flew out of Berlin on the night of April 30, 1945. He fled the city in company with a woman and they made their departure in a Fieseler-Storch plane. They reportedly carried several suitcases and proceeded to a secluded Nazi submarine base in Norway. There a fully-stocked U-boat was already awaiting them.

On July 10 of the same year, Spruille Braden, American Ambassador in Buenos Aires, received a phone tip that two German U-boats had just put into Mar del Plata.

"I acted immediately," he later told the *Police Gazette* in an exclusive interview. "Within the hour I dispatched two of our ace intelligence officers to Mar del Plata. They phoned me and said there was only one U-boat in the harbor—but they confirmed that two German submarines had arrived.

"For 24 hours the Argentine authorities refused to allow our agents to board the remaining U-boat. Nor were they permitted to speak to any member of the crew. When Capt. Otto Wermutt, 22-year-old commander, was finally questioned, he stated it was just an ordinary 'routine cruise.'

"But he would not explain why he had not surrendered on May 2 to the Allies when Germany had surrendered. He would not disclose why he had 54 men on board instead of a normal crew of 18 or 19. He would not discuss his cargo, which had been landed before my men got there. Nor would he explain the luxuries aboard—there were 540 cartons of cigarettes (U-boat men do not smoke aboard), a cellar full of champagne, wine, Scotch whiskey and German schnapps."

Was this the U-boat that brought Hitler and Eva to Argentina?

That mystery still remains unsolved.

Mysterious Cargo

A month later another U-boat landed in the same port, the Ambassador disclosed to the *Police Gazette*, and again he dispatched Intelligence agents to the scene. "Again," he said, "they got a runaround. This time men and freight had disappeared into thin air."

"I know these U-boats came from Norway. I firmly believe they also carried highly secret component parts of Germany's secret weapons as well as the nuclear developments of Nazi scientists. I don't think they had an atom bomb yet but I'm sure they were close to it.

"Our intelligence officers were handicapped in their mission in Argentina by complete lack of cooperation from the government. In fact, the Argentine authorities protected the Nazis and consistently concealed information that would have been of assistance to us.

"We were never able to ascertain the full scope of Nazi infiltration in the country. We traced four hundred million dollars of Nazi funds to Buenos Aires. Then it just disappeared.

"One of Hitler's principal agents was Ludwig Freude, who was entrusted with secret funds. He was our Number 1 target since we knew him to be liaison man for General Freidrich Wolfe, Nazi military attache in Argentina. Freude's son was one of Peron's intimate friends and acted as his personal secretary for many years.

"I tried to have Freude deported to Germany, where we could arrest and try him. To no avail. On Sept. 15, 1945, Argentine Foreign Minister Cooke informed me that despite the gravity of the charges against Freude, the Foreign Ministry was powerless to deport him.

Subsequently Braden reported to Washington that the Nazis had built a virtual fortress in the San Carlos de Bariloche area as an escape haven for Hitler and his close clique of Nazi henchmen.

"I sent our intelligence agents there to check," Braden recalled ruefully. "They were spotted by the German guards and ordered

to leave. We were never permitted free movement in that territory."

   That was in 1945. Since then various efforts of investigators
to penetrate the Nazi stronghold failed, until recently, when the
London Daily Express correspondent obtained the first eyewitness
report—a report that confirms the expose that first appeared in the
Police Gazette, 12 years ago.

THE NEW MANHUNT FOR HITLER AND BORMANN

by HARVEY WILSON

The fact that the Fuhrer and his number one aide are alive is conceded by the West German Government . . .

The conviction that Adolf Hitler and his top aide, Martin Bormann, are still alive now has the support of German officials.

The West German Government, which for 19 years stubbornly rejected any theory but the one that the dictator took his own life, reluctantly did an about-face under the overwhelming pressure of new evidence.

It conceded that Hitler's well-dramatized "suicide" in a bunker in Berlin's Reich Chancellery was Hitler's biggest lie, a hoax that fooled almost the entire world. It made the concession when its Justice Ministry launched a world-wide hunt for Der Fuehrer, as well as for another supposedly dead man, the notorious Martin Bormann.

A few months ago, Werner Naumann, who was the state secretary of the Nazi Propaganda Ministry, confessed to West Germany Justice Ministry officials that he was with Bormann when he escaped. He debunked as "completely false" the report that Bormann was killed when a German tank blew up near him after being hit by a Russian shell. "Bormann made his escape," Naumann now finally admits.

"Bormann is indeed alive," Dr. Fritz Bauer, prosecutor of the State of Hesse, unequivocally declared. "We now have conclusive evidence that he is hiding in South America."

Hitler himself was last reported holed up in a South American wilderness camp guarded by Nazi fanatics, a hideaway to which he assertedly fled by U-boat when the Third Reich tumbled in ruins under Allied bombing and Russian artillery. But there was every likelihood, once the story of the manhunt leaked out, that the elusive Hitler, to say nothing of his pal Bormann, would escape elsewhere.

New proof that Hitler's suicide was a monumental fraud came from none other than a son of Adolf Eichmann, who was seized in Argentina, tried in Israel for the deaths of 6 million Jews, and executed. The son admitted to Dr. Bauer that his father had confided to him that both Hitler and Bormann were still alive.

Hitler's Fake Suicide

Allied intelligence agents have long admitted that Hitler's suicide and Bormann's death were both fakes, but few believed them. Their theory was based, first, on the lack of physical evidence—no corpse to prove either death. And there was the statement of a member of Hitler's staff who saw the Fuhrer minutes before he supposedly committed suicide.

"He seemed more like a man about to take a trip than a man who was going to commit suicide," this witness said.

Ironically the elder Eichmann was captured by Israeli agents seeking not him but Hitler and Bormann. They had followed an intricate trail that led to a remote area of the Argentina's San Carlos de Bariloche, site of the Nazi-guarded camp. There were so many heavily armed storm troopers around the Israelis were unable to penetrate the camp. They grabbed Eichmann in Buenos Aires as a kind of consolation prize.

Even as Eichmann's son was making his admission to a badly shaken West German government, fresh insight on the mind and personality of Adolf Hitler was disclosed by trusted Germans who had lived and worked with him in the last two years of his reign. What they had to say, while only a revelation of character rather than facts, served to prop up the belief that Hitler was still among the living.

These ex-colleagues of the Nazi tyrant painted him as a man alternately friendly, charming, furious, brutal and playful, childishly playful—but always optimistic. Hardly a man to kill himself, unless all means of escape were closed to him.

"Hitler would never commit suicide," an aide of Dr. Bauer told the *Police Gazette.* "He was obsessed with the idea that he had divine guidance, was always too concerned with his own health and safety. The people who were closest to him are convinced he escaped."

To his very last day in Berlin, Hitler was a picayune eater, inordinately concerned with what food was harmful to him, what good. He considered meat deadly. He enjoyed making guests disgusted with meat by spinning horrible yarns about "what goes on in slaughterhouses."

His idea of good food was flaxseed or oatmeal gruel, raw vegetables and vegetable juices. He especially enjoyed a dish of baked potatoes with sour milk, which he practically flooded with raw linseed oil.

He always had coffee boiling for his friends, but he would have none of it. He considered it bad for the nerves, harmful to the body. He preferred caraway tea, or, strangely enough, a tea brewed from apple peelings. For dessert he was especially fond of generous slices of freshly baked apple cake.

He never drank alcohol. He never smoked.

His passion to preserve himself was revealed in other ways. Wherever he went, he was followed by a retinue of Germany's best doctors. He dosed himself with cough medicine at the very first sneeze.

He drove in an armored-car with bullet-proof glass. Even that wasn't enough. He always made sure the car shades were drawn.

Bomb-Proof Hideouts

His shelters during the war were bomb-proof hideouts strong enough to resist the blast of the most powerful air bombs. His principal headquarters was the "Wolves' Redoubt," a series of giant concrete and steel structures hidden in a forest near Rastenburg, East Prussia. The roof of Hitler's shelter was covered with grass, as a means of camouflage.

On July 20, 1944, a bomb exploded in the Fuhrer's "situation barracks." It had been planted there as part of an officers' plot to assassinate him.

He emerged from the barracks with his black pants torn, his hair in disorder, but his belief in his star undamaged. "This is proof, gentlemen," he said with a twisted smile, "that Providence has chosen me for my mission."

Later, when the shock had worn off, he flew into one of his rages. "Those fools don't know what chaos would set in if I'm no longer around!" he cried. "But I'll show them! These criminals, who wanted to get rid of me. . . . Once Jewry with all its hatred gains power over us, good-bye to German and European civilization!"

From Berchtesgarten, his mistress, Eva Braun, bombarded him with letters filled with anxiety for his safety. Touched, he mailed her his torn pants "as a souvenir."

When he visited the mountain eyrie in Berchtesgarten his constant companion, the fear of death, would vanish briefly and then he'd cut up like a kid.

One April evening, just before his birthday, he and Eva and some friends were sitting around the roaring fireplace. He began playing with his police dog, "Blondi."

"Stand up!" Der Fuehrer ordered, and "Blondi" stood on her hind legs.

"Now sing for us." With that, apparently to inspire "Blondi," the dictator of the Third Reich let out a prolonged howl.

"Blondi" did some howling herself, in a high-pitched voice. It rose to falsetto and then Hitler, with mock sternness, commanded, "Sing lower down!"

And "Blondi," with a howl or two of accompaniment from her master, would drop her voice and sing contralto.

Most of the sycophants around Hitler would laugh. A few looked embarrassed. They found it almost inconceivable that the man who was master of a large chunk of Europe could fling away his dignity to howl with a dog.

Banned Smoking

Hitler like many lesser men, got sleepy right after he ate and would doze off in his chair, no matter how important the dignitaries seated at his table. Such moments as this delighted his guests, because it gave them their first chance to rush out of the room and enjoy a smoke. Smoking in Hitler's presence was strictly banned.

Supper was usually served at 8 p.m. in the main house. Guests who were not remaining for the night had to wait quite some time before taking their leave. Hitler had a terror of being alone in waking hours. He wanted people, laughter, conviviality, around him all the time. No guest could leave until 4 or 5 in the morning, when finally the host felt like retiring.

There was only one guest Hitler didn't care to have around long. This was the wife of Baldur von Schirach, formerly Reich Youth Leader and later Reich's Governor of Vienna.

One day Mrs. von Schirach, clearly a compassionate woman who let her heart get the better of her head, broke into the chatter of a tea with this naive statement:

"My Fuhrer, I recently saw a trainload of deported Jews in Amsterdam. They were starving, miserable. And each wore the Star of David on his chest. God knows where they were being deported. I'm sure you don't know, my Fuhrer!"

A thick silence blanketed the room. Hitler suddenly leaped to his feet and marched out the door.

Mrs. von Schirach left Berchtesgarten next day. She was never seen there again.

Hitler loved being a dictator, and yet there were moments when he would have enjoyed being like common men.

"If you only knew how I'd like to be able to walk through the streets alone sometimes," he would say longingly. "Maybe buying Christmas presents in a department store. Or sitting in a sidewalk cafe, watching the people pass by."

He was constantly issuing statements and required a crew of 10 girl secretaries. It was with them that he revealed a Hitler virtually unknown to the outside world, a kindly, almost fatherly boss who quite considerately always dictated slowly, so the girls could keep up with him.

One girl, who had just landed the job, entered Hitler's office all atremble. The man who ruled Germany with an iron fist almost tenderly led her to a typewriter table near his desk.

She noticed that Hitler was wearing spectacles, the old-fashioned kind, with a metal frame. It made her think of a village schoolmaster.

Shakily she removed the cover from the typewriter and tried to insert a sheet of paper. She had trouble doing this, because of her fit of shakes.

"You needn't be so nervous," Der Fuehrer said softly. "You know, I myself make more mistakes in dictation than you possibly can."

That calmed her down.

When she had finished typing a page, Hitler said, "May I see it a moment?" She handed it to him and he read it carefully. He looked up, beaming. "You typed it well."

Fatherly Warning

He got off the subject of typing and questioned her about her family, her schooling, whether she wanted to remain at her new job. Then he issued a fatherly warning.

"You're still young, Miss. And here at headquarters there are so many men. Men who seldom get home. And the attraction of the eternal feminine is strong in soldiers. What I mean is, you must be careful and reserved. And if you have any complaints, don't hesitate to come to me!"

By the last year of the war, Hitler was pretty fed up with uniforms. "You don't know how well off you are," he told one Berchtesgarten guest who arrived in shorts. "That's how I used to go about."

"Surely," protested his visitor, "you can do that here. After all, here you're in private life."

"No, as long as we're at war, I won't take off the uniform. And what's more," Hitler added with a twinkle in his eye, "my knees are very white. That looks dreadful in shorts.

"But after the war I'm going to hang up my uniform and retire. Someone else can take over the government. Then, as an old gentleman, I'll surround myself with witty clever people and I'll write my memoirs."

And that is exactly what Adolf Hitler may be doing at this very moment!

THE SECRET HIDEOUT OF HITLER AND HIS HENCHMEN

by KENNETH KAASEN

One of the most infamous Nazis from Adolf Hitler's Third Reich has now admitted to West German authorities that Der Fuehrer's last deputy is without question still alive in South America. Martin Bormann has been pinpointed in the Brazilian state of Parana, located near the border with Paraguay.

Germany's top Nazi hunter, Hesse state prosecutor Fritz Bauer, and Simon Wiesenthal of Vienna believe it is only a matter of time before Bormann is arrested. It was Simon Wiesenthal, a man with a mission, who hunted down Adolf Eichmann.

Spotlight on Hideout

The Nazi war criminal Franz Stangl plans to throw the spotlight on Hitler and at least ten of his top henchmen still living in Argentina, Brazil and Paraguay, some of them prosperous businessmen.

Franz Stangl, who is now being interrogated in West Germany, was the former commandant of the notorious Treblinka extermination camp in Poland.

Stangl, awaiting trial on charges of war crimes, is talking about ex-Nazis other than Bormann.

After Adolf Hitler, the most wanted Nazis are Martin Bormann, Josef Mengele, and Richard Glucks.

Another most wanted man on the Bonn government's list is Heinrich Muller, the former S.S. Intelligence chief.

In July, 1967, the Brazilian newspaper Folha da Tarde published a report that Hitler's right hand man Martin Bormann was living in the industrial city of Sao Paulo, in southern Brazil. The information came from a Roman Catholic priest who in turn got it from Helmut Bordeon, a former Nazi Elite Guard officer.

Hitler's chauffeur, Erich Kempka, was the first to spread the lie that Hitler and Bormann were killed early on the morning of May 2, 1945.

Kempka told US Army Intelligence that Bormann and Dr. Werner Naumann, the State Secretary to the Nazi Propaganda Ministry, made their way from the Chancellery to the Friedrichstrasse railway station early that morning without incident.

Joined by the deputy Hitler Youth Leader, Artur Axmann, they stopped near the station to discuss how to get away from the advancing Russians.

"Others joined them behind a large German tank and some armored vehicles," Kempka said. "They walked alongside the armored column as it moved toward the Russian lines. The column, preceded by men on foot, passed through a tank trap and had gotten fifty yards or so past it when the tank was hit by a bazooka shell.

"I was about three or four yards behind the tank. Bormann and Naumann were directly beside it. The shell smashed into them and I saw their bodies hurled away. They could not have survived."

However, Werner Naumann did survive and was active in neo-Nazi circles after the war. What really happened to Bormann? Noting that Bormann's companions, Erich Kempka, Naumann and Artur Axmann had no trouble getting away, investigators dismissed the Kempka story.

The fact is that after Hitler escaped, Bormann, Naumann, Axmann and Kempka fled the flaming ruins of Berlin together.

As far as US Army investigators could learn after the war, they crossed through the weakest spot in the Soviet lines, commandeered a German staff car outside the city and drove over back roads to Hamburg, in the British occupation zone. From there, they made their way south to Bavaria.

Among those who confirmed the escape of Bormann were Major General Otto Ohlendorf, an S.S. officer, and Hartman Lauterbacher, the chief political officer of Southern Hanover.

Before Ohlendorf was hanged for the murder of some 90,000 Jews during the year he commanded one of Himmler's extermination squads, he flatly stated that Martin Bormann had escaped Berlin. Bormann was known to have a mountain retreat a short distance from Hitler's Berchtesgaden, called the Halali, meaning "tallyho."

Lauterbacher told British officials: "He (Bormann) told us all many times that 'in a certain circumstance we will meet in Halali.'"

Nazi Youth Packs

Later in 1945, Allied intelligence received reports that Bormann was hiding in the Bavarian mountains with young Nazi youth packs led by Axmann. When American troops drove out the youth packs, Bormann fled to the German-Austrian frontier with its snow-covered slopes, and helped to create a new guerrilla band call the "Edelweiss Pirates."

Bormann hid in the hills for four months, but then apparently decided to risk a visit to an old hangout . . . Munich. He was seen there in October, 1945, by J. A. Friedl, a former Nazi sergeant in the Munich police

Friedl knew Bormann from early days of the Nazi party.

He signed a sworn statement for the US Army and Bavarian authorities. "I saw Martin Bormann with some men in a car parked in front of the Spanish Consulate," Friedl said.

"I approached the car and greeted Bormann. He remembered me and we chatted together for a few minutes. From what I saw and heard, I gathered that Bormann was trying to arrange a visa to enter Spain."

Nine months after this incident, Bormann was again reported seen in Munich.

This time he was seen by Jakob Glas, who was Bormann's personal driver up to 1944. On July 26, 1946, Glas was standing on a Munich street corner. Glancing into a passing auto, he saw his old boss riding in the front seat next to the driver. "I know Bormann and the man I saw was Bormann," he told US intelligence officers.

On December 11, 1946, two Stockholm newspapers, Arbetet and Aftontidningen, reported that Bormann had found his way to South America. US and British intelligence also received word that Bormann was in Argentina.

According to their informants, Bormann left Bavaria in the summer of 1946, went to Switzerland to get travel funds from a secret Nazi bank account, then traveled to southern Spain where a mysterious submarine was waiting to take him to the Argentine. Bormann's destination was the province of Patagonia.

The Patagonian pampas were crawling with former Nazis, including the late Adolf Eichmann.

Arrived by Sub

Intelligence reports revealed that Bormann arrived off the Argentine coast on the German submarine U-435 and came ashore near the small city of Rawson.

Bormann and his staff reportedly had gone inland to lose themselves in the vast grasslands after American agents picked up his trail.

This a far from complete story on how Bormann escaped from the crumbling Third Reich. The full story of how he got to South America may never be told. This much is known: Spruille Braden, American Ambassador to Argentina at the end of World War Two, sent an intelligence group to Patagonia to investigate U-boat landings.

The big Nazis got away.

At various times in the late 1940s, Bormann was reported to be living on a ranch in Patagonia, and in the jungles of Brazil.

At the time of his arrest in Sao Paulo, Brazil, last Spring Franz Stangl revealed that Bormann has been moving about between three South American countries . . . Argentina, Paraguay and Brazil.

Stangl reports that Bormann is now an old-looking man and completely bald. Bormann also has a heart disease. At one time, Stangl claims, he was in the Monastery of the White Padres in Asuncion, Paraguay, where Dr. Josef Mengele, the "Doctor of Auschwitz" was called in to treat him.

The West German government now concedes that it believes Martin Bormann is still alive, something which cannot be denied in the weight of evidence. His arrest may be only months away.

The most wanted Nazi after Hitler's elusive deputy is Heinrich "Gestapo" Muller. Muller's whereabouts are a mystery. But there is no doubt that he is still alive. During the last year of the war Heinrich Muller collaborated with the Russian secret service.

As an S.S. lieutenant general, Muller was chief of Hitler's secret police, the Geheime Staatspolizei, or Gestapo for short. In addition, he was also the Lord High Executioner of the Third Reich.

As commander of the Gestapo, he was partly responsible for some 12,000,000 murders. At his orders, Adolf Eichmann sent millions of Jews to Nazi death camps. At his orders, Gestapo men turned Germany and occupied Europe into a vast slave empire.

A British intelligence agent, Captain S. Payne Best, who was once kidnaped by the Gestapo's intelligence branch, observed that Muller "had rather funny eyes which he would flicker from side to side with the greatest rapidity, and I suppose that this was supposed to strike terror into the heart of the beholder."

Hitler's Gestapo chief vanished without a trace in April 1945, within days of Der Fuehrer's fake "suicide."

S.S. Lieutenant Colonel Willi Hoettle, a former member of the Gestapo's Foreign Intelligence Service, was convinced that his boss joined the Soviet Secret Service after the war. Another former Nazi official revealed that he saw Muller in Moscow. He said Muller, wearing a Russian police official's uniform, was dining in the old Sovietskaya Hotel.

The most reliable information, from former Red agents, reveals that Heinrich Muller was until recently the most secret of Soviet secret police. Reports hint Muller was a colonel in Russia's foreign intelligence bureau.

Muller was reported to have said in 1943: "Joseph Stalin is immeasurably superior to the leaders of the Western nations, and if I had anything to say in the matter, we'd reach an agreement with him as quickly as possible."

William L. Shirer wrote: "Muller was never apprehended after the war . . . some of his surviving colleagues believe he is now in the service of the Soviet secret police, of which he was a great admirer."

In 1950, a German officer who had been a prisoner of war in Russia said he had seen Muller in Moscow in 1948.

Today Heinrich Muller is free to carry on his murderous profession. Recent reliable reports put him in Albania working for the Albanian secret police. Wherever he may be now, he was never captured and brought to justice. The Third Reich's official race exterminator is still free.

Next on West Germany's "most wanted" list is Josef Mengele, the murderer of millions. Mengele has been a citizen of Paraguay since 1959.

While in his early thirties, Dr. Josef Mengele was the chief physician at Auschwitz, where he earned the title of "Angel of Death." At Auschwitz, Mengele tortured and murdered hundreds of thousands of Jews, gypsies, old people, children, and even babies. He would perform childbirths at Auschwitz with the utmost care. Then, thirty minutes later, he would send both the mother and her newborn baby to the gas chamber.

He sent millions of people to their death merely because, according to Nazi racial theory, they were inferior beings and therefore detrimental to the Third Reich.

At the end of the war, the name of Mengele was cropping up in accounts of Auschwitz. He went underground, but soon ended in a British hospital with an unknown ailment, then was discharged.

With war criminals such as Bormann and Muller at large, little attention was paid to Mengele, who held the rank of an S.S. lieutenant.

It is known that Mengele was stopped several times during routine checks. Eventually, he went to Spain and then on to Argentina.

Practiced Medicine

Within the last twelve years, Mengele practiced medicine in the Vicente Lopez suburb of Buenos Aires, where he reportedly specialized in venereal disease and abortions. For more than fifteen years, he has obviously enjoyed high-level protection in South America.

Josef Mengele is now co-owner of an agricultural machinery factory which employs some 2,000 workers. Mengele's factory has two branches, in Paraguay and Argentina. His son is studying in Vienna.

Attempts to extradite Mengele have repeatedly failed. Now in his late fifties, Mengele may die of old age before he could be extradited and brought to trial.

Another wanted Nazi, former S.S. colonel Walter Rauff, last known to be in Chile, successfully fought an attempt to extradite him to Germany in 1963. Groups of wanted Nazis have settled safely in Chile, Argentina, Paraguay and Brazil. Hundreds of other ex-Nazis are living and working in the United Arab Republic.

Hitler's inspector of concentration camps, Richard Glucks, is still alive in South America, although he is now a sick man.

Glucks is the next most wanted Nazi after Mengele. However, before his death in Egypt in 1967, Josef Mengele's counterpart at Buchenwald, Dr. Hans Eisele, was next on the list. Eisele's recent death in Cairo shoved Richard Glucks up to next place.

Glucks is a former S.S. general who worked directly under Heinrich Himmler. He was in charge of training and supervising the men who presided over the extermination of some 6,000,000 Jews in Nazi occupied Europe.

As early as 1934 Himmler created the post of Inspector of Concentration Camps.

In 1936, Richard Glucks, a forty-seven-year-old S.S. commander, was assigned to the first appointee's (Theodore Eicke) staff. Unlike Eicke, missing since the war, Glucks was a confirmed bureaucrat.

"Glucks possessed an unquenchable Rhenish humor and he saw the funny side of everything," Rudolf Hoess, the Auschwitz camp commandant, once said. "He made the most serious matters sound comic, and he laughed over them and forgot them and made no decisions about them."

When the question of genocide was raised, Glucks would say, "These are matters to be discussed with the individual camp commandants, not with me. I'm just an inspector, not a policy maker."

Although his exact whereabouts are at the present unknown, Richard Glucks was at one time in Chile with Walter Rauff.

Big Nazi Still Free

Hitler's henchmen are still free. Some are in South America, some in Egypt, and thousands in Germany. All the big Nazis remain free after over twenty years of running.

All told, there are still over 1,000 Nazis on the wanted list of war criminals, but it is only the top Nazis that the West German government really wants.

Martin Bormann, second only to Hitler during the last few months of the war, is alive in Brazil. He may never be arrested. Race murderer Heinrich Muller is also alive, possibly in South America. Dr. Josef Mengele, murderer of millions, and the concentration camp boss Richard Glucks are still free.

But even at this late date, German and Israeli agents are tracking down Hitler and his top henchmen. But time is running out.

The End . . .
Or Is It?

HITLER STILL ALIVE TODAY

FUHRER'S OWN
DOCTOR DEBUNKS RED CLAIM

One evening last November, Germans watching ZDF Television in Hamburg got an unexpected jolt. Dr. Erwin Giesing, who was Adolf Hitler's personal physician, appeared on the screen to discredit a Russian author's claim that the Red Army had found and burned Der Fuehrer's body in Berlin in 1945.

The Russian claim was a hoax and Dr. Giesing, who was among the few to see Hitler before he vanished, presented the evidence on TV to prove that the body the Red author was talking about wasn't that of Adolf Hitler.

Dr. Giesing pointed out that he possessed the last X-rays of Hitler and that his "Hitler mold" differed from the one made by the Russians of the corpse they found.

Furthermore, according to Dr. Giesing, Hitler had two normal testicles instead of only one as the Russians claimed.

It was the first time that Dr. Giesing had broken his silence to talk about his famous patient. He discredited completely the theory that Hitler's body had been found.

Dr. Giesing didn't rule out the reports that Hitler escaped from Berlin alive.

Twenty-seven years have passed since Hitler vanished from his Reichschancellery bunker. He was 56 years old then. Could he still be alive today at 83?

Contrary to all reports concerning his health, Hitler was in prime physical condition. A health fadist, he adhered to a balanced diet of organically grown fruits and vegetables; avoided alcohol and smoking. His pulse and blood-pressure were consistently normal and he had an especially strong heart.

In Bonn, West Germany's Intelligence Service agreed with Dr. Giesing's conclusions. As far as officials of the secret service are concerned Adolf Hitler is still alive. He is still on the official "Wanted List of War Criminals."

In 1958, Allied Intelligence agents traced Hitler's whereabouts to a remote region in Patagonia in South America—a heavily guarded fortress patrolled by a contingent of armed storm troopers. But official London and Washington policy was not to force the issue; if Hitler were to be captured it would complicate the foreign policy to unite Germany behind the Allies. It could also trigger an emotional frenzy; a revival of Nazism in West Germany.

Final Report

I was authorized by higher headquarters in 1945 to say that: "On the basis of present evidence, no insurance company in America would pay a death claim on Adolf Hitler."

My final report to Washington stated that no evidence was found of Hitler's death in Berlin in 1945. As a result, the "Wanted List of War Criminals," last issued in 1948, carried the cryptic notice: "Wanted: Hitler, Adolf, Reichsfuhrer."

More sinister than Hitler's disappearance was that of Martin Bormann, for Bormann was an organizational genius with a true passion for anonymity. Moreover, he was a true Nazi who believed passionately in that evil political system.

Aside from speculation, there is no ghost in the crumbled ruins of the Reichschancellery more dangerous than that of Hitler himself, and over the deliberations in Bonn as well as Washington, there still hangs the cloud of doubt: "What really happened to Hitler?"

MYSTERIOUSPRESS.COM

Otto Penzler, owner of the Mysterious Bookshop in Manhattan, founded the Mysterious Press in 1975. Penzler quickly became known for his outstanding selection of mystery, crime, and suspense books, both from his imprint and in his store. The imprint was devoted to printing the best books in these genres, using fine paper and top dust-jacket artists, as well as offering many limited, signed editions.

Now the Mysterious Press has gone digital, publishing ebooks through **MysteriousPress.com**.

MysteriousPress.com offers readers essential noir and suspense fiction, hard-boiled crime novels, and the latest thrillers from both debut authors and mystery masters. Discover classics and new voices, all from one legendary source.

FIND OUT MORE AT

WWW.MYSTERIOUSPRESS.COM

FOLLOW US:

@emysteries and Facebook.com/MysteriousPressCom

MysteriousPress.com is one of a select group of publishing partners of Open Road Integrated Media, Inc.

THE MYSTERIOUS BOOKSHOP, founded in 1979, is located in Manhattan's Tribeca neighborhood. It is the oldest and largest mystery-specialty bookstore in America.

The shop stocks the finest selection of new mystery hardcovers, paperbacks, and periodicals. It also features a superb collection of signed modern first editions, rare and collectable works, and Sherlock Holmes titles. The bookshop issues a free monthly newsletter highlighting its book clubs, new releases, events, and recently acquired books.

58 Warren Street
info@mysteriousbookshop.com
(212) 587-1011
Monday through Saturday
11:00 a.m. to 7:00 p.m.

FIND OUT MORE AT:

www.mysteriousbookshop.com

FOLLOW US:

@TheMysterious and Facebook.com/MysteriousBookshop

OPEN ROAD
INTEGRATED MEDIA

Open Road Integrated Media is a digital publisher and multimedia content company. Open Road creates connections between authors and their audiences by marketing its ebooks through a new proprietary online platform, which uses premium video content and social media.

Videos, Archival Documents, and New Releases

Sign up for the Open Road Media newsletter and get news delivered straight to your inbox.

Sign up now at
www.openroadmedia.com/newsletters

FIND OUT MORE AT
WWW.OPENROADMEDIA.COM

FOLLOW US:
@openroadmedia and
Facebook.com/OpenRoadMedia

CPSIA information can be obtained at www.ICGtesting.com
Printed in the USA
BVOW08s0253300116

434562BV00002B/3/P